Mute

By the same author:
Mudsharks

Mute by Dave Barbarossa
© 2024 Dave Barbarossa
Astral Horizon Press
designed by Simon De Rudder
www.astralhorizon.co.uk
978-1-7396630-8-7

Mute
Dave Barbarossa

For Sunna, the lioness of Shepherds Bush

In memory of Roger Stewart Wells 1966 - 2012
Brother, builder, father.

&

Dear Louise.

For my brothers and sisters, my children and their children.

Thanks to Kev Foulkes, Richard Norris and Jem Panufnik for encouraging me after reading the first bloated draft.
To Sue Blunt for her forensic sub edits. She never let me off.
To Charlie Kennedy for his belief. Chocks away!!
To brother Gene for the amazing jacket.
To Kayvon for the introduction.
Special thanks to Kev Whelan for his friendship and genirosity.

Finally, huge gratitude to Mike Carter, editor and mentor, with me line by line, and more than once.

1

London 1999

I heard it.

I was hanging off the bars one-handed in the aisle of an eastbound tube train. Topographical view of the girl I was standing over: pale blue baseball cap, bedraggled honey hair pleasantly spilling from beneath it. Couldn't see her face. Her bag was shocking silver and lay open on her lap. Brimful – there was a purse, weighty dog-eared novel, Tampax, bits of make-up, lippy, a pink scarf and some plastic cutlery. She was subtly nodding to the music on her headphones.

There'd been a huge joining of tourists at Queensway station, lots of laughter and Latin poses. Mums, dads and kids getting bags and elbows trapped in the doors. Open-shut, open-shut, we'd stewed there for five minutes. I hated being late. The wheels screeched, slowing for the next stop. The doors opened. More got on. Hemmed in on both sides, I was forced, knee-wise, to inch closer to her.

Lumbering out, the carriage a-chatter with foreign pronunciations of Holborn, Marble Arch and Tott-en-ham Court Road, I watched her trying to extricate the ticket from an inadequate zipped compartment in her bag. I could see her fingers in there – clear neat nails, a slender pinching, obliviously elbowing the bloke next to her, but only gently. It wasn't coming out.

After tunnelling on for a beat or two, she sighed and tugged forcibly. The action wrenched the headphones from her ears, and what she was listening to reached mine: eight notes, a thoughtful orchestral motif it was, but it didn't sound like it now. She was flustered, attempting to reset the headphones over the peak of her cap, which had gone a little askew. The train was pitching and rocking, the bloke next to her spreading like a virus as he prepared to stand.

Dragged in a blur across the windows, platform adverts lit the carriage, initiating a great shuffling and gathering. I looked left and right for the nearest departure point. Everyone got off at Oxford Circus. Below me, the cameo played on as we slowed and slowed. With her left hand she was cramming the headphones and disobedient cable into her bag, while simultaneously trying to persuade her ticket to leave its compartment.

The train coughed violently, shaking us like chips in a pan. It was too much movement, in too tight a space, in too short a time and she jettisoned the unlidded coffee she had in her right hand all over me.

That got them sniggering, the dumb waiters and pole dancers. And there I dangled, breath held, heart thudding, hot coffee sizzling my scalded nethers.

She raised her head. Her face was heart shaped and her eyes so shockingly green that, for a moment, I felt nothing. Pale pink lips could not form a sentence. I winced a smile as the liquid heat did its worst.

"B-but..." she muttered, looking like the heroine at the end of some weepy old afternoon film.

My smile froze. "It's OK, doesn't, er, hurt …much." My glasses had fallen onto my nose, revealing my eyes. It took less than a second for my forefinger to flick them back.

Gathering herself and her possessions, she continued to blink with utter remorse. "I'm..."

"Not a problem. I'm getting off here."

The coffee was cooling, an expanding continent of wet, a piss-patch growing from my blue-jean flies.

"Sorry," she finally managed. "My headphones…I'll get off too."

As we edged sideways, I could feel eyes on me and on her.

"No, no," I said. "It's cool." But it wasn't, it was warm, sugaring the tip of my penis, the goo molten on my pubes.

Stepping onto the platform – the back in front of me at my tempo, the person in front, at his – I drew my navy cagoule over my cod incontinence, wishing I'd zipped it up. Finally released for the race up the escalator, the stickiness had turned to cold boxer granules. I was going to be at least ten minutes late. Not that there'd be anyone there to see if I was, and not that anybody would care. I just prided myself in being as exacting as I could in all facets of life. Being late, even if it didn't matter, needled me. Sashaying swiftly through the barriers, I thought of what had affected me most just now; the shock of hot coffee, those eight notes or her. The wrench was delicate, but irresistible. I felt as if I'd been lifted and was floating laterally, elbow high, backwards.

"I'm *really* sorry."

Her unruly silver bag swung gently into me. I tapped my glasses just in case, but the frame reassuringly pinched the bridge of my nose. Around us, commuters avoided each other like negatively charged particles. The Tannoy barked a direction. I was getting later by the second.

"It's OK. An accident. I'm fine."

Gently, each of her fingers compressed a nerve on my forearm. "I'm mortified." She was forced to step forward to make way for a huge woman, just as I was shoved in the back by a smaller one. Our faces were inches apart. Her eyes held a forest of sadness when she blinked at me.

"What, sorry?" I said, shaking my head. Trapped in her gaze, I'd not listened to what she'd been saying.

"I said, I'll pay for your dry cleaning."

"Ha, it's a pair of jeans."

"Then..." She ran out of lines.

We'd edged our way to the calm of a sandwich shop window. The glare from it was bright and harsh compared with the ticket landing's monochrome shimmer. Against a background of pasties and samosas I took her in entirely. Even in scuffed white plimsoles, she stood a little taller than average. She didn't seem to be wearing any make-up, but you'd say her cheeks were brushstroke sculpted. She might have had on just enough lipstick to bother.

Beneath an unbuttoned cream mac was a blouse of green and black jungle colours, and a thin cardie of yellow over that. Her cotton skirt was easy and chequered, just longer than the hem of her mac. There was a scarf of indeterminate pink about her shoulders. It was a baffling collection of clobber and styles, befitting this baffling commute.

While I was studying her, she was, of course, studying me. She saw: mid-twenties, in OK shape, black clipped hair. The thick horn-rimmed glasses meeting my stubble was my cloak of invisibility. Trainers, jeans, and lightweight plastic cagoule (why hadn't I done it up), *my* unbaffling uniform.

"Really, it's fine." I insisted.

"Thank you," she said, obliterating her remorse with a cover girl smile.

Because I was one, the word 'professional' came to mind and I realised that what was mesmerising me was a mask, albeit one of flawless, eye-twinkling perfection. At that moment I did something alien to me – unprofessional, you might say – I peered unabashedly at a stranger and to my amazement, that stranger didn't flinch. The Tannoy barked again and in the pastry glare I watched, like some time-lapse bud-to-flower thing, a different smile emerge. Wrinkles spread from her eyes, faint lines appeared above her lip, her brow furrowed and her neck, between the pink, revealed miniscule lateral creases.

Her, dry with mirth and me, wet, wincing, bowing my legs so the now-freezing coffee wouldn't chafe, we ascended into a light summer shower on Oxford Street.

"Sorry, I'm not laughing at you."

"It is sort of funny, I admit."

She pressed those nerves on my elbow again. The sensation was exquisite. "There's a dry cleaner's in Wardour Street!" A part of me wanted to call her bluff, ask if she was going to buy or borrow a pair of trousers for me while my old jeans were being dry-cleaned. Would she wait with me in my coffee-coloured boxers perched on a stool in the window, like a little lad getting his hair cut?

"Nah, 'course not. I gotta go. My boss, he's quite a stickler for time," I said, initiating the first of a thousand lies between us.

"Mine too. Well, sorry again."

"One of those things."

The almost invisible gold fuzz above her pale lips shaped a comedy frown.

"What's your name?"

"Daniel."

Knotting her mac's belt decisively, she re-shouldered her bag and offered her hand for me to shake. I took her fingertips in mine. How soft her gaze was on me.

"I'm Kerry."

"Kerry," I said, nodding my farewell.

Hunching up my shoulders to cross at the lights, I began the short walk to Tottenham Court Road, but even though I was late, I didn't hurry. I knew she was behind me.

2

The door clicked and I entered quickly, glad to get out of the rain. Time had unquestionably stood still in this murky reception area. I remembered Mick Corbossa perusing the pinned-up, black and white glossies of Tin Pan Alley's finest declaring: *'Dead, dead, senile, in prison, dead…*

"*He's* here Daniel." From behind his glass-topped counter, Jake greeted me with a dubious wobble of his beardy head. Was it just with me that he wore that glaze of mild disbelief? It had been his demeanour ever since we'd turned up here last week. He must have thought it was some kind of prank, 'Torin' – *the* Torin – block-booked for three weeks in these damp old arches with the crusty, after-work pub-rockers and kids' drum lessons. But it was no mystery or publicity stunt, we weren't filming some gritty documentary on our band, the reasons were elementary: the rehearsal room was stupidly cheap and its proximity to a certain members club across the Charing Cross Road was perfect for our leader. I'll just add that I was not a member of that club.

"He's been here fifteen minutes."

"Oh, OK, ta."

I passed the ancient drinks machine and the pinboard with adverts for equipment never sold and positions in bands never filled. Halfway down the corridor, I pushed open Room Three's heavy soundproof door.

"The mad professor *finally* honours us with his presence. Time is money," he said, tapping an imaginary watch on his wrist, and uncurling from a red leatherette sofa so knackered it was almost entirely upholstered in gaffa tape. Of course, on the one morning I was late, he'd got here before me.

"Something up with the tube," I said, closing the door.

In leathers as black as his hair, Torin, *the* Torin, directed a limb at my groin. "You shit yourself?" he asked, his shark mouth wide with amusement. Examining my crotch in the studio's wall-length mirror, I winced. Pale-coloured jeans and coffee did not make the most alluring palette.

The one thing unaltered by all the tours and trauma was Torin's smile. Beneath superiorly flaring nostrils, it grew untamed from his generous lips. Pub, theatre and stadium, that smile had swallowed the lot. It stayed on me as I walked past the drums. But instead of the pessimism that had clouded all matters to do with us for the last month, I approached my colony of equipment to a pleasant echo.

'Sorry, I'm not laughing at you...' she'd said, her silver pet bumping me as we ascended, side by side. *She* could laugh at me all she liked. I'd play the clown, the prat, the coffee-coated pillock, just to generate the thing I'd glimpsed on the other side of the barriers.

Walled in by my equipment, I ignited my PowerBook. PA speakers popped and electricity hummed. The LEDs blinked and winked on my effects rack, and I wondered if she swathed herself in that unconfined clobber to disguise who she was.

'*Daniel?*' Ten minutes ago, I'd heard her voice above a bus's wheels hissing through a puddle. I turned around as a pushbike shot by. It was the second time she'd said my name. Standing there, her chin high, she appeared as statuesque as the mannequins in the clothes shop behind her. Her blink was warm and slow. '*Can I at least buy you a coffee, after work? I've caused you so much trouble.*' The strawberry madness cascaded over her bag as she rummaged through those fateful headphone cables to retrieve her phone.

"Daniel!" That *wasn't* the second or the thousandth time *he'd* said my name. I glanced up from the vertical and horizontal lines on my laptop's screen. "It's coffee," I told him.

He was watching me at the mouse pad like a character from antiquity, one arm resting elegantly on a patch of exploded yellow foam that Jake would need to tape down before it mushroomed out of control. Running the program on the laptop for a couple of seconds, volume off, it came to me that recently, most of everything around me was exploding and foaming out of control.

"The big day's here."

"So, it appears, Torin." I could not extract the sulk from my voice.

"Look at you up there, you should wear a cowl, or a cape. The Priest of Pessimism. The Lord of? Well…not laughter."

I buried my hornrims in the screen's creeping detail.

"Every song we do live, Danny boy."

"I thought it was an experiment, only four," I said quietly, hating my obfuscation. I'd known for weeks that it would end up being our entire live set.

"Thinking's never been your strong point. Leave it to your betters."

"Doing it," I muttered.

A fortnight ago, out of nowhere, Torin had asked me to transmute the bass lines on four of our songs to the 'Logic' programme on my computer so that at the touch of the spacebar, the bass would play 'on its own'. I'd been bemused, we'd never needed anything on a sequence because we'd always played live, organically. He assured me it was an experiment; he said he was interested 'on an academic level' only, but his shark-wide mouth betrayed him. It always did.

Alana, the bass player (*'the bass player'* what an absurd underestimation of what she did) had been expelled six weeks ago. I'd been hoping Torin would recant and get us all back together. But as time had passed, it was obvious I'd never go on stage with her again. That there would be another person playing that instrument in front of me broke my heart for the band we'd built together. Alana was a beautiful musician. It had been insanity to let her go.

So, at Torin's behest, in the modest studio I'd built in the shed at the end of my garden, I began the process of duplicating her bass lines on a synth, before grafting them onto a computer sequence. Doing it, I'd felt taken over by someone else, someone I did not like. I'd had to take down all the posters and photos of the four of us together. I could not bear Alana's eyes on me as I turned her into a soulless, digital facsimile of herself. Listening back, the join between 'my bass' and the digital metronome on the computer was audibly undetectable, but so much feel and fluidity had been lost achieving it. It sounded nothing like 'us'.

In the middle of my dismal task, there'd been a rare occurrence, a visit from Torin himself. That he'd bothered to venture into the suburbs to check on what I was doing showed a degree of interest in the band I'd not seen for years. Through the studio window I could see my mum at the kitchen sink peering anxiously up the garden, excited that 'my boss' was visiting our average semi. *'Don't you think it sounds a bit stilted? Robotic?'* I'd asked him. Spread across the sofa in my shed in an absurdly well-tailored charcoal suit, pink shirt and tan brogues, he'd said it was, *'The sound of the future. Perfect'.* *'It's got no...'* He'd interrupted me, *'Nothing personal Danny, but the trouble with the music industry is that musicians are involved in it'.*

The microwaved cauliflower cheese I wolfed down before his arrival turned to acid in my throat when he'd said that. It seemed so callous after all we'd been through.

Things began to accelerate. A week after his visit to my house, he asked me to join him at his club in Soho. Without looking away from the view from the window, he informed me there'd be no new bass player and I should put my sequential synth bass on the remaining twenty songs in our repertoire. I was not rocked back on my heels. From his armchair, he'd turned to address me directly: *'The pressure's on, Danny boy. We've got all those gigs...'*

A British and European tour would take us into the new century. To kick it off there'd be a prestigious show in London. Not knowing who was going to play bass for us was stressful in the extreme. Our line-up had never needed meddling with. It had successfully got us around the world and back, for the last five years.

After ordering up another glass, he asked me if it was necessary to rehearse *'so much'*, as I was doing most of it in my *'potting shed'*, anyway. It was then I realised that this was a cull not motivated by art, or the *'sound of the future'*, but by Torin's extraneous business affairs.

He'd sacked Kev, our tour manager of the previous three years, citing his profligacy with the band account, though none of us could see any new or added extravagance in the hotels we were staying at, or the routes we were taking to them, or even the bus we'd hired to travel in. What was new, was his preoccupation with deals and investments. Snatches of his phone conversations had become an unwanted guest in the dressing room and a distraction at sound checks. In charge of touring now was Barney, a workaholic amateur devoted to him. I think he mentioned he'd been in marketing before he *'got into music, professionally'*.

From his club 'throne', Torin had pointed a sharp, winkle-pickered boot at me, *'I need you to focus now, Daniel'* he'd said.

I knew that if he could dismiss Alana, the person who'd

discovered him, been his lover, mentor and stood by him in the most literal sense, he'd flick me off his world like lint on the knee of his gorgeous suit pants, and where would that leave mum and me?

"Got it! Languor! The Lord of Languor!"

I blinked into the rehearsal room light. "Yeah, funny."

"Come on Daniel. We needed to modernise. There was a 'slackness'. Aged our sound."

"Isn't that just feel?"

He waved me away with his fingers, "...said the bloke who evacuated his bowels on the Central Line."

"A girl spilled her coffee over me." Lining up the click-track the drummer would play along to, I touched my forearm in an attempt to recreate her special pressure.

Torin stood and stretched. "Yeah, whatever. Let's see how the legendary Corbossa gets on with the click-track. Going to make a few calls." He sniffed, winked and left me on my own.

Mick Corbossa entered ten minutes later.

"He about?" he asked.

I squinted up from the computer to give the room a rhetorical glance.

He sighed. "Thank fuck for that."

After a short, statutory battering of his drums, the sticks clicked on the floor tom and he walked over to me. He glanced at the door and ran a hand through his thick brown locks. "Bit concerned with all this, Daniel," he said, alluding to the screen.

"You'll nail it man. It's all fours and eights, you've been doing it years."

"I'm hopeless at clicks, you know that and so does he."

We watched the door open slowly as Barney, our new tour manager, waddled in.

"Greetings band mates!" he said, pushing the door shut with his bum. I felt Mick bristle beside me. We greeted Torin's factotum in silent unison. In his 'box fresh' industrial denim, complete with trendy utilitarian satchel, Barney fell into Torin's place on the foam-blown sofa and rubbed his hands together. "Can't wait to hear this."

Ignoring the sound of silence, he ploughed on, paunchy, bald and energised. "Been working with the agent all morning. A load of very cool venues lined up. Our first tour venue will be…?"

He didn't flinch at the two blank faces looking at him.

"Hull!"

An eggy silence pervaded.

I let him off the hook and inched out a smile. "Cool Barney. Ta."

He took out his laptop and fired it up. "Yes, yes, yes, good, good, good," he chanted, peering animatedly at the screen as if the dates were flying in as he spoke. "We're leaner and meaner now, and besides, there's a few more quid for everyone at the end of the night. Torin's instincts are spot on," he blathered on, blind to the irritation and hurt he was causing the two of us. "That digital bass feel is what it's all about nowadays. We needed to trim down, compete …like a team!"

I gripped Mick's thick forearm and gave him a warning look. He audibly exhaled, returned to his drums to play a ghostly, funky beat that dissipated his anger and calmed me a fair bit too.

"Daniel?" Barney had levered himself out of the sofa to bob up and down in front of my array of keyboards and effects rack. He could just about make eye contact with me. "Can I ask, on 'The Ship That Never Sailed', is that an S900 or S950 on the intro?"

"Nine-fifty."

"You know, that *brrrp, brrrp,* bit on the SH-101 on 'My Life, My Trials', genius mate. I had the SH-101, did I say? Well didn't everyone? I had my heart set on the, er, Korg M1 workstation, but my salary couldn't stretch to…"

"Listen man, could I just get on with this, I need to set up the clicks."

"Of course. Sorry Daniel, big fan…well you know that."

He pushed the door open. "Corbossa. Barney," he said into the mic, checking himself in the wall-length mirror and liking what he saw. "We ready?"

3

On the linoleum tablecloth, beside a plate of sugar-dusted segments of apricot pastry set in custard, a small iceberg of sodden napkin soaked up spilled tea. She examined my groin while balancing a loaded fork. "Thank God it's dried, but the stain!" She had the sort of face that did not suffer when grimacing. I tugged the plastic hem of my cagoule across the brownness and took the seat opposite hers.

"Ha, yeah. Hi, Kerry." We were in the dining room of a double-fronted patisserie in Soho. She'd chosen a table at the back. The silver bag hung off a vacant chair.

"*Had* to get a pot of tea, I was flagging. Normally I'd go straight home, but *she* gets hormonal. I don't mind doing the adding up while she rests her feet. They're swelling, the ankles. Think it's the change."

The green gaze batted. Time stood still. She offered the fork by her mouth towards mine. I shook my head quickly. Her eyes shut, her lips parted and in it went. After a few seconds of pleasurable consideration, she swallowed then blinked at me as if I'd just materialised. "You haven't the faintest idea what I'm talking about, have you?"

"Well, no."

She sighed, "This taste always takes me back. Coffee?"

"I'll get it."

"No, no. After what *I* did? Latte, espresso?"

"Espresso, please."

"Double?"

"Err, that OK?"

"Double it is!"

Pulling her baseball cap down, she rummaged in the bag's silver mouth for her purse then held it up as if it was the winning raffle ticket. "Cake?"

"Oh, no. Not really a cake man."

"We shall see about that," she said, nodding solemnly. She edged out of the door and turned immediately left to re-enter the side of the café that served coffee, cakes and pastries. A couple of men loitering on the pavement made eye contact with each other as she passed them. I watched them shuffle laterally to improve their perspective of her at the counter. She had an effect on passers-by. I'd been aware of it in the tumult of the tube station, and when she stood at the lights on Oxford Street after calling my name. The thing is, all those confusing layers could not conceal an inherent physical charisma. She had attributes I'd only seen in adverts and magazines. She was different.

"Your coffee."

She'd appeared in the doorway holding the tiny cup and saucer in both hands. Peering into it as if it were a crystal ball, she took a step, then stumbled.

"*Oh no!*"

As I shot up from my seat, she righted herself, and her smile flowed into me. For a moment, I felt like telling her how that smile had sustained me through the nauseous hours at rehearsal, but that would be saying too much, too soon. I moved her open bag onto the chair next to mine. She quizzed me with a look.

"Bit near the door. Tea leaves round here."

She shook her head slightly.

"Thieves?"

"Ah those," she said blithely, amused really. "That's very thoughtful, Daniel. Thank you."

She was obviously the sort of person who was quite blind to the criminality lurking in the city. Embarrassed, I addressed the sodden napkin in the saucer. "Nah, just being err, careful. There's loads of signs, you know, keep your bag zipped."

"You laughed," she said, alluding to her cameo just now.

I'd angled myself so that my left side faced her. It was something I'd learned to do when I returned to school.

"Did I?"

She didn't reply as she sectioned off a sliver of cake. I looked out of the window. Her fork chinked the plate.

"Daniel." I logged the sound of her saying my name, so I had words as well as pictures for later. "I want to say, formally, I'm so sorry for the assault on you this morning. I'd actually missed my stop. I was listening to music."

"Forget it."

"Thank you." Pardoned, unburdened, she concentrated on

segregating a bigger piece.

Watching her eat cake was a like an ad break in a film, a thriller or horror, where it's all going disastrously wrong and you're holding your breath and then suddenly, advert time, and there's this ridiculously beautiful female sampling some complex gateau with a voice-over and strings.

When she caught me looking, her eyes flitted like a deer at a lake. She put down her fork, went into her bag and offered me her headphones. "Would you like to hear it?"

I felt something hot flick inside me. "No, no. I don't."

She reared comically. "OK, fine." Returning the headphones to her bag before licking the back of the fork, she confessed, "I'm addicted to that song. It's 'My Perfect Seventeenth'. From the film? I always have it on so loud."

For a second or two, I sensed what resembled a childhood memory: a sepia, degraded image with sound. I must have looked a little strange, drifting off while she was speaking. I shook my head to indicate that I didn't know it.

"Girly movie?" she persisted. "It's on everywhere. I'm a bit old for it, to be honest. Surprised you've not heard of it." She was examining my stubbly jaw line. "Not your cup of tea. I'm guessing you're a bit of a hard rock man?"

"Ha, not particularly."

She'd mentioned she worked near Bond Street tube station. I asked her if that was where she was going when we met.

"I'd been to visit my friend, Francine."

"Oh, she's not local?"

"King's Cross." She moved the handle of her cup away from her with a clear neat nail. "She wasn't in."

"Shame."

"So, where was I?" She began telling me about her job. Her boss was some kind of heiress and had a clothes shop (and should or shouldn't be on HRT), but hadn't a clue about running it, the shop, as a serious concern. She had taken Kerry on as assistant manager, but she didn't do much assisting by the sound of it, she actually did the lot. Licking her fork clean, she said that she was determined to make the shop a success, adding that her twin passions were fashion and eating cake.

"Oh no, I can't believe it!" she said out of nowhere.

Careful not to dislodge my spectacles, I glanced left and right. "What?"

Her eyes had widened melodramatically as she looked past me into the street.

"It's the most amazing coincidence, Daniel!"

I shook my head.

"It's a Citroën Deux Chevaux!" There was an old French motor, rattling to bits outside the café.

"Yes, yes, I'm eating *this* cake today, with you, and that was the car my mum took us in through France when I was ten!"

"That's …mad?"

"Can you not see, the serendipity; the cake, the car and…"

I couldn't face her directly. She was alive with memories I could never compete with. She went on to tell me about the journey in the car and how slow it was and how unafraid of the big lorries she'd had to be as they hemmed them in on the drive across the mountains into Switzerland to visit her mother's boyfriend, Phillipe, who, she said earnestly, was the love of her mum's life, 'the one'.

"When we got there, I must have fallen asleep, but I was so hungry, and he bought me this cake for being such a good girl…Daniel, not boring you, am I?"

Her fingers were lightly tapping the back of my hand.

"No, no," I said, retracting it to push up the frame.

I had to get home by eight, no particular reason, just always did, mid-week. Weekends too.

"So, now you know all about me; dogsbody shop girl for a schizoid heiress, but I'm not complaining. I'd like to know about you. What do you do? You have kids, do you see your mum, go on holidays?"

The woman looked like she was in films, she'd touched my hand and uninhibitedly revealed intimate memories of her childhood. We were sitting somewhere nice, she wasn't constantly checking her phone or looking over my shoulder to see who was there. She patently had time for me. Why? Alarm bells began ringing in my head and in the cacophony, I imagined canned laughter, cameras and a presenter emerging from the steps behind me with an old-fashioned microphone. *'Daniel Earl tonight…'You're A Mug!'* I checked my watch. I'll give it another fifteen. The tubes are pretty consistent this time of night. Should make it home by eight easily. Dinner by eight twenty-five?

"Daniel?"

It isn't a hard question to answer, the *'what do you do?'* one. I could be concise. I'm a keyboard player in a famous band. That it was imploding was irrelevant because I would never let anyone know about the inner working of *my* band. Why would I blurt out the details of my unflagging loyalty to a coked-up power-obsessed, sex- and rage-crazed alcoholic, who had effectively ordered me to assassinate my two closest friends, to a strange woman I'd met on the Central Line after she'd thrown hot coffee at me? I mean, who'd admit to eating copious amounts of shit just because they were scared of going back to where they were from. *No.* There was no way this person was going to learn anything about my living's dark machinations.

One of the men that had watched her earlier had returned and was walking slowly past the window. He was tall, urbane, well-barbered. He paused, feigning necktie adjustment, wanting to catch her eye. She turned to face me directly, enquiringly, job-interview style. "Carry on, your work…I'm interested."

"Kind of preparing?" I flannelled. "It's like a programming thing."

Pointlessly licking the back of her fork, she aimed more guileless mirth at me. She was tilting her head, curiously examining that side. I turned fractionally away. But she was not to be deterred. I was starting to heat up. Did she want a fucking photo? I exhaled, tapping my heel rapidly on the floor. There could be delays, line cancellations. I'd been held at a red signal coming in this morning. I needed to eat by eight-thirty at the latest. After that, it's heading towards wind-down and I wanted to finish the last half-hour of the video I was currently watching.

"You know, I was mortified about what I did. I'm usually so dexterous."

I looked up from serviette island in its sea of spilled tea. "Nah, these things happen."

Her laughter, like wind-chimes, tinkled around my head.

"Just thinking about my mum. We were always knocking things

over between us, miracle we didn't electrocute each other, lose a finger or two at least."

"You live with your mum?"

"Oh no, she's on the coast. Lewes. She's got a weekend stall in The Lanes. Ceramics." She could not lick that fork any cleaner. I gave her nothing. She didn't care. "She was a graphic designer in the seventies, lectured in it. S'pose I inherited my passion for clothes and fashion from her. She was *so* stylish. Taller than me. What's your mum like?"

"Ha-ha, nothing like yours."

There was a mildly uncomfortable pause.

"Tell me about your office, Daniel. I'm technically inept. Barely get my phone switched on some mornings. And I'm probably the only person you know that still listens to cassettes."

She's gonna poison herself licking that fucking metal.

"Although you wouldn't think it, I'm on it to my girlfriends for hours. My phone. God, we can yack away," she said, tamping some cake crumbs on the plate, transferring them to her tongue and pinning me with a lustrous gaze. "Honestly. I'm interested."

"I'd bore you to death with the details." I couldn't raise a smile now. Getting near the witching hour. I could practically hear the platform announcement informing me of *'leaves on the line'*. I needed to finish that video and get down to Blockbuster's for another. It'll be too late to take it back if I hang around here much longer. Her past, her outlook, her appearance, just her – like my band and Jake's clapped-out sofa – it was all mushrooming out of control.

She produced her first frown. It was comedic. I didn't smile.

"You don't want to tell me what you do?"

"It's very boring. Like number crunching, feeding in data and stuff like that. You know?"

"No, I don't know."

"You don't wanna," I mumbled, slouching in my chair.

Bang! The table shook when her knee hit it, hard. I reached out quickly and settled the crockery.

"Thanks for being so understanding, Daniel."

Success. Double-biceps! I'd repulsed her. The microwave pinged faithfully in my head. The brown, plastic tray that transported every meal I ate was on my lap. Home by eight. Press 'play', get that video rolling. Finish it and leg it up the road for another. Happy days.

In a fifteen-second windmilling of her arms, she'd tucked everything in: shirt, scarf, hair. The silver bag gaped open and spoke to me. *She was being nice, and you fucked her off.* She jerked the baseball cap down. When she wrenched the bag from the chair, most of the contents fell out. Emitting a yelp, she scrabbled around beneath the table stuffing her bag with her phone charger, that night's Standard, bangles, crap cassette player, plastic cutlery wrapped in serviettes, Bible-sized book. I watched her wonderful inefficiency with sadness, but relief too. I'd failed to succeed again. Succeeded to fail?

Finally, cheeks flushed, she stood. The mac belt cinched her waist with a gasp.

She did not see me put the sole of my foot on it and roll it towards me.

The gutless, lonely man I was, spoke to the table. "No problem."

She left.

I lifted my foot and picked it up.

4

It wasn't Jake I nodded a three o'clock greeting to at the reception desk, but Jill. Same job, same initial…entirely different establishment. "First floor," she said.

Spread out in a livid yellow Adidas tracksuit, he reared theatrically as I approached. "No nasty accidents on the way in today?"

"Why, what?" From the armchair beside him, Barney's puffy eyes darted mischievously between us.

Torin took a swig of red. "You didn't know our Danny had developed incontinence in his old age?"

"Wondered what the smell was."

Torin enjoyed my chagrin with a tilted smile.

"It was coffee," I said. "A girl on the tube accidentally threw her coffee at me, yesterday." My effects rack had hidden my jeans and the tell-tale stain from Barney.

"Throwing coffee over a pop star," said Barney, admonishingly. "A step too far in the adoration stakes, methinks." His sketch went unacknowledged. It was becoming a pattern. "Nah, joking," he added, filling the vacuum repentantly. "Seriously, I respect you massively, Daniel. I know I like a laugh but listening to those synths on the live stuff. You are a major talent, mate, *major*."

I addressed Torin. "Thought we said the live recordings were for our ears only?"

"You're not in MI5, matey. It's just music, it's all been heard before."

"Daniel," Barney interjected, "I wouldn't dream of passing anything on. I'm a pro, like you."

"God, you're so precious about your noodling, Daniel," said Torin. "No one cares."

Barney chipped in, "Just saying, stellar keyboardist, mate."

Nodding the thanks you'd give to a parking warden after peeling his ticket off your windscreen, I wondered that if Barney was so musically clued-up, why hadn't he stopped Torin from breaking up the amazing rhythm section that had accompanied those 'stellar' keyboards he kept going on about.

"Danny?" With an open palm, Torin offered me the armchair

to his left. I sank gratefully into it. I'd not slept brilliantly. There'd been a bang in the middle of the night; Kerry's knee hitting the table as she stood, her mind made up, *'bloke in rain mac = waste of time'*. But her face had floated above my bed, her fork loaded, poised at her lips, her soft green gaze on me as I hunted sleep.

Mum had irritated the jaded me at breakfast. She'd loitered in the kitchen doorway as I munched on my toast. I knew, that she knew, I wasn't her 'train on the tracks' son this morning. She was so attuned to the mundanity of my journey: bedroom, studio shed, rehearsal room, Blockbuster's, that when there was a kink on the line, she felt a bump.

"You OK, Daniel?"

I said I was.

"You were up in the night. I heard you."

"Lot on my mind."

"Tell me?"

"Nothing mum. You wouldn't understand." I looked into the garden as she turned in the little space in the hallway and entered the front room to watch breakfast telly.

"We have a problem," Torin stated flatly, jerking me back into the moment.

But three months ago, we didn't, we were four, self-sufficient, organic. Other than for me to write sketches and demos, we'd never been in need of 'Logic' and its programming genius. Corbossa would count us in with four clicks of his drumsticks and we played. Simple as that. There'd even been talk of new material and a renegotiation of our record contract (including an advance, which would have covered my mortgage and what I owed on my credit cards for at least six months), and then Rotterdam had happened.

"I remember the first time I heard 'Silent Storm.'" Like an annually tipsy uncle with a party hat on, Barney was bleating into my ear, "…with my mates at college. We were all pretty much into the dance stuff, but when the synths came in, that chorus Daniel, the way you made it rise up and up…"

A dark look from Torin silenced his assistant. I sat without speaking for a beat or three and waited for him expand on the *'problem'*. I'd noticed recently that when Torin was stern, wanted to be taken seriously, a sulk chewed around his mouth. It was a pose that his audience would never recognise. They only ever saw him stage- or photo-lit, offering a wide, wide smile, his eyes like blue neon beams set on unimaginable horizons just above their heads. Mick once said that they'd used Torin's face as the template for 'Action Man', chiselled jaw, sculpted stubble, deep-set brow, computer-generated teeth. But if his handsomeness bordered on the bland, his voice did not. He'd been an avid chorister at school and could hold a note with classical pop vibrato. It worked brilliantly on our choruses (and I did write a big chorus). Our refrains had an epic feel, thanks to that – combined with Alana's street echo (or more accurately, his echo of her) – he could literally move a room to tears.

He was heroic on stage, mesmerising, taking huge breaths and geometric strides, rousing his followers with expansive sweeps of his arms, wringing the very soul from his vocal. During 'The Ship That Never Sailed', a favourite of his, he'd fall to one knee to sob into the mic. Seeing that, we'd 'organically' drop down to a pulse with him for a few bars. We'd watch him whispering behind his hand to an unseen confessor knowing, via some telepathic twitch of his arse, a flick of a clairvoyant finger, that he was about to explode. Mick would meet our eyes, smash a cymbal and electrified, Torin would leap into the air and fellate his harmonica until his lungs gave out.

And between songs, as the applause reluctantly faded, there was intimacy over a glass of red (a couple of uncorked bottles always rested on the drum riser), as he related the 'funny thing that happened to him on the way to the theatre' to the hushed hundreds. He was magnetic, every lad's best mate, every girl's tryst. When he finished his glass, Mick would click his sticks and in we'd go again.

Barney interrupted my thoughts, "Seriously Daniel, 'Silent Storm', I mean, when you're up there playing it, how does it feel?"

Barney's enquiry had me observing myself on that stage; speccy, level with Mick's drum riser, Juno loud, climbing through the final 'semitone up' chorus of our worldwide hit, feeling the room rising to meet us on some undefinable musical summit. *'Silent storm,'* they all sang, *'Oh silent storm...'*

"Fucksake Barney, shut up!" The chewy sulk leaked from Torin's unsmiling mouth as he stared me down from his bitter widow's peak. "Corbossa's not cutting it."

And he was right. Torin was *never* to be underestimated. Although musically inept (a mad thing to say; explanation to follow) he had discerned during the rehearsal before the last one (when we were 'trying it out just to see') that Mick was infinitesimally ahead or behind the digital metronome I'd attached the synth bass to. It is a staggering thing that Torin detected that subtlety, because since we'd got together, he'd shown not one iota of that attention to detail in his own work.

"We've all these dates. The big London one to kick it off. Routing, budget, the usual hoo-ha. A lot of money invested. A lot to be made."

I met his eye. "One rehearsal, Torin."

In Denmark Street, a quarter of a mile away, Mick was practising for his life; in here, I was pleading for it.

"You've either got it, or you haven't."

"He's been a top drummer for five years, man!"

"He's an old woman in a Ferrari."

I stewed in my sumptuous armchair while he sipped from his glass. Two or more beats silently passed. I sensed Barney moving in. Torin cut him off with an inhalation. "OK, Danny," he said. "I'll give it one more go, for you."

He waved his empty glass laterally. With an imperceptible bow, our 'manager' took it from his hand. While we waited for Barney to return from the bar with a refill, I took a breath.

"He's been solid for hundreds of gigs."

"You've got no critique."

"This is mad, Torin."

"It's sanity at its purest, actually." He looked past me. Members were arriving in dribs and drabs. "And what would have happened if I'd abandoned *my* critique in that pub on that fateful day? Not seen through the mediocrity… 'Delta Dawn' indeed."

Well of course, there's only one answer to that and I wasn't going to supply it.

"You came free with a packet of twenty, Danny." When his stage smile was on me, I couldn't resist smiling back.

Summoning up my nerve, I looked straight at him. "We had a

band that took us around the world. You're breaking it all..."

"Barney!" He spluttered, then roared; "Fucking Merlot. I'm drinking Cabernet, you fat fool!" Barney was up and waddling towards the bar like a scolded duck. As Torin's rancid, furious tide ebbed, he nodded coolly at a couple of newly arrived members, then brought his mouth to my ear. "Simply can't get the help these days."

* * *

We took off our headphones simultaneously.

"How was that?"

"Tiny bit loose?" I replied.

I'd walked back to the rehearsal room to see how Mick was getting on with the click track. Torin's red breath was still in my nose. Him roaring at Barney for such a trifling miss-order activated memories of his darkest moments on the road, when coloured by self-medication, grim daylight recovery and the unbearable pressure he felt performing, he edged into states of fury. I'd seen the rictus, teeth-clenched face he'd shot at Barney many, many times. He'd worn it, baffled and buffeted, show after show when he whirled around to face me on the stages of Chicago, Green Bay or Minneapolis bellowing not, *'I'm drinking Cabernet!'* to Barney but, '*What next, what next?'*

What, I wondered – as he reclined like a big, elegant banana with fuck all to do but get smashed into the early hours – could bring him to that hyper, mid-gig touring state?

"How loose?" Corbossa asked.

I shrugged. "Lagging on the fills. Could be a tiny bit tighter."

Mick's face dropped defeatedly, which was tragic because he was such a forward-looking bloke. Broad shouldered, broad forehead, a smile for anyone under those brown curls. His companionship in this mad musical spaceship had been invaluable to me.

"But not in a bad way," I added, feeling a ripple of guilt run through me. "Gotta have some feel in there."

"Yeah, you gotta."

"I'll run it again."

I put on my headphones and pressed the spacebar. Mick listened to the computer's eight-beat count in his headphones, hit the opening cymbal and proceeded to mark time on the hats for a further eight beats.

From the PA, 'Silent Storm' began its creeping, swirling ascent and, as Mick joined in, I drifted back to the moment I discovered that sound on my Casio SK-1. The keyboard was my mum's Christmas present to me when I came out of hospital. In my box room in the flats, that modest instrument instantly became my best friend. Of course, it was in no way a 'professional' keyboard, nothing like the gear I had now, but it had enthralled me with its user-friendliness and zany effects. I remembered how I'd amuse my sixteen-year-old self endlessly swearing into its sampler and playing it back. I don't recall, when writing 'Silent Storm', whether the sounds or the melody came first, but I knew when I'd put both together, I'd created something irresistible. You just do. Playing it to the band in rehearsal the following day, Torin was humble, bordering on grateful. He'd said the synth line was brilliant, 'stormy'.

"Behind?" Through my fading memory, Corbossa was looking up at me from the drums.

I pressed the spacebar and stopped the song. "Bit of both," I said.

His sticks rattled on the drum rims as he lay them down. "Going for a bath," he said. Our eyes met in melancholy at our trusted US tour quip. There they said 'bathroom' instead of toilet, so we were always going for a slash in someone's bath over there.

I'd not listened to the song (without playing on it) for years. Torin's vocal breathed the verse in over my *'stormy'* keyboard part, Alana pumped her bass line and Corby picked it all up with a clever sixteen's hi-hat pattern, understated, but the back-beat strong and solid. I might have played the song a thousand times, but listening to it in this empty room and on a tired system took me back to our first rehearsals together under the railway arches in Shepherd's Bush. Creating our sound, arranging it, then playing it again and again was all we lived for, back then. Nothing got us down, not even the bare musical facts of life that said a band like ours was ninety-eight percent doomed to failure. We never *not* believed we were the charmed two percent that wasn't.

As the song progressed, another musical truth stamped itself onto my consciousness... if you can hear the click track when the drums are playing, the drums are 'out', and if they're out, the whole thing slides arrhythmically, it stutters and sounds shit, basically.

I glanced at the door. My best mate was gonna lose it all 'cos he couldn't keep that clever, tricksy sixteen's hat thing he'd invented in perfect digital time, for four minutes.

Studying the vertical line on the screen, I tried to remember how the hook had got to the Casio from my imagination. What was I looking at, what had I been doing, what was I about to do? I turned off the computer and flopped onto the studio sofa. Behind my shut eyes I saw, not my cascading keyboards on their heavy-duty chromium stands, but my Casio, resting on a length of hardboard between two bar stools.

"Daniel, you're doing 'versions' of these songs, again."

I'd gone back five years. Standing next to my set-up at the back of the tiny stage in the local pub, Miss Ferguson was watching me place the Casio into its cardboard box, post gig. She had on her red check shirt, flared skirt and cowboy boots. "People want to hear them exactly as they are on the records. We're a country cover's band, Daniel, not Gong, or whatever."

I loved 'Delta Dawn' and 'Ring of Fire' but wanted to do them my way. It wasn't a 'Blanket on the Ground' for me, it was a magic carpet. On those Friday nights, mum driving me to the pub on the edge of the estate, I always had the best intentions, knew that I should stick to the arrangements, but something reckless got into me when I was up there. Because I couldn't release that teenage energy and rebellion with mates; drinking, smoking pot, flirting (I didn't have any mates and no one flirted with me), I 'rose up' against a set of innocent country hits, inserting an arpeggio where one didn't exist, fuzzing up a bass line or extending a solo. I'd wrench those faders to breaking point at the back of that old pub. It's a miracle I didn't tear them off.

As I was about to deliver my well-worn apology to Miss Ferguson, tell her I'd play *properly* next gig, she blinked past me in disbelief. I turned and followed her gaze. Against the flock walls and faded denim clientele *he* strode towards the stage. The mums, dads, in-laws and local outlaws were as bug-eyed as her, the bloke was wearing a fucking dress!

"I'm Torin. What's your poison?"

"Err, Daniel Earl. Lager, please."

Returning to the table, he raised his glass and scanned the room. "You don't see many boozers like this anymore," he announced, as if he could buy the place, flatten it and park his car on it.

"Nah, suppose not," I floundered, looking around the room.

He told me he'd just stopped in to buy cigarettes when he heard us. "I caught the last couple of songs. You look like you're in pain up there?"

I was aware that all eyes were on me and the tall bloke with the Zapata tash, swept-back mane and skirt. He gently rapped on that corner table's scratched surface to get my attention. "Ideas are the currency, Daniel."

That phrase hit home, because all I had were ideas.

"The way you play." He subjected me to his all-encompassing smile for the first time. "What's in your head will make your fortune."

"But you've only heard me play covers?"

He traced the edge of his moustache with his thumb. I'd made sure my good side was on offer.

"You shit ideas, my friend. You cannot contain yourself." He turned over a beer mat and wrote down his address. "Midday tomorrow."

It wasn't a request.

A thud on the bass drum snapped me back to reality. Corbossa had returned from the gents and picked up his sticks.

"Right, let's have another crack."

Our headphones went on. I pressed 'play'.

5

The train doors opened, the bloke opposite me crushed his tin and left it on the seat. A teenager flicked it off, booted it along the aisle, then sat down. We laboured through the black walls until a flash of bright sunshine lit me, him and the half dozen people in our section. Emerging from the underground depths, I looked at the line-side properties etched against the deep blue of the stratosphere. I knew every garden, window, curtain and blind (on this side of the aisle and the one opposite). I knew when the wheels would screech in defiance of a minimal corner and the junctures that would rock us in our seats. An on-going loft conversion, big tree with kids' trampoline beneath, alley with motorbike, tilting shed and splintered fence marked the countdown to my stop. 'Staz', 'Crow', yellow and orange graffiti, then, forward, back, right, erect.

The train decelerated to a halt. The carriage speaker scratched into being. "Just waiting for the train to depart on the platform in front of us."

I yawned and shut my eyes. I'd lived with my mum in leafy West Acton for four years now. Nothing much distinguished the homes from each other; grass verges and front garden gates, no one parked across anyone's drive and the bins were always put out the night before. It might sound dull to some, but I treasured it.

On my knee, I played the eight-note pattern I'd heard in the seconds before Kerry had thrown her coffee at my groin. It had happened three carriages back from this one. My mind slowed as I tried to decipher something hidden in the notes of that modest hook, then my chin fell on my chest in hopelessness. *'Jesus, Mick,'* I opened my eyes and stared emptily at the grubby slats between my feet, *'can you not do what a thousand other less talented drummers than you can?'*

***

Mick Corbossa had taken me to my first gig, *ever*. Although I played in the pub on Friday nights, I'd never actually been a part of an audience – literally 'faced the music'. Everyone in the covers band was married with kids, and were ten, fifteen years older than me, so I never mixed socially with any of them.

It was after an intense session under the arches, perhaps our third or fourth one there, that Torin, Alana, Mick and I had gone to the pub. We were sitting, heads together, discussing songs and sounds, when Mick said he'd take me out.

"Me?"

"Yeah, we're in this great band together. Let's celebrate."

I thought Torin and Alana would go with us, they were lovers back then and never apart, but Torin had said he wanted to work on the lyrics to the thing we'd put together that afternoon, and he never worked on anything without Alana. Thinking about it now, it was the Friday I'd played them the music to the then untitled 'Silent Storm'. In the studio Torin had turned to Alana: *'Told you'*, he'd said.

Mick stood with a belch. "Right, Daniel, we're gonna go to where the darkest of denizens gather."

Blinking beneath my spectacles, I uttered, "Where?" I'd had two pints of lager and felt ready to be led. If only the three of them had known, that at nineteen, I'd never stepped foot in a club. I'd heard of the place Mick was talking about. Some very cool bands played there, and it struck me looking at Alana – cropped-haired tough waif; Torin – ethnic poncho, leading-man handsome; and Mick – B-Boy fit, that I was in a pretty cool band myself. I finished the inch in the bottom of my glass, stood and followed my drummer out.

In his fawn-coloured jacket and green Puma trainers, Mick, at twenty-five (the age I am now), was a man of the world as far as I was concerned. He worked for his dad who had his own plumbing business and like his son, an affable, obliging nature. Mick was attending evening classes to get his exams for some advanced plumbing/ engineering thing. I was aware he'd had some trouble after he left school and that was the reason he was going for his qualifications 'a bit late'. I wouldn't say he was excited about a career with boilers, rads and shower units, but he knew it was important to have a trade.

Steaming through the glorious avenues of Notting Hill towards Portobello, we talked music. Mick was as obsessed with beats as I was with sound and melody. Like me, he was self-taught and a fervent practiser. We agreed it would have been good to have had lessons from a young age, but what we lacked in technique we made up for in the will to *make* music any way we could. "We've got *'chemistry'*, he said, gently barging me with his broad shoulders as we walked beneath the Westway, "and style too."

We were talking about getting into rehearsals early and jamming out ideas when my voice trailed off. We'd hit the queue, and suddenly I was being scrutinised by a score of funky West Londoners. Mick was already chatting to some of the people lined up. I remember the pride swelling in me when he introduced me to a couple of blokes as the 'keyboard player in his band'.

Inside the venue, the PA volume sucked the wind out of me, and I swayed on my two pints, feeling like I'd come from a world of monochrome into Technicolor. The band on stage was by far the loudest thing I'd ever heard.

Back from the bar, Mick handed me a frosty bottle. "What d'you think?" he boomed.

It was fascinating listening to a band that were our contemporaries. I remember the singer was a tuneless but energetic Asiatic. The guitarist had a scruffy mohawk, gallons of reverb and attitude. The bassist played like he was doing the rest of them a favour; he was that much better. The drummer was a bit of a plodder, but they had their thing and were doing it passionately. Despite my ambivalence (born out of envy, because they were playing and we were not), my feet were tapping along.

I realised Mick was no longer at my side but leaning on the bar talking to a girl with blonde hair, red lipstick and an embroidered coat. When something knowing passed between them, he levered himself forward to remonstrate, affably, obligingly.

A lot of flamming tom-toms and vocal wailing signalled the next song, but I couldn't take my eyes from Mick and his friend. He said something else, her eyes flared and her red lips pursed. They both laughed. When her coat parted I gawped at the patent, thigh-high platform boots compressing her long, slim thighs. The song dropped moodily down to just bass and kick drum. A held note of feedback initiated her eyes closing and her lips brushing his.

As Mick pulled away, I spun around and faced the stage. Bang! The drummer was smacking the fuck out of the snare like a gleeful blacksmith. A verse and chorus passed. Somehow, I'd found myself right at the front of the stage.

"*Cheers!*" Mick was beside me with another bottle: "*They sound better the more of these you have.*" Around me, groups posed and gyrated in varying degrees of revelry and style. I'd never seen so many attractive women in one place at one time. It was like turning the pages of one of the i-D magazines I'd flicked through at Torin's flat weeks before. A round of cheering greeted the end of the song. I raised my bottle to the guitarist. He saw me, leaned over and clinked my bottle with his.

Eyes were on me suddenly. When a man a few feet away winced, a bolt of angst shot through me. I clenched my fist. The urge to readjust my specs was compelling, but I didn't want to draw further attention to myself. The man nudged his mate and nodded towards me. I scanned the room for Mick. He wasn't there. I felt like a toddler abandoned in the supermarket. Sidelong glances were being aimed at me. It was unbearable, like the first weeks back at school. Back then, I'd just walk out, today was no different.

The doors shut behind me and I strode from the club drawing in big mouthfuls of air. But at the sound of tinkling laughter I slowed. Below the roaring overpass, beneath the awning of a shop in the arcade, Corbossa and the girl with the straight blonde hair were kissing. When the club doors opened again and music burst through, Mick looked up. I poked up my specs, smiled the best I could and went on my way.

I didn't know Mick *that* well, I'd only ever seen him on his drums. In breaks at rehearsals, we'd walked around the corner to get a Coke or whatever, chatted a bit about him being a plumber like his dad, me and my covers band, but in the main, we talked about music. I knew he was nothing like me in the respect that he 'had a life', had friends and of course, some of them were female and lovely, but it still burned. At nineteen, when you've had almost no experience of girls, it just does. Knowing that not one of those attractive, stylish, music-loving women back in that club would take a second look at me, I rammed my hands hard into my pockets and chin down, marched on. I'd get into the studio early tomorrow and work and experiment and create. I might not be accepted in a cool club, but I was an intrinsic member of a cool band. I was positive of that from the outset.

"*Oi, Daniel!*"

I turned. He was running towards me. I waited until he caught up.

"Where you goin' man?"

"Home. Getting on at Westbourne."

"Nah we're out tonight, you and me."

 "But...you, had your friend."

"*You're* my friend." I looked past him. Like an album cover, the girl in the thigh-high boots was posed in the half-light beneath the Westway. Mick cupped his hands over his mouth, "I'll bell you up, Tracy," he bellowed.

"Oh no, Mick," I said, watching Tracy shrug and turn towards the club doors. I couldn't imagine walking away from a girl that looked like that.

His arm went around my shoulders. I tottered on shaky legs. "I know a place." he said.

Somewhere down Portobello Road, I recall a metal grate being slid across a door and stumbling into a space not much bigger than my front room.

"Starvin'. You?"

"No."

"Nuvver one?"

"Yeah, OK." I slurred. I'd fallen into a leatherette niche with the rummy pineapple thing Mick had bought me.

While he chatted through the serving hatch to the cook, throbbing dub rattled the foundations. The place was comfortably seedy and everything, including the glasses, seemed sort of third hand, but it was electric too. People grooved in slow motion. I floated with pleasure; I was patently having the best night of my life.

Mopping up a huge plate of curry with about six rotis, he told me that Hendrix and Bob Marley had played here years ago and that there was an even chance Mick Jagger might pop in for a swift one. He laughed when he saw the look on my face. I never found out if he was taking the piss or not.

Time passed in a broth of side-sticks and reverb. I might have consumed two of those pineapple things, maybe three.

"You alright bruv?"

I could barely hear him over echoing trumpets. "What?" I yelled. The brass seemed to be coming at me from every crack and fissure, under the table, up through the floor.

"You know you're a bit special, don't you Daniel," he hollered.

"Owjewmean?"

The music dropped to just bass and hats. He leaned in. It was like a scene in a film. "You got it, you know, the way you play." There was no need for shouting now. "That thing you showed us today, it's…like, majestic…Alana said you're 'unique', yeah, unique. You look at music, melody and sound, different… you don't copy no one, you follow your own?"

I listened for four beats before answering. "Furrow?"

"Is it furrow?"

The guitars joined bass and drums, jangling over and over and then the trumpets returned chest out, blaring, forceful. He had to raise his voice again.

"Listen man." He downed whatever it was he was drinking. "Trust your instincts. Don't be no fucking doormat, yeah?"

I managed to nod.

"Well, in life too," he added with certainty.

"I will," I said, standing and aiming for the tiny staircase, but reeling into the wall.

I awoke on a front room sofa. Lucy, Mick's mum had brought me a cup of tea. Mick and his dad had already left for work.

***

The cacophonous trumpets from that night out with Mick five years ago were abruptly interrupted by the carriage speaker, "We've got a green light. Sorry for the delay." The train lurched forwards and when the doors opened, I dashed off.

The house I'd bought was halfway down a pleasant, tree-lined avenue. As branches swayed in a light summer breeze, I was put in mind of certain untamed strawberry tresses and a silver fork chinking on the China dish.

"Kerry," I whispered.

She sectioned off a piece of cake, *'I always have a slice or two…or three, when I'm in here'*, then, seemingly inspired by the Deux Chevaux rattling away outside the patisserie, she exclaimed *'Grindelwald!'* *'What?'* I'd asked.

'The little town in the German-speaking part of Switzerland we drove to. We…' She stopped mid-sentence and carefully set her fork on the plate.

I detected the sadness that had enthralled me in the carriage that morning. Her eyes flashed with energy when she looked up at me. She had gone from dark to light in half a second.

"Ha-ha, your face, Daniel. Mum and Philippe used to go skiing there. It's in the shadow of the Eiger. Huge, jagged cliff-faces leaning over you, quite scary and awesome. Remember Heidi? It's like that, fairy-tale houses, gingerbread? I'd go on the nursery slopes while mum and Philippe went off 'somewhere else', ha-ha. We had a chalet, shared it with another family. They had three kids a bit younger than me, I liked having siblings…yeah, their dad was a journalist on the Observer and that's how my mum got her column…what? Oh, so mum wrote about our holiday, the journalist dad chap, said she should write an account of her stay? Cut a long story short, pun, pun, pun, they published it. It didn't last long, her column, two summer holidays and that one, in Grindelwald."

Another forkful was consumed, and to be honest, so was I. I'd never been near anyone as absorbing and unpredictable. I was so enrapt I'd forgotten to face the right way.

"Oh Daniel, it was so dreamy. We had a hostess who'd cook for all of us. You couldn't afford it now. Huge fry-up breakfasts and really posh dinners and, of course, *this* amazing apricot tart."

And the comic way she had turned the plate left and right in her slender fingers, the TV advert face she made spread warmth though me after the icy hours in the studio with Torin and Mick.

"It'd all be laid out when we came back from skiing. I didn't care about the fry-up, just the cake, ha-ha. Philippe was quite accomplished, army I think, and he went off with his chaps, you know, to do daring stuff? So, mum and me would spend afternoons on our own walking and just being close, mother and daughter. Natural."

She paused. Suddenly dry and blank. When she resumed it was as if she were reading from a board behind me and the font was fractionally too small. "There wasn't anyone around, only us, the cold and our breath, the mountain keening over us, only the snow crunching beneath our feet, unspoiled, totally unspoiled…" Her voice had grown so quiet, I had to lean across the table to listen. "There were little huts nestled into the hillside. A farmer…mum spoke French and knew a little bit of German. He was so friendly, kindly with a huge bushy beard and fat forearms. Me and mum went inside, and in this pen there was a new-born calf, and he asked me if I'd like to come and say hello. He told me to put three fingers in its mouth…my hands were little, and the calf suckled them hard, she wanted her mother's milk but of course, there was no milk, just my fingers…"

Her face had fallen. A well of sadness flowed from her eyes as they studied the empty plate in front of her. I was clueless as to what to do or say to return her to her brilliant self. I went for my cup and sipped, when I looked up, she was again, beaming. The centrefold glam had returned to that quirky old café. With a toss of her head and an impish wink, she said, "I repeat, I *know* I can yack a boy's ears off."

"No, no," I said, but I was thinking that my mother – whose jobs, between stultifying belts of depression, had variously been cleaner, dinner lady and super-market check-out staff – would have probably been employed to do her mum's ironing. I had no stories to tell about us, apart from the big one, and the details of that had been told only to the band in the confines of a tour bus on a dark desert highway, a continent away.

"Kerry," I said out loud as I neared my house. I'd reached my front door and imagined her standing on the other side. It was mad. I fingered the thin tube in my mac pocket then took out my phone. I sent a text: *'Sorry to trouble you, but after you left the cake place, I found your lipstick under a chair. Can I return it to you? Mail it?'*

Done. Key in the lock.

Before long I was watching a video, mum was in the doorway.

"Took that old chair to the dump."

"Oh mum, I said I'd do it for you. Weekend. Weighs a ton."

"Don't be silly. You make me sound so old and frail."

"No, I meant…"

She nodded at that night's steaming microwaved offering: "Don't let your dinner go cold. What is it?"

"It's cannelloni. Italian."

She chuckled. "Sounds like Mick."

I paused my video. She wanted to speak. Just then my phone pinged.

"What's wrong with the band, Daniel?"

I opened the message.

"Nothing mum."

"Really?"

"Yeah, all good."

She left me to the film, which though epically convoluted plotwise, paled in comparison to the complexities developing in my life. I pressed play on the remote but couldn't concentrate. Pressed pause again. Things used to be so simple. I hated what Torin was doing, but still loved him for what he'd done for me. Striding into that moody pub in his sarong, impervious to the sniggering and pointing at his back, he'd not given a fuck. He still didn't. I remember Miss Ferguson asking me who the hell that was. *'Just some bloke'*, I'd said, stunned, nursing the pint he'd bought me, not wanting to finish it in case I broke the spell.

'Just some bloke…' For once, instead of different, I felt special. The most magnetic human that anyone in that bar had ever seen had singled *me* out for attention. Ten minutes later, crossing the car park to mum's Toyota with my keyboard in its disintegrating cardboard box, Torin's words played in my head. If ideas are the currency, was I to be his banker, his mint? He'd given me the address of his flat. He expected me there with my gear the next day and it struck me as absurd, because although I bordered on the reclusive with mum on the estate, there was no way I *wouldn't* be at that address, and at the appointed time.

That morning, standing at the front door with my Casio and cables in a plastic laundry bag, mum studied me from the end of the passage. Her eyes, as they invariably did, pleaded for forgiveness as I turned the latch.

"You never go out on Saturdays Daniel."

She was right, but, as was soon to be the custom when Torin called, I came *and* at a time of his choosing.

"Go and watch telly mum, I'll be fine."

***

Standing outside a pristine, jasmine-strewn town house, ten minutes' walk from Holland Park Station, I double-checked the address he'd written on the beer mat that he'd given me the night before. I peered up and up. Flawless, white stucco pierced the bluest sky. There were too many windows to count. I wiped the sweat from my forehead, climbed the broad stone steps and lifted the brass knocker, but before it fell, the door had opened. He was topless and shoeless in a brown sari. It was a bit after twelve on a blisteringly hot Saturday.

The exterior and lobby were immaculate, the red carpet on the stairs spotless and the winding banister polished to a glow. On the first floor he opened a door and ushered me into his flat.

"Shut the door behind you," he called over his shoulder.

Hairline cracks ran down the architrave by the door, and the area around the light switch was blackened with handprints. The scuffed and dented passage ahead was an obstacle course of shoes, boots and coats. Stepping over a skateboard with only three wheels, I followed him into the room at the end.

The dimensions spun my nut. You could have dropped my kitchen, front room and hallway into it, and they wouldn't have touched the sides. The chipped ornaments and icons parked randomly gave the impression of a ransacked museum, but there were no paintings or posters on the walls. Wine glasses and bottles, half, quarter full and drained, occupied every surface. Across the breadth of parquet floor, both sets of shelves either side of a gothic fireplace had spectacularly collapsed. Cracked and splintered CD sleeves were strewn, magazines, paperbacks and coffee-table art books were stacked, hip high. It was as if everything that should have been spread out, had been bulldozed into the end of the room.

"Put my stuff down?" I asked, blinking the sweat from my eyes.

For a second or two he seemed not to understand the request, then he smiled. "Anywhere you like," he said, padding across the scarred floor to light two long yellow candles at either end of the mantelpiece.

As I lay down my bag of gear, my shoulder rose to meet my ear with a sense of relief.

"Wine?" A cork popped. Dust motes danced in the sunlight streaming through the windows.

I cleared my throat. I did not want to squeak at this juncture. "Yes, co..."

"...is the right answer," he said, filling two glasses. "To planetary peace, *and* more importantly, world domination!" We touched glasses. I'd had a few glasses of wine in the past, but they had never tasted like the glass that Torin poured for me that afternoon. The heavy scent I inhaled and the spiciness I swirled around my mouth, had me craning my neck, squinting up at the thousand droplets in the vast chandelier above my head. It was delicious. His bracelets rattled as he refilled his glass. I took a further sip, and through the slowly receding dregs, watched him stride to the netless street-side windows. He addressed the road outside as if faithful legions stood in ranks beneath him.

"My band will be great. Tremendous actually. And you, Daniel, will be its banker." He spun around and shot a dazzling smile at me. "And why is that?" he asked.

I cleared my throat. "Ideas are the currency?"

"You're getting the hang of this, m'boy."

"Err, anyone else coming?"

Refilling my glass, spilling loads, he flopped onto a weathered Chesterfield.

"Yes, Alana," he replied. "She should be here any minute. Set your stuff up over there."

As my first day with Torin beneath his vast chandelier fled into memory, I whispered "Alana" into my bedroom ceiling. Torin was coming to the studio tomorrow. He wanted to hear Mick beat-perfect on all our songs, but Mick couldn't get thirty seconds into one before lagging or chasing that fucking metronome. He was no robot drummer, Torin *knew* that. Mick guided us with feel and instinct. But there wasn't an 'us' anymore to guide.

I picked up my phone from the bedside table and, for the fifth time, reread the message that had pinged up when mum had come into the front room while I was eating my cannelloni.

6

I could hear him as I approached Room Three, our cadence, the intrinsic sound of 'us'. He continued drumming as I put on my headphones. The track stopped. He glanced up, his warm brown pupils asked the question.

He was out.

"Miles better, Corby."

"Been here since ten. I'm determined."

"Ninety percent of it, man."

"Next."

After what I'd achieved in the dead of night at the back of my garden, I could barely endure placing the tips of my fingers on the computer keys.

"Play it," he insisted. I pressed the spacebar and put my conscience in a box on a high shelf in the shed because today, *I* was determined as well. This shitty time *had* to be got through.

By how slowly the door opened, I knew that Barney was pushing it (and finding it a struggle). Torin followed him in, sipping from a double espresso.

"Men," he said, exaggeratedly wincing at the brew. This 'men' thing was a recent character posture. One of the many he'd adopted over the years. Day to day, you never knew who he really was. Alana had once mentioned that there was some military component in his background. Recently, he'd fancied himself a Savile Row, off-duty guardsman, replete with 'brolly rifle' swinging at his side. It was as bogus a pose as the cod ragamuffin act he'd performed for her at the tube station five years ago.

While Barney squeezed into an armchair, Torin took his place on the sofa: classic grey suit, the shoulder blades pushing against the gaberdine, his kneecaps doing the same to his suit pants. I could smell his coffee and was envious. When he'd come to my studio last week mum had offered him a cup of 'instant'. I'd cringed.

The drumsticks clattered against the rim of the floor tom as Corbossa picked them up. Torin eyed him over his witches' brew. The atmosphere was absurdly strained. Untightening my jaw, I reminded myself again, that this *had* to be got through.

"I won't sing," he said. "You men get playing. Let's have 'Silk'."

'Silk' was a basic fours groove, straight as a dye for all its verses with a subtle change up in the chorus – the tempo never wavered. Like an ace barrister who'd found the weakness in the suspect he was grilling, Torin had chosen the one song that would, in seconds, lay bare Corbossa's timing abilities.

I pressed the spacebar. Through the PA, the keys played a couple of sequential bars and Mick played the fat flam that brought the song in.

***

From the studio, I walked diagonally across Soho from Denmark Street and onto Oxford Circus. It was a little after six and mobbed. Heading west, I realised my heart was beating faster than normal, which was silly. I'd say I was pretty nerveless; huge festivals, live TV shows, flying, none of that upped my pulse, but the next ten minutes or so, did. Access to St Christopher's Place was via a passageway across the road from Bond Street tube station. Comforted that in a few minutes' things would return to normal (band, mum, tube journeys in and out) I ducked in. Beyond the sheer alley walls, café and restaurant tables were laid with white linen, the punters gathered against the inky black railings and bollards were languid in pose, their glasses amber coloured, their cigarette smoke, like the daily grind, blown into the air. It was so 'of this city' that just thirty feet behind me the populace barged and scurried in their avid commute, while here an easy continental ambience pervaded. I walked directly through the square onto the road beyond. *'It's sort of brown'* the message had said. Detecting a faint russet glimmer on the right-hand side, fifty feet ahead of me, I took a breath and quickened my stride.

A small tree grew from a terracotta pot beside the shop door. Its foliage tipped the maze of precarious pipework that ran over the window. The legend 'SIENNA' was printed in black against the goldy-brown façade.

I took a breath. *'Smile and get through it'* I said to myself and pushed the door open. Ding went the doorbell.

She was sitting behind the counter, set on a small dais at the back of the shop. Hearing the doorbell ding, she'd looked up from her phone and put it aside. Up went my apologetic hand. I knew how I looked, but I didn't detect displeasure when she saw me. There was no *'God, there's that miserable bloke'* about her beckoning hand from behind the counter.

Leaning in, I placed her lipstick with thumb and forefinger on the glass case in the middle of the shop.

"Thank God. Naked without my lippy."

I found the courage to look into her eyes. "That's OK. Thanks for the coffee."

"Ha-ha, that a joke?"

There was a furry orange armchair by the door. I couldn't see myself sitting in something like that. It was time to depart. "No. Anyway, I'll err..."

"Where are you going?"

"Just home."

"Don't rush off. Come in." Instead of something pleasant shooting through me at her invitation, my 'hook-making mind' composed a dismal verse and chorus: she was being charitable, or was bored. Was she making a lover jealous? But in I stepped, anyway. "How have you been?"

"Alright." Hands in pockets, pirouetting on my heels, I took in her shop. Gowns, dresses and coats hung on long rails on my left. I lifted a sleeve of one and looked at the price tag. "Three hundred quid!"

"Oh, the vintage rail. They're all designer. That's a Valentino. I actually found that in a second-hand shop and bought it for forty quid."

I nodded, suitably impressed. "You did all this?" I said, extracting one hand from my pocket and casting it about me.

"Yes. Re-merchandised the whole place."

"Re-what-ed?"

"Arranged everything. Looks cool, doesn't it?"

"Yeah, think so," I replied, flicking through the T-shirts and blouses at the end of the rail. "Eclectic," I managed.

"I merchandise by colour, some do it by designer, but I love colour. That way, people find pieces that they wouldn't normally be looking for."

Shoes were arrayed on circular plinths on the other side of the shop. Heels, flats, sandals and trainers all seemed to know their place. I discerned a pattern. Care and thought had been put into everything in here. My focus was on a pair of fake crocodile skin loafers.

"Patrick Cox, they'd suit you."

"You think?"

Willing myself to smile, I loitered by the lingerie display on the gravity-defying shelves to the right of the counter. Feeling her eyes on me, I switched to the bath salts, sponges and moisturisers suspended on the other.

"I'm not the most fashionable," I muttered, returning to the glass island to examine the earrings, bracelets and rings exhibited in and on it. Hands behind my back, I bent at the waist to sniff a crystal perfume bottle.

I knew she was looking at me and knew she was smiling. "Still listening to 'My Perfect Seventeenth'?" I asked.

"Such an ear worm, but I don't care. I think you like it too, secretly."

"Nah. Each to their own, I s'pose."

"Does it bother you that much that I like it?"

"No accounting for taste," I said, rocking on my superior heels. Waiting.

"So, you're more of a classical man, Daniel?"

"I like some classical music, yes."

"Me too. Not against the law to like both."

"I can't see how you can, but..."

There, I'd done it. I saw myself crossing the square, speeding up the alley and clipping down the escalator at the tube. I was thinking about how average that video was last night. I'd ejected it, not even bothering to see what happened to the bloke who got shot. If I could get on the tube in the next ten minutes, I could dive by Blockbuster and get something else, a comedy maybe? I'd be behind, re time, for dinner, but that was OK, once in a while.

"Well, I do," she said. "I guess I'm a bit of a freak, taste-wise."

I poked my glasses up to make sure.

"I'm not bothered. You've a right to like what you like."

"You said you were in IT?" I balled my fists in my pocket and delved into my box of sour replies. My heart racing properly now. *Get through this.*

"Something like that."

"You're a little above it all?"

I raised my eyes. There was a wryness about the corners of her mouth that I could study endlessly. "I mean, I'm not interested in that sort of err, 'distraction', musically," I said. "Of course, I wouldn't dream of telling anyone what they should or shouldn't listen to."

She began typing on her phone. I stood there, barely able to breathe. She looked up finally. I flinched from her gaze. "You're a proper B-52, aren't you?"

"Sorry?"

When she stepped from behind the counter, I kept the gasp behind my teeth. She had on skin-tight, black plastic trousers, black T-shirt and tiger skin brothel creepers. Her pale lips parted in the smile I'd searched my bedroom ceiling for.

"Dropping little bombs, clusters of provocation?" She kind of toe-stepped in rhythm around me and picked up her lipstick. I looked away while she applied it.

"Sorry. Just my way."

I heard the soft catch of the applicator snap shut. "Really?" she said, fluttering around the room, tucking and tidying.

"How's business?" I asked.

"We have bursts," she said, fastening buttons and flattening lapels.

It was so weird. I'd become hooked on the mirth that shaped her mouth when she regarded me. Usually, when people laughed in my direction, it stung like hell.

"Err, that's good then. Keeping the wolf from the door."

She glanced over her shoulder. This particular smile lit me up. "No, I think I may have let him in."

While she patted a pile of sweaters into neatness, I spoke to her back. "You done any acting, Kerry?"

She suddenly ducked behind the counter.

The doorbell rang and a chic-looking woman with a handbag like a wicker basket entered the shop and began perusing the rails with what must have been her daughter. A cat-face sweater caught her eye. She extracted it from the rail and held it up.

"Cool, isn't it?" Kerry had appeared beside her, beaming.

In the seconds I'd stepped aside for them to enter, Kerry had tied her golden mess into a tight bun. A wispy, pink blouse had taken the place of the black T-shirt and subtly jewelled sandals replaced the brothel creepers. The skin-tight plastic trousers had stayed on, but now meant something else entirely.

"Yes, I adore this sort of thing, and cats, of course," said the lady.

"Do you have a cat?" Kerry asked the little girl. She must have been about ten years old.

"We live in a flat. Mummy said I'm not allowed."

"Oh, I'm sorry."

"But we will, Cara, as soon as we move. Promise."

"That scarf, Hermès, isn't it?" Kerry was tilting her head inquiringly. "Reminds me of the one I lost in the Gorges du Verdon."

"You know the gorge?" asked the woman.

"Adam had a '*manoir*' there. We were having a picnic, some friends. We think the wind must have taken it."

"It's a heavenly spot."

Kerry glanced at the ceiling as if she could see this magical land. "I'd swim in the rock pools every day. Naked. The water, so clear."

"My husband and I were set on living there, but the bank posted him to Zürich."

"I hate Zürich," the little girl said.

"You won't if mummy gets a kitten for you."

When the little girl hugged her mother's arm, I noticed Kerry's focus waver momentarily, as if she were waiting for the OK from some unseen director. Mother and daughter continued to peruse the rails. When the woman parted a section of cashmere sweaters, Kerry stepped back and pointed at her handbag. "Limited edition?"

"Yes, there are so many impersonators, but I always return to Yves Saint Laurent."

Kerry's eyes batted in appreciation. "Classic."

Then, as if letting the sun into a gloomy room, she brushed aside some hangers on a rail. "This is *so* you?" The robe, like a kimono, seemed to flow from Kerry's arms.

"Really?...I wouldn't normally."

Like lining up a six-foot putt, Kerry's eyes flitted from the woman's body and face, then back to the garment.

"Who cares for normal," she said, exchanging a wink with the little girl. "Let me tell you about the designer. She's new and terribly precocious, but her designs, the embroidered pieces…look, you can see the work, the detail…"

With their head's inches apart, all three examined a gold-flecked garment embossed with creeping green liana as if it were actually growing on the thing.

"We've only got a few of her pieces here, but we're thinking of having a trunk show in a few weeks. I'd love you to be our guest. I could put you on our mailing list."

Kerry held the garment up against her customer and it seemed to me, that the fact that she was holding it, and the way she did, went three quarters of the way to convincing the woman that she'd look good in it. "Doesn't mummy look glam?"

The little girl nodded enthusiastically.

"Would you like a coffee?"

The woman sighed, "I'd love one. We've been shopping all day."

"Would Cara like a nice strong coffee?"

The child laughed toothily. "No thank you."

"Coke?"

She looked expectantly up at her mum.

"Well, OK," said mum.

This time, the girl returned Kerry's wink.

Over their heads, Kerry addressed me with mirth flicking at the corners of her mouth. "Daniel, two lattes and a Coke please." For a quarter note I blinked, then just got on with it. You just do, don't you?

Returning to the shop I saw that the 'open' sign had been switched around. Kerry gestured me in. I presented her with the coffees and Coke. I could see a curtain moving across the changing room and heard mother and daughter speaking. Kerry nodded me towards the door: "Give me fifteen minutes."

Fifteen minutes later, almost to the second, I watched the lady and her little girl leave the shop with four fat bags of clobber and head towards a waiting black cab. Kerry was pulling down her black T-shirt, her back towards me when the doorbell dinged. She spun around. I wanted to speak, but her face stunned me into silence. She skipped across the floor like a ballerina.

"Three grand! High five," she said, laughing and holding up her hand, I raised mine reluctantly. Our palms touched.

"Thank you, Daniel."

7

Pouting, Torin moved one long forefinger left, right, left, right, imitating the hands of a metronome.

"Didn't go well, did it," he stated.

I was back in the ersatz living room at his club, lunchtime, the day after visiting Kerry's shop. "Seemingly not," I said.

He offered me a glass of wine. I shook my head. "You know, it's nothing personal. We'd have to say goodbye if you didn't cut it."

I rubbed my face. My stomach was churning.

A smile crept around his mouth. "You look knackered. The coffee chucker?"

"No, no, nothing like that."

"Stressful for you."

"Yes. Breaking up the band. Losing good friends."

"Corbossa isn't going to die."

"It's a sort of death."

"So theatrical. Your weakness, Danny. But then, your music needs that 'woe is me' element."

"What are you saying?"

"Time to burst that creative bubble you've been floating around in and step into the real world." He inhaled the aroma from the glass, then sipped appreciatively. "Concrete and steel, Danny."

I said nothing.

"So, Corbossa. You'll be having a drink with him, *dahn the rubber dub?*"

It was surreal. I was sitting here thinking about the gentlest way to let my best mate know we weren't going to be in a band together anymore.

"The past is holding you back, Daniel. Remember who plucked you from mediocrity and gave you your living?" he said, affecting a loaded 'cough, cough'. Then, tapping his metronomic digit on his chest, he leaned in. "Look, Alana might have been a great organiser or whatever, but her sound is obsolete. We serve the machine now. End of the century, Danny boy. You *have* to trust me on this. Hear *my* voice now, not hers."

'Torin!' His name was the first thing I ever heard Alana say. She'd bellowed it at the windows, breaking the spell between Torin and me over our debut glass of red that first Saturday. *'Bass'*, he'd said, as if it were a word he'd just invented and thundered down the stairs. I could hear him speaking excitedly as he sprinted back up.

Breathing hard, she stepped into the room in a sodden, ridden up, T-shirt. She set a small amp and portable cassette recorder on the floor.

"Daniel," Torin said, his voice bubbling, his eyes flitting eagerly between her and me. "Allow me to introduce Alana." She shrugged the huge 'burden of bass' over her shoulder onto the sofa as I stepped out of the shadows. I can remember her handshake. I went gingerly into it, but she gripped my hand like a wrestler.

"Daniel Earl," she said, wiping her forehead with the back of her hand. "Heard a fair bit about you."

I felt the usual unease as she studied my face but knew instinctively that if I were to survive with the likes of her and Torin, I'd have to bear the scrutiny. There'd be no walking home from school in the middle of the day with these people.

"Alright, Alana."

The formality of the occasion elicited a broad smile from her, so I smiled too. "Wine, wine, wine!" Torin sang, dancing across the room to the marble hearth where the open bottle stood. We listened to the 'glug glug glug' of liquid into glass.

"Cheers," we said in unison.

Although a head shorter than me, from the moment I met her, Alana radiated authority. There was a sense that she knew exactly what she was doing. I think that both Torin and I cleaved to her because we really didn't.

She acknowledged my Casio. It looked like a transistor radio against the expanse of wall I'd set it up against. "Can't wait to hear some," she said, taking out her bass and strapping it across her body. Her amp hummed ominously when she plugged it in. I played a couple of notes, jarring and dissonant, loud. Like a vampire, Torin drew the curtains and laughed into his over-reverbed mic. The scene was set.

You could tell there was something there in minutes. Magic just happened. Low-end poured like lava from her fingers, prompting me to wrench my faders and bully melody from my little machine.

Torin, framed between the flickering candles on the cracked marble mantlepiece, looked like the avenger from a horror film. Alana had encouraged him to sing lines written on numerous A4 pages set out on a big table by the window, but I recall him being reticent, occasionally chanting and howling off-mic but not committing to anything. He seemed content to pose and stay on the periphery.

But I wasn't paying much attention to him, I was entirely focused on meeting Alana at the junctions of the musical map we were drawing together. It was the most exhilarating afternoon of my life, so far.

I remember, around twenty minutes in, Torin leaving the room and returning with a huge upright mirror which he wheeled in front of the fireplace. Seeing himself in it switched him on. While we played, he must have tried on half a dozen sarongs and saris, matching them with vests and shirts or nothing at all. There was a moment when he left the room and returned wearing a full, Red Indian headdress. I met Alana's eye with incredulity. We started laughing, and when Torin saw us, he did too.

Posturing and pouting, mic in hand (it could have been a hairbrush for all the vocalising he did into it), he leaned over an imaginary stage, picking out the eyes of his prospective adoring public, oblivious of what we were creating behind him. After a timeless jam, Alana flopped onto the sofa, and I slid down that high white wall. We were both drenched, breathless. A hillock of clothes lay in the middle of the room.

"Sounding OK," she said.

I checked the time. "We've been playing two hours!"

"Definitely something to build on, Daniel."

At home, I'd noodled endlessly, creating verses, bridges, choruses, key or chord changes, but none of them left my box room. But in here, under Alana's direction, tangible structure was emerging from the jigsaw of my imagination. When she nodded at my right hand, or I anticipated a move up or down the fretboard from her, it was known we'd end up in the same place. From minute one, we had a unique and instant musical telepathy.

Torin was stunned. *Real* music was growing in his living room; a seed in the earth, in seconds a flower, a meadow in minutes. I recall him rushing to fill Alana's glass and then mine, but halting, realising we hadn't made a dent in his last refill and that it hadn't been anything artificial or chemical powering us, it was simply the love of music.

Looking from her to me and back again, his blue beams awed and penetrating, he whispered; "Is this how it's done. Is this how they write songs?"

I was levitating with excitement at the musical possibilities we were putting together with blinks and nods when Alana brought me down to earth. She always did. "It's all well and good jamming, but I've been here before. What we've got won't get us around Hammersmith, never mind the world." Looking away from me, she smiled at Torin. "But you were right, he's got it."

Pride filled my chest. I poked up my glasses and watched Torin slowly walk to the sofa and tilt up her chin.

"*Never* doubt me," he said, standing her up, taking the small of her back in the palm of his hand and lowering his shark-wide mouth over hers. He could have eaten her.

When he let her go, she buckled at the knees. He'd turned her from wrestler to waif with a kiss. As his laughter spiralled into the impossibly high ceiling, Alana began pummelling that huge Fender Jazz with her fists. The sound twanged and thrummed elastically and I joined in, turning the oscillator full on until the low throbbing sound I'd used a minute ago, morphed into a child's squeal of delight. In that overwhelming moment, my old covers band, the estate, even the accident, became an irrelevance.

Afternoon turned to evening. Pizza was ordered and more bottles uncorked. We selected favourite CDs from the mess on the floor and Torin delighted us with his uncanny impersonations of Iggy, Bowie, Rod and Jagger; pistol-pointing into the mirror with a slice or a glass in hand, never, ever, fully dressed.

'*I've got a lusty wife*,' he sang, causing me and Alana to snigger over our dripping mozzarella. And later, we laughed even louder when he sang, "*Maggie, I wish I'd never seen your car.*" I saw, for the first time, that baffled, posh-boy look of hurt, when Alana chided him gently. "It's *face,* Torin. 'Maggie, I wish I'd never seen your face.'"

"Whatever," he'd said.

Alana had recorded the key musical moments. She reckoned there were solid ideas for four songs: basic melody, a keys riff and bass line. "Huge element missing boys," she said, "The beat."

To keep time, I'd programmed a cheesy four/four thing on my Casio. It was totally inadequate. "Yeah," I said. "We need a drummer."

Torin stood up. "Let's go and get one."

A trendy grown-up clientele populated the sparse underlit bar we three ended up in that evening. From our table, I noticed a tanned, brown-haired man talking to a girl with cornrow braids. He was making her smile and frown in turns. When Torin went to get drinks, I watched the man swap an aside with the barman before stopping in the middle of the room to engage with a girl dressed in denim. She looked like she was ready to leave, but as he walked towards the modest percussion set-up by the DJ booth, I could see her struggling with the decision.

When the brown-haired man got behind the bongos and began to play, Alana and I were taken aback. The music being pumped out was hard industrial stuff, it was rhythmically unsmiling and rigid and did not lend itself to swingy Ibiza bongo grooves, but that was what this bloke was laying down. I watched him gazing heavenwards, his muscular arms hammering away, and even though no one was paying him much attention, his lips remained on the verge of a smile, an inner smile. He was lost in music. I liked him for that, instantly.

"He's not giving up, is he?" Alana said, as we watched him swap rhythmic jabs with the DJ. Some missed, some hit.

Another track blasted in and this time he challenged it with his left hand, patting the bongo skin on the 'off' beat while, with the drumstick in his right, he struck a timbale with double hits on the 'on'.

I looked around the room. Instead of flinching, people were tapping their feet. He'd managed to convert something inflexible into something that flowed.

"I like the way he did that," said Alana.

"Yeah, like he switched the accent on the 'on' beat. Made it go backwards."

Torin was paying attention now. "Is he any good?"

"He's playing with his hands, so he's probably no use to us, he…" But before Alana could finish her sentence, the percussionist had picked up the other drumstick and was playing a pattern on the timbale and cowbell not dissimilar to the one on the bongos, but louder and harder.

I turned to her. "Wouldn't it be amazing, if on the same day we had our first jam, we found our drummer."

"Can he play a kit though?" she asked.

Torin stood. "I'll find out." He strode across the room to bellow in the brown-haired man's ear. Fifteen minutes later, he was sitting at our table.

"Can you play 'kit' drums?" Alana asked.

"Yeah, course. That's my main thing. I only do this for pizza and beer."

"I'm Alana, this is Torin and Daniel."

"Mick, Mick Corbossa."

After jamming all afternoon in Torin's stately room with Alana and then meeting Mick, I left for my flat on the estate in a daze. Another life had opened up for me. Since leaving school, I'd dreamed about being a musician in a cool band, with real character and creativity – amazingly, in one afternoon, that dream had come true.

"What did I just say, Daniel?"

"Hear my voice, not hers," I replied, returning to the dismal present.

He topped up his glass. "Not entirely sure this coffee chucker is a good influence. You seem awfully distracted."

Kerry would be forever the 'coffee chucker'. His sobriquets were only ever demeaning: 'the damaged professor', 'the bass bitch', 'the lesbian', 'the plumber', 'the bog cleaner'.

His fingers tapped lightly on my knee. "You have to tell him, Daniel."

"Surely we both should."

"He's always used you as a crutch."

"A crutch! He's my mate."

"All right, all right. But do try to live in the now."

"I am. And it feels shit."

He waved my angst away. "The shittiness will pass, Danny. It always does. Clear your mind and focus on the job at hand."

"What about the record company?"

"They are absolutely in accord." He paused a beat. "OK, well, they've not been totally informed, but at the risk of repeating myself, I'll ask you what the name of the band is?"

I said nothing.

"*Exactly*. We'll present them with a new sound, and they'll eat it up. They always do."

He caught my eye. "Don't worry, your retainer won't stop. The mortgage'll get paid and you'll be able to look after your dear ol' mum. How is she by the way?"

"She's alright."

"Fragile, though." He draped an arm across the back of the chair. "And you're so devoted. Such a responsibility for one so callow."

I winced.

"Ha-ha, come on Daniel, lighten the fuck up." He took a drink before continuing. "And that's why you've got to *'get ya nut dahn son 'n' graft'*. Those bods in the glass towers aren't going to pay our advances if we're average. Clear the melancholy from that genius mind of yours and let's get – this – done!"

The irrefutable black and whiteness of his words permeated the conflicting emotions in my head; work equals reward. Since we'd put the band together, it always had.

I looked up. "You can't make me search for a new drummer on my own."

"No, I won't let you do that."

He gestured at some men by the bar. I stood up to leave

8

Lowering myself into the furry orange chair by the door, I watched her stabbing her calculator, totting up that day's receipts. "Fucksticks!" she exclaimed. Her head fell forward and, caught in the sun's dying rays, the sheen of perfection fled and the great sadness crept in.

"Admin's not my strong point," she said quietly.

"Can I help?"

"No, no, I *must* learn all this." Her words surprised me. I'd assumed she was experienced in all matters of shop management. After all, she said that was what she did. "Been a long day, but it's been productive. You're my lucky charm, Daniel. You were the other day as well. Pam was so pleased with me."

"Nice, Kerry." I felt good being lucky for someone, I certainly wasn't for my band mates.

"Wasn't it lovely. Mother and daughter out together," she continued. "Do you go shopping with your mum?"

"What for clothes?"

"Ha-ha, no, but you know what I mean. Do things together?"

"Well, not really. But we live together, so I suppose…" I could remember going shopping with mum when I was at school to get uniform and football kit. And there were trips to FDS and Argos when I was fitting out the new house. I couldn't recall any more expeditions than those.

"You miss your mum, Kerry?"

"So much, yes," she said, scribbling away. "Been dying to have her visit, but I'm in the spare room. They're doing up my flat. It's broken, the gutter and the whole of that bit over the sink, you know?"

"You're insured?"

"Uh-huh. It's all rotten, needs replacing. Thing is, I'm on the third floor. They can only access it, the builders, through the hallway, so I'm in the spare room and everything that was in the front room is in my bedroom. I've got all my mementoes and silly little things from holidays in there. Most sensible people would put them into storage, but they mean so much to me."

"Scaffolding up?"

"Yes, yes. It's just chaotic, a mess. These blokes everywhere and dust and plaster."

She looked so dismal. I felt an overwhelming urge to go to her side.

"Surely, they'll finish…"

"Done," she announced, hitting me between the eyes with a bolt of blinding charisma. Renewed, her cover-girl smile beaming, she undid the bun on the top of her head and shook her hair free. Honey cascaded onto her shoulders. She opened the safe behind a poster on the wall and placed the card machine, cashbox and receipts inside.

"Do you play snooker?" she asked, locking the safe and covering it with the poster.

"What? I mean, I don't have a cue."

"I can show you."

"What?"

"You said you didn't have a clue."

"No, I said…" I returned her smile. "Very good, Kerry."

She made a shooing motion with the back of her hand. "Go," she said, manoeuvring me from the alarm keypad by the door. She punched in the code. "Two, five, seven, seven, five…Yes!" The bleeps bleeped. The keys jangled when she dropped them into her silver bag.

As I turned away from the shop, I felt the exquisite pressure of her fingers on my forearm. "Look at that glorious green, Daniel." She was staring intensely into the tree that grew wild from the big terracotta pot by the door.

"Yeah, it's got quite err, big."

"Look at its depth, the different shades of green in it. You know, I have the privilege of seeing it every time I come in or out of work and it's never, ever the same."

Out of respect for her words, I actually bothered to look and there was something. It held me, but it had gone in a second.

"There," she said. "You saw it."

"Saw what?"

She pulled me away. "Come on then. I'll thrash you within an inch of your techie life!"

Wading through the masses towards Covent Garden, I asked her how long she'd been at the shop.

"Six months, next week."

"Where were you before then?"

"Oh, I had different jobs."

I had planned on asking her a series of fashion-based questions. After my apathetic performance in the café, I wanted her to know that I was genuinely interested in what she did.

"Did you start out in retail, err, department stores, before you decided to go it alone in err, boutique management?"

She glanced at me. The mirth obvious. "Someone's been doing their research."

I sagged. "Come on Kerry, it's not a world I know much about."

She took my hand. It was the first time she'd done it, but she had to let go to allow a couple to pass between us. I felt like pushing them into the traffic.

"I appreciate your interest, Daniel. It means a lot."

I swallowed. "I can be a bit distant. And…"

"You're making an effort."

We were quiet for a block. "So yeah, what shop were you at before? West End?"

"I've never worked in a shop before."

I slowed down. "Really? I thought…"

As we walked, she told me that she spent a lot of her time ducking in and out of clothes shops and had wandered into Pam's one afternoon. The layout, she said, the 'merchandising', was a disaster and it was obvious to her that whoever was running the shop hadn't a clue about what to buy and sell to suit the season or what was trending in that 'high-end' way they have in St Christopher's Place. Over tea and cake, Pam had told her that her husband had died and left her a 'little money', and that she'd always loved the area (and stylish clothes), so when she saw the vacant property, she went for it. But she'd not sold anything in weeks. Kerry had told her, there and then, she'd restyle the shop for fun and that Pam didn't have to pay a penny for it.

"I've got hundreds of old Vogues and Elles blocking up the passageway at the flat. I'm completely absorbed with it all, designers…

trends…the history, just like blokes are mad about football."

"Yeah, I get it."

After seeing what Kerry had achieved in one afternoon – the increase in traffic and the way the place looked – Pam offered her the job as manager. "I couldn't have been happier," she said.

"So, the pay's OK?"

"We're here!" Beyond a weathered red door somewhere off Kingsway, I could see myriad snooker tables in a vast low-lit room. "My treat," she said, rummaging in her bag for her purse.

Walking in, I was shot back to when we started; me and Mick playing snooker after rehearsals at the club on Shepherd's Bush Green. The clacking of balls, cue tips being chalked and exhortations of *'Shot mate'*, *'Bad luck'* issued from the twenty or so men in there, filled me with melancholy for those happy days five years ago. But my backward thoughts evaporated when Kerry took my hand in her soft fingers for the second time in an hour and led me to our table. All eyes were on her as she leaned over to rack-up the balls. They'd been on her since she'd slalomed between the tables in a loose orange dress and scuffed sneakers.

Taking up position beside the table, "Fire away," I said.

Placing the white with care, she bent long and low. The sound of ball on ball and tapping cue tips subsided around us as she slowly drew back her arm. She was hopeless, smashing the white at whatever was in its way regardless of colour in the hope that something might go in. Triumphant and dejected in turns, she was quite a sight to see.

"Good shot, Kerry," I said, as some random red fell into a pocket. "Who taught you to play?"

"Mum's boyfriend in Paris, Gene Alexander," she said, anointing first one cushion with her cue, then another, and then another, mathematically calculating the travel of the balls *after* she laid into them.

She got over the table. Squinting with one eye, she took aim. "He was an artist, huge canvases. His trousers were always paint-spattered…Damn!" She missed.

She was quiet as I took my shot.

I missed.

"Bad luck."

She got over hers again. "*And* he wore a different scarf for every day of the week and socks that didn't match. Translated English into French…or was it the other way around?" Smash.

"After or before Phillipe?"

"Oh, before…no, after, after…"

I missed again.

Back went her cue arm. Smash. She stood up brightly. "I like brown best, looks like a giant Malteser. Funny the things you remember from when you were little. The detail. There was a pool table in the back of the bar at the bottom of his flats, so trendy in the 11th Arrondissement. Him and mum used have their coffee there and I'd play pool on my own. I could hardly reach over the table. Gene would come and show me how to play between bites of croissants. They'd get me a pastry…he'd lick his finger and dab up the flakes I'd dropped on the table…it was purply/red, not green like this. Got me a little stool. I'll never forget the smell of coffee in that café. *Always* think of mum when I have my coffee in the morning. Did today."

"That's difficult, in the kitchen with the builders in?"

She looked up, comically addled. "Why?"

Even though it was my turn, she decided she'd have another go. What order there had been, had disintegrated frames ago.

"What about your mum?" she asked.

"She likes a cuppa in the morning. Tea, that is. Bit bland, basic. I've not had the adventures you had, as a kid."

"Sorry. I didn't mean to be insensitive."

"No, I didn't mean to sound all, 'woe is me.'"

"I know," she said, shouldering her cue, rifle style. "We're all accidents of birth, aren't we?"

It seemed that any prop or setting enhanced her shape, her length of leg and narrowness of waist. Even with the jumble of hapless clobber doing it's damnedest to wash her out, her movements gave her away. Stalking the table on tiptoes, or bent low, to get a level perspective, I was entranced. The thing is, so was every other male in there.

The reds were scattered. I had my eye on one at the baulk end. The cue ball was near the black spot. I did like the long shots. I nailed it. When I glanced up, her eyes softened with pride.

"Shot, techie boy."

I missed the colour and stepped away.

Down she got. "Does she make you one?"

"Sorry?"

"Tea, in the morning?"

"Yeah, course."

"Every morning?"

"Yep."

She whacked the white into a pack of balls. Nothing went down. I missed and stepped away again. "You know the posh lady with the little girl?" I asked. "Was that true about the South of France, the chateaux?"

"It was a '*manoir*' Daniel. Of course. You can't make up *everything*."

Narrowing her eyes, she retracted her cue a good few inches further back than she normally did. I feared for the plaster on the back wall. Her elbow shot forward like a piston. She'd grazed the cue ball. It moved about half an inch. She immediately replaced it with her hand. "Whoops."

She hit it aimlessly.

"You know the sequence yeah, red, colour?"

"Sometimes, but when I see a nicer shot, I go for it. That's OK, isn't it?"

"Of course."

I missed.

She spoke as she meticulously chalked her cue. "...'Pam's Paradise', I mean seriously, *and* she refused to change it. So, we had a sit-down and, hang on..." She hit. I watched her ball miss everything. She looked up at me out of one beautiful eye. "Let's start another game?"

It had always irritated me when people hopped from topic to topic without introduction or warning. Why begin explaining something, place the listener's focus on that track, and then 'bang', switch direction, derail, confuse and create chaos. I thrive on order, a to b to c. For instance, my synths must 'cascade' perfectly on their stands. My effects racks must sparkle (I'd even get out the Mr. Sheen before a gig). I like my cables and leads colour-coded, I like my clothes colour-coded too, mainly black or navy. I double-check times and locations, and have back-up plans just in case. This methodology is proven. It has given me a trade, wonderful friends and taken me around the world. I don't know where I'd be without my daily 'box tick'. I get up, take a strong coffee to the shed and I create (although a bit pointless at the mo), I check on mum, I go to the shops (where I get my micro meal for every day of the week, except Saturday when it'll be take-away; Chinese or Indian on alternate weekends) or, I get the hornrims out and get on the tube to work (which is rehearsals right now). In case there's a delay and I have to change my groove, travel wise, I'm always on the platform twenty minutes before I need to be. When I get into the room, I turn everything on (wall switch first) and prepare. I don't like leaving it to anyone else. And, when its home time, dinner is pinging by eight thirty. I check on mum and watch telly with her until she goes up at nine. Then I'll put on this week's offering from Blockbuster. A bit before or after midnight, I wake up on the sofa and turn everything off at the socket.

Torin, decimating the band had left me feeling like a sailor staggering in a hurricane, and now Kerry has come along and torpedoed the fucking ship! But weirdly, I wasn't repelled by her randomness. The whizzing, ricocheting bullets of her interjections (exotic or mundane) actually drew me in. I found myself excited at the prospect of her next cache of meandering, verbal disorder with all its green and honey stops and detours.

I racked up the balls.

"I'll break" she said, from the other end of the table. "It's my favourite shot, anyway."

All eyes were on my opponent as she leaned over her shot like an archer warrioress from antiquity. Her arm hurtled through. She cannoned the pink straight into the pack.

I knocked a red in and lined up the blue.

"Daniel?"

"Yeah?"

I looked up from the table with one eye closed.

"...but I hung in there. *She* said, 'What about the sign? Believe me Daniel, the sign was as tacky as the name."

We *were* talking about France, her ex, swimming, coffee and pool, but she'd returned to the topic of the shop and how she got the job as manager there.

Missed the blue.

"God knows who she got to design it, a brickie? Anyway, I stuck to my guns and said, 'Sienna'. She *knew* it was perfect. I painted the exterior myself over the bank holiday."

"On your own?"

Over she went with her bow and arrow. The cue ball crashed into an innocent group with some force. She stood and posed like a muscle man. "Yes, I'm quite strong, you know." She was trying to be comic, ungainly, but it was impossible for her to ever not look statuesque.

I potted a red but missed the easy yellow afterwards.

"Bad luck, son," she said, with a wink, skip and jump to her shot. Her yellow rolled in after kissing the blue.

"Shot," I said.

Eyes were tracking her from the monochrome depths as she sauntered around the baize, cue angled elegantly between the fingers of one hand, the other on her hip. Over she went. Her white missed everything, rebounding from cushion to cushion to finally rest on the tip of her cue. "Sorry. I do rabbit on. How are things at work?

"A bit fraught. Got some personnel issues."

"In the factory, the shop? Where you practise your techie ways."

"Where I practise, yes."

"In a shop?"

"I travel."

"Home visits?"

"Ha-ha, sort of."

I could sense her impatience. I couldn't continue this pretence if I was going to keep seeing her.

I took my shot. The white went in off a colour. "You win, Kerry."

She raised her cue. The bow was now a spear. "Yes!"

As we exited, she hugged my arm. My heart thudded pleasantly. "Wasn't that fun?"

"Ha-ha, really was."

She lived off Shepherd's Bush Green. One of the mansion blocks on the way to Hammersmith, so we headed west. "You look like you needed a break, huge pun intended," she said, barging me gently. "You're quite anxious at the moment, aren't you. I can tell."

"Just a stressful sort of job."

"Number crunching?"

She was eyeing me as I squirmed in obfuscation. When she stopped to speak to a young man with his dog in a doorway, I realised that the 'O' word was much like quicksand, in that the more you struggled to deny a thing, the further it sucked you under.

She returned to my side and blinked wonderfully into the present. "What a gorgeous creature, like half Staffy and something else?" Again, she took my arm. "Copper or drug dealer?" she persisted.

It was becoming harder and harder to scowl, so I poked my glasses up and laughed. "I'm a musician." My dark secret was out and what a relief it was.

"And?"

"Keyboards, synths."

"Wow. Are you famous?"

"Not personally, but you might know who I play for."

"Really?" The green gaze batted expectantly, when I glanced to the side.

"Torin."

Nothing. In fact, quite weirdly blank, as if she'd popped off somewhere. "'Silent Storm'?" I said, that invariably nailed it. She was squinting cluelessly. Something wasn't right. "'Silk', 'Jesus Boots'?"

I felt myself heating up. *Everyone* knew Torin. Wasn't it enough that I'd told her what I did without her having to pretend she'd never heard of us? 'Silent Storm' was a hit, worldwide. I started tumbling, abysmal thoughts kicking at the inside of my skull. I changed sides on the pavement and poked up my glasses again. I couldn't figure out why this person was with me. What was the endgame? She'd already said she'd been with some bloke who had a chateau in the South of France. Did she *really* not know my band, my brilliant band that I used instead of a personality? Was this some social experiment? Was she going to ask me, in the middle of Tottenham Court Road, to perform some shit karaoke impersonation of a song that I wrote…that said, because I didn't want to leave her side, I probably would!

"Torin DeVere. Handsome. Black hair. He used to be on every chat show on telly about three years ago. The wide smile, bloke? Did the advert for teeth-whitening? That advert on the tube?" I took a breath and grudgingly sang, "*…you told me so many times…*"

She suddenly screamed – me, and everyone within twenty feet of us, stopped dead.

"I didn't lock up!"

I jogged behind her. "Kerry it's OK."

"You don't understand," she said, sniffing tears, "I *cannot* lose this job Daniel. I…No, no!"

9

Torin set his glass on the table in his club's public living room and nodded encouragingly at his sidekick. Barney patted my knee with his fat palm. "Daniel, it's all in hand."

Hopeful, porcine eyes searched mine for a connection that was never gonna be made. "Change is good. Change promotes newness and revives energy. To be honest, it's basic marketing strategy."

They were handling me. I could imagine Torin briefing Barney about his keyboard player, *'Daniel Earl? He kicks up for five minutes, but then he just gets on with it.'*

"While you've been working manfully on the computer," Barney continued, "Torin and I have put a new exciting production together."

"It ain't a production, it's a band!"

Torin gave me a warning look. "You need to listen to Barney, Daniel."

I shook my head and stared into space.

"Tell him again, Barney."

Barney was pointing at some diagram on his laptop. "What I'm saying is, the music business is changing. Look at this line here, that three thousand pounds. I've gone back through the tour accounts for the last couple of years. The fact is, we aren't getting the fees we did. We need to cut our cloth. I know the business model might sound a little austere..."

"Fuck's sake, we aren't a 'business model', mate."

Barney looked at Torin, who was looking at me impassively.

"But we aren't," I pleaded.

"Come on matey, grow up."

***

Debbie, behind the bar, nodded in the direction of the alcove we had used for all our band meetings back in the day.

"Where's Alana?" she asked, as I passed.

"Err, having a break," I said over my shoulder.

Corbossa pushed my chair back with his foot. He had a pint

waiting for me. We did not greet each other in the smile we'd swapped all over the world.

"Guess what I did the other day," I said, sliding in.

"Got up late? Bought a round?"

"Played snooker."

"Didja?"

"Yeah, with this girl."

"Bet she won."

"Was a draw, but I had a laugh."

"Which is more than we're having."

A vintage bass line and drum beat, soulful and warm, oozed through the speakers. A short blistering guitar solo followed. The music paused a beat. Debbie always played this classic for me. *'Every day I spend my time drinking wine, feeling fine…'*

"What you thinking, Daniel?"

"Thinking of how lucky we are."

"Don't feel too lucky, mate."

"I mean, the serendipity. How it all came together. I honestly thought Torin was behind it. The mastermind."

"Torin DeVere, the busking mastermind!" Mick said ruefully.

"Her chucking fifty pence in his hat."

"*And* he took it!" Corbossa laughed. "He's probably the richest bloke I've ever met."

From the moment I saw Torin kiss Alana beneath that absurd chandelier in his apartment, I'd wanted to know how they'd got together. He was so different from anyone I'd ever met.

Remembering that Friday night, him waltzing through the pub crowd in a dress, I wondered if his introduction to her had been as cinematic as mine. So, when Torin had gone out for wine at an early rehearsal, I asked Alana how he'd discovered her.

"He didn't discover *me!*" She said, her brown eyes flaring with affront. "I discovered *him!*"

She lifted the bass off her shoulders and flopped onto that room's ubiquitous tatty sofa. Mick set down his sticks and came over to listen.

"A few months ago, I was coming up the stairs at Notting Hill tube. I was short of dough, had some CDs for the Record and Tape

Exchange. I could hear this harmonica wailing away. A right racket. It was Torin, sitting cross-legged at the top of the escalators, blowing into it like a nutter."

"He was busking?"

"There wasn't a penny in his hat. He looked pretty desperate. I chucked in my last fifty p."

"Yeah?"

"So basically, I was heading for the barriers when I felt my guitar wrenched back and it was him. He asked me if I could actually play the thing. I almost told him to fuck off."

From my keys, I watched her pass her palm over an orange buzz-cut. A softness came to her eyes as she paused for a moment. "But that smile…anyway, he bought me coffee, cheesecake too in some posh café in Holland Park. Put it this way, he *didn't* pay for it with his busking money. The rest is history, I guess. He was totally convincing as a rough sleeper…even the smell."

We laughed.

"Master of disguise," said Mick. "I thought he was a…"

Just then Torin returned to the room. I remember he was wearing leathers, the purple hippy hat with its owl feather, box-fresh sneakers and of course, that smile. Box-fresh too it was back then. The cork popped, plastic cups were filled with red and passed around. After taking a sip, Mick asked Alana what she was doing before she was with us.

She allowed a Hammersmith-bound train to rumble overhead, then said she'd been playing since she was seventeen and had been in about six bands already. Not only had she played scores of gigs around the London pub and club scene, she'd been on the road crew *and* tour managed her own all-girl three-piece two summers ago. Without a budget, she'd managed to plot and plan the entire thing, borrowing gear in different towns and having friends put them up. She'd even designed and printed T-shirts. The cash they made from selling them at the gigs had practically paid for the tour. They'd nailed fifteen dates from Edinburgh to Exeter and "still had money for a bag of chips when we got back," she'd said, not cracking her face, until Mick cracked his.

I remember thinking that I could only dream of such an adventure. She really was a bit of a hero.

Alana was the only one of us who knew how to put a live set together. She had that 'song vision', a gift that I, with all my abilities, did not. It was because of her that we all headed in the same direction, musically. Her methodology was exacting too. She'd drill us through verses and choruses, intros, outros, middle 8s and breakdowns over and over until they were second nature. Six songs were written by the end of our fifth rehearsal.

On the day she'd told how she met Torin at the tube station, she announced she was going to contact her mate and get us a support slot with his band. I remember no one saying anything. We'd been happy enough just rehearsing together. Taking this entity outside and exposing it to strangers was momentarily incomprehensible. But two weeks later we opened for her mate's band in a pub in Hackney. We drove our gear to and from in Corbossa's dad's work van.

It was the first time I'd tasted applause for music I'd not copied but actually created. It was fantastic!

From the outset, Torin's gig experience differed from ours. Firstly, there was no way he was going to sit at the front of a vehicle with, *'Dave Corbossa – Your Friendly Plumbing & Heating Engineer'* emblazoned on the side of it. And forget about sitting in the back with Alana's amp, Mick's drums, the U-bends, sprockets and sockets. He wasn't about to endure the headline band's extended and obviously 'vital' soundcheck, either. It was only when we finished setting up our equipment, that he materialised with a bottle half full, his blue eyes flitting, collar up, failing dismally to be anonymous. But we were fine with that. We didn't want anything to distract or derail him. He was already becoming irreplaceable.

In six months we were selling out places, show after show. People could not get enough of us. From impassioned clothes horse, Torin had turned himself into the archetypal frontman. Whether singing or confiding between songs, when he opened his mouth, a room held its breath.

After a dozen gigs, an A&R man put us in the studio and boom! 'Silent Storm' emerged as the song of that summer. It became routine to have photographers snapping Torin and Alana in dressing rooms and bars, through car windows, or as they went to the shops to buy milk.

I remember showing mum a picture of both of them in the Standard showbiz section: him in brown sarong and Cuban heels, hair pinned back by Ray-Bans; Alana, her shaven head on his shoulder, spitting her prettiness unwaveringly into the lens. They looked like people I didn't know, but of course I did and was so proud.

They became regulars in the gossip columns. One week, when the record was at its peak, they appeared on three separate TV chat shows on consecutive nights. They'd become the great underground celebs of the season, wild lipstick-smeared fuckers seen late and often, falling out of places, he in his dress, mouth laughing wide, she the impassive, cropped-haired elf with the huge guitar, middle finger up. Promo shots had them eyes and fingers locked, Mick a little behind, handsome and smouldering with his sticks, and me, the shaded background lurker, just as I liked it.

Early reviews described Torin as the 'Architect of an emergent new sound', a 'Musical strategist of rare inspiration!' In interviews, he was coy about the workings of his band, and that was understood – after all, no alchemist reveals his formulas. But *we* knew, Corbossa, Alana and me, that his onstage panache and swagger, that gaunt, open-armed glare across the sea of adoring heads, cloaked the most unbelievable secret.

It remains the most extraordinary thing that Torin DeVere is a musical dyslexic. Live, in a song, he's a dog a chasing a balloon...and we're chasing him. I'll explain. Torin has *never* been able to get to grips with how a song sequentially travels. Half the time, he literally does not know where the blimmin' words should go and often, what the words are.

Of course, he is far better now than when we started, but right up until that last gig at the end of the European tour, he remained unsure of which part was the verse and which was the chorus, and occasionally – incredibly – which one of the two came first. During the honeymoon of our first few months, I was able to talk to him about it. I wanted to get to the bottom of this mental block and try to help him around it. To see him as I did, facing away from the gawping crowd, terrified and vulnerable, traits so alien to him, broke my heart, because he was the man who had looked past *my* deficiencies to encourage and inspire me.

"Torin, you know the one that starts with, '*You could have told me*'?"

"You're calling that the chorus, now?" he'd snap. "Can you not make up your mind?"

He had left the room for fags or some such during our second rehearsal, a dismal one for him. He knew he was repeatedly 'getting it wrong'. But because of that blind spot, a kind of degeneration, or retardation in the muscles of his brain that aided concentration and retention (we three discussed and sort of agreed it was that), he had no hope of fixing it himself.

I broke the heavy silence as the door shut behind him. "He can't remember what he sang two minutes ago."

Torin hadn't been able to get through a verse without stopping or hesitating to make sure he was where he should be. Subsequently, the music with his vocals on it sounded shambolic.

"He's..." Corbossa had muttered, pointing at his temple. "Nothing's sticking."

Alana had her arms folded on her bass and was staring at the wall behind the PA. "We must find a way, or it's over," she said. I recall wanting to cry. "I'm gonna try a few things," she said, after a quick nod to herself. When Torin returned, she gently sat him down and told him not to worry about arrangements and getting the lyrics right, she'd take care of all of that for him. "We won't let this stop us," she said, stroking his brow. "We'll stick together and make it. I promise." His eyes shone like a puppy on a Christmas card as she re-shouldered her guitar. "Torin listen, if you can't find your way in..."

"...way in where, exactly Alana?"

"Don't worry, darling."

Aiming him at the big mirror, she ran through the songs (maybe only three or four at that stage), singing the opening lines to various verses and choruses, prompting him to join in. But try as he might, he just could not locate the 'b of the bang'. Doggedly, she pushed into the evening pre-empting his inevitable miscues with a held-up finger and gentle 'no, wait' into the microphone. But her vocal orders seemed only to elicit a flat-footed 'Hokey Cokey' in and off the microphone. It might sound funny, but it was really depressing. We were glazing over with fatigue and not a little hopelessness when Alana shoulder barged him (probably a little harder than she should have) just as she began to sing the opening line of the chorus and his vocal landed beautifully, milliseconds after hers. By some miracle, the physicality of the nudge had caused the tumblers in his brain to unlock. He'd sung the part infinitesimally late, but *not* out of time.

"That's it, Torin!"

"You nailed it, see?"

"I am doing it, aren't I?" he said breathlessly, his eyes expanding with wonder at his own abilities.

"Yeah man!"

We were ecstatic. After months of chasing it, he'd finally caught that fucking balloon and trodden on it.

"Piece of piss," he announced, clenching his fist into the big mirror. "Come on you shirkers, let's do it again."

Torin's gift was his uninhibitedness, the ability to let himself go without fear of ridicule (who else would stride through some dodgy council estate boozer in women's clothes?), but he turned up at the soundcheck of our first gig with an implement that would undermine that gift totally.

From outside the pub, Mick and I watched him exit a black cab on Hackney Road, arse first, before striding towards us.

"Is that a…?" Mick's voice trailed off.

I couldn't believe it. Torin had brought a music stand with him. He was going to go on stage with the lyrics printed on pieces of paper, replete with crib notes for the stops and starts – and they were *his* notes, so fuck knows what they would have instructed him to do – then he'd peel the pages away, one by one as we went through our songs. We were aghast. We told him it'd look appalling, amateur. Mick said he'd look like a pissed-up karaokist and be laughed off stage. Torin was so dejected by our response and its irrefutable truth, that when he fell against the alley wall outside the pub I feared he'd go through it. Alana had put her hands on his shoulders and looked into his eyes. *Her* gift was the ability to fill you with confidence when you most needed it. She told him to trust her. She'd be right by his side and, apart from a stage and people watching, it'd be just like rehearsals back at the Bush.

But the early gigs were challenging. Oftentimes, he'd forget to stay near her, go blank and mumble erroneously, and she'd have to compromise her own playing just to get him back on track. When this happened, we'd compensate by slotting in an extra couple of bars in lieu of his late arrival. If we saw him draw breath to sing a part that was early, we'd make eye contact and in that split second, go with him. It was exhilarating, a test of skill and perception on our part. That intuition got us through the band's first six months and was convincing enough to draw the ear of the A&R man who eventually signed us and put us in the studio.

Major difficulties occurred when we began playing larger venues with lighting, dry ice and inconsistent onstage monitoring; we simply could not connect with him, and he could not connect with us. He'd had a hideous sixty seconds at our first big festival. While we wailed away behind him, he'd stood there, open-armed, smiling cluelessly at the expectant thousands who were waiting for him to sing the opening line.

Sensing it was all going tits up, Alana placed her mic and stand, which had been set up a good twelve feet away, next to his. A tug on his sleeve, a gentle calf kick and theatrical push or pull made the connection. It was as if they were back in the rehearsal room with all the intimacy and support he thrived on. And it looked great too; them welded together at their mics, touching and breathing the same air.

In the dressing room afterwards, Torin was triumphant, drinking straight from the bottle, bragging about the way he had them all in the palm of his hand.

Alana had shut the door on the hubbub outside. "That can *never* happen again," she said, quietly.

Torin reared. "What? They loved me!"

"We nearly lost everything. The record company blokes, the agent, publisher, they were all watching from my side of the stage. Thank God my mic had a long enough cable." She opened a bottle of beer and swallowed. "Really scary," she said.

I was probably the only one who noticed something dark and dense expand in Torin's eyes as they darted at his girlfriend. In that moment, with our band not even a year old, I knew that her genius for making him competent would be something he'd never forgive her for.

On the way back to London, it was decided that we'd never chance Torin flying vocally unaided again. Whatever the gig – club, theatre, festival – Alana would be there, touch-tight, from the opening bar. We were about to put our first record out, there was a debut album to follow, as well as tours and shows lined up for as far as the eye could see. We weren't going to let him fuck it up.

I was with him in an empty record company office a few days after we'd recorded the album. He was sifting through scores of live shots of the band, trying to find the right one for the cover. When one of the stills on the table caught his eye, he brushed the others aside. The shot was of Alana in profile, bass slung low, her finger pointing at him as he nobly drew breath at the microphone. Torin recognised the power of the image in an instant. You could almost hear our music coming from it. The photograph appeared to capture the intimate connection between two unique creatives, careless of the myriad eyes on them but in truth, it was 'the nudge' immortalised in celluloid.

We *think* we see Alana gesturing to Torin in a moment of passionate, musical telepathy, but in reality she is poking his sternum with her finger, commanding him to wait, or drop, or do that bit again or cueing him for a harmonica solo (that was never into a mic, but played by me on the sampler), or telling him to cool it because there were eight/sixteen bars of music ahead, or mercifully, the song was ending.

Only we knew that while the audience clapped along to her stamping feet, she was about to hit her knee against his, cuing him onto a vocal bridge he'd sung a hundred times, but one he would *not* make his way across that night in Newcastle, or Portland, or Madrid unless she *physically* led him on and off it.

But I do Torin a disservice. It is an undeniable music fact, that however tight, however intuitive and resourceful under the spotlight the musicians may be, it is the person up-front who sparks the fire, and live, Torin was the most glorious accelerant. To observe him, as I had many hundreds of times, strolling debonair and handsome in a sarong or Portobello militaria, exploding into a spider shape, sobbing into the microphone, desperately panting words and notes, is the privilege of my life. From the very first gig, perhaps the very first song, at my post in the far corner, stage right, I witnessed how he hypnotized the half-dozen or so who had bothered to lever themselves off the bar to watch us before the main band came on. In less than a year, that paltry few had become thousands.

'Don't push your luck too far...' Memories of how Alana and Torin met, his inability to keep an arrangement in his head, and the nudge, fragmented and dispersed. Five years had passed. I was back in Debbie's pub and, most weirdly, Mick was laughing.

"What?" I asked.

"Remember when he got out of that cab with the fucking music stand!"

Turning the glass in my hand, a pang of sadness went through me for Torin. He only brought it with him because he didn't want to let us down. That we could remember every second of every song always amazed him.

"Just remembering," I said. "They were the good times, those first gigs. Your dad driving us, me sitting on the bog seat cos it was so chock-full in there."

There were light years between those early gigs and the ones we did now, but however disunited we'd become off stage, we *always* came together on it.

Mick sighed. "I know he thinks I took the piss, but I tried to get on with him, Daniel, I really did."

"I know you did, man. He's a complex bloke." But they'd never bonded, him and Mick. Their personalities and attitudes were so entirely different; Mick an open book complete with pictures, Torin, the darkest byzantine thriller. From the start, he wouldn't stand next to Mick in photos, he'd pair up with either me or Alana. I think he'd have preferred the line-up to have remained as it was in the Holland Park mansion on day one; the petite, love-struck female and the wincingly shy noodler. But that wouldn't have been a band, it would have been a fan club. "Same again?"

"Ta."

I brought two pints back to the table. "My nut's spinning with all this, Mick. I miss Alana."

His warm brown eyes looked up dolefully. "Me too."

"She taught him everything he knows. Taught me loads too."

"And me."

"He was all over her when I joined," he said. "Flowers and perfume waiting for her. Didn't he whisk her off to Paris?"

"Monaco." Mick shook his head. "Like some bloke in an advert."

Torin had always seemed other-worldly to us. He did things on a whim with money that left us open mouthed. More than once, walking the West End streets with him, I had spun around to see him not at my side, but in some flash store, buying another coat, another set of speakers for his stereo. Once, he bought a painting for five hundred quid on the way back from rehearsals. I wondered if he'd ever put it on a wall.

"They were inseparable, then," I said quietly.

"It started getting ugly when the album came out. Just as it was all going right."

"Nah, it started the minute he had to rely on her for the nudge."

Our eyes met. Obfuscation. The secrets we keep. Sitting there, I felt its muddying energy pass between us. We had watched Torin slide into a lifestyle that would be unacceptable in the real world, but we'd made excuses, shrugged and jogged on into the lights and applause regardless.

"Where did it all go wrong?"

"It was the stuff going on outside, Mick. Never the music. And it all came to a head in Rotterdam."

"What was that all about on the phone…Ibiza? He was such a mess on stage."

I looked up quickly. "Ibiza! So, you heard that as well?"

"Yeah, he was going on about flights and money? To be honest I just wanted to get on and play."

"He was speaking to this Conrad bloke. You know him?"

"Nah." For a moment we were lost in the memory of the final date at the end of the spring tour when Alana had left.

"The huge fight they had."

Mick was referring to the scene in the dressing room after the gig. It wasn't much of a fight. Torin had steamed into her. Brought up personal stuff about when they were together years before. I'd sat there, sick with shame, and not said a word. "You were lucky you weren't in there to hear it all, mate," I said.

"Too right. I've never seen Alana like that…sort of beaten."

Before the gig, on the way from the hotel to the site, Torin had festered, glancing darkly at his phone, then at the hordes making their way to the venue. After being dropped off backstage he paced around in his pretend military commander's kit getting in the way of the crew, shouting into his phone about Ibiza and money. Imploring this Conrad person.

"He was still on his phone when we went on stage!" That had infuriated Alana. She couldn't abide anyone disrespecting the performance. It went against everything she'd instilled in us.

"He was in such a state."

That night on stage, never mind the odd line, whole verses went missing. He started choruses that weren't there, fucked up the get-ins and get-outs of songs he'd been performing for years. It was as if we were shot right back to the first couple of hopeless sessions below the Shepherd's Bush arches. Alana tried, gently at first but then more forcefully, to get him in on time but he looked straight through or around her. In the middle of 'Silent Storm' he actually missed the chorus that thousands were singing. She let go of her bass and took his wrist, but he barged her away. She was left alone, belting out the vocal the best she could. I could see the people at the front squinting bemusedly. I can't remember ever leaving a stage to such half-hearted applause.

"Maybe if we'd had a real manager like the rest of the bands, we wouldn't be in the state we are now."

Mick leaned across the table. "What is it with him and managers? Trust? Fear?"

I looked up. The second pint was getting to me. "You know that thing he always used to say, that *people are after what is rightfully mine*?"

"Yeah, never quite worked out what that meant."

"He was *never* gonna allow an 'outsider' in to run the band, and do you know why?" Mick shook his head and I felt imbued with a rare energy. Fuck obfuscation – for now, anyway. I had a big drink and finished my glass. "He can't stand to be around people that are able to do their job properly, cos he can't fucking do his!"

Mick got up and laughed. "Fuck me Daniel, that's bang on. Like Alana doing his work for him. I'm havin' annuver, you?"

"Yeah, yeah, ta."

Alana had consistently advocated that we hire 'professional' management, but he always shouted her down. Instead of someone with authority, Torin had hired 'helpers', 'advisors', but they'd never been any more than blokes that could book a hotel or get the requisite wine on the rider. He had a penchant for out-of-work marketing types that called our fans and friends 'assets', obsessed with stats and pie charts. They were frauds, pretenders, attendees at the 'opening of an envelope'. They never understood the way we felt, our passion for music. It would drive the agent and record company nuts that we didn't have someone appropriate at the helm. In the end they gave up on us and we drifted across the years, riding on the success of 'Storm' the first album and our amazing live show.

"Cheers!"

Mick had slid a pint in front of me.

"Here's what I think," I said. "It was that club. When we got back to London after the first American tour, joining that club meant he had to leave ours."

"Yeah, he was addicted to the place."

I took a swallow. "Still fucking is."

"Let's face it, we weren't TV actors or movie producers. Hanging out with us was never gonna compare to that lot, popping corks and dropping names like a plopping horse."

We roared with laughter and Debbie looked across with a smile that curled out of the corner of her mouth.

"Play it again," I called to her. For a moment me and the drummer listened to the opening bars of the song.

"I couldn't stand it there, Daniel."

"You were the first to stop going."

"We were like ducklings, waddling behind him, through the doors and past reception. Fuck that, man. I ain't no one's ducking fuckling."

"Quack that!"

And we were laughing again and for a minute, it was as if all this wasn't real, a nightmare hangover evaporating in our lager.

"Poor Alana, having to stick it out with him and his shitty mates."

Witnessing Torin's nightly disintegration over four slow hours wasn't so much a hell, she told us later, but a waste of a perfectly good evening – weeks of them. The narrative never changed. Nothing interesting was mooted with his new friends, no original thought, no insight or humour came of the cokey repetition, spat at each other's faces while they tapped their feet, out of time, to whatever was playing. The evening's high point, she always maintained, was tipping him into the cab at three in the morning and dragging him up those spotless, red-carpeted stairs to his pit in Holland Park.

As our laughter died, I looked through the now thinning cloud of obfuscation at Mick and replayed a poisonous dressing room exchange:

"Where the fuck were you last night?" he'd asked over his glass.

"In bed."

"What? You should be out with me. Important, the band?"

"Nothing to do with the band."

"Disloyal. Unprofessional!"

"No. I just can't handle you when you are in there with those people."

"They're called friends, Alana. You got any?"

She had flicked him a *fuck you* and he came back with some really low stuff about her personal hygiene. On stage, ten minutes later, I witnessed the nauseating sight of her coaching the person that had just called her a smelly cunt. I don't recall what gig it was now, but I remember, as soon as we got back to London, she moved out of his flat.

Mick drank from his glass. "Do you think he got into 'that scene' before or after they'd split up?"

"I dunno. So hard to think of dates and times now. We were having such a laugh. I mean, a record deal, Mick! A wage, people setting up your gear, it was mad, wasn't it? Remember his school chums coming to the shows in their Land Rovers and Jags when 'Storm' got to number one?"

"Arrogant wankers, taking the piss out of him for going out with her, calling her a crusty and an urchin. That tall one, asking her if she'd like to earn some extra money doing his ironing."

"She was fucking ten times the human those chinless tossers could ever be."

"And he never stuck up for her," Mick said. "I know I'm not brilliant with women, but I'd never let that go."

He took another long drink and leaned across the table again, "I mean, if they'd split completely and never seen each other again that'd be 'normal', but to go on stage and sing together, photos, interviews, years of it, that's tough."

Days, a week, a month after she'd moved out, we were doing some photos for something, and the photographer asked them to hold hands for the shot. Alana refused.

A new way emerged; him turning up at rehearsals moody, miserable, hung-over or still embarrassingly coked up. However inconsequential Alana had felt living with him, she at least got him home in one piece and made him breakfast when he got up. There were no 'checks and balances' now they were apart. We wasted days of rehearsal listening to him castigate the industry and characters he'd met from it the night before. When we finally managed to coerce him into doing the thing that we'd all turned up to do, he'd flounce irritably and accuse Alana of bullying him. Of course, she wasn't, she was running things with the same dutiful professionalism that she'd always done, but it stuck in his cokey craw that she wasn't his anymore *and* was patently the better for it. After two hours of doing sod all, we'd stumble through the songs, him getting the same parts wrong, her trying to coax him to get them right.

Our sessions became a broth of distraction and acrimony and because of that, we never really progressed as a band. In eighteen months, what was a joy had become a chore. The second album was an ill-conceived disaster and as for the third, it never happened. Perhaps a manager with a strong enough personality would have whipped it all into shape? All I know now is, the musical ideas I'd had about where we could take our sound and the themes for subsequent albums, are gathering dust on MiniDiscs and CD-Rs in my shed or clogging up Torin's unopened emails. Two years into our life cycle, we were running just to catch up.

Our glasses were empty. I realised I was singing to myself. *'Right now, is where you are, in a broken dream…'* Our conversation had driven into a cul-de-sac and there was no reverse gear. I was overwhelmed by a sense of finality. My dreams were well and truly broken.

"But we had the gigs Mick, those amazing tours. Tokyo, San Fran…We went to fucking Hawaii man!" Corbossa didn't acknowledge me, he was looking through the pub's open door. His eyes had lost their warmth. No humour or energy remained. "Mick, you OK?" I felt his recoil. The metaphorical bracing for the knife between his shoulder blades.

"Mick?"

He spoke quietly. "I'm not coming in to rehearse with you tomorrow then?" My reply stuck in my throat like a sideways fish bone. He knew I was going to spend the entire night programming his beautiful drums next Alana's bass parts on the computer grid. A lone tear ran down his face, and in the same way it was incongruous to see Torin cowed, it was equally so to see Mick Corbossa sad.

"You're a great talent, Mick. Look at the work you've done, that album is timeless."

"Best days behind me, now."

"Never!"

He stood suddenly.

"Mick, sit down."

"Nah, fuck it."

Debbie reared as he stormed out of the pub. I held up my palm to assure her everything was OK. I was such a fucking liar nowadays.

***

Leaving the pub, I took the left into Denmark Street. In the reception area, Jake began fanning the booking diary pages. "You aren't in till next week," he said.

"Yeah, I know. I was in the area. You got a room with a keyboard in it? Just want to err, work something out for a minute."

He glanced at the clock. It was four-thirty. "Two's got a piano, but you'll need to be out by five. There's a band in."

Studio Two was hoovered and carpet-cleaner scented. I shut the heavy door behind me, made my way to the piano and played those eight notes. I thought about the sound and rhythm of them leaking from her headphones, how tacky and nonsensical they had sounded. I couldn't work out why I kept going back to them. I *must* have heard that hook in an advert or on a car radio as it passed me by. Most musicians absorb music even when they're not listening. Little scraps lodge in the memory and pop out when you least expect them to. That had to be it. I left the piano, lay back on the rehearsal room sofa and allowed my eyes to close.

"Daniel, it's five. That band are here." I awoke to see Jake's beardy head looking around the door and got up quickly. Huffing and puffing, with his arms either side of a bass cabinet, a man of around my age walked into the room.

"Hang on! You're Daniel Earl." He lowered the cab to shake my hand. "Torin! Was playing 'Jungle Ocean' the other day. Great album."

"Thanks man." I could feel his eyes on my bad side.

"Great sound, those keys, so big. Ken," he called over his shoulder: "It's Daniel from Torin."

A second man awkwardly switched the keyboard stand in his right hand to his left to shake mine. "Love Torin mate. You rehearsing?"

"Err no, not today. In next week."

"So, you've got gigs coming up? I'm there. Alana's a real inspiration. Tell her, when you're rehearsing. Love her style."

"I will mate. Have a good rehearsal."

10

After breakfast, I crossed the roundabout near the take-aways and Blockbuster shop and entered the park. Although it was warm and the trees were green and abundant, I could sense summer coming to an end.

I'd woken up to an email from Barney entitled, *'The New Way - Meeting One'*. It was scheduled for tomorrow with him and Torin at an address in North London. I felt sick at the prospect. The best thing in my life had been going on stage with the band, and now the band didn't exist. What had anchored me had been cut away, and I felt as if the earth was receding as I rose inexorably, from it. As they regularly did these days, my thoughts turned to Kerry. She'd become a final, flimsy tether to the earth. It was absurd that I was relying on her for gravity in my life. I didn't even know her second name, but when I was with her, or even when I thought about her, the band stuff didn't edge in. She kept my feet on the ground.

Corbossa hadn't replied to any of the messages I'd sent him or answered my calls since he'd left the pub. Six weeks ago I would have called Alana and we'd have gone looking for him. But I couldn't face her. When I listened to my stiff, soulless versions of her bass lines, a little of my heart flaked away. I knew that hearing her voice would drive a stake through what was left of it.

The wind gusted up and shook the branches above me, I slowed, recalling Kerry's panicky sprint towards the shop the evening before last. I'd got on the train home. Emerging from the tunnel, I'd received a text, *'thnx for everything. Don't take the snooker thrashing too badly LK xx.'* And that had been it for the last forty-eight hours. No mention of the keys drama at all.

Exiting the park gates, my phone buzzed in my pocket.

'u x with me?'

'X'? what the fuck was x?

I typed quickly, *'What is x?'*

'Cross.'

'No'

'Come to the shop, I've got something amazing to show u.'

***

We were standing outside.

"Well?" she asked.

"I did notice, the tree, the green in it, I think…"

"Not that, Daniel. The window!"

Did the mannequin have a friend with her? I vaguely recalled there being only one previously.

"There's two?"

"Don't tease."

A girl leaned against a section of plastic, silver-sprayed tree bark and leafless twigs, while another sat on a milking stool. They had on shirts: chequered, one red, one black. Both were embossed with roses and crossed pistols in white and yellow. There was a lot of denim, tilted Fedoras, brown leather boots and something green and sinewy wrapped around them, vines? A foot-and-a-half section of white picket fence cordoned off the scene.

She put her palm on my arm again. "Took me all day and we were so busy. Our new seasonal look."

"Oh…erm, you did all that on your own?"

"Well, the fairies didn't come in the middle of the night. And those mannequins weigh a sodding ton."

"Ha-ha. Reminds me of Texas. Been there with Torin a few times. You been there?" I said, thinking that I could finally connect with her on an 'exotic destination' level, but all she did was grip my arm and press me to her side. "Looks good, Kerry. I'm really impressed."

The sun went behind a cloud, etching our reflections in black in the shop front glass. When she tilted her head, wrinkles and lines became sentences and paragraphs, childlike freckles appeared. It was perverse, she seemed suddenly drenched in sadness. She bowed her head. Her voice was almost inaudible. "Are you truly?"

"Truly what?"

"Impressed."

"Of course, I am."

She looked up as the sun burst through and shook her hair

free. I sensed people looking at her as they passed. That she drew the eye everywhere we went reminded me of being with the band at our peak and I wondered if I were happiest in the shadow of naturally charismatic people because then, no one would bother to look at me.

She found her voice. "People have been coming in all afternoon saying they love it. We've sold two shirts and four of those scarves. Pam's delighted with me."

"So am I, Kerry."

"I'll let you off a snooker thrashing for that, techy boy," she said, gently punching me in the shoulder and pushing her tresses back under the cap. "Anyway, I'm starving."

We swapped a knowing look when she exaggeratedly rattled the keys and locked up.

"In here." I helped her push open the heavy glass door of a Chinese restaurant on Old Compton Street. She said she wanted to sit at the back, but there weren't any tables free, so we got one halfway down. She fell into the red leatherette, removed her cap again and ran her fingers through her scalp with comical vigour.

I studied the wipeable laminated menu. "Blimey," I said, amazed at how inexpensive the dishes were.

"I know, *very* competitive."

We ordered. The starters were brought and in she went, chopsticks flicking and clicking, items vanishing between her lips as fast as the words emerging from them.

"Yes. Took a fair bit of badgering on my part before she let me put those pieces in the window. She's very conservative about style. 'Of an age', if you know what I mean, so it was quite a leap for her to let me dress it, the window. Anyway, they're clearing a huge shop in Baker Street. I found those bits of plastic fence and vines and stuff in one of the skips outside it. A bit of cleaning, touch of gluing and voilà!"

Reality began to recede. I'd become transfixed by the way her fingers, as if shaping wisps of cloud, trailed the air when she spoke. She appeared to me a woman out of time, involved in the mundane tasks of our era, with the elegant actions from another.

"She's lucky. Sounds like the place would fall to bits without you," I said, biting a piece of sesame prawn toast.

"Do you think?"

"She's never there, is she?"

She patted the back of my hand for a couple of beats. "It's never a chore. In fact, I can't wait to get up and run at the day."

"But you're well paid?"

"It's complicated. We're hoping this new therapist will work out." She chewed energetically for a couple of seconds. "She's looking to open another shop. Chelsea perhaps."

"Hang on, she's just opened this one."

"I said it's complicated. She's talking about Sienna being a brand."

"But you said she doesn't know how to run a shop, so...?"

She shook her head beguilingly, "I told you, it's complicated, Daniel."

"I just worry…"

"Anyway, this medication…Hoping it can give her some energy. We said we'd look at my money when she's done a business plan for the new shop."

I was starting to heat up inside, and it wasn't the squid in chilli. "Come on, Kerry, you're doing the lot. You open and close, you clean the place, you work six days on your own. Paint the sign, get stuff out of skips! I mean, she should be paying you top dollar. How much is she saving, not having another person working in there? And opening another shop while she's getting therapy? It's taking the piss."

Behind the chopsticks, she darkened fractionally. "You don't understand retail, Daniel."

"You do everything in there."

"Adore tofu," she said, turning a glistening cube between her chopsticks. "Try some." She aimed the cube at my lips. I had to open my mouth. She poked it in with a triumphant grin and scanned the menu for her next foray. I shrugged and sat back as she ordered. There was something animal in the way she set about her food, as if her plate was going to be whipped away at any second. "That's a Goyard," she said, she was pointing at the window with her loaded chopsticks.

"A what?"

She signalled for me to wait, while she chewed and swallowed. She was drawing my attention to one of those immaculately aged, rust-tanned women you see dotted about Mayfair. This one was standing with her bald, Crombie-wearing hubby, reading the menu on the wall outside the restaurant. She gulped some water. "Goyard bag."

"Oh, her handbag," I said.

"A wealthy female is defined by her handbag, Daniel."

"I shall bear that in mind, Kerry."

"Remember the woman who came into the shop with her little girl? She had an Yves Saint Laurent rattan bag." She flicked her chopsticks between her eyes and mine. "The second she opened the door, I saw it, and made my move."

"You react to things in split seconds. I'm like that," I said. "When I have too much time to think, I get indecisive and lose my way. That make sense?"

She was looking straight at me. It was wonderfully unnerving. "Kindred spirits," she said, stabbing the last piece of spicy chicken on my plate. She leaned back patting her tummy. She'd devastated the half-dozen dishes we'd ordered.

"Feeling better?"

"An army marches on its stomach," she said, with a little burp and then she looked past me. "Can I have the bill, please?"

"No, no." I took a note out and put it on the tray.

She sagged in her seat. "Thank you, Daniel. It'll be back to normal once she's sorted out the cash flow issues."

I remember her card being declined at the snooker club. It was obvious she wasn't making any money at the shop. She kept saying it was a 'labour of love', but that doesn't pay the bills. I couldn't imagine the rent on a flat in Hammersmith being cheap, and there was the service charge for the new guttering on top of that.

"No problem. You're alright with the rent though?"

She tried but failed to give a look of disdain. "Darling, I own the flat, well mum and me, do."

"Oh yeah, of course."

"Thing is, mum's been really generous. Once Pam's sorted it all out, I can pay her back. Thank you for dinner Daniel…and snooker. I haven't forgotten," she said, pulling that pale blue cap over her eyes.

"All good, Kerry."

Strolling through Soho, her arm in mine, she stopped at nearly every clothes shop window 'to see what people were doing' and talked endlessly about dogs, the moon and children. "Stop me rabbiting on, Daniel. All I do is talk about myself."

"I don't mind listening."

"*Please* tell me about you. How was your mum today? Did she bring you your breakfast cuppa?"

"Yeah, she's kind of devoted. She hasn't got much going on in her life. I've tried to encourage her to err, retrain and all that."

"She must be very proud, you looking after her. But then she did look after you, right?"

"S'pose so. I put a deposit down on the house with money from the band, our first advance. The mortgage is a bit steep, but it's a nice place."

We walked on, me thinking that I might not have any friends left, I might not be in a 'great band' anymore, but at least I'd hold onto my retainer and keep a roof over mum and me. Thing is, you know from a very young age what it is to be poor. In seconds, when you're with other kids, you discern that the basic juvenile accoutrements – this season's trainers, tracksuit, an upgrade on your bike – will not be afforded to you. By the time I was fourteen, I'd learned how to duck out of the after-school newsagent splurge, 'forget' we were all going to the pictures that Friday and defer my football subs for yet another week. My frugal attitudes, and my creativity to an extent, were shaped by single parenthood, council housing and school dinners.

I let Kerry squeeze my arm, I was more than content that I'd be able to buy her the odd cuppa and posh cake, a Pad Thai and a frame of snooker.

"The new guttering at your place up yet?"

"Oh, don't ask. They're talking about something else that has gone wrong now. Going to take ages, I know it."

"They putting a damp course in?"

"Yes, That's it! The man said it's going to take a long time preparing…?"

"Yeah, it can do. Rising damp, is it?"

"Yes, that's it."

We walked in silence for a minute.

"How did you get into it? Did you go to uni for music, do a degree?"

"I was discovered in a pub."

"Really?"

"Yes."

She stopped and gave me a quizzical frown. "Daniel, I insist, no reticence or modesty. We must be open about our talents." And even though there wasn't anything hilarious being said, we were both laughing.

"All right. There was this music teacher Miss Ferguson. She took a shine to me. I'd missed a bit of school, had an accident. When I went back, she was really kind. Let me play around on the piano in the breaks instead of having to go outside. Then, the Christmas before I went into the sixth form, my mum bought me a Casio. It's like this real entry-level keyboard."

"Your *mother* got you into playing keyboards?"

"Yeah. Then, Miss Ferguson asked me to play in the pub band she sang in, mainly country music, some standards, and Torin...you sure you've not heard of him? Anyway, he walked in one night and asked me to be in his band."

"I understand," she said, but something in me wanted her to be a little more enquiring. After all, she'd been on at me about what I did, but since I told her, she'd not really followed it up.

I cracked on. "There's a lot of politics involved in a err, pro band."

"OK," she said quietly. We stopped at the tube station. She stepped up to me and adjusted my specs. "Thanks Daniel. It was so nice to see you again."

I didn't have the guts to say that being with her was the highlight of my life. A kiss bumped my lips. She fluttered her fingers and pointed at her phone as she backed away.

***

The next morning, after a short walk from the station, I found myself standing on an expansive gravel driveway outside one of those classically, double-fronted town houses not far from Highgate Woods.

Parked either side of a glorious oak was a cement mixer and a white van. I stepped out of the sunshine through an open front door and into the cool passageway. In the reception room on the right, up a ladder, a bloke with a scraper worked away on the coving. In the room on my left, a drill whined, stopped and started again.

I was peering up the stairs when I heard Torin's voice, "Come through Danny boy. We're in the garden!"

He was silhouetted at the end of the passage that ran the length of the house. I raised my palm and he turned away. At the end of the corridor was the open-plan kitchen. In it, a huge cellophane-wrapped fridge-freezer and pale blue Aga were waiting to be plumbed in. Half a dozen trendy stools, their legs still encased in the cardboard sleeves they'd arrived in, were tucked under a weighty, slate breakfast bar. Extending from various apertures and sockets were a score of electric cables and wires.

When I turned it, the handle rattled on the battered old kitchen door, its panes taped up with yellowing Sellotape. I stepped into the sunlight squinting at Barney, he was sitting, his laptop open, at a table in the shade of a cherry tree. "Sit down man, have a glass."

Torin swept up a bottle from the middle of the table. Pop went the cork.

"No thanks."

Barney peeked up. "Any groupies chuck their coffee over you this morning, Daniel?"

I dredged up a jaundiced smile and looked around me. The garden had the dimensions of a small park. A wrought iron pagoda featured in the distance. I turned to Torin. "Whose place is this?"

"Chap I was at school with."

It was always weird seeing Torin in nature. To me, he was an inside, late night person, existing in the dark of a gig, or beneath the artificial light of a club or hotel bar. Meeting him in the sunshine at an early hour with birds twittering made an unnerving situation worse.

"You sure, Daniel? This is cause for celebration."

Drinking wine before twelve wasn't usually my thing, but noticing the meaningful look he and his manager exchanged, I took a glass from him. "Cheers," I said.

All three of us touched glasses. When the liquid made contact with my digestive juices, I felt instantly queasy. Knowing that this meeting held ominous portents, I'd passed on breakfast. I regretted it now.

Torin leaned towards me. His face looked bloodless in daylight. His stubble black and abrasive. "We're in a time of revolution. Great change."

I let the wine swill around my mouth before swallowing. "Yeah. I'm aware of that."

"And I know you are feeling it acutely."

"I called Corbossa. He's not got back to me. Two days. I'm concerned."

"You've been a great friend to him, but the time has come to let go. You can't carry him."

"*Carry!* He's a better drummer than I am a keyboard player."

Barney leaned in. "You're doing it again Daniel, selling yourself short."

"I'm not, I'm saying that Mick Corbossa is a great drummer and..."

"He can't keep time," Torin said emphatically.

"That's not fair, he can't keep time to a digital..."

"But it's the digital age. We have to embrace the new way. That's the job, *Mr* Earl."

Barney turned his laptop screen towards me. "The dates, Daniel. Thirty in so far. Excited by that? Opening at The Shepherd's Bush Empire in a few weeks."

I'd be lying if I said I was not relieved to see that I'd be earning a living and that the band had a future, and I was part of it.

I turned to Torin. "I'm worried about Mick?" He gave me an admonishing smile and topped up the glasses.

"Are you your brother's keeper?"

One of the builders appeared at the kitchen door. "Guv?" he called out.

Torin stood and turned to Barney. "Brief him. I'll be back in a mo."

We waited until Torin had reached the door and entered the house. "Daniel, you need to know that Torin thinks the world of you."

"Yeah, bet you said the same to Corbossa."

He flinched at my harshness. But didn't he know he was just another of Torin's dispensable factotums and his days were irrefutably numbered?

"Let's focus on the new way," he said, "You are an intrinsic component. The main one, actually."

The wine was getting to me, numbing me and making me sensitive at the same time.

"I'm a musician, not a fucking component."

He sagged a little. "I'm just trying to explain. Look, I'm not from a music background. My thing is marketing and finance. I monetise product, strategise…"

"Thought you worked at Currys?"

"That was between jobs. Perhaps I don't express myself in the right way. Let me state again that you are irreplaceable, a great musician, a…"

I held my hand up and refilled my glass. "Just get on with it, man."

As Barney droned on, I began keying into the bird song from a far region of the garden. Thin rays of sun pleasantly warmed patches of my jeans. I took another drink. A lone bee buzzed over the table for a moment. I peered through the branches and remembered Kerry's lips on mine for that half second before she fluttered her fingers and retreated into the Oxford Street throng. Dry and perfunctory it may well have been, but she'd *definitely* kissed me. I'd turned and jogged down the station stairs in a daze, stopped, then jogged back up.

She was fifty yards ahead of me, the belt tight around her cream mac. Her holey white plimsoles rapid on the flags. I was mildly surprised that she walked past Bond Street station towards Marble Arch. She said her flat was off Shepherd's Bush Green, one of the roads that led from it.

I lost her, but I didn't fret. She was easy to track in her trusty baseball cap, but scanning the street ahead, I couldn't see it. A second before, she was walking past Debenhams, I was sure of that, but there was nothing pale blue ahead and the department store was long shut.

I knew where she'd gone in a split second and turned around. As I lurked in a darkened shop awning on the other side of the square I saw her cap – like some pale blue nocturnal thing – flitting past the rich green of the small tree. I stepped out to see better. Opening the door with those hefty keys, she punched in the alarm code. No lights went on. I stood there for half an hour. I could have stood there all night.

I'd finished the bottle on my own. Torin had returned to the table.

"Is this really happening?" I asked him.

He clapped me on the back. "Ha-ha, you're drunk, Danny boy."

"But fucking miming!"

The sun was over his shoulder. To look at his face would blind me. When I stood up, the flora seemed to swirl around. I walked through the passage towards the driveway with his laughter booming over the drilling and scraping.

On the tube back, so pissed, rocking sickeningly, the 'new way' played itself over and over in my head. There seemed no exit, no way to change direction. I was trapped in my band. The abuser I loved. The shopping bags next to me protested at my spread legs and unruly elbow.

"Miming!" I said aloud. I slid a little, sat up straight and opposite me saw a lit-up stage and Alana in platform heels, her huge bass slung over her bare shoulders, slender neck craning at a microphone that was always an inch too high for her mouth. On his drum riser behind her, Mick Corbossa, tattooed schoolboy baller, my best buddy, laid down one of the swingy grooves that separated him from the 'sit up and beg' drummers the other bands had. And there, at the arrow's head was Torin DeVere, on his back, his penis flopping about under his dress, blowing into his harmonica, sucking the wide-eyed crowd into his darkness.

"Drunken idiot!" The woman beside me stood and moved herself and her purchases to a far section of carriage. A couple of teenagers were seated diagonally across from me. "Go on mate," one said, playing an imaginary piano, "Sing us another one." I looked down. My fingers were poised over an invisible keyboard. I lowered my hands and blinked around me. Apart from one bloke who was smiling and nodding, no one could meet my eye. "Come on mate, don't stop now, we're all enjoying the choons," said the kid across the aisle. The carriage lurched. I must get a coffee. I stood up. The doors opened, I alighted, but it wasn't my stop.

The two women resplendent in their Texan setting seemed pretty lifeless, I peered into faces that didn't exist and lost my balance.

The bell dinged, the shop door opened and she pulled me in.

"Daniel, you look ill. Was it the chow mein?"

"I'm drunk, Kerry."

"It's three o'clock. Is that common for Fridays?"

"...'ad a meeting..."

"Hell of a meeting."

"Nah, nah..."

She set me in the fluffy orange chair. I peeked through the fingers of my hand at the baffling miscellany around me. Too much going on. I closed my eyes.

"I'd get you a coffee, but I can't leave the shop."

"Nah, nah..."

"Is that one of your songs?"

I squinted at her. "Nah, nah?"

"Ha, ha." Dancing a showy, Latin hip glide towards me, she sang, *"Nah nah, ha ha."* Her gyrations in such an intimate space sobered me momentarily. I exhaled an appreciative, rubbery smile.

"That's better," she said, her hands on the rests either side of me. I drank in her minty breath and chocolatey body lotion. A scintilla of energy returned.

"Can I use your loo?"

"Downstairs, second on the left."

I made it through the arch at the left of the counter and arrived at a narrow corridor at the foot of the stairs. The door on my right was ajar. I peeked in. It was rammed full of stock; boxes stacked, garments hung, labelled, all very ordered. I closed it quietly.

There were three doors on my left. I walked past the first and into the toilet; functional, clean. I peeked into the cupboard behind me, before splashing cold water on my face. The door after the toilet opened onto a galley kitchen. Microwave, small fridge (which I opened). Again, clean, functional, a cupboard above the sink, a dish cloth folded, a tea towel (map of Paris on it) on a little hook. I heard her voice above me. Someone was in the shop. I turned and made for the stairs.

"Getting coffee," I said, opening the door onto the street. The last thing I saw through the window was the irresistible smile she aimed at the person looking through the vintage rail.

I mumbled my order and took it to a stool by the window. I knew that the 'customer smile', although a brilliant and dazzling thing to behold, wasn't the one she gave me. It might have been a drunken conceit on my part, but I'd never seen her smile at anyone the way she did at me. As I tried to conjure it up, Barney's voice, from a couple of hours earlier, rose with the coffee fumes.

"The world is changing Daniel." I'd been gazing at the pagoda in the distant reaches, locking into the bird's twittering. "Kids today, they don't care how music gets to them, as long as it does. People travel light now; they don't need all that 'gear'. It's a win–win. Thirty dates mate. You earn, Torin earns and even little ol' me makes a few bob.

Two girls, not teenagers, not bimbos, they'll look the part, sort of actresses, I suppose. They'll have a clue…No, no, no, Torin was very specific that they look like they're playing. He's really thought it through. Bass player *must* be a bass player and the drummer must know which is the right and which is the left stick. The beauty is, nothing comes out front-of-house. It'll all flow from your laptop. You'll be the 'Great Oz'. *They* won't know and as I said, they won't care anyway. As long as those songs are belting out, and they can see you and Torin doing what you do best…You alright mate? You want a top-up? You can see it, can't you, Daniel?"

"Such a waste." I muttered, sipping my coffee. I no longer felt drunk. I felt dull and heavy. "Such a fucking waste."

As office workers scurried past the window, it came to me that the tirade he'd aimed at Alana after the debacle on the last date of the tour, was the precursor to the charade Barney had set out in Highgate earlier. A burgeoning red wine headache triggered the memory of Torin in Rotterdam, grudgingly placing his phone on the drum riser with his wine and harmonicas. When the audience thought he was having his customary swig (not that he wasn't doing that as well), he was peering at his phone's tiny screen. Such was his obsession with it, that Alana, coaching like a second in a boxer's corner, just couldn't get him in and out of the songs that night. Halfway through the gig, she had bellowed at him to turn the thing off. He'd snarled and barged her away. Thousands of people watching, and he'd done that. I remember feeling sick at the sight of him. During the last song, he had it in his hand. He was reading it instead of singing!

As Mick had smashed the cymbal on the last song he'd ever play for the band, Torin swept past the waiting crew, down the ramp and through the open dressing room door with the phone glued to his ear. Incredulous, me and Mick waved at a crowd already turning to each other to ask what the fuck it was they had just witnessed.

With that ability to remember every note from the set list of my old covers band to every nuanced second of my own songs, it isn't hard for me to recall precisely what Torin had been saying into his phone when I entered the dressing room with Mick. It had almost become an addition to our repertoire, an encore, albeit an ill-fitting one.

"Conrad, I'm away somewhere, fucking Belgium. Anyway, trust me. I can get it to you on time. Guaranteed. You know how big my band is, right?"

Alana had walked into the room as he was speaking. She opened a beer and leaned against the wall…"*That* was fucking garbage, Torin. What on your phone is more important than the show?"

He turned away shielding the screen. That was when I heard him say 'Ibiza'. Mick had heard it too.

"Call me man, please." Torin put his phone away and sneered at Alana. "They clapped, didn't they? Fucking sheep."

"What the fuck happened to you, man?"

At that point Mick had stood up, took a couple of beers from the ice bin and let himself out. I wish I'd followed him.

Torin shut the door on the prying eyes outside and, between the fruit bowl and kettle, proceeded to chop out a post-gig line. He turned on her, rubbing his nose. "Give it a rest *darling*. Been doing this five years, I don't need lessons from you."

I sat there sweating, wishing I had the guts to say, '*but you'd be fucked without them*'.

"You're jeopardising everything," she said.

He opened a bottle of red with a violent pull of the cork and glugged straight from it. "As if I give a shit."

"Seriously, what is happening, Torin?"

Sniffing, he eyed her maliciously. "You! You put me off, always in my face." He was actually looking at his phone as he spoke.

"If I wasn't, we wouldn't finish a song."

"Crap, Alana."

"We'd be going round and round, waiting for you to come in."

"Rubbish. You heard them, they love me."

"They love the *band*, Torin, the *sound*. All our efforts."

"You've always been ugly with jealousy. You're after what's mine, like the rest of them."

"What?"

"You bottled out of the press cos you were in my shadow. Never at the club. Left me to do all the, the…to make connections."

"All you were doing is whoring and taking coke!"

"Are you surprised, fucking dry old lesbian."

"You utter bastard."

He waved his bottle at the room. His eyes were neon strips boring into the prefabricated walls. "I've outgrown you baby. This whole fucking band is so small-time."

"You wouldn't know what to do without us."

At that moment, his phone flashed on. As he read the message, Alana stepped across the room and gently put her hand on his arm. "Tell me, Torin. Has something happened, something serious? Your parents?"

He threw his phone into the sofa. "I can do this fucking job standing on my head. I don't need you to tell me anything."

We had nobody to blame but ourselves. We should have deferred those first gigs and worked on him until he developed the mind muscle that came naturally to ninety-nine percent of musicians. He'd be standing on his own two feet now, not balancing on Alana's shoulders. From the minute she nudged him, he'd hated her.

She was shaking her head.

He took a step towards her and yelled in her face. "*What!*"

"You're unhinged, man."

He pointed the wine bottle at her as she flattened herself against the wall. "Take your bass and your fascist orders and get the fuck out of my band."

She wasn't noble then. She winced like a little girl who'd banged her knee and there was no one to rub it better. Tears streamed. Feeling like I wanted to vomit, I watched her slowly walk into the commotion of crew and musicians outside.

"You got something you want to say, *Mr* Covers band?"

I left the room with a couple of beers and sat on a flight case by the trucks parked behind the stage. I finished one bottle and opened another.

This is it, I remember thinking, gazing at the flat fields stretching away, *It's over.*

On the bus back to England, Alana didn't speak. Her final words to me at Paddington were, "Take care, Daniel." That was two months ago.

11

It was getting on for eight o'clock and while all the shops along the road were shut, hers looked aflame. Backing into the shadow of the doorway that I favoured, I watched silhouettes chink flutes to a muffled house beat. I couldn't believe you could cram so many people in there.

Looking as waxy as the mannequins, Kerry, hair tied in a severe bun, appeared with a tray of full glasses. She had on a starched white shirt and black pencil skirt. It was odd seeing her not enthused and expansive in her domain, theatrically exhibiting the fine fibres and gorgeous colours of some eye-wateringly expensive garment, buzzing around the rails, tucking and tidying. No one was paying her any mind. She was neutral, blank, waiting to be told what to do. As an arm protruded from the chattering clumps to relieve her of a glass or two, a sadness radiated from her that made me short of breath.

I'd been trying to come to terms, reconcile and organise my feelings for Kerry. I knew our relationship was tenuous, predicated on a comic vignette on the underground, but like mum, I was compelled to make sure she was fed and cared for, which was absurd as she had a job, a past, a flat in an affluent location and, of course, her mum, and *she* sounded pretty minted to me.

When a camera flash went off highlighting Pam, sandwiched between a couple of barbered young men, all teeth and designer stubble, I lost her momentarily. She reappeared waiting on one of those wrinkly 'handbag women' who, on seeing her, turned her back. I watched Kerry take a couple of side-steps to re-present the tray. The woman flicked the back of her hand at her then cricked her neck at the tall tweedy man she was clearly beguiled by. He must have been a top comedian because she didn't half laugh when he finished speaking.

Kerry didn't join in. She shifted her weight from one foot to the other, her eyelids batting slowly with fatigue.

"Fuck her off and walk away, Kerry," I muttered.

It was as if she'd heard me and obeyed. But the woman tapped her hard on the shoulder and glaring, removed two glasses for her and her funny mate without a word.

I began to heat up again. We said we'd go and celebrate with cake. Tonight, was our fifth Soho Stroll, an *'anniversary'* she'd written in her text to me this afternoon. She'd not sent a follow-up message to say there was party at the shop. Strange.

Then she saw me. Looking left and right, she placed her tray on the island and rushed across the road into my arms. She held me tight for a moment and whispered hotly in my ear, "Go home, Daniel, I'll be here ages."

I was stunned. It was one thing to have my arm squeezed looking at some 'adorable' dog across the street, or her pale lips press mine for a quarter beat at the top of the stairs at the tube, but to be held by her like that, outside, the full body press, made me feel like I was levitating. But I couldn't relish the moment, because Kerry was already backing away, her eyes so sad and tired. "You never said..."

"It was a surprise, Daniel."

"...can't."

She shook her head and turned around. Pam, waiting at the door, pulled her aside.

Instinctually, I'd not made myself known to her boss. Pam was a squat woman, with a bit of a beak, a cruel one, I thought. As well as a Hermès scarf, there was a sulky plumpness about her chin that seemed to crave attention. My stomach curdled watching her berate Kerry. The goldy woman was looking on approvingly, the tall bloke in tweed jabbing in a punchline. I stepped up to the door from my shadow. Kerry's eyes left her employer's for a second. Pam winced when she saw me. Ah yeah, that wince. While I'd been seeing Kerry, I'd forgotten how easily I elicited it. I turned and steamed off.

Halfway across the square, I slowed as I thought about what had just happened. Kerry had left the shop to see me even though she knew she could get into trouble for doing it. Instead of walking up the alley to the tube station beyond and home, I poked my glasses up and turned right for an anniversary stroll on my own.

Entering the alley and then the square an hour later, I saw Pam, the goldy woman, the comic and the himbos outside The Lamb having a smoke and a joke. Keeping to the shadows, I made my way towards the shop. It was bright, but empty, save for Kerry.

"I'll put the rubbish out," I said, through the open door.

She didn't even try to smile. Wordlessly, we worked for twenty minutes, her taking the glasses and plates to the kitchen downstairs to wash up, me filling the bin bags and putting them by the terracotta pot outside. I vacuumed the floor while she tidied the rails.

"Team," she said, raising a tired hand for a high five. A smile was swapped as she tapped the code into the pad. "I didn't know until about three thirty."

"Still, I'd never have…"

"If she'd have caught me on my phone," she shook her head quickly. "I didn't have a minute. You saw what it was like in there."

"No, no, of course."

"First it was going to be a few friends, nothing late, then she started inviting everyone, getting me to order champagne, catering."

"Jesus, weren't you…?"

"Look, she does this sort of thing. She's capricious and spontaneous," she said lightly, comically, as if her boss had her fun, unscripted moments and it was all part of the 'Sienna experience'.

She forked some chocolate-speckled gateaux between her lips. We were back at the double-fronted patisserie. I leaned forward and spoke in a low tone, "She treats you like shit, doesn't she?" Invisible motes of charisma danced in the air around us as she sat back, tossed her head and laughed loudly. The couple on the next table gawped at her. She locked onto me with that cover-girl glare. She seemed…well, a little deranged. I put it down to fatigue.

"So, the first time I came here was with my mum, when I was about five or six. I was *such* a little chatterbox. Doesn't surprise you, does it? We used to…well mum used to dress us identically. That creepy?"

"No," I said, conceding ground to further memories of her mum and childhood. I was tempted to ask where her mum was tonight. She'd never have stood by and let her daughter be treated like that. She would have packed her into whatever car she currently had, and driven her to the coast to make, I dunno, tea and crumpets? Tuck her in nice and tight.

"…Patent black shoes, Mary Janes, and immaculate red princess coats. Bows in our hair. I loved that. Did your mum buy you nice clothes when you were a little boy?"

"I don't think so, Kerry." She aimed some serious, closed-lipped expectancy, at me. "Well, you know…I'd get something hardwearing… football kit, school uniform, I suppose."

"But she did spoil you a bit?"

"I wouldn't say spoiled me, but she did care. Does care. I'm thankful of that, I suppose. Can't all have mums like yours."

"Yes true," she said quietly. Revived by tea and cake, she hugged my arm as we strolled towards Wardour Street and the tube beyond. "So, we *did* get our anniversary walk, see."

"I'm glad, Kerry. Err, thought I'd tell you, we'll be playing soon. I mean me, Torin. A few weeks' time, at Shepherd's Bush Empire."

Thousands of people had seen me on stage, but right now, she was the one person whose approval I wanted. She'd finally see what defined me, what had sustained me all my adult life. I felt giddy at the thought of meeting her eyes from my cascading synths.

"Oh, I shall definitely…Ah, *that's* what I'm looking for." She'd pulled me towards a shop window.

"What?"

"The cat, there." I scanned a window with innumerable and varied ornaments in it.

"Oh that," I said. The statue she pointed out was a foot-high porcelain cat: cartoonishly elongated body, creamy coloured, a whiskery smile and black bow tie. "Yeah, nice."

"It'll go perfectly on the ledge beneath the big window. I adore cats, but the lease says we aren't allowed to have pets, and anyway, I'm on the third floor. No garden." She tugged me away and on we walked. I glanced at her. She was lit up, eyes dancing. "It's French themed, my flat. Well, the front room and bedroom are."

"Cos of your mum in Paris?"

"Uh huh."

"Same with me and music. Those early influences, they stay with you."

"You like France?"

"Yeah," I said.

We walked in silence for a few steps. "I managed to find this adorable nest of coffee tables. *Had* to have them. I didn't have a Scooby about where they were from. Turned out…"

"…French?"

"*Naturellement.* Saw them in a second-hand shop in Portobello. I adore boot sales and bric-a-brac, *vous*?"

"Yeah, me too…*Oui.*"

"Ha! *Parfait.* Let's go to one soon. A *brocante*, somewhere in the South of France, you and me." She hugged my arm harder. "I'm always on the lookout for something to add. I try to keep the Gallic theme going. I'm quite girly, habitat wise. I adore cushions. Do you like cushions Daniel?"

"Kerry, you sure you should be waitressing at the drop of a hat."

She didn't break stride. "It's all warm a cosy in my place, especially this time of year."

"Seriously, you've been taken on as the shop manager, right? I mean, the way she spoke to you." She didn't respond. "I heard her," I said.

"She was a bit squiffy. Tends to get a little…uninhibited after a few. Creative?"

"You told me she's not paying you that much, but blimey, she certainly got the Champers in, a few hundred quid's worth…and canapés. You gonna be paid for all that extra work tonight?"

"The universe will reward me."

I sighed and shook my head. "The universe rewards fuck all," I muttered.

We walked silently in step.

"Daniel?"

I don't know what came over me when I opened my mouth. "I've got to do something for money. Something I definitely don't want to do. Shameful. I'll be betraying really good people. You know, money ain't everything Kerry, sometimes a little…"

I thought she had tripped on the kerb crossing the road, but realised when I tried to steady her, that she was veering towards a woman huddled in a doorway. We encountered a panoply of street people on our walks and Kerry always gave them the time of day. Fishing into my jeans for coppers, I followed her to the other side of the road. The woman's clavicles were unusually prominent, they stretched the wafery skin of her neck when she tugged a grimy sleeping-bag tighter to her shoulders. Her eyes were blue and set deep in dark gaunt sockets. They expanded when she saw the person kneeling in front of her. Kerry seemed oblivious to the stink of piss that had me backing off and standing a little way away. Cabs and motor bikes were roaring past. I couldn't hear what was being said. When I saw Kerry stroking the woman's face and pulling the lank hair from her eyes, I wished I had something antiseptic on me to wipe her down with afterwards. After a couple of minutes, she stood and left the woman in the doorway.

"Phowar!" I'd said, fanning my nose. "Nothing a jet spray couldn't remedy." She raised her head and a smooth, clear smile shone at me from beneath her cap. She looked eighteen. "Nah, seriously," I said. "People fall through the cracks. Shame."

"Yes," she'd nodded.

Later I realised how unreal that smile was, dead-eyed, devoid of any sort of warmth. It was the smile she'd given to those wankers she was serving at the shop a few hours earlier.

***

"Doesn't he put you off? Surely you can find someone a bit more presentable, a fashion conscious girl like you?" Just after three thirty that morning, Pam's vocal critique of her manageress's boyfriend prodded me awake.

Did I look that bad? I suppose there was a lot of light falling on me from the shop, and that was never gonna help. Evenings were usually a good time for me as I could be *'tastefully concealed'*. Kerry not looking twice at my appearance, had fostered a blitheness in me that Pam's scant review had undercut.

I placed my hands behind my head, stared into the fathomless ceiling and remembered myself amidst the white, melamine cupboards and drawer's downstairs in the boutique. Although drunk and reeling from Torin's 'new way' meeting in the garden, I'd instinctively made a 'setlist' inventory of the contents of the cabinet above the toilet: moisturiser, make-up, shampoo, some product that took the grey out of blonde hair, toothbrush and paste, other feminine bits. In the kitchen cupboard above the sink: tomato and chicken Cup a Soup sachets, crackers and sugar cubes, tiny salt and pepper packets you get in takeaways, more plastic cutlery and tea bags. The small fridge could just about accommodate the half carton of semi-skimmed and the few cheese slices it contained. Then I'd heard voices in the shop upstairs and closed the door.

***

We'd arranged to meet up two evenings later, but when I awoke there was a text from her to say she had an appointment and wouldn't be able to see me. I wondered what she'd be doing after work and who she'd be doing it with. Closing her message, I received one from Torin asking me what I thought of the *'new way'*. I didn't reply.

Through the kitchen window morning dew glistened on the patch of grass in the garden. All I could I think of was Kerry.

My phone began ringing.

"Not sulking, Danny?"

"No, not at all."

"Why the radio silence?"

"Coming to terms with it, that's all."

"Everything is riding on this phase."

"OK."

"Barney will contact you with dates for rehearsals."

"OK, got it."

I switched off the phone and shut my eyes. The fridge hummed, and I felt that sickly untethered sensation drawing me away from the breakfast table.

"Eggs alright, Daniel? Made them a bit hard yesterday..."

My mother was standing at the open door behind me, a location from where she could access the stairs behind her, the front room on her left or the kitchen she was facing. Emergency exits for non-emergencies.

"They were fine mum. These are good too." She gave the space above my head a short smile. It was the highlight of her day, I think, making me breakfast. "Really nice," I added. "The toast's got seeds in it, you said?"

"Seeds are good for you. Full of vitamins. Better than pills. Wish

I didn't have to take so many. Doctor said I should cut down, but…"

"I'll have another a word with him."

Breakfast TV chatter permeated the kitchen as she opened the door to the room on her left. As it shut, the fridge noise refilled the space. She'd been an only child like me. Her mum had 'gone away' when she was thirteen. She said that she'd come home from school one day, and there were some people from the council in her house. 'Your mum's gone somewhere nice', they told her, and they would look after her, now. With that impish little smile, she sometimes allowed herself, she told me that she'd given various foster families hell. She liked her own company, she said. She promised she'd never let other people look after me. But she wasn't on her own for long. A week after her seventeenth, she got pregnant with me. We were provided with the flat on the estate, various benefits and leg-ups, clothes allowance, food allowance. We wanted for nothing really.

Growing up, there were always 'people from the council' scrutinising me from the front door, or kitchen table or sitting room armchair when I came home from school. Those 'people' their benefits, surprise visits and hair ruffling, their thin smiles and 'once-overs' of my bedroom, had fostered a cold resolve in me. I hated that we were 'cared for', 'checked in on'. From a very early age I wanted nothing from anyone. By the time I was twenty, I'd achieved that goal. I'd got us this house. What little I had in my account, I'd earned myself. We were independent, mum and me.

The TV jingle seeped into the kitchen. She'd returned to the doorway. "I know I'm not a great mum, Daniel…that it was all my fault."

"Your fault I've got them?" I replied, nodding at the platinum and gold discs that lined the hallway behind her. She looked down at her slippers.

"Another slice of toast, then?" The more concern my mum had for me, the more food she wanted me to eat. If I really troubled her, there'd be all sorts from the deli on the high street: exotic fare, stuff she couldn't pronounce, never mind cook. "What?" she asked, with that impish smile. "What's funny?"

"Nothing. Thing at work." I was smiling at her innocent mispronunciations of continental dishes and that had put me in mind of her early attempts at my bandmates' names: Colin, Alan and Ponderossa. I'd even told them, and for a couple of days, on some giant haul across America, they addressed each other with mum's malapropisms. But tour jokes invariably wear thin. I stood up and took my breakfast things to the sink.

"I could pop up the road, get you some gravel-smoked salmon. You liked that."

"Oh mum, it's OK." I remember being small and her pressing me close, humming to me, big black lashes blinking at me with love and care. She'd hold my hand in the park, push me on the swings and tuck me into my buggy. We'd even booted the ball to each other when I was older. It was all she could do. She didn't have a job, had done nothing at school. She could barely cope. Once, we went to the science museum. I was so proud to be there with *my* mum. It was like I'd taken her. But since the accident she'd not been able to touch me. She'd hold out her hand, then retract it, fiddle with her beads or a hankie or just wind her fingers around each other over and over. I rinsed my cup, turned around and placed a very light palm on her shoulder. She stiffened. "It's alright mum. Ta for breakfast. I'm going to the shed."

"Don't forget your glasses."

I picked them up from the table, left the kitchen and arms folded, walked up the path knowing she was still there in the doorway. After turning on the speakers and computer, I selected the file of song ideas I'd intended as the base for our third album. I'd recorded around a dozen themes and hooks on the file. Eighteen months ago, I'd sent them to Torin via MP3 and waited on his approval so that Alana, Mick and I could start working on them together. He never replied, so we never did. Funny, even as I pressed 'send' that afternoon, I knew they were doomed. The idea of Alana and Torin, heads together, arranging his lyrics into melodies and then, her coaching him to sing them in the right place was as likely as him buying her another coffee in a chic Holland Park café.

As the cursor moved laterally across the screen, the two or three colour-coded parallel lines that constituted the demo filled my little cabin with an ethereal string movement. I slowly nodded my head. It sounded good!

"Fuck," I muttered. I'd poured everything into this new music, and he hadn't even got back to me.

With my precious, moribund theme playing, I lay down on the sofa at the back of the room and thought of being alone in here with Kerry, kissing her properly, feeling her bare skin beneath the palm of my hand, pressing her against me without fear. Closing my eyes, I imagined us a couple, living together, laughing and caring – all that fantasy stuff.

The string piece faded and a mechanical thud emerged. An offkey, jangly organ in six/eight stabbed across a discordant, stifling progression.

I sat up and peered into the space between my feet. How could I dream of being a part of the South of France lifestyle Kerry was accustomed to; the bobbing masts in the harbour silhouetted against a cinematic 'end of epic' setting sun. Could I see myself in a white James Bond tux? I could certainly imagine her in a flowing thing; gossamer, shimmering gold, her waist and behind as graceful and willowy as the sand dunes we'd walked along that afternoon.

As the track introduced a manic two-note top line, I giggled dismally. Swimming in the lake of some chateaux? Had she seen me swim? And her mum meeting mine. I actually squirmed at that scenario: *her* mum all tall and chic, reaching down to shake my mum's hand. My mum, head bowed, examining her slippers! Her mum looking at her, then at me, then back at her. I suddenly laughed like a nutter into the ceiling.

The track ended. I exhaled in the silence. But opposites attract, don't they? I mean, look at Alana and Torin at the start. She was from Reading, her mum was a nurse, single parent, and Torin was from fuck knows where, but he was undoubtedly different gravy; creamy, rare and, above all, rich.

I peeked through the square window at the kitchen. My mum was at the sink, pretending to wash up the breakfast things, peering back at me. "Alan and Colin," I muttered.

As was often the case when I was in here, my mind would trip back to those contented days on the road, but then I remembered that Torin had not found my mum's mispronunciations as funny as we had. He revealed 'Torin' had been his great-grandfather's name, a celebrated industrialist in the days of Empire. Torin thought mocking the name, disrespectful. When had that uncomfortable exchange taken place? Pacific Coast Highway? Up or down it? California had been spectacular through our tour bus window. After the volley about us 'taking the piss out of his heritage', he'd sneered and left for his quarters upstairs. Mum's funny names were never used again.

It was on our third American tour that the gigs, although rapturously received, began to go stale. There was a crustiness around the edges of our live show. We were dipping below the standards we'd set ourselves. Alana cited disunity as the cause. On previous tours, we'd travelled, laughed and argued as a unit, a band. We'd go on together and in the dressing room after the show, there was this sublime feeling of satisfaction as we allowed ourselves a minute or two to bask in the afterglow. But none of us relished the way we felt after the shows on that tour. Crisscrossing the continent relentlessly, the divide grew ever wider between singer and band. At his irritable behest, Alana began doing his soundchecks. Consequently, we only interacted with him for fifteen minutes before curtain and the time it took for him to open a bottle after we came off.

It was in some hotel lobby as we waited for the bus to come from the parking lot, or it may have been as I slid into the seat opposite him while he pushed the granola around his breakfast bowl, that I attempted to broach the topic of disunity. He must have known that the shows were suffering, but he wasn't having it. "Piss off, Danny. They clapped, didn't they?"

His 'come-downs' on this tour induced incredible moments of distrust and paranoia. He'd send food back if he didn't like the look of a waiter. He'd corner the driver and ask him why he'd taken a particular route, as if he'd been ordered to take him into the desert and leave him to the coyotes. He would sequester me, Mick or our soundman Roy, and quiz us on what we perceived as each other's weaknesses. He seemed intent on dividing us, but that only made us closer and him more detached.

Mick and I had never quite got our heads around Alana's devotion to him when we started out. Being so savvy in all other areas of her life, it amazed us that she'd let herself be broken and disrespected by him. She had the most acute bullshit detector of anyone I'd ever known, but I suppose that love, back then, was blind, or at least had no sense of smell. She had done everything for him; ran his errands, fought her way through the massed ranks at the bar to get him his glass of red, cleaned up his flat, and boy, did it need cleaning. To see her, back then, shiny eyed with adoration was quite magical. But you could tell it wasn't a two-way street. Her attention was only reciprocated in front of a camera or on a stage.

So, on that final tour of the States, it would be just us three watching the highway's endless white lines flashing past the window. Those mundane miles, like they do to everyone eventually, prized Alana open and she told us about how a rare man had totally swept her away one afternoon in Notting Hill Gate.

Alana and I were sitting in the tour bus's back lounge waiting for Corbossa. This was common. That night he'd fallen for the waitress in the truck-stop diner. She was a blue-eyed Southern babe, petite, feline, and she liked Mick a lot. Through the bus window I could see her at the side of his table smiling, swishing her blonde hair while he looked up from his plate, beguiled.

We sent the tour manager to go and get him. Minutes later, the bus door hissed open.

"Why do we *always* have to move on, Danny?"

"It's the job, man," I said.

"Her voice was…there seemed no need to rush."

Placing his beer in the well on the table, he began to map out the life they might have had together if he wasn't on the road, and lived in another country, and she wasn't married with three kids.

"I think I love her, mate."

"No Mick," I said from my seat. "There's a kind of chemical urge, surge, initially. Endorphins rush in…"

"…where angels fear to tread."

"Yeah, all that, and then they fade. Scientists have sussed it all out."

"You're a cold-hearted fucker, Earl. One of these days you'll fall backwards in love and I'll laugh my arse off."

"No such thing as love, Corby old mate, I assure you."

"Yes, there is," Alana said from her unlit corner.

My eyes met with Mick's over our bottle tops.

"I'm just saying that..."

"The thing you *shouldn't* do," her voice came from her vast, black leatherette chair, "is fall in love with the wrong person. *Never* do that."

We rocked in our seats as the driver turned the bus around. Soon, the white lines were once again accelerating past the window.

"But don't take relationship advice from me," she said, "because, as you both well know, I did."

"Did what?" Mick asked.

"Fell in love with someone I shouldn't have fallen in love with."

I could tell Corbossa was itching to ask the same questions as I was. How? Why?

Only her voice, and inching into the interior glow, one unlaced DM boot, was physical proof she was in there with us. Her opening words were unexpected. "I had a passion for geology at school. I wanted to be one – a geologist, studying the earth, rocks, minerals. It was all I was interested in when I was fifteen."

"Ha-ha, and you ended up in a *rock* band," said Corbossa.

"Don't think I haven't chuckled about that to myself over the years," she said, edging into the light. She nodded towards the ceiling at the front of the bus where Torin lay comatose in his bunk. "I fell in love with him. You both know that. You were there. Why? Well, there are the obvious reasons, he's a beautiful-looking guy and back then he was a laugh, exciting to be around, so different from anyone I'd ever known. And, as time went on, I admired him for transforming himself from what he was when I met him, a kind of drifting trustafarian, into a great frontman. I mean, he's a star, now. But it was more than that."

She backed into the darkness. The bus rumbled on. "From that first coffee we had after I saw him busking at the station, he had me like a cat has a mouse in its claws. How many times have I gone over that first meeting. What was in my head, thinking that he was some kind of potless crusty? He took me to the poshest coffee shop in Holland Park!" She leaned into the light. Her eyes flitted between us with incredulity. "But boys, the people in there knew his name, they brought him his macchiato without him even asking for it! I sat there, his smile eating me up, refusing to accept the evidence of my own fucking ears and eyes!"

Through the window, the night stretched into black infinity. The driver had on the gentle, pedalling sounds of a local country station.

"From the very start, this odyssey, this travelling band we are all in, was predicated on a lie, a con." We were rapt, we'd never heard her speak so freely. She was a person of short sentences and long patient smiles. "He was a fabulous hunter...but maybe he wasn't. Maybe it was me. I was the model prey."

I sort of got that, but she still hadn't explained the 'more than that' part. On we went into the night. An advert on the radio broke the spell.

She spoke from the darkness again. "I loved him because he wanted 'justice'." The drummer's eyes met mine in puzzlement. Justice for what, for who? A truck going the other way illuminated the cabin and for a moment and I thought I saw a tear trickle down her cheek.

"It was as you said, Daniel, I was overwhelmed with that chemical urge, endorphins going crazy. I'd never felt like it before. I couldn't bear to be apart from him. In his bedroom, with the ceilings so high, the soft cotton sheets welding us together, we spoke passionately about the iniquities of the world while we drank the champagne and ate caviar he'd ordered from the place around the corner."

"Justice, Alana?" I asked.

She took a breath. "It was frustration with 'culture'."

Of course, she got nothing from us.

"I'll try to boil it down. Unlike the seventies and eighties, the hippies and punks, our generation seemed apathetic, causeless. Is that even a word? Pointless then. But, I mean, you can't keep endlessly whinging and moaning with your mates about the evils of the system, and he said – I can remember that moment so well, he was standing naked, the windows flung open, like he was addressing a crowd in the street below – *We have to do something about it. You and me, Alana*. The only way we could think of changing anything was through music. The idea of a band began to grow. He asked me to move in with him. He said we needed to be 'hugga mugga'."

She looked at our bemused faces. "I know, I'd never heard that before either. Anyway, that's how we had to be to get this done properly, he said. We began writing these incredible lyrics together. We had the enemy in the crosshairs; Third World debt, misogyny, racism and the rampant, careless capitalism that had created the environment for it all to thrive. By candlelight in that beautiful front room, the chandelier like a glass spaceship hovering above, we decided we'd put a band together. A band that would 'shake up the world'. He knew I'd done it before, knew the practicalities…and all I could see was a beautiful, charismatic man who could sing, who spoke *my* language and loved me."

She paused, took a serviette from the table, blew her nose and sniffed. "He said, we'd take on the system and beat it with art, passionate art that came from the soul. He was not only the man I loved, he was my champion. But…"

I could see Mick across the table, barely able to contain himself. I tapped him with my foot. We waited.

"I realise now, well, I realised after the awful shit at the club years ago, that it was mainly me that had done all the talking, it was *my* cause, *me* mouthing off and writing the words. He'd just nodded, his blue eyes piercing me, making me literally weak at the knees. He swallowed me whole with his smile."

My brain whirred and ticked. Scanning the lyrical content of the thirty or so songs we'd written, not one contained anything about the subjects Alana had spoken of. Torin sung about getting wasted, taking drugs, how it all felt, the good and bad parts. The good parts were sitting in the sun with your pals and getting cunted, the bad, the same pals helping you out the next day when you felt shit. There was representation on the subject of betrayal, lovers (he was always wronged by them), a smattering of war, battle and heroic stunts from a vague kind of heraldic era. There were a few set in the biological confusion of teenage angst. Subdivisions of 'my shitty parents who never understood me'. When you stepped back and listened to our catalogue in its entirety, Torin only ever sung about himself.

"He promised he'd be our spokesman," she said. "The righteous vein running through the granite of our music. I decided that this band would be the one I'd give everything to because of the indelible rightness it was going to propagate. Daniel, Mick, for six weeks, we spoke of nothing else. Was I wrong to have fallen in love with him?"

Corbossa spoke. "I never heard any of that in the lyrics."

"No one did, because he never sung about it. All the lyrics 'we' put together, reams of them, were binned in one huge temper tantrum a couple of weeks after we met you both." Shaking her head, she backed into the darkness. "When I asked him what was going on, what happened to our cause, he lost it, called me a Trot and a commie, other stuff, dog on a string, smelly Camden tramp; I was living in Dalston! He said I was leeching off him and, like everyone, 'wanted what was his'. It went on all night and into the next day."

"But he seemed so devoted to you," I said, remembering how perfectly 'in love' I thought they were.

"An act," she said, "on his part anyway. I hung in there. I couldn't stop loving him just like that. For weeks, I tried to reach him, reignite his conscience and, pathetically, his love for me. But as time went on, and we had all those issues with him not remembering how the songs went and then, you guys wanting to get it moving, and the sheer joy of being under the arches creating that sound, I thought, fuck it, and let him write what he wanted."

While a banjo plucked the stars out of the Texan sky, I thought about obfuscation and how even the most noble of us succumb.

"I've been working with the geezer for four years and I don't have a clue who he is," said Mick.

"He's from big money," she said. "His dad's a major property owner: London, New York."

"Did you ever meet his parents?"

"Only ever met the cleaners. He said he has to leave the house when they come back. They live in Monaco."

"Blimey. What happened with them?"

"It's sketchy. He's not spoken to his dad for years. It'd piss him off if I pushed it. God, he hated his father."

"Imagine hating your father," said Mick.

"I know that he sacked Torin over some money 'discrepancy' when he worked for the family business in Manhattan. A serious amount went missing. His dad never trusted him. He said that in the band he could at least make his own decisions. Guys, his goal was never to reach down and pull people up; it was, in his words, to be 'independently wealthy.'"

"That's seriously fucked up."

"He was sick of asking his father for 'permission' all his life."

"Well," Mick said, "he certainly doesn't give a shit about what we think."

"So, all the lyrics you wrote together, he replaced with his," I said, remembering the first jam we had in his living room, the pages of A4 she set out on the big table, discarded while he gooned about, yelping and changing his outfits.

Mick interrupted my reminiscence. "Alana, when it was all going off at the club, the whoring and drugs, his horrible mates at the gigs, why didn't you just fuck it all off?"

"I have my reasons."

I suppose we should have been satisfied with that, she'd confessed all the whys and wherefores of their doomed romance, but I sensed there was more to come. Alana didn't tolerate loose ends.

"You guys had given it everything, jacking in your apprenticeship with your dad Mick, and I know you have to look after your mum, Daniel. I just couldn't dump him on you, the way he was."

"We'd never have made it," said Mick.

"When we split up, Torin and I made a pact. We didn't announce it to you, or anyone. We'd do the shows, the photos, go to the opening of an envelope together, even act 'passionately' in the video, for the sake of the band."

I exhaled. "Well, thanks for that Alana."

"Yeah, ta," echoed Corbossa.

"When we started, I was twenty-nine. I'd given everything to music since I was seventeen and got fuck all to show for it. I'd hit my head on so many glass ceilings I was thinking of wearing a crash helmet on stage. And then, with him, there was this aperture. Your amazing musicianship, too. It had all come together at the same time. I could see that people were turned on by us in a way *no* other band I'd been in had got within a hundred miles of."

She sat forward. In the lounge light's jaundiced glow, her resolve had returned. She rapped the table twice with her knuckles and met our eyes unwaveringly. "Boys, we are the one-in-a-thousand shot, the camel that has passed through the eye of a needle and made our dreams come true. You just don't throw away your career because you've had your heart broken. It's fucking rock and roll. You suck it up and crack on."

12

And that was what I was doing, sucking it up and cracking on.

Jake wasn't behind the desk when I walked into the rehearsal room in Denmark Street, he was bending from the waist, assisting an attractive green-haired woman in a biker jacket with an issue on her phone. Sharing the bench with her, were another two girls similarly dressed: studded heels, fishnets, 'attitude' – the traditional Camden kit. He looked up, quizzically. I nodded. I was late. Mum had had a bit of an episode.

Entering Room Three, I resisted a 'morning comrade' to a clean-shaven Barney, his gut popping two buttons on a khaki shirt a size too small, his military calf-length boots two sizes too big. He was moving mic stands about in front of the panoramic mirror between the PA stacks. When he saw me, he touched the star on the front of a Castro cap.

Torin was in full repose on the battered sofa. He was wearing that red guardsman's tunic. Years ago, he used to wear it with a dress. Today he matched it with razor-pressed suit pants.

"We'll have no shitting your knickers today, Daniel," he said, unbinding his limbs to stand.

I stepped up to my gear. The computer screen flashed with life. It was day one of the new, dismal way.

"You know you wear this perpetual...?" Torin winced handsomely as he approached me. "Like your nose is too near your arse."

"I left a message on your phone. Said I'd be late. Something up with the signals." I lied.

Mum had not got up and made me my morning cuppa. When I went into her room, she was sitting by the window overlooking the street fiddling with her fingers. It was the pose she adopted in the dark days before we managed to get off the estate.

"I feel a bit lethargic, Daniel," she said. "Sorry about breakfast." Much like Torin, she could detect uncertainty in me. If I was OK, so was she. If I wasn't, if I was actually feeling down, she'd plummet – in fact, she'd fly past me on the way to the bottom. I had to be careful about the way I presented myself to her. I had to temper my tone of voice, keep a smile in it, repeat everything was going to be fine with the band. I couldn't allow her to see me brooding. She got it that I was sometimes tired, but she was so attuned to my moods that when I was unbalanced, she'd fall over.

I'd made tea for us both and sat with her for half an hour. I assured her everything was fine and we weren't going to have to go back to the flats. But as she listened, I noticed familiar darts of anxiety flitting around her eyes. When I left for the studio, I knew she wouldn't leave her room.

Torin's fingers encapsulated my shoulder. His breath was twelve o'clock Merlot. "Could you lighten the fuck up for Uncle Torin, pretty please?"

I gave him a smile so bogus it physically hurt to produce it.

"Better. Now this shouldn't be too painful, a dozen gorgeous females trying their damndest to make the best impression on us. Let's give them the benefit of the doubt, yeah?"

"I'll set up."

Walking back from the mixing desk, I listened to him and Barney discussing the prospective tour dates, promo, t-shirts, etc. A minute or two later Torin cleared his throat at the mic. "Music, maestro, please."

For a split second, I imagined my old band in here with me; Alana ready, looking over her shoulder at me after tuning up, Mick setting his hi-hat stand just right, then a couple of thuds on the bass drum before giving me a nod. I blinked and they were gone.

Pressing the spacebar, I remember thinking, *'I'm in complete and utter control of this thing, this shitty thing that has to be got through.'* The intro to 'Silent Storm' oozed through the PA then the worst thing I'd ever witnessed in a rehearsal room occurred – the drums and bass kicked in with no one playing them.

Torin's voice boomed over our famous anthem. "You're a genius, Daniel. The new way is ignited. Allow me to fill your glass for you."

I let him. I needed alcohol's numbing powers. Last week I'd spent an afternoon and evening programming all Mick's beats onto a drum machine and then uniting them with Alana's synth-bass on the computer program. They sounded as they were supposed to: dry, faultless rhythmic data. As ever, Daniel Earl had nailed it.

"Right Barney," Torin said into the mic. "Let's get the first two in."

By the time we'd gone through the third couple of auditionees, I didn't give a flying fuck what individuals mimed Alana and Corbossa's parts, as long as they looked like they were playing, and I got my fee, so that mum didn't spend her days staring out of her bedroom window wondering when we'd have to move back to the estate.

I switched off my gear and watched Jake bin-bag the empties. Torin and Barney had left for the club to discuss strategy, pincer movements and beachheads.

"Was that, err, the new line-up?" he asked me. No doubt he'd enjoyed the glam cavalcade in the reception area. I'd lost count of the number of earnest, attractive young women who had passed through Three's soundproof door.

"Side project," I slurred. I'd had far too many plastic cups of Torin's red. "See, err…next week."

Edging my way through the glut of commuters on Oxford Street, I was muttering away to myself, "You did it, Torin. You actually did it!" My beautiful band had been dismantled and replaced by a half-baked, income-generating, pastiche. Our live set would now have the predictability of my weekly microwaved meals. "Bullshit!" I yelped in grim acknowledgement. There wasn't going to be any new albums, any new songs, or any more goodness in my playing. It was quite stunning.

I managed to duck through the alley into the square without hitting the wall. Weaving towards the shop, my favourite fantasy played: a Mediterranean stucco façade, a gravelly village square, strolling hip to hip with Kerry in warm sunshine, our fingers entwined. We passed between olive and orange trees to tables set with spotless white linen. Cicadas chirruped and buzzed as I pulled the chair back for her, but one of the legs was caught. As I tugged it free, I staggered outside Sienna's window.

Reality had me wiping my numb face with a palm. My glasses fell off. I caught them before they hit the pavement. "I'm in a covers band of my own band," I told the faceless mannequins.

I blinked at the ding of a bell.

"Daniel, what's wrong?"

I was truly going nuts. They were speaking to me.

"Daniel!" Kerry raised her hand to my face and gently felt the hard ridges and dents in the flesh below my right eye. "What's happened to your glasses?"

"Oh," I said, quickly putting them back on.

***

When I finally got up the following day, there was an email from Barney formally introducing me to my new band mates, Daisy and Bluebell. He was good enough to attach their CVs giving details of their am-dram experiences, adverts, extras work and modelling forays. At the foot of the email was the running order of the songs we would be 'practising' as well as times and dates of 'practice sessions'. I was listed as 'music producer (live)'.

Most musicians would be delighted at the prospect of confirmed work ahead, but it burned that I was being emailed by a stranger about other strangers I'd be performing with.

"I've got another busy day, mum," I said, toeing open her bedroom door and sliding the tray of tea and toast in front of her.

"That's nice."

"We're going on the road, and I've got to organise it all."

"That was what Alan used to do, isn't it?"

After yesterday's inertia, she'd upped her antidepressants, but she remained indecisive and vacant, incapable of coming downstairs and making breakfast.

"Alana. Yeah, sort of. Eat up, mum."

In reality, it was only for the first few months of our existence that Alana was the organiser. She booked rehearsals, sorted out soundcheck and stage times at gigs and negotiated the fees. Another thing she did was arrange fortnightly meetings for us at the pub on the corner of Shepherd's Bush Green. Back then, Torin wasn't concerned with *'band prattle'*. He'd been pissed and disruptive at the only one he showed up for. At a favourite table, Alana would get out a school exercise book and list the outgoings against what little dough we were pulling in from our shows. Corbossa's attention span wasn't very long, he'd spend most of the time with his phone trapped between ear and shoulder, peeling the label off a beer bottle, cooing with a girlfriend. But I tried my best to stay focused. Mick took the piss at the paltry amounts, but Alana insisted we were cognizant of the income we generated, even if it was only fifty quid for a forty-minute set at a pub. She said, she'd seen bands split up over a fiver.

Soon the gigs were flying in, and her notebook was set aside in favour of a 'band account' set up at the bank on Goldhawk Road. I recall Torin laughing at her when she brought the cheque books and forms into rehearsals for us all to sign. Despite his derision, she said that the account should be sacrosanct, set up only to pay for necessities: rehearsals, recording demos, sticks, strings, leads and other sundries. She'd arranged it so that it was impossible for one of us to take anything out unless two of us signed it off.

When it opened, it had about thirty quid in it, mostly to cover the petrol for Mick's dad's van. Sometimes, it stretched to a sarnie after soundcheck, perhaps even a round of drinks when we came off. In six months, with our first recording smashing through the charts and the shows selling out, we had upwards of ten grand in the account. But the money remained untouched, because by then the record company was shelling out for everything, including our retainers. With 'Silent Storm' getting ridiculous amounts of airplay, and the band tons of media attention, Torin scrapped Alana's meetings entirely. He stated that we needed, "Professional businessmen to take care of professional business." From then on, he and his accountant, Pinky Forbes, took control of the band's finances. He and Forbes had been in Durnford House at Eton and Torin trusted him, completely. We weren't to trouble ourselves with the 'in and outgoings' anymore.

It took just two weeks to record our first album. The nine songs on it were the ones we'd written in Shepherd's Bush and gigged to death during the first six months of our existence. After signing with a top live agent, we were packed off on tour to promote it. It was obvious we were generating real money now: every show was sold out, the merchandising stalls looked like they'd been ransacked at the end of a night and, of course, the album was palpably doing the business in the charts.

In rare, quiet moments between gigs, TV appearances, photo sessions and travelling, I sensed things running away from me regarding our money, but I never uttered a dissenting word. Why would I? I was on a healthy retainer, ferried about in limos, my gear set up for me, smiled at by attractive women, and cheered to the echo of what was a dream come true and then, one evening, things got even better. Torin invited us to the club and greeted us with bottles of champagne.

"Men," he said, his eyes brimming with wild good humour. "This is for all your hard work."

"Fuck me! Fifteen grand!" I said, peering disbelievingly at the cheque made out to me. We'd signed a deal handing over the publishing rights only a few days earlier. This was our share of the advance.

I was standing with Alana.

"What you gonna do with yours?" I'd asked, gulping my champagne.

"Property."

"With fifteen grand?"

"You're on a wage, retainer, whatever they call it. Get a sensible mortgage, use this for a deposit. There'll be royalties coming too. Our album's going ballistic."

My nut was spinning as I stared at my name and the figures after it. Me and Mick had mucked about at the 'signing do' at some chintzy gaff in Mayfair, the photographers shuffling us about like playing cards, while the publishers, execs and accountants looked on. We thought it was just another back-slapping session with faceless industry suits, them telling us how great we were, us knowing that if we hadn't got a record in the charts, they'd have called security.

"You know what," I said to her. "I'll do that. Get my mum out of that dump."

"Best thing you can do, Daniel. Tell Corbossa to think about it too."

"Yeah, I will. Amazing amount of money."

Her brief smile was not one of joy.

"What's up?" I asked.

"Nothing. Look. I'm gonna make a move. This place isn't for me."

I didn't see her leave but later I found out that fifteen thousand was the *minimum* we'd deserved for *'all our hard work'*. Alana knew it, but she wasn't one to piss on anyone's chips.

Draining my glass, my eyes were drawn to Torin. He was wearing some amazing Italian suit, as blue and intense as his stare. His dark mane was swept back and his roguish tash, trimmed and tapered. As he laughed with his mates, a well of gratitude rose up in me. That man had discovered me, believed in me and despite the shortcomings, given me the benefit of the doubt. Because of his genius, I was going to save my mum, and it was so welcome because at that particular juncture, she really needed saving.

I was away a lot now. From being with her practically every day since I'd left school, I was suddenly absent for weeks at a time. Before the accident, she'd worked in the kitchen at school and did morning's waitressing in the builder's café next to the bookies. She went to the pub with some friends she'd been at school with, and a bloke she'd met at the café took her to Hastings for weekends. Now, she was on sickness benefit and went nowhere. Her confidence was shot. A week before we embarked on our first European tour, Mr Wilson, the widower next door, passed on. For as long as I could remember, mum had done his shopping and checked in on him. Even though he was going deaf, he still enjoyed her company, and she enjoyed his.

I wasn't to know that on the opening date of that tour, the council would move a family into his vacant flat. The parents were the same age as me and already had three kids. They fought and rowed, banging the walls and screaming at all hours. Someone called the police. Of course, the couple thought it was my mum, so as well as the half-life she'd been living because of the accident, she'd had hostility and suspicion literally plonked on her doorstep, and I wasn't there.

The day before Torin's cheque and champagne surprise at the club I came home and saw the police on our balcony. Peering up, I imagined they were sorting out another domestic explosion next door. An acrid tang had me gulping and squinting as I climbed the stairs. Heart thumping, I sprinted along the walkway. The police told me the fire brigade had been and gone. One of mum's scented candles had set fire to some magazines and the curtains had gone up. She was OK. The people downstairs went mental because water had poured through their ceiling and ruined a new three-piece. That night, with her room uninhabitable, I moved her into mine. Lying on the living room sofa, my knees curled unnaturally beneath me, next door's rancour oozing through the wall, I thought seriously about chucking in the band. She needed looking after. From the time I'd started going away on tour, she'd begun shrinking and flinching before my eyes. I left for the club the following afternoon thinking that this might be the last time I'd go there. I couldn't leave her on her own on that estate.

Four weeks later, we moved into our quiet, two-bedroom semi in West Acton.

"I'm so proud of you Daniel," she said, as we stood together at the kitchen door and looked up the short, winding path that cut through a postage stamp of lawn to a crumbling shed in a bramble patch.

"You deserve it mum."

A couple of twittering robins landed on the branch of a small bush next to us and she started to cry. "But I don't. It was all my fault."

She accepted, for a few seconds, a perfunctory cuddle. "Come on now. You have to move on."

The mortgage repayments have always been steep, and perhaps I should have gone for something a little more modest further out, but I needed to move quickly. I've never been one for drinking or drugs, flash cars or clothes. As for holidays, travelling the world with my band superseded lying on a beach for a fortnight. So, when the bills came in, I covered them. Anyway, concern about repayments paled in comparison with the anxiety I experienced leaving mum alone on the estate and besides, when you're twenty and literally living the dream, you don't think about what might happen in five weeks, never mind five years. The band was flying and there seemed no reason, with the tours and prospective albums ahead, that my advances and royalties would ever end.

After flattening the bramble patch at the back of the garden, I realised another teenage fantasy. With help from Mick and his dad, I built a breeze block structure, soundproofed it and filled it with synths, samplers and a mixing desk. In there, wilfully ignorant of what might be going on in Soho, or the accountant's office in Holborn, I spent my hours creating music.

You can imagine how enthused we were at the prospect of making a second album. We discussed it endlessly in tour buses, hotel lobbies and dressing rooms. Because our time was squeezed, we made the decision to capitalise on the gap between soundcheck and the venue doors opening, to work on ideas. Our soundchecks soon began to rival the show for excitement as we put together templates for new songs. But all this spontaneous stuff going on with 'his' band irked Torin. He couldn't control our enthusiasm and although we invited him to join us on stage (and in those lobbies and dressing rooms), he showed scant interest. As the gig doors opened and the punters streamed in, we'd pass him skulking in the wings, muttering, *'This is live, not for writing'*. He finally put a stop to our creativity by ordering the stage sound to be switched off immediately after we checked. He said we were wasting our energy and the performance was suffering.

When we came off the road, he asked me to email my song sketches directly to him. He wanted to sift through them for *'quality control'* before passing them onto Alana and Mick. He told us that this was a far more organised and methodical way of writing music. *'Everything in its proper place, men. Organised and methodical'*, he'd repeat often. At the time I remember thinking, *'organised and methodical?'* He was the most chaotic person I'd ever met.

It was a strange and remote process writing music this way, sending him MP3s of a minute or two of music for his approval, but it didn't derail us. Despite his negativity and the obstacles he chucked in our path, we still managed to create something of merit in the recording studio. In fact, those very obstacles caused us to find new ways of communicating, musically. We'd been placed in a situation that most bands would not usually encounter and surmounting the problems (because more than anything, we wanted to make a great second album), engendered a unique feel to the music we made, defiant, sort of.

In the control room on the final afternoon of the album session, listening through the finished versions, we all agreed the work sounded amazing. Darker, deeper, more emotional than our first album – which was like popping a cork from a bottle with all its brashness and attention seeking.

That last listen through was one of the most satisfying times of my thus-far short career. The producer, Torin, all of us were beaming, hugging and shaking hands after the final track had ended. It sounded stellar. Thoughts of where it would take us as a band were tantalising. Alana spoke of levels and tiers, and said this would take us to the next one. I hoped it would. Another positive element was that we'd fulfilled our contractual obligation to the record company, the advance would be paid, and my income would be secured for another couple of years at least.

That night in bed, the songs played over and over in my head, happily nudging me awake just as sleep threatened to take me under. No way could I just lay there. I got up and barefoot, walked around my little castle in Acton humming my songs. After a glass of water at the sink, I opened the door to the garden, sat on the iron bench and gazed contentedly at the stars. My band was the gift that kept on giving and giving.

A week later, we were invited to the record company offices to hear the finished masters. As each song went by on the posh system they'd set up in there, our collective faces drained of blood. Even Torin's most sycophantic supporters could not ignore the evidence of their ears. We left quickly after the last track. There'd been very little hugging and shaking hands.

Around that old table at the pub on the Green we turned solemn pints in our hands unable to meet each other's eyes. I'd asked Debbie, to put 'In a Broken Dream' on the juke box. The title summed up our second album completely.

I dared to look at Alana. "Anyone know where he is?" I asked.

"The press girl said South of France? Not in the country."

"Not fucking surprised," I said quietly.

"That's it," Alana said. "You know it can't be changed. They're already pressing the thing."

Mick tried to speak, but the words wouldn't come out. Alana went into a denim jacket pocket and handed him a tissue.

He blew his nose. "If he walked in here now, I'd rip his posh-boy head off. How fuckin' dare he!" Mick's normally mirth-filled irises were furious indignant slits. I'd seen him lose it a couple of times, and when he did, he didn't know where to draw the line. "The fucker never told no one. He snuck in there with some two-bob engineer and shit all over it."

"Is there no way we can remix?" I asked.

"No," Alana said.

"All those people around the world are gonna hear that garbage, that mutilation and think we're frauds."

"Mick, calm down."

"It's all him," he said. His was glaring across the pub and I was thankful my singer was at least a continent away. "And the fuckin' truth is, he ain't all that."

"He hates me," Alana said quietly, "Any semblance of my presence is an affront to him."

Torin's final clandestine mixing session had ripped out the very thing that had made us unique. It was as if he'd superglued Alana's vocal fader to zero. Her voice had been completely eradicated from every track.

"Talk about cutting off your nose," said Mick, standing up. "Same again?"

We had another round, but not much more was said. The deed was done. That was the second album, for sale at all good record shops and some crap ones. The thing is, that whenever I listen to that album, I feel like I've lost someone close and that around the family table of my music life, there is an empty chair where a close friend, a young one, full of potential should be sitting and growing old with me.

On his return from the Côte d'Azur, a bronzed Torin was carpeted by the record company suits for the album's bang average impact, reviews and initial sales. Of course, they'd not said a word when they were listening back on posh speakers of their own. Not one of them had piped up. There was no "this is rank", "we have to remix", "where's Alana's vocal?" They'd obfuscated and lick-spittled, and we had let them.

A meeting was called in a sectioned-off living room of his club's fourth floor. Mick occupied a minimalist armchair, all angles and not made for slouching. Torin in jeans, flimsy cheesecloth shirt and hippie sandals, opposed him on something statelier; claw-legged, velvet and gold braid. Taking the extended chaise longue between them were Martin Reed, the agent and Stewart Winters, our tour manager. I was drawn to the spectacular scene from history set high on the wall behind them. Clashing in watercolour, bug-eyed horses railed up, their riders, Hussars, hacking at each other one-handed while booming cannons splintered the trees around them.

Torin was well away when we arrived and sadly Mick, finishing his second large vodka tonic, was only a pace or two behind. I stuck to coke, the cola variety, and leaned against a pillar, totally absorbed by the ancient bloodbath suspended above my colleagues.

I think that if, like the other bands at our level, we'd had a manager, the following twenty or so minutes would have been less damaging, but because of Torin's fear of people *'after what was his'*, there was no referee and it went proper nuclear, PDQ.

"I'm shocked," he said.

He didn't look it, all bronzed, topping up his glass.

"Are you?" I replied.

"The bollocking I had from Sebastian and Mark-Alexander, I mean, when did those musical masterminds grow the balls to speak to *me* like that? After all I've done for them and their poxy record company. 'Silent Storm' has paid for their little darlings' school fees for the next five years, right?"

"What did they say?" I asked.

"The phrase 'underwhelmed' was used a fair bit, and 'disappointed'."

Mick's voice cut our chat in half, "fucking bottlers".

Torin squinted across the hand-woven Afghan rug at his drummer.

"They should have called a spade a spade," continued Mick. "It's shit mate and it's all your fault."

The harder I peered into the scene on the wall, the more detail I saw. For every upright hero, swishing a blade, there was a terrified-looking foot soldier, eyes on stalks, knowing he was about to die.

"You don't know what you're on about, Señor Cor-bossa," Torin said, with a flowery tongue roll on the 'r' and a gaseous release on the vowel at the end.

"Don't fucking Corbossa me. *He* knows," Mick said, nodding at me.

I cleared my throat. "Torin, you shouldn't have remixed it. Not without us being there. It's…".

"Neither of you are aware of the big picture. That's why you are, where you are."

"Who the fuck do you think you are!"

"I'm Torin Fortescue DeVere and I get things done!"

I lurched across as Mick shot out of his chair. Torin laughed into his glass as Stewart and I held Mick back. "Look at you," Torin said, "fucking menial thug. You're going to assault me with your plunger, are you?"

"What the fuck did you do to us?" roared Mick.

With Stewart's help, I backed him into his chair. The room seethed. I returned to my post and peered deeper.

The earth was covered with limbs, muskets, helmets and sabres. A house, some kind of villa, lay in smithereens on the horizon. In the oily silence, I recalled the grim exchange Mick and I had had walking down Old Compton Street towards the meeting.

"He's turned the songs inside out," I'd said. "There are parts I don't even recognise, but I know it's us playing."

"Months of work reduced to that. Sounds complete and utter shit."

"I know man."

"I need a fuckin' drink, Daniel," he'd said, accelerating ahead.

As well as eradicating any semblance of Alana, Torin and his henchman had mercilessly cauterized us. Sections where I'd gone off-piste had been excised and the bars edited, causing the songs to be unbalanced, top- or end-heavy. It was nothing we would have done and it hurt so much, because as artists, we only ask for what we do to be heard the way we designed it. But all the mix stuff paled in comparison to the obliteration of the magic blend Alana had invented to help him achieve his dream and be a singer. That heavenly anticipation, the two voices in unity, was the genius Torin had stupidly extracted from our second album.

Mick, becalmed, spoke again. "Torin, if you're such a hotshot businessman, into making money and all that, why did you change a production that didn't remotely need it?"

"What would you know about generating income. God knows

what would have happened if we still ran the thing around those pathetic little band meetings in the pub with her. Talking of which, where is our little Marxist?"

"Her train's delayed," I said quietly. "She was staying with her mum."

"We had a winning system and you fucked it up, Torin," said Mick.

Torin sneered across. "You're a plumber by trade, right? What on earth would you possibly know about systems?"

Moments later Alana entered. She told me afterwards that she'd arrived late on purpose, knowing there'd be a period of macho posturing before she could get a word in. I remember that heads turned when she walked in – she was wearing a purple two-tone suit, creepers, her hair cropped to the bone. Her elfin face directed an unwavering gaze at each and every one of us.

"What's done is done," she announced. "We're the people that are going to have to go on the road and do the work. Let's get things nailed down."

While everyone around her swayed and lurched, she began asking direct questions about the tour, road crew, routing, press and of course, the budget.

Torin had just returned from the toilet as Alana was speaking. He'd gathered a few acolytes around him. Album and band matters had lost their fascination.

After affectedly craning his ear, sniffing and swallowing, he pronounced, "Boys, take no notice. It's her hormones. Seen it all before."

"What the fuck are you on about, now?" spat Mick.

"Can't you see, she's on the blob. She's mental!"

The air left that corner of the room as if sucked out by a giant hoover. I stared into the face of a horse laying amongst the detritus of battle. I imagined it in its paddock with its hay and grass, moseying aimlessly, petted on the nose by passing children. There was no going back to that sunny field for it now. Its head had been brutally detached from its body. The ragged, bloody sinews of its once beautiful neck told me that.

Torin was laughing and soon those around him joined him. I said nothing, neither did Mick. Obfuscation abounded. You see, on and off stage, when Torin opened his mouth, people stopped, listened and then they clapped.

We toured that second album hard for six months, but it didn't move any more units. We were aware of the substantial profits we were making. The tour manager (sacked on the last date – seemingly a tradition of ours, now) was happy to show us the books. But two weeks after that knackering stint, I'd still not received my tour bonus.

Alana called me and Mick to our local and confirmed our worst fears regarding the bonus. She told us Forbes had it (along with our royalties and payments) in some limited company he'd set up. He and Torin were the sole directors. She told us she'd done some digging and discovered that our publishing splits had been decimated to fuck all as well; accountants and lawyers, talentless bores, criminals really, were now embellishing their lives with my money. She said, that as we'd already had the advance for the second album, there wouldn't be another. She said we should strike.

Mick didn't meet Alana's eye when he explained he'd got himself into trouble buying some money pit of a supercar and was now on the bones of his arse, living back at his parents. I was equally sheepish. I feared for my mortgage and, to my shame, I didn't want to lose my status – the keyboard player in a cool, world-famous band. People would pay to have my job, I said to myself.

Alana insisted we weren't getting a fair day's pay for a fair day's work and were earning little more than the bloke who wheeled the gear into the van after the show. Our silence established she'd been outvoted. Before leaving the pub, she told us she understood, but we'd live to regret not addressing this now. But we weren't miners, or nurses, we were fucking rock and roll musicians and we didn't give a damn as long as they clapped and we were fed and watered.

That meet at our local had taken place two years ago. Because I never received that tour bonus or any other advances, I'd got a second mortgage on the house. The repayments caused me night sweats. Mick had to let go of his flat and was now back with his parents, permanently. I imagined, after Torin's most recent decision, he was sitting next to his old man in the van on the way to work.

13

In Room Three, Barney, laptop open, squished himself into the sofa more chubbily excited than ever. The PA speakers hummed. We were about to go through our running order; the numbers we'd play on the upcoming tour. We would start with *'Brothers'* a song founded beneath the Shepherd's Bush arches five years ago. We'd never written a better opener.

Torin stood at the mic and I at my station, finger poised over the spacebar, the all-powerful, two-inch, plastic strip that started and ended everything.

Previously, Alana and Corbossa would make eye contact, Mick would click his sticks and start the straight 8s beat that Alana's pumping two-note bass line would accompany. I'd give it four bars, push up my specs, and play an arpeggiated synth line on that groove. The audience, as if controlled by a greater power, were compelled to jump and clap in time. It was the most amazing high; thirty seconds into the gig and we *knew* we were irresistible.

Thereafter, a degree of patience was required because Torin had to find the door into the song, and if he'd had a little too much red before going on, or somehow managed to avoid Alana's double tap on his outside thigh, this intro could last up to two minutes. But there was no drama, convinced it was part of the night's great entertainment, the public would clap along harder.

'Was the best of times, we were the best of them, brothers we're here to rock...'

But on this new day, none of the above happened. With the subtlest of nods from Torin, I depressed my forefinger. To the left of me were my new band mates, Daisy (drummer) and Bluebell (bass, backing vocals), two attractive, gum-chewing, punky actresses. I watched Daisy register the 8 beats of the digital metronome ticking in her earpiece, she clicked her sticks, and we played.

Although I was set up next to the drums, I couldn't hear them. The sticks thwacked snare and hats, but the kit made no noise. The heads were covered in thick white lino, the cymbals bronze-sprayed, plastic discs. Bluebell thrummed her bass, her amp lights glowed, but the volume level was set at zero. There were a few wrong moves, miscues and hits, but after the song had ended no one was unimpressed. The girls had obviously done loads of prep in their bedrooms.

We were in there for five hours and ran our fifty-minute set three times. Torin was buzzing at the end of the day. "No fuss and blissfully, no egos," he said. "Well done girls. It'll be a well-oiled machine on the night, and speaking of 'well oiled.'" His shark's mouth widened and a warm blue glare settled on the purveyors of his new way. "Let's celebrate a monumental rehearsal!"

Setting off for the short walk from Denmark Street to Soho my phone buzzed in my pocket. *'Come to the shop sevenish? I'm sooo hungry! LK xx.'*

After reading the message my tread was a little lighter following Barney, Torin and the two girls. In an hour I knew I'd be with Kerry watching her eat and expound and then, with her arm in mine, point at various dogs, shop windows and aspects of London architecture as she walked me back to Oxford Circus Station. There, I'd receive my customary lip-bump. I lived for that half a second.

Torin wafted past Jill at the desk and we followed in his wake. Soon glasses were being raised in salutation of the day. Understandably, Daisy and Bluebell were effusive. They'd told me that they'd had brushes with fame, call it 'success', but this was by far their biggest career opportunity.

"Thought we sounded really good," said Bluebell.

She was earnest, pretty, and no mug, but I couldn't believe she'd not thought that sentence through before uttering it.

"Will Torin sing, you know 'properly' at the next rehearsal?"

"Yeah, of course."

"I get it that he was checking us out today. I know you were too, Daniel."

"And you both did great."

"Thank you. So cool you can turn on his vocal like that, but I can't wait to actually hear him sing, like, live. His voice is amazing."

Daisy batted her eyes and shook her head. "I can't believe in… eight days' time, I'll be playing the Shepherd's Bush Empire with Torin."

Bluebell giggled and sipped her cocktail. "It's like a dream."

I pushed up my specs. "Really enjoyed it."

What an accomplished liar I'd become. In truth, rehearsals had been stultifying, boring. Torin made a half-arsed attempt at singing before flopping onto the sofa, stating that it'd be "More beneficial if he went 'UN' and observed." So, I'd ignited the red line – the lead vocal on my screen – and on we went, perfecting our grand delusion. There was little to observe, in reality. From the first beat of the opening song to the cymbal crash on the final note of the last, the outcome was identical. By the second run through, I'd not even bothered to inject the occasional run up and down the 404.

From the bar, Torin met my eye and nodded towards the windows. I met him there.

"Sure, you won't? Sharpen you up," he said, with a sniff.

"Nah, not for me."

"Corby was into it."

"For a while."

He tilted his smile. "But you, with all your 'disadvantages', have never dabbled. Extraordinary willpower, Daniel."

"I know it...it enhances your personality."

"You have to have one first, ha-ha!"

Nobody was near us. Torin wasn't using a lighter, but I distinctly heard the flick-flick of one.

"To Corbossa and the saintly Alana." He raised his glass. "Lest we forget." I smiled flatly and raised mine.

"No, you know I'm only ribbing you. You're my lieutenant, my strong right arm."

"I don't know anything about the military, but..."

He leaned forward. "Don't you know it's a war out there."

"I'm just a keyboard player. I make stuff up."

He ran his tongue over his gums and tilted his noble head. "The kid with the big specs in the pub, off on a mad one on his synth in the middle of 'Jolene'." He made a screeching sound and mimed a keyboard player wobbling a fader on his instrument. "Still so charmingly naïve, Daniel. S'pose that's why you play the way you do." He sipped and waited a beat before continuing. "Can't tell you how pleased I am by that rehearsal. Pretty good, don't you think?"

"Yeah, good for the first one. But we need you to come in and go through the set properly with us."

He dismissed me with the back of his hand. "We've got loads of time."

"Seriously, the girls need to get the cues spot on."

"Just play my vocal on the computer like you did today. They'll learn from that."

"But you change every performance," I said, knowing how whiny I sounded. "Your err, presence. The way you interacted with Alana…she isn't going to be there. Bluebell needs to learn your ways."

"Everyone's miming. Get Mr Blobby to rehearse with them."

"What?"

"Him, the fucking bane of my life, Barney."

I couldn't see Barney. I remembered he'd asked me to have a word with Torin about the money, he needed access to the various accounts for the tour. "He isn't equipped, Torin. He's hasn't got the experience. No way will he be able to handle managing a tour. Even this show is too much for him. He's told me he's skint. His wages…"

"You've seen where he lives. Askew Road. Not cheap."

"We need to get a professional in. We…".

He patted my knee. "Look, the girls look great. The songs sound great. We've sold out the gig. Martin Reed is bombarding us with dates." He turned the wine bottle label towards him. "Do you like this? Portuguese."

Topping up my glass, he regarded me with a hammy sad smile. "You've gone all 'Daniel looking'. Talk to Uncle Torin."

I heard that flick-flick. It was deep inside my head. It was a lighter trying to spark a flame. "Just, so difficult to gauge the way it's going to sound without actually hearing you sing."

"Sound, Daniel? I just told you."

"Yeah, but about your singing."

"Are you doubting me?"

"No, just saying."

"Don't you think I can cope?"

"It's not that, it's just Alana, you know…"

When he looked at me, I felt like a mouse with a cat's claw

hovering over its eggshell cranium. "Let me put your mind at ease. I'm practising every day."

"Are you?"

"I know how important this is. I told you, I wanted to observe today." He sampled his Portuguese and set his gaze on the horizon I'd never been able to see.

"The destiny of Torin DeVere is in his own hands."

He returned his focus to me.

"You keep pressing your little buttons, matey. What'll come out will be irrefutably *'Torin'*. All the work we've done over the last five years…a couple of very attractive young women will present it to the public while the two most important members of the so-called *'originals'* will perform it. Do you seriously think, that when we're up there playing to three, five, ten thousand people I'll mess it up?"

I didn't reply.

"There'll be no need for me to be nudged."

My stomach buckled. I'd thought he'd been deaf and blind to our code words and glances.

"You've gone a little pale, Daniel. You think I've not listened to you 'musos' chatting about me over the years. I'm never as pissed as I appear, my facially flawed friend."

"We only did it to make you better."

"You make *me* better?"

"Just…you were the least experienced out of us, Torin. You must remember. To make it work we *had* to help you."

I felt sick. The tide of obfuscation was overwhelming. That he was wiping from history the fact that he'd literally cried in Alana's arms in the rehearsal room when she said she'd start the choruses for him, was like the two of us agreeing that we were born with ovaries.

"I'm six years older than you, *sonny*."

When he leaned in, it was not with cokey bonhomie, it was with the wrath that lay like a scummy pond just behind his dazzling blue eyes. He glanced left and right to check that we were not being overheard. "You thought you could manipulate me."

"Torin man, what are you on about?"

His whisper was harsh, scratchy. "So, who's going on stage

now? Who's playing a European tour now, not Corby or 'her'. For all I know, she's eating lentils seven days a week, running some lesbian bookshop and he's got his arm up some shit-caked u-bend. It's *Torin*. And you, my tame mad professor, should count yourself lucky to be up there with him."

I'd forgotten how his mood fluctuated when he was 'on one'. Friend or fiend, you never knew what variety of Torin was standing next to you after midday.

"What the fuck did I ever see in that harridan dwarf and her incessant practising! Fucking scales up and down, up and down into the morning. All she ever went on about was repetition. Boring cow."

"But it's served us well."

"Hated rehearsing."

My heart broke at those words. He didn't, surely.

"No, Torin."

"Yes Daniel. Doing it over and over. Oh, for fuck's sake, don't sulk!" He tossed his head and drained his glass before leaning in again. "Just so you know, those two actresses are taking a third of the fee your erstwhile band mates were *and* they're a damn sight more attractive."

When he walked over to the girls and put an arm around each of their waists, the spluttering lighter flickered inside me, and I remembered the 'fair day's pay for a fair day's work' speech that Alana had given at our local on the Green. *'Boys,'* she was standing over us, her palms flat on the table. Both Mick and I were too ashamed to look up and meet her eyes. *'If we don't stand up for ourselves, address this now, we'll live to regret it.'*

Someone began playing the piano, a voice was raised, a huge belt of laughter followed, and Torin was again at my side. With a sniff and a gum rub, he placed his hand on my shoulder. "Sorry. I do get a little caught up in it all."

I nodded.

"Come on Daniel, drink up. A new day has dawned. I feel reinvigorated." He raised his glass and waved his hand at the space around us. He was my best mate again. "Torin is reborn."

"I'm a bit knackered. Been a long day. Gonna call it a night."

He came in close. "Don't mean to chow at you, old boy, but you could be a little more friendly and accepting. The girls are not the enemy."

"All good, Torin. I've been talking to them."

"Then why the long face?"

"Sorry. A lot on my mind."

He sighed. "OK. Understandable. You're doing the job of three now. Huge responsibility."

He was looking at the girls, posing and laughing with his friends.

"But you need to work on your acting, Daniel."

"What?"

"The girls, me, we can all see how miserable you are. Try to act, man. Pretend you love it. It's showbiz, after all. A great illusion. You get that?"

"Sorry. Not been sleeping too well, what with all the changes."

"How's your mum?" He'd not asked about her for years.

"She's alright." We looked at each other. The resentment coming off me and the boredom radiating from him were an equitable and heady repellent for us both. I turned and walked towards the door.

"Oh, and give her one for me," he winked with his pop-star eye.

I squinted back.

"The coffee chucker."

"Yeah, ha-ha."

"I know you better than you know yourself, Danny."

***

Kerry was tidying the stock. When she saw me skulking by the great bush outside, she opened the door wordlessly. I fell into the fluffy orange chair.

"Tired and emotional?" she asked, sniffing the air as she refolded some sweaters. "And I'm guessing drink has been taken."

I exhaled. My glasses fell down my cheek. I didn't bother to poke them back up.

"Yeah, a bit. Lot of pressure. Some shitty stuff with my band. Torin…I know you don't know him. It's like he's run a Rolls-Royce into a cesspit."

She spun around. Her smile was brilliant, too much to behold.

"We're going to get something tasty and nutritious in you as soon as I'm done here."

The day at Jake's diminished as I watched her totting up at the desk.

"Good day?" I asked, my head falling, staring at the carpet between my boots.

"Yes, sold even more snow to the Eskimos."

I heard the rattle of a hanger and looked up to see her posing in an arctic-white, pillbox hat. Folding one knee across the other, she blinked at me coquettishly.

"Blimey Kerry, you are so…"

Even the most mundane actions delighted her. Stopping at a shop window invariably caused her to squeeze my arm excitedly. It was as if she'd been kept away from the things she liked, or not been allowed to do the things she'd wanted? And she didn't care who was watching her. I recalled her flamboyance at the snooker club. The bending and pouting after a miss, the stretching and calculating, theatrical forefinger on her lips, batting her lashes at the ceiling, twirling her cue. I wanted to tell the quiet men in the shadows she wasn't performing for them, it was just how she was.

"Use the loo?" I asked.

"Of course. Nearly done."

I walked through the arch by the counter and down the stairs. I could hear her humming as I entered the toilet. Before going back up, I nudged the door on the right with my foot. This time it wasn't locked. But I couldn't open it fully, something was blocking it. I lowered my shoulder and pushed hard. I'd managed to squeeze my head in for a second before, *'Bang!'* An obstruction in the room caused the door to slam into my temple. I fell backwards, smarting.

"Like the Tower of London," Kerry said, holding up the keys before locking the shop door. She punched in the code, hugged my arm and on we walked. It was a Friday evening, and the West End was throbbing and hungry. We found ourselves sitting at the front of the generous Chinese restaurant on Old Compton Street that she favoured. She kept her cap on which saddened me. I'd come to look forward to the dramatic reveal when she removed it and shook her hair free before our food arrived.

"Yummy," she said, perusing the laminated menu she knew like the back of her hand. When they came, she attacked the plates with a frenetic energy, chattering ravenously about the various clients that had come through Sienna's doors and had bought this garment or that scent. "….so, just because they appear well off, doesn't mean they'll buy anything. And this woman, I'm not a snob Daniel, but you'd never have thought she'd splash three-hundred quid on that dress, but she did."

"Well, you can't judge a book, I s'pose."

"You not going to eat that chicken?"

I poked my glasses up as her chopsticks darted across the table. "You missed lunch again?"

"Yes, full-on today. Are you still feeling queasy?"

"I hate drinking."

She was smiling at me.

"I know," I said. "I'm pissed every time I see you, but…"

"Daniel, I know you aren't a drinker."

When she put her hand on mine, I wanted to tell her everything: the betrayal of my band mates, the charade Torin was perpetrating, the untethered way I felt, but she was already speaking.

"Have I told you about Christina? We had a marathon phone call last night, catching up. She's bought another dog!"

I blinked in bafflement.

"I've told you about her, surely?"

"No, you've not mentioned her before."

"OK. My mum used to go out with her mum in the sixties, clubs and parties. They lost touch, then they met again at a friend's in Oxford, who coincidentally, was in fashion too. Anyway, they were both pregnant with me and Chrissy…Oh Daniel, sorry, I do rabbit on."

"No, no. Carry on," I said, nodding, trying to key into her details while in my head, Alana (avoiding the condiments) pressed her palms into our table. *'If we don't stand up for ourselves, address this now, we'll live to regret it.'* Her words of three years ago still resonated. Well, they more than resonated, they drowned out the entire restaurant and Kerry's shop chronicle.

"Daniel?"

"Yeah?"

"So, we're kind of sisters, although they were in North London, more…" And on she went referencing holidays they had together, how having kids affected her mum's graphic design career, teaching at college.

"Daniel." She'd paused and looked concerned. "What's that on your head, there."

Her right chopstick was pointing at my temple, which still tingled after its encounter with the angry door downstairs in her shop. *'Flick-flick'* went the lighter in my head. I covered the redness with my hand.

"Daniel?"

On the table next to ours, two blokes had been yakking about Gucci loafers since the sesame prawn toast landed. They'd been going *round* and *fucking round* about how you tell which ones are snide and which are pukka. The family behind us were singing bits of poxy Evita with atonal fervour. Standing over me was Alana's apparition with her, *'fair day's pay for a fair day's work'*, oration. And of course, by the stairs that went down to the loos, smiling irresistibly from his sofa, was Torin telling me he knew me *'so well'* and that pissed me off, because I clearly didn't.

I drew breath. "Bumped it."

"Poor you," she said. "Eat up."

Tipping my oily chow mein over the heads of the tuneless family behind me was more inviting than eating it.

She brightened suddenly. "Did I say my mum rang? She's found that seventies lamp shade I told you about. The Lanes in Brighton…I didn't?"

I shook my head.

"It'll look so cool in my flat. French. It's gathered cotton in Turkish blue, oh such a lovely thing. She was going to parcel-post it, but I said I'd come down. Introduce you. You'll come, won't you?"

"Yeah, course."

She appeared electrified by my compliance, her eyes flitting around the bowls, chewing as she spoke, "But, you speak to your mum every day, right?"

I nodded. She swallowed.

"Do you tell her about the band? Is she concerned?"

"Nah, she's alright. Used to the, like, chaos."

Her mum, my mum. The comparison shamed me. Alana shamed me. Torin shamed me. Mick's programmed drumming, his very soul extracted by an alien hand, made me want to cry. The blokes next to us were onto socks and Taiwanese factories, and the musical family were now mangling other show tunes – *Annie*, *The Sound of Music* – eliciting wincing smiles from the usually taciturn staff. The side of my head was starting to throb. I felt overwhelmed. Breathless.

"Kerry, need to get out…walk around the block for a minute. Clear my head."

She looked like she did when she threw her coffee at me: like an animal, startled by a predator.

She gripped my forearm fiercely. "You *are* coming back?"

Were there tears in her eyes, or was my vision as skewed as my fucked-up thinking?

"Yeah, course."

I turned right, moving fast. Like baby birds, their beaks snapping air for food, the myriad questions in my head demanded answers. What was Torin guaranteeing on his phone in the dressing room in Rotterdam? He'd been more impassioned leaving that message than he had been on stage. I moved my forefinger to my eye. It itched. I pulled it away. I longed to speak to Alana. She would know, but I'd bottled it so completely back there. Ibiza and Conrad? Mick had heard that too. Mick, my mate, my brother. I'm so sorry man. I rubbed my sore temple, my fingers strayed to my eye. I pulled my arm away roughly. Sienna's basement had revealed more doubt and puzzlement, more snapping, hungry beaks. I'd wilfully ignored Alana's words of warning, her truth, and because of that, Torin had run riot. Was I doing the same with Kerry? Obfuscation. So much I was prepared not to challenge, just to be.

On Barney's open laptop today, I noticed that the tour itinerary was dotted with these weird shows, deviations from the norm. There was one for a debutante's twenty-first party, a private corporate 'do' and a set of naff slots at seaside resorts. I imagined the grilling Alana would have given Barney if she'd seen dates like that inserted in a tour. It just wouldn't have happened. With her gone, we'd lost our 'quality control'. But what was I thinking. There was no 'we' anymore. It was just me, a job of work, a mortgage to be paid and mum, sitting in her bedroom, knotting her sheet in her fingers, staring out of the window, waiting for the bailiffs.

I stepped off the kerb to skirt a clump of revellers spilling out of a restaurant and nearly got hit by a motor bike. Its horn blared angrily as I strode on.

Had the agent anything to do with those deviant gigs? Surely not. Was Barney sliding those into the tour just to make an extra few bob behind his back? Fuck it. What did I care anyway? This wasn't the same as a *real* tour. It wasn't even a real band. I wouldn't have to concentrate, apply myself like I used to, because I didn't have to play an instrument. But the travelling, mile after mile with these impersonators, strangers – *that* would be a real chore. And *she'd* just asked me to go to Brighton to meet her mum. One look at me, and she'd wonder what the fuck drugs her daughter was on.

I was steaming along Wardour Street, hands rammed so hard into my pockets that the seams on my trousers were splitting. *'Ibiza's a certainty. You know how big my band is, guaranteed!'* What was he guaranteeing this bloke? And those dates on Barney's laptop would stretch for months and where would Kerry be by then? I worried about mum when I was on the road, but a ten-minute call from the lobby would settle her. Kerry would need more than a verbal post card, she needed someone to watch her eat cake and listen to her while she told them about 'her day'.

Nut down, I turned into Oxford Street my visage grim. Would she still be working in that piss-take of a shop? If the bloke in the South of France clicked his fingers, would she even be in England?

She told me on the way here that the thing she missed most was swimming. *'What's stopping you'*, I'd asked.

She said that her apartment block had a pool on the roof, but because of the building works they'd shut it down. She simply had to have a daily swim. Her mother was the same. She listed off the various lakes in Italy and France that they'd swam in. She couldn't wait for us to have a dip together, she said. My taciturnity almost cracked at that absurd notion and I laughed out loud. While I watched my mum cleaning the stainless steel in the school canteen, Kerry had been motoring through the continent with hers in their *pas de deux*, or whatever it was. And while I hid in my room (every mirror banned in the house because of what they made me do), she was strolling through super-quaint fishing villages, smiling and beguiling…captains of industry and fucking film stars pulling her chair back at some local eatery.

My hand went gingerly to the side of my head. It throbbed. That forbidden room was as mystifying as her.

I was almost jogging now. She'd been the only female in that snooker club and whenever I looked up from my shot, and whenever she was over the table taking hers, eyes were on her. Was I wrong about her indifference? She *must* have felt their scrutiny, the masculine heat on her.

Kerry's smile had become the one good thing in my life, and I knew for certain that while I was away, pressing that fraudulent spacebar on my computer, she would find someone far worthier than me to aim it at.

"Oi! Fuckin' *idiot!*"

I felt myself shoved hard before I lunged into a mound of cardboard stacked against a lamppost. As my head rocked back, my glasses fell off. Trying to find my feet, I trod on them, snapping the bridge. Squinting, left eye, right eye, a burly, red-faced geezer in a Fred Perry loomed into focus over me. My immediate thought was, he must be hard, he's wearing a T-shirt and it's freezing.

His wincing girlfriend held onto him, rubbing her knee.

"Watch where you're fuckin' going, pisshead."

With his arm around his girl he walked off. Aware that eyes were on me, I got to my feet and tried to put my glasses back on. Hopeless. I put the two halves in my pocket.

The guy in the Fred Perry had scared some perspective into me. What a pillock I must look to her, legging it from the table like that. I resolved to make it up. Not only would I pay for dinner, I'd take her for tea and cake afterwards.

As I approached the restaurant, I could see someone sitting in my place. I crossed the road and secreted myself in a dim doorway. From this vantage point, the other person was hidden from me. I could see only Kerry at our table. She was downcast, nodding robotically. My heart raced when a hand reached across and, for a few seconds, lifted up her chin.

When the interloper stood and revealed himself at the side of the table I saw a tall, heavy-set man with medium-length flaxen hair resting on the collar of a navy suit jacket. He had a chiselled jaw and a hunter's glare. He shocked me when he extended his arm and removed her cap. The action betrayed real intimacy. A knowledge of her that I did not have. But Kerry did not shake her hair free or direct that gaze that so enlivened me, at him. She remained still, staring at the soy-sauce bottle and chilli dispenser in the centre of the table.

Speaking, the man gave his pockets a perfunctory pat. Kerry's expression, when she looked up was hidden from me, but his smile was not. It had broadened, and I thought, why don't I own a brilliant, clear-eyed smile like that?

I crossed the road and walked into the restaurant. The theatrical family were exiting messily, pulling kids' hoods up and wiping noses, seemingly bidding a farewell to every diner in there. As I edged past them, I was aware of a low, mellifluous tone emanating from my table but couldn't hear what was being said.

He squinted at me as he passed and shot an inquiring look back at her when I sat in his seat.

I felt his residual energy.

"Who was that Kerry?"

Her smile was of the front of house variety: flawless, lineless and efficient. "Someone I used to work with."

"Ah, yeah. In the shop before this one?" My sarcasm was as obvious as her vagueness.

"No, in France." She glanced up, saw the look on my face and began rummaging in her silver bag the way she did on our first encounter over tea and cake. She stood, on went her cap and mac. Over-cinching her belt, she blinked in discomfort. She put a tenner on the dish.

"He give you that?" I called after her.

Her flimsy leopard-print scarf almost choked her as she went through the door. The chaps to my right were finally silent. When I looked at them, they offered me twin, sanguine smiles of sympathy. I caught up with her in one of those incongruously empty streets that lead from Brewer to Carnaby.

"Look, Kerry. I think I understand, you and me…" And it was weird, because inside, I *still* wanted to buy her the biggest, fuck-off cake she could handle, but what was coming out of my mouth would make her puke it up. "I dunno what game you've been playing with me, but I know who that was."

"You don't know any…"

"I do. I know what you're used to, your mum, and the holidays and yachts and all that swimming naked in lakes. What was I, some kind of social experiment?"

She'd gone waxy and still. She could have been a mannequin herself.

"Not so chatty now, Kerry?"

Our faces were inches apart. The wax melted. Lines and freckles appeared and the faint sagging beneath the eyes emitted such profound grief, that I had to look away.

I felt her fingers gently caress the ridges below my right eye. "Your glasses."

A shiver shot through me. "Don't touch me," I said, backing away in tears.

14

Through a milky sun struggling to light up the grey outside my bedroom window, the drama of the night before came seeping in. I'd let myself in and hovered at the foot of the stairs. Mum had called out from the front room and asked me if I'd eaten.

"Yeah. Going up. Tired."

And I was, but I couldn't find sleep. The ill-fitting jigsaw pieces, the disparate events and coincidences of the last couple of months, bumped and repelled each other in the molten liquid of my thoughts. Ugly words. Ugly face.

The final moments of our parting were quite cinematic. I had sped along Carnaby Street, through the station barriers giving myself an inner pep talk. *'What's wrong with being in a covers band of your own band? Doesn't make you a criminal.'*

On the platform a child's cry brought me around. A family – mum, dad, two small children – were looking at me. They wore matching Puffa jackets that had neat Italian flags on their breasts. Even with my spectacles on, I knew how unsettling I could appear if scrutinised too closely. One of the children hugged her mum's thigh while dad stood protectively in front. I attempted to poke my glasses onto the bridge of my nose, but they were in two pieces in my pocket. These unfortunate tourists were being subjected to the full 'Daniel Earl Prosthetic Experience'.

I raised an apologetic palm. Suitably appalled, they edged their way further down the platform, and it brought back memories of the *'pizza, pizza, pizza'* they sang to me when I returned to school.

The train roared in. The doors shut and, as it attempted to pull away, Kerry ran onto the platform, capless, her mac open, bedraggled scarf and hair.

The exit was agonising with coughs and judders, doors opening and closing causing her to hop forward and back, her silver bag trapped between her arm and side. Sitting there, I wondered if she appreciated the irony: these tubular actions were the same as the ones that had caused her to toss her coffee over me three weeks ago. Knowing her, I'm sure it did.

I tracked her tears and read her lips: *'Please Daniel'*. Was that continent of sadness in her expression regret, was it fear? Was she flinching from cruelty? Had she suffered that in her life? Passengers seated on my side of the carriage observed her resigned futile effort, her green gaze on me, her hair a fountain of gold in the filthy underground draft.

The woman one seat away from me stifled her double-take. *'I know,'* I wanted to tell her, pointing at my face and then at the platform and back again, *'Doesn't match up, does it?'*

Mercifully the train accelerated. There was a final, garish flash of advertising and where she had been, my reflection was looking back at me from the black cables in the window across the aisle.

The replay from last night faded and in the void, a sensation – a sickening, but not unfamiliar one – enveloped me and I found myself gripping the mattress and breathing through my nose. The strain of dread I felt at fifteen, on my back in my box room on the estate, knowing that I *had* to go to school tomorrow, was the same one I felt now, a decade later, in the house I owned as an adult. Although unable to exhale or move, a part of me marvelled that I was back in the grip of my past.

"It was him," I said in a gush of breath.

That, I was sure of. The man that had taken my place in the restaurant last night was a vital player in the legend she spoke of so longingly. He'd jetted in from the paradisiacal 'Gorges du Verdon' to rescue her from totting-up duties and worse at Sienna. How lit up she was when she spoke of those gay times.

You could tell he was wealthy, had investments and stocks, bonds? I imagined her in the passenger seat of his Ferrari, laughing into an azure sky as he took a stealthy left-hander, descending the panoramic hills behind Nice. How could I compete on Torin's few hundred quid a show plus expenses? *He* certainly didn't live with his broken-down mum *or* had stabbed his best friends in the back. But more than those agonies separated us. The bloke framed in the restaurant window exhibited momentum and promise. My one-eyed outlook opposed that, diametrically.

My phoned buzzed. Kerry for the third time. I didn't even open the message. What a grand delusion I'd enjoyed, arm in arm with this goddess, my mystery dinner guest who delighted me when she nicked the food from my plate, my gloriously crappy snooker opponent, my green-eyed dream. And what the fuck was I thinking…walking through that white, bright Sicilian square with her…*idiot*. I deleted and blocked her.

I got up and stared at the mirror. After a moment of nothingness, I fancied a hundred microscopic wasps, their wings beating in multiples of sixteen, swarming below my eye. Their buzzing and activity became unbearable. I swayed and felt something crack deep inside.

As the blood embedded itself in my nails, I hectically clawed at the location relishing the profound relief that this action brings. I fell backwards onto my bed, the blood now blending with tears of disgust.

"Daniel?"

Heart thudding, I pulled my hand away from my face.

"Daniel!" As she had back then, my mother was speaking to me through my closed bedroom door.

"In a minute."

"I'm a bit worried, Daniel."

"It's alright."

"You broke your glasses. I saw them on the shelf downstairs."

"Just tidying up. Down in a minute."

As she padded softly down, I slid through the bathroom door. When, ten minutes later, we met at the junction of the front room and kitchen, she staggered backwards, gasping at the sight of me. I was aware that I'd made a mess of my face, but it's not until you see someone looking at you after an episode do you realise the damage you've done to yourself.

"Oh God, you've picked."

With the TV moaning for attention and the washing machine tumbling, we went back in time, my mum and me. *Then*, my teenage logic dictated that if I scratched the scabs off my face, my skin would miraculously smooth and flatten, but it had never once worked out like that. From my hospital bed I'd watched her pass out when, for the first time, the nurse had removed the bandages from my face to clean the injury.

Her voice interrupted the memory of that moment. "Why Daniel?" she asked, as the washing machine changed gear to begin its spin cycle.

"Bit of stress at work, mum," I told her, but equally could have said, *'some kids at school'*.

Twisting her fingers in the doorway, she asked if we'd have to move back to the flats. I understood her fragile 'adult' logic because since we'd moved here, I hadn't picked at all.

"No, mum," I said, walking towards the kettle and turning it on.

White light coated her face when she opened the fridge door. "I'll make you a nice big breakfast."

"Just a cuppa this morning."

When I returned to school, the headmaster had assured us it'd be fine, but it wasn't. It was hell. For the first couple of weeks, a gang of kids would stand behind me in the lunchtime queue, or as I walked through the alley to the flats singing *'pizza, pizza, pizza'*. A breaktime didn't pass without my appearance being referred to. It didn't matter if the words were cruel or sympathetic, what was unbearable was the incessant focus.

Back from school, I'd race up the three flights, dart along the balcony and slam the door on the world outside. Sliding the bathroom lock across, I'd be gripped by a febrile energy. The abuse, the songs and rhymes, the day's bug-eyed scrutiny caused me to claw at the scars in a pitiful attempt to flatten and smooth them so that tomorrow, walking through the school gates I'd just bolted out of, I'd look like the other kids...*was* just another kid.

Initially, the action delivers relief. The red bumps and bloody crusts of skin vanish after a messy few minutes' work. But within an hour, the recovery process resumes, the skin reddening and hardening over the weeping lumps. Witnessing this healing, I felt as if my body was betraying me and I'd return to the mirror furious and vengeful, doubly determined to get it right *this* time. Such was the urgency, I'd occasionally forget to lock the door and she'd nab me literally 'red-handed' leaning into the mirror, digging into my skin. She'd scream and I'd jump. Then, there'd be a pathetically comic minute or so with me pushing the door shut while she tried to force it open. That was when the 'speaking through doors' protocol began. Her telling me to *'leave your poor face alone'*. Me telling her to leave *me* alone. Her pleading forgiveness for it all, me telling her it wasn't her fault. I told you it was pathetic.

We utilised all the strategies suggested to us by the hospital psychiatrist: ban mirrors, wear surgical gloves (to negate the effect of my nails – file them right down too), try to find something to occupy my hands. There were jigsaw puzzles, Gameboys, squashy toys, knitting for fuck's sake! All futile. There seemed nothing that could halt the irrepressible urge to flatten, and to flatten I had to pick, and when I picked, the livid red welts would erupt and I'd claw them away, and it'd all start again. For a year, I didn't come up for air. And then, my mother presented me with her gift on Christmas morning.

The packaging wasn't spectacular. Mum's traditionally inelegant Christmas wrapping. I honestly had no idea what it was. "Open it then, Daniel."

It was a Casio SK-1.

I was hooked before we pulled the first cracker. Her finding something for me that was more digitally compelling than my face was a moment of genius on her part. In a couple of weeks, I had learned all the songs I liked on the radio (and some I didn't). Although the bathroom still called, it had to wait until I'd mastered an advert's jingle or the theme to a detective series. I surprised myself. After one or two listens, I seemed to know instinctively where the notes were (or were going to be) and could remember the precise journey of a song just as easily. As much as playing the notes, I was fascinated by the sounds stored within the instrument. After learning an arrangement, I'd add weird, wobbling effects, spirals of electricity and randomly dissonant stabs. My goal was always to change it into something that was indelibly, and imperfectly, my own. I remember mum asking why I had to *'spoil that nice tune'*, but I was drawn to the imperfect, because that was what I was.

"Just a cuppa," she repeated doubtfully, closing the fridge door.
"Yes."

Showered, I patted my lapel flat in the mirror by the front door. The glasses (I kept four spare pairs at home, identical thick, horn-rimmed ones) and strategically barbered stubble would make the deformity (unless peered at from a foot or two away – and *nobody* got that close to me) manageable until it healed. And it would. I promised myself. I wouldn't go back again. I poked my head around the kitchen door. She was at the sink looking into the garden.

"Going now mum."

"You've gone back to picking." It was if she was speaking to the robins on the little bush.

"Nah. It was a one off. Overtired."

"You have, and it's all my fault. They'll send us back to the estate."

"Course they won't. We own this house. They can't take it off us."

Walking towards the station I felt cool and focused. It was time to start rehearsals in earnest. Over my one cup of tea, I'd opened copious emails from Barney re our live spec: backline and stage set-up. It was unnerving that he was asking me for answers that any road manager would know by heart. His indecisiveness betrayed a man who was way out of his depth and watching the tide come in.

I would *not* be indecisive. Minus pleasure and pride, I would give the job (and the people paying good money at the door) my professional respect. The new way would arrive on stage well-rehearsed and totally convincing.

Jake nodded. "Alright, Daniel."

"Fine thanks?"

He leaned across the reception desk conspiratorially. "So, all change then? Mick Corbossa and Alana," he made inverted commas with his fingers: "no longer involved?" It was a bit of a shock to hear that fact vocalised, but not as big as the shock he got when he looked at me. The pathetically underpowered lighting illuminated last night's handiwork in scabby relief.

"Appears not," I replied. He responded to the damage by ignoring the evidence of his eyes and pressing on. It's what people did, invariably.

"Blimey. Would you tell me why?"

The dismantling of the band, like most criminal acts, had been committed in secret, but the news would soon be out. Barney would be setting up Torin's press for the tour. I wondered what the party line would be for ejecting fifty percent of the band.

"Err looking for a new sound? New challenge?"

"Right. They doing anything in music?"

"Not sure."

"Well, let me know. Brilliant rhythm section."

"Yeah, they are," I said, turning for the corridor.

I pushed through the door into a wall of sound. The lights were low, set at stage level for performance effect. Daisy and Bluebell were hard at it: posing and throwing the regulation shapes in the big mirror. For once, Barney wasn't on the sofa with his laptop but pacing back and forth in front of the girls, head bowed, as if searching the beer-stained carpet for an anomaly in the faultless production emanating from the big speakers. As the song moved inexorably through the program to its climax and Torin's vocal soared, he clenched a pudgy, triumphant fist. I caught Bluebell's eye, we swapped a smile and any loathing from me for our tour manager evaporated. As the last chord rang and the cymbals echoed, he looked up and seeing me, shrugged sheepishly and returned to the sofa.

Daisy got off her drums and pressed the spacebar before the next song could commence. As the speakers hummed, I felt the flicking lighter in my brain.

"Hope you don't mind, Daniel," she said, "We thought we'd get an early start."

She reared when I removed my glasses to wipe them. I smelled school dinners, heard the rattle of cutlery on the trays and the murmur of hungry, queuing children.

"Your face."

"Think it's an allergy."

"Sorry," she said, gently.

As I said, most people ignored the state of me, but a minority didn't.

"Let's crack on."

She nodded and got back to her drums.

I'd returned to the classroom tubbier than I'd been before the summer holidays. I no longer played football over the park with my friends and the sight of a pushbike made me sick. Where once I joined in, I now spent the lessons looking out of the window at the playing fields. The teacher's drone had become as relevant as the grumbling traffic on the high street beyond. Evenings, like weekends, saw me supine, watching telly and letting my guilt-ridden mum fatten me up. Surprisingly, my exam results weren't abysmal, but they weren't noteworthy either. There was nothing extraordinary about me, apart from my appearance.

Emerging stubble at the start of the sixth form changed my outlook. I could see a future in which the scarring might be concealed. The habitual examination in my mirror, with the urge to pick the scars and make them vanish, had been replaced by the daily inspection of burgeoning black shoots of facial hair. By my second sixth-form year, the weight had fallen off me and unbelievably, the bottom of the pear drop, an area of about two millimetres, was peppered with welcome shadow. But however successfully I camouflaged my face, the acute shyness and distrust I'd developed in the years since the accident lingered.

Perversely, on the stage, playing those country covers for Miss Ferguson, had been where I felt least heavy. Twisting the knobs and pushing the faders as if I were at war with them, released all the teenage rebellion I stored up watching telly and inspecting my mirror. While my pub band mates chatted with friends and family at the bar, I would sit in the dark at the back of the little stage. At the sound of Miss Ferguson at the mic, I'd step up to my Casio like some capeless, coffee-coloured Rick Wakeman. If they wanted to look at a monster, I'd give them monster sounds too.

"Pizza, Daniel?" Barney was smiling bemusedly at me from the old sofa. "If that's what you'd like, I'll pop around the corner. Bit early?"

"Sorry mate, miles away. He err?"

"No, not today. He said he'd come down and 'top and tail' for a couple of hours before the Empire on Saturday. He's got meetings."

Torin *'topping and tailing'* would be interesting. In five years, he'd not been able to grasp which end of the animal shits or eats.

"You're joking!"

"He said he'll call you. See you up at the club soon. Something big's come up he needs to focus on."

So, I was to accept that there was something in Torin's universe bigger than a sold-out gig at the Shepherd's Bush Empire with a new line-up and a completely different way of delivering the music.

"And what's that, Barney?"

"Sorry. What's what, Daniel?"

"This other thing. Music?"

"Not entirely sure."

The lighter flicked. *'Come on now, pizza boy.'*

"Not entirely sure?" I stared at him. "We go on stage in three days, man!"

He cowered. I sighed. It was pointless kicking up. Why should I have an issue with the band, its gigs, personnel and future no longer fascinating Torin. They no longer fascinated me. *'This shitty thing has to be got through,'* I said to myself.

"OK girls?"

I put the lead vocal up on the computer and off we went.

I was relieved that Jake was on the phone with the booking diary open when I ducked out of Room Three and headed for Tottenham Court Road. I didn't want to answer any more questions about the band and its new line-up. I couldn't deny that it hadn't been a good day. It hadn't dragged as I feared it would. Daisy and Bluebell were as diligent as ever and I took energy from their enthusiasm. Barney had been in my ear asking advice and guidance and I was cool about that too. I had accepted that I was the only one that had done this, so why shouldn't I help my less experienced colleagues. After all, we're all prawns in Torin's salad, aren't we? I poked my glasses up and actually laughed as I jogged down the tube stairs.

Mum was sitting at the kitchen table looking into the night-time garden when I walked in. It was as if she hadn't moved since I left the house.

I turned on all the lights.

"Alright mum. Nothing on telly?"

"No, rubbish."

"Yeah, no law says you have to watch it. Gonna put this curry in the microwave."

As I set about puncturing and timing. I glanced at her again. She was twiddling her beads and muttering. Instinctively, I glanced at my phone to see if I'd got a message and realised that I'd blocked her. I felt bewildered suddenly. Untethered.

"How did it go at work, Daniel?"

Even though I saw mum's lips pucker and say the word 'work,' I heard 'school' and was shot back half my life; her making me egg on toast after my first day back there. I had dropped my rucksack and blazer on the kitchen lino with tears tumbling down my face. *'Oh Daniel'*, she'd said. I could hear the frying eggs crackling. I pulled hard on my tie to take the thing off, but only succeeded in tightening the knot. *'They laughed at me, mum'*. She buckled at the knees and slid to the floor. *'They chucked my homework over the fence. They called me 'Monster Munch' and 'pizza face''*. The eggs exploded, jolting me from my sobs. Mum got to her feet and shrieked as she tried to lift the pan from the hob. Her palm was crimson and bubbling. I had to call an ambulance.

Ping.

I shook my head.

"Your curry."

"Ah yeah. Ta mum."

I emptied the plastic tray onto a plate and put the plate on a tray. "Gonna eat in the studio. Watch some telly mum, go on."

"I will, I will."

With my dinner steaming into the night, I walked along the mosaic path to the shed. Backheeling the door shut, I set down my tray and from a dusty, high shelf, retrieved a half-dozen CDs.

Ideas that had been dammed-up on the estate came pouring out of me once I'd set my equipment up in here. Verse sections, sixteen bars of strings, brass parts and piano for choruses. Longer pieces as well, two or three minutes of music complete with tempo changes and breakdowns. As well as making further albums with the band, I'd imagined a future writing music for film and TV, but our shameful second effort had pulled the plug on those projections. For the last three years I'd only composed music for me and the robins.

When we moved in, as well as caning IKEA (refitting the kitchen and furnishing the house), I splashed out on the latest Apple Mac and was able to store entire libraries of music on its hard drive. The days of recording individual MiniDiscs and CD-Rs, endlessly writing titles, dates and duration with a biro, appeared steam-driven compared with a few taps on a keyboard.

Although I'd stockpiled hours of music on the computer, sifting through the selection of CDs I'd taken down, a melancholic longing overcame me. I'd made music so innocently back then. Reading the handwritten track lists was like seeing your signature in a textbook or paperback that you'd signed when you were a kid, and for a moment I was fascinated by how my writing style had changed. It was as if it wasn't me that had, so neatly, inked those titles and dates on the inner sleeves with the varied coloured biros I'd kept in a battered pewter tankard on a shelf in the box room. Projects from as far back as the Christmas I'd got the Casio were in this ancient batch. I remembered I'd put down so many ideas that I'd had to title the tracks in different languages, so for example, the word 'mountain' 'lake' or 'tree' would be in French, German or Swedish.

After a moment's sifting, I found the CD I was looking for and returned the others to the shelf. Swivelling 180 degrees in my office chair I played the notes on the CD on my 404. The world slowed. A glob of cream, rice, chicken and cardamom stayed unchewed in my mouth as I stared into the blank section of wall between the speakers. I felt unbalanced, sort of drunk, but sharp for a second too. Snorting a laugh of incredulity, I swallowed hard, scooped another spoonful and allowed my mind to trip back to the sixth form and an assembly a few weeks before the Easter break.

My reputation at school as a visual oddity was well established, but there was a creeping recognition that I was an interesting musician as well. While the other kids in the music lessons trod the tried and trusted curriculum, I was left to my own devices. One day the headmaster himself asked me to 'perform for the school'.

I played them my 'Water' album – a blend of sounds, moods and riffs with a liquid feel, from rainfall to stream, waterfall and ocean. Fingering the opening notes on my Casio to the hundreds of seated children, I felt, for the first time, the unique thrill of communicating without using words.

The suffocating hush when I'd finished lasted only for a couple of seconds before a deluge of applause overwhelmed me. I remember looking behind me to see if someone had walked onto the stage, but it was just the headmaster and the deputy head, and they were applauding as well.

While the hall cleared and I packed my keyboard away, Miss Ferguson, offered her congratulations and told me she ran a covers band that did gigs at the pub on my estate. It'd do me the world of good to play with other musicians, *'learn the craft'*, she'd said. I jumped at it. It gave me the chance to go out and stay in at the same time.

Of course, the reality wasn't quite what I had in mind. What I had in mind would come two years later when a man in a dress singled me out and bought me a pint.

15

"Dreadful worrier, Daniel." I was taking his call in Room Three at the end of the day's session. "Always have been, always will be," he continued. "Which isn't a bad thing, makes you diligent, but a little wearing...Daniel?"

I could hear his club in the background. Someone plinking and plonking on the piano. Walking in small circles, I glanced at my face in the big mirror. I was making a real mess of it. The impulse to pick had become irresistible.

"Just that I'm kinda running everything, and the girls wanted to go through the set with you. They want to know what you think of them."

"Come on Danny, they're miming, what's to think?"

"It's more a case of err, coordinating the live moves?" I winced as I spoke. It was such drivel. "They need your approval, man."

"Ah, women and their insecurities."

The clock was ticking. The girls had been on at me about getting him down. Bluebell needed to spot his cues on stage: she didn't want to blunder into a vocal just as he was starting one of his fire-side chats.

"But you're practising Torin, yeah?"

"I said I was."

The atmosphere behind him seeped into our call. "Barney's losing it," I said.

Barney had admitted to me on Monday that he wasn't a marketing ace. He'd never been backstage at a gig either, never mind gone on the road. He'd been sacked from his last job: salesperson at the big Currys showroom in Edmonton (specialty VCRs and TVs), for fucking up the orders. He said he couldn't get his head around the addresses and delivery dates – he had more of a creative brain, he added.

Sitting with him and his open laptop on the blown sofa, I quizzed him as to why this or that thing hadn't been taken care of. Van hire and driver should have been nailed weeks ago, hotels booked and stage times confirmed before then. There was regional TV and radio promo people that he'd not got back to because he'd been running around trying to get a few quid out of our singer to print up the tour T-shirts he'd designed himself to save money. We'd not even settled on an opening act yet. There were half a dozen contenders all tuned up waiting by their phones for a 'yes' or 'no' from us.

While Torin breathed into his phone, I glanced at the studio's closed door and replayed the conversation I'd had with Barney after the girls had gone.

"I need to hire all these amps and drums and stuff, and the insurance, deposits for hotels, and…You've got to call him, Daniel, he'll listen to you."

"I'm the keyboard player. There's tour support for that. Ask the accountant, Pinky Forbes."

Chewing his lip, the poor bloke said the accountant was getting pissed off with him calling. He'd told Barney that it wasn't his job to tour manage Torin.

"But you *need* to get that money."

He'd looked around him nervously. "I don't think he's paid the girls Danny. Daisy's got a daughter. Bluebell's cool, but she's no mug," he said offering me his phone.

I shook my head. "You know where he is. Wait for him there."

He lowered his pallid pink dome and didn't reply.

"What now?"

"He told me to stop stalking him." His hands went to his face. He was peeking at me through his fingers. "He said if he saw me in there again, he'd have me thrown out."

"What!"

"He's very angry Daniel. What are we going to do? We're on the road next week." He was wearing a medium-sized, homemade 'Torin on Tour' T-shirt. Not only was it crap, it should have been an XL. I gave his shoulder a friendly squeeze.

"You chip off, Barney. Leave it for tonight. I'll give him a bell."

"Daniel, are you still there?"

"Torin."

"How long have we both been doing this thing, five years? Just get on with it. I've not gone into details, especially with that fat incompetent hovering, but there's a healthy bonus for you at the end of the tour. You are the senior pro, the MD no less. The way I've calculated it, you'll be five K richer in March. How does that sound, m'boy?"

"Well, it sounds pretty good. But Torin, the record company need to release the tour support money. Barney…"

"Will you please not mention that fool again! I'm trying to communicate with *you*!"

"Yes, I get that, but stuff needs to be booked and paid for. You know that Torin. Barney only wants to…"

"Did you not hear what I just said!"

He'd tipped his champagne over the sides. Lost it. Echoes of his tirade in Holland six weeks ago sent a shiver through me.

"For fuck's sake," he hissed through clenched teeth, "I've told him. I'll deal with it."

"Easy Torin, we're all doing the best we can."

"Grow a pair man! Run the thing! It's what you're paid for. I'm incredibly busy with important matters."

"What could be more important than a tour starting next week?"

"Ha. And there you have it in essence. You, her, the plumber, you honestly think that music is the be-all and end-all. You sound like an eight-year-old."

There was a moment of silence as he seethed, and I hurt. This shitty thing *had* to be got through. I took a breath. "But what about rehearsing?"

"What about it?"

"You know."

"Know what?"

"I'm going through the set with the girls with your voice on playback and…"

"Yes?"

"Come on man, you've always had issues."

In the silence, the skin around my eye began to itch. My forefinger went to a minutely raised scab on my cheek. I smashed my right hand into my first to stop myself.

"I think I've proved I can handle that issue now," he said.

'Do you?'

So, all the years of me, Mick and Alana shitting it onstage, the icy dread we endured watching you with one graceful arm on the mic stand and your handsome head tragically bowed, *you* having no idea whether to open your mouth and sing – all that was an illusion? If it wasn't for Alana's nudge or flick, or her opening the chorus or verse for you, we'd have been there all fucking night!

With the piano tinkling down the phone, I thought of how well that rock and roll conceit had served us, how beautiful it sounded, that split second: her voice before his, then the heavenly blend of both. I could hear him saying my name on the other end of the phone but was swept away by another memory: Mick and me in a dressing room with the previous night's reviews scattered about us, clutching our stomachs in paroxysms of laughter at some journo's loquacious wonderment at Torin and Alana's vocal telepathy, waxing on for paragraphs about the musical synchronicity and timing of the two great rock and roll lovers. So much bullshit.

"Daniel!"

I turned away from the mirror. Blood was dripping into the corner of my mouth.

"Yeah."

"Are you listening to me?"

"I think you need to come in, man."

"But it's sounding and looking good, right?"

"Well yeah. But the whole show, apart from me, is on playback. Three quarters of the thing is miming, an act."

"And your point is?"

"The girls, Torin."

"OK, OK. I *promise* to come down tomorrow, but make sure Fatty Arbuckle is not in the same fucking postcode."

***

At end of the session the next day, I crossed Charing Cross Road into Soho. The hood on my mac was invariably up now, regardless of the weather. I'd ceded to nightly facial tidying. Repair and disguise had become the breakfast priority. I could cope as long as I limited my appearances to the tube into rehearsals and home straight afterwards. An audience with him and the ogling elite at his club was the last thing I wanted, but his no-show today, after last night's promise, had caused me to text him, steam up there and have it out.

Girding myself for the inevitable doubletake from Jill behind the desk, I stepped off the kerb and almost walked straight into him as he exited the building. I quickly knelt behind a car to tie my shoelaces. I was wearing Chelsea boots. Why I didn't intercept him as he crossed the road – *'Torin, thought you said you were rehearsing. We've got two days, man'* – was not clear in that moment, but I stayed low and watched him pass. I was half a block behind him when he nipped into an open doorway on his left. As I walked past, I saw the sellotaped pieces of paper advertising the 'models' who rented rooms on the various floors.

Initially, Mick, Alana and I had been baffled by Torin's addiction to prostitutes. Ever since he strode through that pokey old pub in his dress, I'd been aware that women could not take their eyes off him, and when 'Silent Storm' hit, the attention he got became absurd. Knickers, bras, hotel keys were tossed at him from the wilting front rows, he'd be dogged at the tour bus doors and airport check-ins by avid, gorgeous women (and a fair number of gorgeous men). Wheeling my case through a hotel lobby, it was not unusual for me to be casually threatened for his room number.

Amazingly though, Torin wasn't 'one for the ladies' in the way Mick was. Mick was an unashamed hound, but an open-hearted one. He sincerely loved the company of women, delighted in their presence, their sounds, scent and opinions. You never got that feeling with Torin.

The only woman I'd witnessed him be affectionate with was Alana, but I don't recall him putting his arms around her or holding her hand in front of me or Mick, yet there are hundreds of photos of him 'performing' those actions in public with one azure eye piercing the camera lens.

One evening, a few months after he'd become a member of the club, we stepped out together, Torin and me. It was around ten o'clock. Alana and Mick had stopped attending weeks before. He'd had a bugle full and could not stop rabbiting on about all the deals he'd lined up and how he was going to 'beat the system' and how 'they' were all thieves and frauds, after what was his, et cetera.

We reeled along the raucous, drunken cobbles of Soho, him in Elvis black leather and me, in acolyte jeans and DMs, wedded to him, obedient and *so* proud.

After a third or fourth compliment from a passer-by, he put his arm around my shoulder. "Danny my boy," his red wine voice so close in my ear. "Ideas are the currency, and you are my mint."

I was twenty years old and the singer who was top of the charts favoured me above all others.

Then he stopped, asked me to, *'give him fifteen'*, and ducked up some stairs. While I waited, a bloke asked me if I was in the queue. I backed into the dark shaking my head.

Torin was out in thirteen minutes. "These Slavic's keep themselves in such good shape. Here, take this. Call it a bonus. Get up there."

"No, Torin."

He tilted his head. "Must be tough right, with your eye. No oil painting? Anyway, your call. We're number one, man. Woohoo!"

These ten o'clock excursions became routine. It disturbed me that Torin needed or liked, or that it added to his sexual frisson, that I go with him and then, like a dog he'd tethered to a lamppost, wait for him to conclude. He'd study my face from inches away while relating the details of the intercourse he'd paid for in a second-storey room on Green's Court, then laugh into the air, lead singer style, when I gulped my embarrassment and distaste.

Like Alana and Mick, I stopped going to the club. He didn't like that. He protested for a bit, called me disloyal and weak willed, warned me to be wary of Alana's commie instincts as well as questioning my sexuality and potency, then he left it.

Footsteps clattered down the stairs jolting me back into now. As Torin appeared on the street, I stepped further into the darkness. I gave him half a block and resumed my shadowing. When he stopped at the Marquee Club, I feigned interest in a restaurant across the road. Minutes passed. I watched him dog his cigarette, look up from his phone and break into a broad smile for the man who had just walked past me.

From the rear, the stranger's frame stretched at his suit pants and jacket, but not because he was out of shape – the reverse in fact. If it wasn't for the tailoring and the bragging bass voice, that even a roaring taxi couldn't dampen, he could have passed as a doorman, an unforgiving one. Shirt unbuttoned; he surveyed the street with a sniper's eye. Torin was like an excited puppy around him. The man laughed uproariously when Torin hitched up his ball-sack and nodded in the direction of the address he'd just visited.

***

Materialising in the kitchen doorway, knowing not to comment on the handiwork that had sent us both tumbling back through the years, my mother addressed the space beside my shoulder.

"Where are you going?"

"Just up the back to the shed, mum."

"But you've just got in. Do you want some dinner? I've got you some nice whitebait. I can make you scrambled eggs."

"I'll have this," I said, extracting yesterday's lasagne from the fridge and turning on the microwave.

"Oh, alright. How was Torin?"

"He was good mum."

Ping!

"Just doing some music," I said, shutting the kitchen door behind me.

Heating on, music on, I manfully chewed the rubbery day-old pasta. When my phone rang, I turned the volume down on the CD. A piano accompanied the club chatter in the background.

"Yes, Torin."

"You sent me a text. I was expecting you." I was baffled for a moment. But he was right, I'd not spoken to him about his absence at rehearsals, even though I'd been following him all evening.

"Doesn't matter." There was a short pause.

"I bet you've gone all 'Daniel looking'?"

"Torin, you were supposed to come to rehearsals today."

"You know who you're beginning to sound like?"

"Torin, I told the girls. Bluebell…"

"Fuck the girls!"

With my stage instincts – the ones that could tell he was going to end a chorus prematurely, or extend the fucker for another one, and round we'd all go again – on full alert, I sensed something grave in the offing.

"What, Torin?"

I pictured his shark mouth widening but not in a smile. I closed my eyes as he drew breath. "The record company haven't taken up the option."

"What?"

"The wankers have kicked us off the label."

"No, Torin."

"End of the month, which is next week. It'll all stop. No more retainer."

"But the band's account."

"Been using it for tour support."

"But Barney said..."

"Don't fucking Barney me, *man!*" He sounded seriously unhinged. The ambience behind him faded. He'd moved to somewhere quieter, less public, less embarrassing. "But it's OK," he managed calmly. "I know you've been concerned about new material. Ideas are the currency, right?"

Through the window, I peered into the kitchen. She was by the sink looking at the shed. Was she a witch, my mum? When she peered over my shoulder just now – did she know our time was up? Instead of the piss-stained walkways, dismal views of car parks and red brick walls she'd inherited as a lone teenage mum, for the last few years she'd enjoyed fresh air, trees and space. Twittering birds had replaced the screaming threats through the front room's peach anaglypta. She wasn't half going to miss those squirrels darting across the kitchen sill while she made me breakfast.

"...new ideas Daniel?"

"Right, Torin."

"I need you to get your brilliant, nutty head down, magic up some demos. Stuff that means I can walk into a label with my dick swinging proudly. I want to be irresistible, back to where I was. Get us our money back, Daniel."

"So, I'm not on a wage."

"None of us are. Look at me, I'm as fucked as you are."

No mate, rumour has it your old man's got a few bob under the mattress. My mum's on sickness benefit and what I've got in the bank is already allocated. Appreciate you might be unable to cover this year's sojourn in Jamaica, or front up *all* your club memberships, but it looks like I'll be signing on by the start of winter.

My thoughts turned to the chances of me – without Alana and Mick – writing material palatable to an A&R man after our moribund three years: pretty fucking slim.

I glanced up. Mum had left the sink. A hot belt of panic had me wondering where she'd gone. He was droning on about this new album I needed to knock off in a couple of days. "…current themes, stuff with a 'contemporary' groove. We need to get out there, expeditionary force, Danny boy. Clubs, 'out of the way' gigs. See what's happening in the underground, *maaan*. You and me, we can get it back…Danny?"

"OK."

But I couldn't even get the bloke to practise his own charade in Denmark Street for a couple of hours, never mind sit together somewhere without a bar and write music for an album. The thing was so utterly fucked. And the truth was that Torin was always the icing on the cake, the lit-up fairy on the Christmas tree. It was us that came up with the song arrangements and melodies, and us that had patiently squeezed his giant-sized ego into them.

As he continued listing clubs and producers and people he knew, my thoughts about the future were icily clear. Without *quality* new music (music that could only be written by quality musicians like Alana and Mick), the law of diminishing returns would come into effect for the band. The old material would be all there was, and however good it had been at the time, those units were sold. Nobody was going to buy them twice. As the seconds ticked by, our catalogue (along with our fanbase) incrementally decayed. To make up the gigantic shortfall in our earnings, the tour itineraries would need to contain even more holiday camps, debutantes' balls and festivals of nostalgia. I thought of how casually that line 'new music' is tossed around. Only when you are in the eye of the storm as the composer, do you appreciate what a Loch Ness Monster of elusiveness it is.

As if someone had opened the door and let the chill into my shed, the atmosphere changed on the end of the line. He'd moved closer to the piano. I could hear his voice over some well-worn, honkytonk blues.

"So yeah. Daniel?"

"On it, Torin, but…"

As I was speaking, a low vocal tone smothered the piano in the background.

"And get some new beats on them…" His voice faded out. He was speaking to someone instead of me.

He was back again. "I can't be doing with those mouldy plumber *chops and fills* old what's-his-name used to play. Everyone's heard them before…"

Again, he'd faded out. I listened to laughter blending on the other end of the line.

"And dust that sampler off. No more steam-driven noodling, young man. Give me fresh meat…*ha-ha!*"

The piano stopped playing. He left me hanging there for about ten seconds.

"Rustle up another 'Silent Storm'. I know you've got it in you. Ideas are the what?"

My mouth refused to form the words.

"Correct," he answered for me. "The currency."

"OK Torin, try to get down to rehearsals. We've only got two more. The girls need you."

"I will, I will. *Dreadful* worrier…Look, gotta ring off."

He and the club were gone. I examined the crusty ends of the lasagne that were too tough to chew. Inedible. I turned everything off and walked back to the kitchen.

***

While my eyeballs flitted behind my tightly shut eyes, my stomach churned like a cement mixer. My world was crumbling, but who cares. It's entertainment, a job, right? The new way is the only way: gigs, gigs, gigs. If I had to take over the whole shebang, I would. I'd do what I had to do to survive. I'd get this shitty thing done, and done, and done. My forefinger fluttered below my right eye. I stood up. I *must* get laughing boy to rehearsals, I needed to check whether Barney had got hold of the accountant, I needed to get the girls paid. I flopped back onto the bed. I needed to sleep.

Gripping the edge of the mattress with my left hand, the fingernails of my right excavated the area around my eye until the blood ran down my cheek. The itching thereafter was sensual, calming and I drifted off. In minutes, my unseeing eyeballs were dancing again and the cement mixer below my heart had recommenced its sickening rotation. As my thoughts bashed into each other, breaking and chipping, I sat bolt upright.

"It's him!" I said to my empty bedroom.

The person who had taken my seat in the Chinese restaurant and tilted up my beloved's chin as if he owned her, was the same person that had embraced my singer like a long-lost brother last night.

"Fuck!" I said, turning on the light.

The sound of the sea whooshed in my ears. I was back at Sienna, squeezing my head around the door of the room downstairs, trying to marry up what she'd been telling me for weeks with what I'd seen in there. I fingered the area on my head the door had slammed into, hoping again to feel that tenderness, but instead found myself reciting that restaurant menu in Wardour Street: *'Shellfish bisque with chervil cream, potted shrimps with Melba toast, griddled South Devon sole…'*

His voice was unmistakable. Low, penetrating, it had drowned out the happy family, singing their goodbyes through the Chinese restaurant exit and it had leaked down Torin's phone when I spoke to him from the shed last night. I looked away from the menu on the wall to study the two of them when they'd met. He was obviously not one of Torin's cokey sycophants. All the actions I'd seen him take, from removing Kerry's baseball cap to the condescending pat of Torin's cheek on greeting, were those of a man not used to taking a backward step. I'd followed them to the corner of Dean Street before scuttling off to Oxford Circus station.

The floorboards on the landing creaked outside my door as I stared into the mirror.

"Daniel?"

"I'm sleeping mum."

My reflection was a mess, but I did not attempt to repair it. All I could ask it was how the fuck did that bloke know Torin and how the fuck did he know her? And then, an even more mind-bending question began forming itself.

16

As well as old CDs and MiniDiscs on the lofty shelves in my shed, there is a sizable plastic container shoved behind the desk. The container can only be accessed by pulling out the boxes of cables and bits of old circuitry that block it in. I packed and pushed it up there after Rotterdam, then reopened it a few weeks ago to hide the photos and posters that I took off the walls when I committed the synth-bass to the computer program. I'd vowed not to open it again.

With the birds twittering in the early morning garden, I lugged it out and lifted off the lid. After removing a stack of past tour T-shirts, a nest of backstage lanyards, fraying set lists and obscure CDs and vinyl, I pulled out a wedge of US tour itineraries – twenty or so pages detailing the hotels and gig dates of our many trips across the pond – and spread them on the carpet in front of me. Selecting the pamphlet from our last tour, I flicked through the pages, incredulous that I'd actually visited all those towns and cities and made a unique connection with the people in them.

I remembered how we, as is the tradition in these matters, would give these printed tour schedules sarcastic titles: 'Book of Lies', 'Book of Dreams', 'The Agent's Great Work of Fiction', as if the 'oh so jaded us' knew that the details were inexact and amateurish, put together by office jockeys who hadn't a clue about the geography of their own country and were careless, bordering on sadistic, with our stage times, the distances between shows and rest days. Reclining in our Silver Eagle luxury, we'd play the seasoned blasé rockers, *'Oh no, we playing there again?'* If obfuscation could ever be acceptable, it would have been in the smiles we swapped, knowing the 'pamphlet' was fantasy literature made amazing fact for us – dozens and dozens of destinations, each one a gig and each gig a guaranteed, unbelievable high.

I turned a page and a blizzard of images: hotel and dressing rooms, smiling strangers, opening acts, shopping malls and meals passed through my mind. I remembered how cities, like glass and steel stalagmites, sprouted out of the plains and valleys or loomed hypnotically at the end of dead-straight highways through the bus's front window.

Although I was sitting in the daylight, English soil a foot or two beneath me, I imagined the tour bus gently lurching as its countless wheels, gears and levers lulled me in the small hours after a show.

"All those overnighters", I said quietly.

There are some that can't sleep in a tour bus bunk, they're preference is the immobility of a hotel room (and a lot more than eight inches of space above their heads), but I always slept soundly in mine.

I turned another page and found myself reading the list of dates we played in the Deep South. I smiled, remembering Mick remarking "Magnolia doesn't mean council house wallpaper out here."

We'd just completed the last of three shows in a row with long overnight drives in between. It was a slog and we had only enough energy for playing and climbing the stairs into the bus afterwards. I was trying to think if there was a day off in Baton Rouge on that Thursday. It says that we played Charlotte, but I vaguely recall the dates being swapped, so it was Birmingham maybe? Had they, the careless sadists back at the agency out west, slotted in an open-air gig in Atlanta on the day off? A funfair, fluttering flags over the festival stage, a rollercoaster? I *do* recall Torin finding it very tough and I felt for him. To watch his on-stage steely jaw soften and a startled lip-chewing wince emerge when he turned away from the hordes never failed to sadden me because this game had not, and never would, come naturally to him.

On the night I'm thinking of…it *was* North Carolina, things got really hairy on stage and Alana had had to nudge him maybe twenty times. Gradually, we'd got the 'interventions' down to around six or seven a gig, but because we'd not stopped for days, his concentration had left the building, and she'd had to 'do the business' loads. Halfway through the first song he was going absent in places he'd usually attend. Concerned looks were swapped when he sang the chorus of *'They've taken everything (from me)'.* over the opening verse of *'Brothers'*. For the entire fifty minutes, Alana, as well as playing bass and having to nail vocals of her own, had to mind him much as you would a toddler playing by a busy road. That we'd got away with it was far more satisfying than the many encores we garnered that night.

In sheer relief we fell, ramshackle with beers and towels into the back lounge. Upstairs, Torin lay in his bunk over the driver's cabin, dead to the world. The engine purred soothingly below and soon, the suburbs flashed by, and darkness engulfed us. Extracting, then opening a couple of bottles from the ice bin, Mick handed one to Alana. "That's the worst I've seen him since, maybe the first gigs we did when we warmed up for your mate's band."

"He was a touch trying," was Alana's rueful reply.

"Four years ago," I added, nicely tipsy and resigned to the monotone miles ahead with my best mates.

"If I had a dollar for every time I've had to mouth where the speaking part comes in *'Spell'*, I'd have…?"

"Three hundred dollars?"

"Three fucking thousand!" There was a moment of quiet before she spoke again. "Don't know if you boys know, he was doing three grand a week on Charlie, as well as two or three hundred on hookers for him and his pals."

"What, when?"

"When we got to number one. No, let me correct that, four grand a week. God knows how much he spends now." Her words cast a pall over the gentle euphoria. Not for years had we questioned the moody 'guests' that knocked on the dressing room doors after soundchecks, 'friends' that barely glanced at us before scuttling off with our singer somewhere private in the empty pre-show auditoriums. We and the crew were on a modest per diem. The wads of cash weighing down Torin's harem pants could not have been accounted for in the tour budget. Our American TM had mentioned something about a private account, but he was purposefully vague and as bound in music business obfuscation as we were.

"However tight he was with money for us – from *our* advance – he was always generous with his friends down the club." She swigged. "Yes boys, you've given a lot of wankers a fine night out with your graft."

"Four grand a week," Mick's black lashes flared. "We were on a hundred and fifty quid. I was still living at home!"

As we passed a ubiquitous truck stop, the lounge was lit up suddenly.

"A major part of us breaking up was that he couldn't get hard," she belched. "He said it was because I was a dry old bat or something horrible, but it was the coke and the wine. Hate to think of what he asked those poor women to do for him."

"When you two stopped going to the club, he made me go with him. Not actually in the room, but I'd wait outside, until…" My voice trailed off.

"We know, Daniel," said Alana. "We used to wonder how you put up with it."

The bus rumbled over dim memories. The thing was, going home to mum and the flats after playing live on TV, or having been photographed in some creative location in Docklands, or whisked from the airport in a limo and dropped at some posh eatery in Kensington, was like admitting that however well I did, I would always be the funny-faced kid with the depressed mother on benefits, and I fought that image with all my heart.

"Because of what happened to me," I said to Alana. "Being unpopular at school, and then this bloke, you know, such a brilliant 'star' wanting me to hang out with him."

"But we're all brilliant in our own way Daniel," she said with a smile.

We fell silent. A steel guitar leaked from the front to the end of the bus.

"Innit funny how they always put on country late at night," Mick said, *'Gypsies tramps and thieves…'* he sang, before gently elbowing me. "Perhaps they know there's a 'good ol' English country boy' on the bus."

"You should be made to wear a Stetson, Daniel," said Alana. "A fucking huge one that completely dwarfs you. You should actually be made to open the show with a little banjo solo…Oh no Daniel," she said (I'd probably gone all 'Daniel looking'), "I'm only joking."

"I'll do it if you say I should."

"I know you would," she said gently. "You're such a trouper. And *you're* not getting away with it either," she said, focusing on Mick. "*You* should be made to sit on a bog seat instead of a drum stool."

"What about you," he replied.

But we didn't come up with anything, because there'd never been an obvious way we could take the piss out of her.

In the world of nine-to-five and train schedules, it would have been the right time to call it a night, but because of the late gigs and the stress and chaotic sleep patterns, we were wide awake, wrapped up in our own exhausted thoughts, and an incident came to me when the piss *had* been taken out of her, but with none of the levity we were enjoying there and then. It was at the beginning of the tour. The record company's publicity department, grateful that they had Torin and Alana to themselves, had arranged an extensive press day. At the end of it I was sitting with them both in the Gothic bar of our hotel in Manhattan. No idea where Mick was, well I had some idea.

After being guests on a couple TV breakfast shows, the two of them had been in photo sessions and interviews well into the afternoon. They had been glued to each other in the limo since breakfast, so it was a mercy that the final couple of interviews were taking place in the hotel bar. After the last one, Alana said she was going up to her room for a lie-down before we set off for soundcheck. She'd been having stomach cramps all day.

As the lift doors shut on her, Torin exploded in a frenzy, running around the bar clutching his stomach "Got me period, got me period!" he squawked, causing the hotel denizens to rear up fearfully. He then proceeded to lay on his back, open his legs, insert an imaginary tampon and screech (in a voice that was like Alana's, but never with words she'd use), "Fuckin' curse, boohoo, ooh muvvah, got me mumphlies!"

Flopping breathlessly beside me, he studied me with a twinkling, triumphant eye.

"Save some of that for tonight, man," I told him.

"Fuck all that relationship shit." He was panting, turning a large glass of red in his hand. "If I want it, I put my money down and get it done. What do I need some hormonal female for? I've got it on tap without the ball-ache of having to listen to her whining, or remember her fucking birthday, or buy her clothes, or whatever."

I couldn't imagine Alana wanting a man to buy anything for her or remember her birthday.

"Why the pout, Daniel. We've sold out New York."

I felt a subtle deceleration as the bus changed gear. Cher sang the last lines of 'Gypsies, Tramps and Thieves' as the tour manager popped his head into the lounge. "Stopping for gas. You guys wanna get a bite?"

Back in my shed, it came to me in a flash. It wasn't North Carolina, it was the drive north after the college gig in Austin.

At one in the morning, we found ourselves walking the vast aisles of a hypermarket. There were endless racks of guns and ammo and, wandering about, huge humans who were as curious about us, as we were about them.

Because he fell for the salesgirl's warm brown eyes and warm brown voice, "Y'all from outa state, right…?" Corbossa was obliged to buy a pair of cowboy boots. Hilarious, him looking so bow-legged, scowling at us as we pointed and hooted behind him, the assistant smiling encouragement. Never one to back down, he promised he'd wear them on the drums, but I don't remember that he did. He left them in a hotel somewhere. Alana bought me that Stetson, a very nice item, grey and smooth. Actually, suited her better. It's probably still hanging on a dressing room hook out there.

Having returned to the bus, boots and hat purchased, huge breakfast consumed, we were soon back in that intimate world of tour bus confessional. The week before, Mick had opened up about his trouble with the police when he was a kid and how it drove a wedge between his mum and dad and split them up for six months. A day or two after, on the Pacific Coast Highway between San Francisco and LA, Alana told us about her sister Elska, who was special and had burned so bright, but had died young. Later that night, I heard her crying quietly in her bunk.

I was the youngest, so they were patient with me. But that night, after the cowboy hat and boots, and the heady relief of getting away with it on stage, I sensed the conversation funnelling in the direction of my outsized leatherette armchair. Driving away from the hypermarket, with the smell of Texan leather permeating, I knew my turn had come.

"It's not much of a story," I said. I'd told them what had caused the damage (people always want to know that), but I'd not told them how. "When I was fourteen…"

Me, Sean and Rio were racing through the estate on our bikes. Rio was behind me, Sean in front. It was towards the end of the summer holidays. My birthday was in a week's time. Mum had had to use my front door key because she'd left hers in the café where she worked.

"If she hadn't, I probably wouldn't be sitting here. Mad isn't it?" My friends did not respond. "Mum had made me a sandwich in the morning so I could stay out until she came home from work at four."

We could have gone to Rio's and played on his PS2 if we'd got bored on our bikes, but his big brother didn't like us cramping his style. He was seventeen and had a girlfriend. They'd snog on the sofa, and we'd giggle through the living room door and wind him up. But it was irrelevant, because we never got bored on our bikes. How could you? So, we headed for the park. It was where we hung out almost every day of the summer holidays.

There were always broken bottles and stuff in the alleys and walkways between the blocks. A shard punctured my front tyre and I ground to a halt. Rio shot past me. I called after him to tell him, but he'd gone. I had a puncture repair kit at home, but mum had my key. My friends were already over the park. I was hamstrung with a flat and the knowledge that the holidays would be over soon and I'd be stuck in a classroom with the days getting shorter.

There was a mechanic called Steve who serviced my mum's car. He had one of the garages under the railway arches between the estate and the park. He'd fixed a puncture for me before. He'd also lined up my wheels and tightened my handlebars and brakes.

I wheeled my wounded bike down to the big doors, but they were shut. I realised that the small side door was ajar and lifted my bike over the step and into the garage. There was a car on the ramp. I called out, but no one answered. I noticed there was a rectangular blue bucket with a black box on top of it. The box was upside down and set at an angle. The top (now the bottom of the box), had nodules on it. It had been wedged diagonally on the bucket so it couldn't slip off. I don't know why, with the hundred and one things I could have investigated in there, I was attracted to the skew-whiff, upside-down box on the big blue oblong bucket, but attracted, I was. I walked over and peered in. The bucket was two-thirds full of opaque gunk. I noticed there was another black box next to the bucket. This box was the right way up. It was old and scarred and had greeny-white furry stuff encrusted on the nodules. It also had two circular holes in the ends of it.

Peering into the bucket, it was plain that the gunky liquid was being drained from the box placed over it. I spotted three similarly empty boxes nearby. Steve had left this one to drain while he'd popped out somewhere. I could see that it wasn't dripping anymore, and I thought, I'll help him, after all, he'll be fixing my tyre any minute. The box was resting at an angle, so I gripped both corners and attempted to lift it off the bucket's rim. It was very heavy. I managed to get one end up, but I couldn't hold the other. It came to me a second too late that this was a man-sized job.

What occurred next plays in my head as a series of frames, sections of time that I can isolate and control. In reality, what happened took less than three seconds. I felt the left corner slip from my fingers and watched the box begin its modest, ten-inch descent towards the liquid. But as it was falling, and before it broke the surface, I leaned in to try to rescue it. I was concerned that I was mucking up Steve's careful 'box draining arrangement'. My face was directly over the bucket at the moment the corner of the box fell in.

"The last thing I saw was..."

I looked away from the bus window and into the lounge. I became aware that 'Wichita Lineman' was playing on the radio, the strings pulling me backwards in time. My bandmates were waiting, and I realised that I'd never vocalised this exact sequence before.

"My mum had a lava lamp, and you know how sluggishly it moves, that coloured stuff inside, when you switch it on. Well, it always seems like that in my memory. A fat blob of lava lamp-shaped battery acid rising from the bucket and splashing into my eye. But I'd closed it tight, so my sight was saved."

Like that slow-motion action of years ago, the strings seemed to lengthen on the driver's radio.

"I can remember the ambulance. Steve in a state. The police. I couldn't feel much in the way of pain just then. Later though, I did. I remember mum sitting in a chair next to my bed in the hospital. She was twisting a hankie or something in her fingers. A nurse called Elaine...that's it. Then I was home."

"What about the scarring, Daniel?" asked Mick.

"That wasn't from the accident. Well, it was, and it wasn't. When it started getting better it itched like fuck and was right down to my lips and across my nose. Like someone had coloured in a purple pear drop on my face."

Their silence begged further details.

"It's because of what *I* did."

"You'll have to explain," Alana said. I could see only their eyes in the dark of the lounge. There was a burger jingle on the radio now.

"When I went back to school I got bullied for the way it looked. I mean, you can't rationalise things at that age. And you never think that you'll recover." I paused as 'Galveston' oozed from the radio, there must have been a Glen Campbell special. I exhaled. "Look, I picked the scabs off. The scars were healing, but I picked them. It was a completely destructive thing to do, OK!"

Mick leaned over and patted my knee. "Easy man, we're your friends."

I suddenly felt exhausted.

"It wasn't the battery acid that did this, it was me when I came back from school. Some of the kids were merciless. One real bully would be at me every day for the way I looked, a kid called Craig, he's the one that would start the 'pizza face' chant and everyone'd join in. At home time, he'd hang about on the alley bars smoking, knowing I would have to get past him – it was brutal. So anyway, a dermatologist told me years later, that if I hadn't picked at my skin, it would have healed completely."

"Your mother?" asked Alana softly.

"She's never been the strongest. Single parent. Stupidly young when she had me. The guilt she suffers, leaving her keys at the café, her having mine so I couldn't go home and do the repair myself, it never leaves her."

"Poor woman."

"She's on antidepressants. Never went back to work. She likes to know where I am. Even if I'm in Tokyo or somewhere mad like that, I have to call her. She has these weird rules about going out. Drives her little car down to the shops even though they're a five-minute walk away. At the same time, she gets very anxious when I'm quiet, because that's what I was like, when I used to pick. Funny game we play. She thinks I'm hopeless and need to be cared for, when it's her that does."

***

On that Thursday, during the penultimate rehearsal before the Shepherd's Bush show, Daisy, Bluebell and I had an interruption in Room Three. It was from the guys in the band that had woken me up on the sofa last week. But it was naughty because Jake would have told them we were in there. It was during a gap between songs that two heads peeked around the big, padded door.

"We didn't hear anything, sorry..."

"Wrong room..."

After a quick scan, they shut the door and I pressed the spacebar. Daisy and Bluebell's eyes narrowed as the 'tick tock' leaked from their earpieces and bang, we were in.

After we'd run through the set, Bluebell reliably asked if Torin was coming in. I told her I was working on it and not to worry. She tilted her head in a precursor of a smile, but the smile never materialised.

"Let's have a break," I said.

I left the room. Approaching the reception area, I could hear conversation. I paused. Jake was speaking.

"No, not seen Torin at all this week. He came in on the first day last week though. Daniel's been in here MDing those two tasty birds." I heard a male laugh. For the last couple of days, the girls had been rehearsing in their stage gear: leathers, heels and lipstick.

"Yeah, but the sound of it," someone said. "People are gonna know it's playback. How can you have Torin without Corbossa and Alana?"

"Daniel Earl wasn't miming, and Torin will be singing. I mean, it's not what it was, but I dunno...Loved that first album. It's all a bit sad."

I was going to step in, but another voice piped up. "Why do bands do that, become a covers band of their own band. The same set of session men rotated at those festivals. Interchangeable. You see it all the time now."

The sound of that lighter flicked inside me. I coughed and stepped in. Jake was behind the glass-top reception desk with its strings, sticks and Mars bars arrayed beneath. The lads who had 'accidentally' popped their heads into our room were on the sofa.

"Alright, Daniel," they chorused.

I nodded and walked towards the toilets. When I returned to Room Three, the girls were in jeans and trainers.

"Tomorrow's our last day," Bluebell said, shouldering her bag. "We can't wander on stage like strangers."

"I'll get him down."

"You're sure?"

"Definitely."

"We'll go home then. This is pointless. We've gone as far as we can without him here. There's stuff I just can't do on my own. I mean, when should I join him at the mic the way Alana does on the video? He said he'd go through it with me. He's been here once. On my first day. I don't know when to come in and out Daniel, especially on the choruses. It's stressing me out. See you tomorrow at eleven."

"But we can still…".

"I don't think so."

I hated these sorts of confrontations. In the past, it was always Alana who dealt with issues with the crew and tour managers, fall-outs, stuff like that. "I understand. Just so you know, he's practising every day." She was shaking her head as I ploughed through the obfuscation. "He's been overwhelmed with promo and stuff. Lots of meetings. I think he's had a throat infection too…mild. But he is going through the set at home. He told me."

Daisy interrupted me, "We know you resent us being here. We're not real musicians, but we've got a job to do, and we won't be able to do it properly unless we rehearse with the frontman."

"I get that. I don't resent you, I..."

"You don't have to sugar-coat it, Daniel." Bluebell smiled at last. "We were fans. I had a poster of Alana on my bedroom wall when I was at school. But I'm a single mum now, and I need this gig. Daisy does too."

The primary reason Bluebell had been selected above the other candidates was her exhaustive knowledge of our repertoire. She knew every word and nuance, a true fan. During that 'getting to know each other' run through at the beginning of last week, she'd been so consumed with getting her parts right and impressing us, she'd not paid much attention to Torin's pitiful efforts. And anyway, even if she had thought he was a tad sketchy, who was she to comment on the great man's performance.

Resigned that the girls would shuffle off and I'd see them tomorrow, I flopped onto the sofa and stared at the islands of tea, coffee and beer, indelibly stained in the carpet between my feet.

"OK," I said, "I understand. See you then."

But when I looked up, they hadn't moved.

"Sorry. I get it, I really do."

Although I'd known them for a bit less than a fortnight, I regarded them as colleagues. But standing over me, I felt no mateyness radiating in my direction. I'd not prepared myself for negativity from them because I thought of them as I thought of myself: cogs in the machine, turning, rubbing along, getting through the shifts. But they'd turned hard, and the wheels had stopped.

Bluebell hitched her bag up. "Both of our cheques bounced."

"For last week as well?"

"Yes. We checked our accounts this morning."

"Fuck."

"This is shit, man. I've got a kid to feed."

"Fuck. Sorry, I'll..." I stood quickly and walked to my set-up. I took the cheque book from my pocket and wrote out two cheques. "This is from my personal account, so there won't be any problem."

Wordlessly, they took the cheques.

"Look, sorry about this," I said. "I know what's happened. There's been a communication hitch with our accountant. Barney's been trying to remedy it. The wrong amounts were err…ascribed? And then there was some problem with the insurance and…don't worry. It'll all work out." They were cool, folding their cheques away, and I felt ashamed that they knew I was flannelling them. As they opened the big door I stood up. "Bluebell, there's something else. It's quite important, actually."

And because they now knew the true nature of the thing in which they were involved, the absolute, flaky-as-fuck amateurishness of it, they knew too, it was worth paying *proper* attention to the arch obfuscator, offering them a place on the knackered sofa. I closed the big door and like a barrister, took the floor. "Sometimes. When he's under a bit of stress, Torin can go missing."

Daisy squinted up. "Missing? Like not coming to rehearsals for nearly two weeks?"

"No err, something even more…unprofessional?"

"Daniel?"

"This happens three times, maybe four times a show."

"What does?"

"Torin. He forgets where he is, arrangement wise."

They didn't get it, but who would?

"He loses his place in the songs."

"The songs he wrote?" said Bluebell.

Daisy added. "The songs we've all seen him sing?"

"It's a very strange phenomenon." I stopped pacing and leaned against the bass cabinet. "So, practicalities. Bluebell, on the night, you might need to err, cue him in."

"Cue him in?"

"Yeah, just start the line off for him in the verses. When you see him hesitate?"

"Hesitate. How will I know?"

"Believe me, you will."

They continued to squint up at me. "He will have a…a certain look on his face. He'll lack confidence. Get his attention, face him, count him in, perhaps give him a poke in the chest, tread on his foot."

"Tread on his foot?"

"Yeah, then sing the line."

She blinked. "What the fuck?"

"No one will see. You'll have your back to the crowd."

"Won't that look a bit rubbish?"

"Nah, on the night it'll be mayhem. It'll look like he's ad-libbing… fashionably late, ha-ha."

Just then, sweaty and breathy, Barney entered the rehearsal room. "Sounding good, ladies and gents?" he asked.

"Better than ever," Daisy said, as they both stood.

His double-take would have been comic if it wasn't for the stress lines embedded in his pout and the bloodless pallor that the room's cod stage lighting cruelly emphasised. "Going so soon girls?" he called as they opened the door. "I've paid my twenty pounds and demand music, music, music!"

As the door shut, he fell into the sofa. I stood over him.

"I've just written the girls a cheque for their wages for the last two weeks. What the fuck, Barney?"

He gave me his best 'allow me to show you this thirty-eight-inch Sanyo flat screen television' smile. But all I could think of was my decimated current account. After five years, I now had about a grand left in it.

Humming the chorus to 'Brothers', he began to retrieve his laptop from his satchel. I wanted to ram it between his teeth. "Seriously though," he said, turning it on, "how's it all sounding?"

The lighter flicked a couple of times in my head.

"It's sounding like it does every fucking day, man. It's playback! The girls sound the same and Torin sounds the same. I'm so depressed with this shit that even I sound the fucking same *and* I'm paying for the pleasure. That was my mortgage money, man!"

"I only meant..."

"This," I said, waving my hand at the walls, "used to be a place of expression, passion…joy! In here, we play music. Fuck knows what you'd call it now, but it ain't what I signed up for!" I picked up my mac. "How's it all sounding? Fuck me," I muttered, walking to the door. Before I wrenched it open, I glanced behind me. Barney was sitting there, dumb and beaten, his faithful laptop pressed to his ample bosom, in a vain bid for comfort.

I sighed. "Sorry mate."

His bottom lip was quivering.

"When was the last time you spoke to him?" I asked.

"He hasn't answered my calls for three days. I had the agent on the phone for an hour this afternoon. Torin sent him an email behind my back, said half the hotels were shit and we are going to drive back to London after the gigs."

I shook my head in disbelief. "So, we come off stage, get on the bus and drive back? But he's not even travelling with us. He hasn't for years."

Barney wiped his palm across his face. "He is now. Everything's being cut back. Not even getting a rider or per diems."

I held up my palm. "Hang on, you're telling me we drive three, four hours after a show back to London, drop our bags at the door *then* get back on the bus and drive back up!"

He nodded.

"To save on fucking hotels?"

"Yes, anything south of Leeds. The agent managed to get us hotels for Scotland, but Torin's flying back. Telling you, that agent is furious, Daniel. I think he might bin the whole thing."

"He can't!"

Because I'd lost my retainer, this tour had taken on life-saving portents. I'd calculated that the first few gigs would reimburse me after I'd given my ring-fenced mortgage money to the girls. I shut my eyes and had a brief vision of mum, looking into the garden for the last time.

"Tell me that again, Barney."

He was looking at me through the fingers of his hand. "He said he's got meetings he needs to get back for. '*Real* business', he said. And he thinks the girls are taking the piss asking for stage clothes on the budget. The last thing he said to me was to look for a couple of replacements. He's not turned up for promo, interviews, even radio ones."

"The show's in two fucking days!"

"Read the email from the agent, Daniel. He found out…"

His voice trailed off. He looked totally beaten, even paler now than ten minutes ago.

"Found out what?"

"Torin's raided the tour budget to pay his dealer. Well, I think it's his dealer. Pinky Forbes told me. *He's* after Torin too. The money for the crew and bus, petrol, the girl's wages, mine too. I don't think I can handle much more, Daniel."

I flopped down next to him.

"What do you think has happened?"

He shook his head. "It's to do with a property deal and Conrad."

"Conrad," I echoed.

"Do you know him?"

Although I'd never even met him, this person was looming

larger and larger in my rear-view mirror.

"No."

"His financial advisor, I think he said he was."

The sweat was trickling down his temple. The sound of the bands either side of our room seeped into the doubtful silence in ours. I stood up and gave his shoulder a gentle pat. "It's alright mate. We'll go down there and see him."

As we exited the room, Jake walked past us without a word. Selecting a key from the jangling bunch on his belt, he locked our studio door.

Passing through the reception area, nodding at the two men who were discussing our 'personnel changes' earlier, I heard Jake clear his throat.

"Daniel, Barney?"

He'd returned to the stool behind the desk. Pressing his palms into the glass, he leaned towards us and gravely drew breath. "There's a bit of a problem."

I could not imagine things getting worse, but the way Jake averted his eyes when I looked at him indicated that they had.

"What's up?"

"The boss, he told me to lock your room."

I suddenly realised how unusual it was: Jake locking our room right after we'd finished using it.

"You owe a grand. You haven't paid your bill since you've been in here."

Barney would not meet my eye when I looked at him. I held my finger up and pulled my tour manager into the corridor. "The band account. I need to go to the bank and get this money out."

He shook his head.

"There *has* to be a grand in it."

"No, there isn't. It's empty. That's what I've been trying to tell you. Torin has had the lot."

I felt sick. That account Alana had set up was sacrosanct, independent of tour budgets and contracts. It was for rehearsals – the place we did our work. It always had about fifteen hundred quid in it, money we'd all chipped in. To empty it was impossible. She had set it up so that two people had to sign before anything could be withdrawn.

"I haven't been paid in a fortnight," Barney whispered, wide-eyed. "I've been shelling out for everything. I've got nothing left."

I looked past him at Room Three's door.

"All my gear's in there, the girls' stuff. We've got our last rehearsal tomorrow, Roy's coming down and Torin *has* to be there, he's not sung for months."

Eyes were on me when I returned to the reception area. "Administrative error," I said with a smile. "I'll write a cheque."

With Barney wheezing at my shoulder, I got my pen out again and emptied my account for the son of a multimillionaire.

It was drizzling as we crossed Charing Cross Road, Barney babbling in my ear, jogging to keep up as I steamed towards Dean Street. "Seriously, all he ever talks about is this property and Conrad. He's drinking loads, never off the Charlie, or pilled up. Just won't address the band stuff. I told you; he stopped taking calls from me. Last time we spoke he really had a go, said it was an error of judgement bringing me in and it hurt, cos I've given him everything, bought him dinners, given him cash for taxis, wine. I…I…"

I stopped. "Alright man. I get it. Go home. I'll take care of it."

"Thanks Daniel. I knew I could rely on you. You're the strong one."

I watched him waddle away with his fashionable leather satchel and exhaled.

That I'd just paid eight hundred quid of my own money to rehearse in that 'modest' room was dire, but what was worse was the neck-burning embarrassment I felt writing the cheque out in front of Jake and the two blokes from the other band. We had played the four corners of the earth, our records had sold in their hundreds of thousands, and here I was, in public, bailing out my band from the current account that paid for my mum's shopping.

Jill looked up immediately from behind her desk when I walked in. My heart sank. Her look said everything as she took me to one side.

"He's not here?" I asked.

She shook her head. "They are not best pleased. He owes over a grand on his tab and he's behind on his membership, too."

"When was he last in?"

"About three days ago."

I nodded. That was when I saw him outside The Marquee with Conrad.

"Gonna sort it all out."

Approaching that amazing property, my head spun in memory. Had it been that long ago since I'd stood outside it on that broiling summer's day, mouth hanging open, gawping at the flawless stucco and countless glinting windows?

I peered up at the first floor and recalled how the sun's rays had lit up the chandelier's glass droplets like a sci-fi special effect. In my head, I heard my Casio giving it everything and Alana driving and weaving her bass lines in between. I was back at the birth of our sound. Our big bang. I almost smiled remembering Torin, standing at the microphone, bewildered that two people who had never met each other could create music in front of him, instantaneously. But I didn't crack that smile, I muttered his name bitterly instead. Five years later he *still* looked like that at the mic, the commander of a world he had no authority in. It wasn't the fact that Torin hadn't any discernible musical talent, it was that even with the hit records and tours and acclaim, rose petals strewn at his feet, he had not loved it. It was profoundly sad that all the joy I'd had, all the love from the audience directed at us, hadn't touched him. He'd not even known there was any.

I blinked into the present as the double doors opened. In her sixties, she was of that tribe of cut-glass, coiffured aristocrats that a person I once knew could spot through the misted-up window of a budget restaurant. When I last stood here, I would never have known that the handbag she carried in one diamond-white glove was worth as much as a decent second-hand family car. Despite the wispy grey, she'd retained a timeless equine beauty. The upward tilt of her jaw, the uninterruptable gaze, and the fact that you could not take your eyes from her, meant she could be only one person.

"Mrs DeVere?"

"Yes?"

Her appraisal of me was detached.

"Err…you don't know me?"

"Daniel Earl."

"Ha, yeah."

"Of course," she said with an affronted blink. "I know you and Michael and Alana."

I stuttered mentally. She was having the same effect on me that her son had on the first few heaving rows of fans when slowly, he raised his head from the rutted wooden boards of a stage.

"Oh...err, how are you? Nice to meet you, finally."

She calmed me with a small, unaffected smile that vanished in a second.

"He's not here."

"Oh, OK, I'll..."

"Has he absconded?" she said, as I turned towards the tube station.

"Sorry?"

"Taken off."

"Ha-ha, kind of."

"Was there money involved?"

"Well, the band..."

The sound of tyres crunching at my back caused me to pause. I stepped aside for a cap-wearing driver to park the Bentley, scoot around the front and open the door for her.

She stayed him with her hand. "You don't need to go into details, Daniel. I imagine you've found out about everything a little too late?" She set that special gaze in the direction of the corner property on Campden Hill Square. "I was relieved when he joined Alana's group. He'd been floating around doing nothing for a couple of years." She looked at me directly. "You know, I never spoke to Alana, Torin wasn't keen for us to meet. I do know she was a good, strong woman, but there you have it, strong and good are not happy bedfellows with my precious little boy."

'...*nor women neither,*' I said to myself.

Although she was as beautiful as her 'precious little boy', she had something not bequeathed to him. Something inside that can be read from outside. I thought it might be integrity, honour?

"He's done it before, Daniel. He's stolen thousands from the family. I don't know what he's like as a musician, but if it's anything like he was as a property investor…Oh, I see. I am sorry." The pause she gave me to collect myself was a gift. "It has taken his father and me fifteen years to finally accept that Torin, has not a jot of decency in him." She stepped into the car. The chauffeur shut the door. Her window came down. "Live and learn, young man. At least you have the time to."

Up came the window and she was gone. Walking towards Holland Park station, I saw her car's brake lights flash, before it turned left. The baffling thing was that I had cared for Torin as much as I did for Alana and Mick. Watching him skid to a halt at the front of the stage with his arms open wide *never* failed to delight me. And later, in the blinking, rheumy chaos of his club, his foppish, trust-fund ways and cod-trampiness endeared him to me just as much. He was the attention-seeking, cross-dressed, leather-clad, party animal supreme. The deep thinker with the attention span of a four-year-old, and as I've said, he'd given me my life. But, stepping out of the lift and walking onto the platform, I knew I'd finally reached the tipping point we all come to with people who take advantage of our good nature, the 'users' of this world. As the train roared in, I ruminated on how it takes seconds to recognise that someone is taking the piss out of you, but a long, long time before you do anything about it.

***

You'd have thought that after the day I'd had, the *week* I'd had, I'd want to drink myself into oblivion, swallow a maraca's worth of pills or inhale clouds of conscience-deadening weed, but here I was, concealed, squinting through a curtain of drizzle at the mannequins in the shop window across the square.

No hint of yellow splashed the pavement. Sienna was in darkness. The leaves of the great green bush looked like they'd been coloured in, in black marker pen.

I could hear a beat, housey, swinging from a place behind me. A tight, more rocky counter challenged from a café nearby. For a couple of seconds, they were synchronised perfectly. Glass flashed as the door opened. She wore her waist-pinching spy mac, collar up, perfect for the moment. I might buy one myself.

She got the alarm sequence wrong and, although it was too far away for me to see, I knew that her eyes were screwed up in consternation below her pale blue cap. When she turned from the shop, the streetlight caught her face. She looked young. More accurately, she wore her 'young look'. To me, it was her most tragic guise. That girly tossing of the head, the stunned blink and waxy shop-front smile grieved me because I knew the effort it took for her to make it. Kerry was never happier than when she *wasn't* trying to be.

Ramming the baseball cap over her eyes, she trapped the silver bag against her side and walked purposely into the weather. I felt responsible for her doing that, the trapping thing with her bag. I'd nagged her about leaving it open for the dippers around here. I wondered if she heard my voice when she performed that cautious action. I'd not left much of a legacy. No show-stopping memories. A few budget Chinese meals, the weird fusion thing in Beak Street, a frame of snooker, some long walks and tea and cake. Yes, tea and cake.

I followed her into the mall in Bond Street station. She bought a burger and chips, and covering the Styrofoam carton with one hand, consumed it on the way back to the shop. I was surprised by the state of her white, now grey/brown, tennis shoes as they padded through the wet ahead of me. Holey and worn at the heel, they now seemed totally inadequate for the season.

She was punching in the code when I came up behind her.

"Don't forget your keys," I said.

She stepped into the shop without looking around or closing the door. I sat on the fluffy orange chair in the gloom and she, on the step that led to the counter. My gaze fell on the mannequin's cowboy boots and I thought of Mick asking Alana and me what we thought as he strode up and down that vast hypermarket aisle, and us laughing behind him. Alana had tilted up her Stetson and said that for the full effect he really needed to buy a horse.

I traced the eight notes on my thigh before touching the ridges and ruts around my eye.

"Who was that bloke in the restaurant?"

She didn't hesitate. "His name is Conrad."

"Is he your ex? Is he trying to get you back together?"
"It's complicated, sort of."
"OK."
"But we aren't…we've never been an item."
"An item?"
"I mean, he's had sex with me, but we've not ever liked each other, in that way."
"He knows my singer."
"Yes, I know. I know him too."

Lighters flicked, gigs played, smiles and grimaces of the years passed through my mind.

"So, you lied?"
"Of course."
"Of course?"
"It's what I do, Daniel."

I don't know how long it was before I spoke again.

"I know you do."
"I know, you know I do."
"Obfuscation."
"What?"

I sat forward in my chair. "It's a muddying. Like there's a bare fact, the truth, and it's unpalatable. Say, Torin being a not very nice person in private and having a reputation of saintliness in public, and those who work with him, work with him closely, never calling him out. But worse than that, never calling him out to themselves, because… you just want the dream to go on and on."

"At least yours was a dream."
"It was. It was brilliant."
"Is brilliant?"
"It's shit now."
"I'm lying again. I know it's shit."
"He tell you?"
"I just know. Some people are shit."

Kerry had an amazing eye for detail. Ambling along, she'd point out the ornate gable ends, never-noticed balconies and gravity-defying brickwork that I'd spent my 'collar up, chin down' life shuffling past.

She'd ask me questions concerning dates and influences and because I hadn't a clue, answer for me. About seventy percent of the time we spent together, she'd be having a conversation with herself. I missed her steering arm randomly pulling me across a road or her hand, yanking me to a halt outside a shop window.

Once, she stopped me in my tracks to stare at a brick wall. "This has been standing here since seventeen thirty-two, Daniel!"

"What has?"

"This building. Imagine the people who have passed through this door, geniuses, kings…"

"Rogues and murderers."

"Exactly."

"It's a hairdresser's. Did they have them in the eighteen hundreds?"

"You're being obtuse."

"Maybe for wigs?"

Before the obfuscation set in, I speculated that she may have been a tour guide, but I couldn't imagine her ever sticking to a script.

"Oh, look at those cakes."

"Yeah, nice."

"Which one would you have first? I'd go for that black cherry… oh no, the lemon. Do you like a lot of glaze? No, me neither. I would have a different one for breakfast every day of the week, if I could."

During our time together, she became an educator and breaker-down of barriers the accident had caused me to erect. Her looking like she did, and me looking like I did, I'd never have gone into those patisseries to buy her cake or sat in a restaurant with her. I'd have felt unworthy, batting above my average. I'd always been Mr Takeaway, Mr Get-the-fuck-out-pronto. Blockbuster sponsored my nights in. I wondered if she'd always been so garrulous, or if there was something in me that gave her license to illuminate the world the way she did. I missed too, the reasonless pole vaults between topics, the reassuring pat of the back of my hand and the meeting of my bashful eye across the soy and chilli dispensers. But mostly, I missed the laughter lines that spread, like a fractured icy puddle, when she looked at me, and me only.

She stood and ghosted down the stairs. The toilet flushed, and when she returned, she had two glasses of water. She placed one on the floor next to me before returning to the step by the till.

"You live down there," I stated.

"Yes."

"I mean…"

"But you knew I was lying."

"I did, but I didn't want it to be true."

"Neither did I, believe me. But it was good, our little bed of lies, don't you think?"

"It was the happiest I'd ever been."

"Living a lie?"

"Living a lie."

I couldn't see her smile, but I knew she was. "Why are you smiling?"

"Just remembering when you went to use the loo. And bang! That door is a death trap."

"Yeah, the mattress."

"If you don't know how to open it, it'll curl up against it and the recoil…So sorry."

I laughed. She did as well. "I had to keep a straight face watching you rubbing the side of your head the whole evening."

I'd wondered why her clothes were always crumpled. I thought it may have been some fashionable, 'anti-smart' aversion to ironing. Or, maybe like me, her mum did it for her. But when I'd peeked into where she slept, I saw that her clothes were crammed into council refuse bags at the end of the bed, so I settled for the 'Big O' and just got on with it.

"What was he like?"

"Who? Oh him. You *don't* want to know."

"I do," I said.

I thought about her dramatic reaction when, walking away from the snooker hall, I told her I played for Torin. She'd screamed and sprinted away from me, saying she'd forgotten to lock up the shop. Sitting here now, I realised her histrionics had nothing to do with the shop and everything to do with my disclosure. She'd been repulsed that I was in his band. Simple as that.

"Drink some water," she said, like a copper with bad news.

"So, your flat," my voice was tremulous now. "The one they're doing up?"

"Are you being cruel?"

"No, just that you said…"

"You've known for a while that I live downstairs."

"But you said, Kerry."

"Have you come all the way here to tell me what a liar I am? I've already admitted that I am. What's your point?"

"I'm just confused. Your mum?"

"I never knew her. I was left on the steps of a church in the west of Ireland when I was a day or two old."

"Kerry."

"The nun's called me that."

"But why didn't you tell me?"

"Don't take it personally, Daniel. I always lie about her. It doesn't matter who it is." She took a sip. "Sometimes she's a happy divorcee, lots of young chaps. *Mum, you're so embarrassing.* Sometimes an academic, wise, bookish. She's actually been a musician, a cellist. I didn't use that one on you for obvious reasons. She's often up north with dad. They are trying to make it work again."

"You always asked about my mum. I don't get it."

"I do that. I'm fascinated to know what it's like to have a mother's love. To have access to a thing more powerful than money or even a devoted husband. Unbidden care, just a step behind you during your entire existence. To me, the thought of that is like laying on the grass, looking at the sky and wondering where the universe ends."

I sensed she was entirely focused on me now.

"What's it like to know that you are not alone, Daniel, that there is a biological element in your life that's as natural as night following day. However clever or inept, rich or destitute she is, your mother will never abandon you. She'll advise and comfort you for no other reason than you are the wonder she produced and *that* will never change?"

"I thought everyone had a mum," I said quietly. I could feel her shift and look directly at me. She wasn't crying or impassioned.

"Do you remember your mum holding your hand when you

were a little boy? It's just there, isn't it. You don't look for it, it's…just there. Wherever you are, however spectacularly you mess up, that hand will always be there for you to hold on to."

"It isn't all that, Kerry."

"You will go home now, and you'll be upset, I know. But she'll be there, right? She'll ask you if you're OK and, even if she can't help you and you don't want her anywhere near you, she'll not leave you. I've seen it dozens of times. I know it's not unique to you, but to me, it's everything I've never had."

An instance from an evening out together popped into my head. Walking through Leicester Square after tea and cake, we came upon a crowd and a red carpet laid out in front of one of the big cinemas. I told her I'd actually been to the opening of some trashy horror flick in LA. The band had been celebrity guests. Me and Corbossa had ducked out halfway through the gory bore for a drink in the bar around the corner.

"I'm impressed Daniel, a Hollywood premiere," she'd said.

"Ever been to one?" I'd asked.

"Ha, no. I was once in a lift at the Cannes Film Festival with Quentin Tarantino."

"What?"

"At the Carlton. One of the girls I was with practically passed out. So funny."

The shop was in complete darkness now. The music outside had stopped. I glanced at her silhouette by the till. "Was the girl in the lift, the one that passed out in Cannes, Francine?"

I sensed her attention move to elsewhere in the shadows.

"You play the innocent. Daniel, but you join the dots so well."

A couple scuttled past the window, bowed, sharing an umbrella.

"Francine, my sister from another mister. So beautiful once. Now, as you've seen, a broken addict. I give her all the spare money I have…when I can find her. The life…rips everything from you."

"The life, Kerry?"

"Ah well…" And I heard in her voice a distant brogue.

We listened to the rain falling hard against the window. She finally drew breath. "It's always frustrated you, and I can understand that, seeing me put up with the way Pam treats me. And I know how angry you are that I sleep down there and that I don't have much in the way of cash."

"It's never been about money, Kerry. Just fairness."

Her laugh was the bark of a junkyard dog. The harshest sound I'd ever heard her make. I feared her, suddenly. I was frightened of what she'd seen and what she'd done. My obsession with her history was not going to provide me with a cosy reveal, the credits rolling down the screen to dreamy violins.

"I was brought up by nuns who beat me. They beat everyone, even the good girls. I ran away at fourteen and lived with various men. In and out of hostels, shelters, sleeping rough. All the men that 'took care' of me were ruined, irrational, drinkers, violent, users. At seventeen I was a streetwalking prostitute in Dublin, but not for long. I was 'discovered' and taken to London where I worked for other men, the same as the ones in Ireland, but with more money and more… ambition. And yes, I was in Cannes, and the Gorges Du Verdon, but I was sucking dicks, having fingers and worse inserted into me and all for dinner and a nice frock."

Listening to her was like standing in front of an open furnace. I looked away.

"I cannot be with you, Daniel." She was standing over me when I looked up.

"But why?"

"Because you know the truth, and that shines a light on me I cannot endure."

"I don't see any light."

"You have always known, not the details, but you've sensed that I'm…not right."

I nodded. I'd wondered why, at times, that shadow of gloom befell her, and now I had my answer. "You're right for me," I said quietly.

She tilted her head. "No lies."

"No lies."

"Then, the truth is, whenever I see you, I'll know you know."

"I don't…"

"I couldn't bear waking up and seeing you, all smiles and tea and cake, knowing that you know about where I've been and what I've done. God, the humiliation. I'd break down, end up joining Francine in her doorway and how long would I last then? I've got years of pretending ahead of me and I'm content with that. Living a lie is far more palatable than the reality I've had to put up with all these years. I'm sorry that you have become a part of that reality."

"You shouldn't be sorry; you should be happy."

"Happy? Yeah, right. I'd say I was content pretending that I had a mother who took me to France, that I went to boarding school and we drove around in her boyfriend's car and all that rom-com stuff. Eating burgers on my own downstairs with a book is good enough for me Daniel. And Pam? She'll never compare to the monsters I've had to bend over for, who burned me with cigarettes, shared me like some cushion on a sofa with their friends. She's not Conrad or Torin, the pimps and sadists I've had to please to survive. And I did survive. Do you understand Daniel? I'm a forty-three-year-old ex-whore. No address, bank account, savings, nothing. Your superficial disfigurement is trifling compared to the running sore on the inside of me."

She'd led me by the hand to the door. "So, goodbye, my love, my one true love, perhaps?" My head swam as I digested those words. It was as if I'd been waiting to hear them all my life. As I tried to gather myself, she reached over my shoulder and turned the lock. "But it has to end now."

I felt the rain on the back of my neck.

"Goodbye, Daniel."

"Kerry…"

'No, no," she mouthed, locking the door and backing into the darkness as I rapped gently on it.

Even as she descended, I kept knocking. As much as her grim disclosure, I was stunned by her resolve – the efficient way she'd eliminated me from her life. Turning from the shop into the squall, I imagined her opening the stockroom door with that single mattress that took up all the floorspace; no window, no telly, nothing in there but echoes of her inventions ricocheting from the dry grey breezeblocks.

***

I heard two soft knocks on my bedroom door.

"Daniel, are you alright?"

"Yes mum."

"I've got your breakfast ready downstairs. Poached eggs."

"OK mum. Down in a bit."

"You sure you're alright, you're not…?"

"No mum."

The floorboard creaked. She wasn't going to move. And where once I'd have had metal in my demeanour, I opened the door and put my arms around her and hugged her gratefully. I know it's not particularly funny, but I actually laughed when she wilted in my arms.

17

"How's Torin?" she asked as I finished my eggs.

"Trying to find him."

"That's not good."

"No. He'll turn up though."

She blinked a smile at her garden. In the morning rays, last night's rain had made all that was green drip and glisten. "You excited, all those gigs?"

"Very mum."

She'd turned from the window to look at me. "You look better this morning."

"Sorted some things out."

"Oh. Mick and Alana coming back?"

"Nah, Torin wanted a new direction."

"I suppose he knows what he's doing."

"Yeah."

I took my plate to the sink.

"You going to the shops?" I asked. "We're running out of washing-up liquid, butter as well, I think."

"We've got butter."

My dream broke through. A tall man behind me. He had butter-coloured hair. I wouldn't, couldn't turn and stare at him, directly. His footsteps were in metronomic time with mine. When I stopped to look into a shop window with cakes and clothes, he loomed behind me, darkening everything. My heart was racing when I opened my eyes: *'Come with me, you might see something you like, Daniel. Continental stuff?'*

I turned the tap off and the dream fled.

'Can't, got a meeting.'

'Now?'

'Yeah, forgot.'

I was out of the house in ten minutes.

I'd left Torin three messages before going to sleep and had called him a couple of times since I'd got up. Nothing. So, I did not alight at Oxford Circus to wander over to Denmark Street and wait for Jake to open up at eleven, that would have been futile. I changed at Tottenham Court Road and took the Northern Line out.

When I was last here, the exterior needed a lick or three, now the sash windows gleamed white against a cool, grey finish. The gravel drive had been ripped up and paved with geometric precision. The surrounding privet had had a severe haircut, but the oak, as it had for hundreds of years, stood indomitably in the centre of the space. The front door of the house was open wide. I passed a navy Porsche, parked at an angle by the garage doors, and entered.

"Hello," I called, sniffing at the scent of fresh gloss and caulk.

I followed a glistening herringbone passageway to the kitchen. Bulbs and cables dangled from the ceiling waiting to be housed in their circular apertures. White goods, still wrapped in cellophane skins, were ready to be plumbed in. I noticed that where the rattily old garden door had been, sleek grey bifolds sealed the room in silence.

Hearing a voice, I turned and walked towards a reception room but before entering it, I paused at the bottom of the staircase and peered up. The carpetless steps were as scuffed and raw as they'd been the last time I was here. The old gripper was still to be ripped out. The right-hand banister had been wrenched from the wall leaving machine-gunned craters in the plaster all the way up the stairs. On the landing someone had peeled a scar of yellow wallpaper away exposing the ancient gold and red flock beneath. Half the ceiling was down. Daylight flitted through the dusty slats from the level above. Top to bottom, the house was like a 'before and after' advert.

The reception room's satin-painted door was faintly tacky to my fingertips when I pushed it open. Standing by the Georgian windows overlooking the drive was my dogged dream companion, Conrad. His back was towards me. He pulled his face away from his phone when he turned around.

"Shoes," he barked, before returning to his call, speaking in French.

My socks sank into a cream carpet that stretched away from the doorway into the bright white skirting beyond. Dado rails glinted against a flawless mushroom finish. Like the kitchen, electric cables protruded from various points in the ceiling and walls. The marble fireplace and hearth were spotless. The only furniture in there was a three-piece Chesterfield, classic burgundy, and a smoky glass coffee table, although I spied a metal ladder, encrusted with filler and paint, hiding behind the door.

With much bass laughter into his phone, Conrad offered me an armchair with an open palm and returned to the window and his call. Asleep on the couch bisecting the armchairs, hands in foetal prayer between his knees, was the famous rock and roll frontman, Torin DeVere and it struck me just then that this furniture arrangement mimicked the lay-out in his beloved club. There was one notable difference though: in his club, they'd *never* leave their cocaine wraps, credit cards and rolled up bills on the coffee tables. It was strictly toilet business in there.

Returning from the windows, Conrad flicked at Torin's overhanging leg with his stockinged foot. "Visitor," he said, pulling the phone from his mouth for a second and taking his place in the chair opposite mine.

Opening one eye, Torin licked his lips. There was no acknowledgment that I was sitting a few feet from him. Unnerved, I looked though the curtainless windows at the twists, whorls and knots of the branches of the oak in the drive. A gust of wind rattled the panes with a portent of the season to come.

Some intimate Gallic whispering signalled the end of Conrad's call. His foot flicked at Torin's shin again, harder. "Visitor," he repeated.

The sofa creaked as Torin sat up. Wheezing, one hand supporting his lower back, he froze bending over, then, with a gasp, pulled himself upright. Extracting a bent roll-up from a pocket in his leather jacket, he shuffled towards the fireplace hacking huge bolts of phlegm. He put the rollie between his lips and flicked at the stubborn lighter in his fingers.

"Outside!" Conrad's voice bounced off the walls like a whip crack and I knew at that moment (I might even have sensed it in the restaurant when he vacated my seat, or when he'd embraced Torin the other night) that there was something about him that was inimical to me. I did not want to be near this well-tailored man, his bulging biceps and flaxen hair. I would cross the road if he was walking towards me.

He was a person outside of my experience. He repelled me.

As Torin left the room, I listened to the tap-tap-tap, the alternative click-track of the nineties. Conrad was chopping out a line on the table. After snorting, he leaned across the divide and offered me the note. I declined. He shrugged.

"I know you're not from the agent," he said with a sniff.

When he looked me up and down, I was reminded of a stone god on the plinth of some Greco-Roman temple, one that you'd glance up at and think, I bet he was an evil bastard in his time.

"No, I'm in the band."

His phone rang. He stood and walked to the fireplace. I could understand this call because it was in English. When he'd finished, he retook his seat. "Yes, I thought I'd seen you before. The drummer, right?"

"Keyboards."

"Ah yes, the drummer was dispensed with. Didn't mean to be rude, about the shoes. It's all new in here."

"I can see. Nice. Your place?"

"Temporarily only, I hope. We're trying to sell it."

"We?"

"No, I'm wrong again. *I* am trying to sell it. It appears my business partner cannot run a bath."

"We've got a big gig at Shepherd's Bush Empire tomorrow. It's sort of vital that he rehearses with us today."

"Always the worrywart, Daniel." Torin was framed in the doorway, hair and face soaking wet.

"Alright, Torin. Been trying to get hold of you."

"Join the queue." He entered the room and picked up the note.

"Try not to drip on the gear, old boy," Conrad said.

"Wouldn't dream," Torin replied, camply, hoovering up a line.

I could sense him searching for that shark smile, the winner's grin, but it was elusive and neither Conrad nor myself could be bothered to help him find it. "God, what a couple of old women," he muttered, falling onto the sofa.

Conrad's phone rang. He stood and walked toward the window, speaking French again.

I leaned forward to get my singer's full attention. "What the fuck is going on, Torin? I've had the girls in the studio for two weeks. Come on. This is the last day."

"I've got to focus on, err…"

I wanted to shout: 'Focus! You can't even see the hand in front of your face, mate!'

He looked up at me sharply. "What?"

"Bluebell really needs to work on the vocals with you," I continued. "She doesn't know when to come in and out. She's been in tears, man. They want to know when to back off, when you speak between numbers. She needs your signals. We've sold out the gig. You haven't sung a note since Rotterdam!"

He tilted his head. "Is there never any wine?"

When he left the room, I could feel myself heating up. Flick, flick went the lighter in my head.

He wandered back in with a glass and popped the cork on the bottle. "Look, I know *my* fucking songs, man."

"Torin, I had to write a cheque out for a grand from my own account to pay for the fucking room *and* pay the girls. Barney said…"

"Don't fucking 'Barney' me, Daniel." I saw a flash of energy at last. "Serious lack of judgement on my behalf, hiring him. Incompetent pygmy."

"But our account Torin, the one Alana set up, it's been emptied out. Remember, we said that was only for rehearsals and equipment."

A shrug. "Speak to Forbes."

"I did. He wants you to call him urgently."

He raised his palm. "Calm yourself, we'll be well paid for Shepherd's Bush. The tour will salve all your monetary wounds."

"Tour? The tour support, Torin. The label dropped us. You're not listening. I've been blanking the agent all morning. We ain't got the money to hire a fucking van!"

"This is what I mean, Barney has been so wasteful."

"No, Torin, he said *you* haven't paid him."

I sat back, heart racing.

"Fucking obsessed with money," he muttered, finishing his glass.

"We're all obsessed with money at the moment, Torin," Conrad said, falling into his armchair. He chopped out another line. After a sniff he passed the note reluctantly to his left. Like a puppy, Torin followed on, nose down, truffle hunting, the way he did.

For a moment, we three sat in our telly-less sitting room while the soft cream moss grew beneath our socks.

Conrad sniffed. "That estate agent called while you were having a fag."

"Oh," said Torin, his hand trembling with the note in it.

"Confirmed. Timothy, and now Sandro have pulled out, even though we dropped the price. As it stands, we have no buyer for our, 'half a house'. Shit show."

I could feel Conrad's baleful focus switch from Torin to me.

"I *do* know you."

"Yeah, I'm the keyboard player."

As if some unseen film director had called 'action', he tilted his head and pointed his finger at me. "You were with Sorrow in Soho last week."

"Kerry, you mean?"

"Is that what she calls herself?"

Torin leaned in. "Who, Conrad?"

"Your pianist here, he was with Sorrow."

Torin blinked, his jaw hung open. "No."

As I studied Torin's stupefied face, I could hear Conrad, rumbling away, "…Rafael's yacht? Strawberry blonde. Lovely round bottom." He paused and turned to me. "But you didn't have the bins on."

I looked out of the window again. "No, I'd broken them." I could feel Torin's eyes on me, now. I turned and faced him. What an ugly thing his smile had become.

"I must be paying you too much, Daniel." He sipped from his glass and chuckled. "Conrad, see his face? In the band, we call it the 'Daniel face'."

"Only you call it that, Torin."

"The coffee-chucker. Oh no, Daniel." Laughing, he turned to his right. "Conrad, you'll never guess what he's done?" Conrad glanced up from his phone. "He's only gone and fallen in love with her! Ah, ha, ha. Didn't your mum tell you, *never* fall in love with a working girl?"

Their laughter was welcome, if only because it stopped me from bursting into tears.

"But, what an arse! When you're behind her…I bet you give her right old portion, you dirty little synthesizer."

Smiling he shook his head, content he'd finally got me to share the same woman with him, albeit him carnally and me romantically.

"What turned me on was that she always looked so dismal. As if in mourning. You felt as if you were fucking the joy into her. Damn, when this nonsense is over, I'm up for a return visit." He was sparkling now. "With your permission of course, Daniel. Ha-ha!" He roared.

A train crash was taking place in my head. Through the screeching of mangled metal and oily hissing steam, I could hear them mumbling and chopping.

"…see Conrad, we *did* have good times, and those times will come again. Trust me."

Conrad's perfectly shaped consonants and vowels were as soulless as the room we sat in. "I did trust you, and now we are fucked."

His gaze fell on me. "Sounds like you've been fucked by Torin too, Daniel?"

"I haven't fucked anyone, Conrad," Torin bleated, "I…"

"Shut up!" Conrad's voice was like a magazine slapped onto a table.

A deflated Torin looked down at his lap.

"This is a big gig, Conrad," I said. "Thousands of people have bought tickets and we need the money from it."

"What are you asking me?"

"Just that, if you could allow Torin to come into rehearsals today…"

I bought him a fried egg sandwich in the café on the corner of Denmark Street. He looked shattered, flinching at the sound of the espresso machine, dribbling the yoke down his chin.

"Here," I said, handing him a serviette. "I'll set up. Come in when you've finished your sarnie."

Jake unlocked Three, his eyes squinting with contrition. "Sorry about last night, Daniel. Hated doing that. Boss just said, lock it until they pay."

"Only doing your job."

"Cheers mate."

Unaware of the 'locking us out of the room' drama that had taken place after they'd left yesterday, the girls arrived a few minutes later. I wasn't going to tell them about it. Everyone needed to concentrate on tomorrow night. This shitty thing *had* to be got through.

Before either of them could speak, I held up my hand. "He's in the café around the corner. Here any minute." "Well done, Daniel." Bluebell rushed across the room and hugged me. When she stepped back, she looked concerned.

"What's wrong?"

"Oh nothing, my err…injury…plays havoc with my sinuses sometimes. All good. Going for a slash."

I left the room as swiftly as Daisy went around her silent drums. I held back the tears as I passed through reception and fell against the toilet door. Bluebell's embrace had cracked me. I'd been patting myself on the back for my stoicism: shutting Kerry out and treating Torin as I did the girls and myself: as a cog in the wheel, a component in the machine that would do the business tomorrow night and the many nights after. But her unguarded gratitude, the undiluted friendship in it, was too much, it opened up the real me, and I found myself staring at the mirror, untethered, silently asking, 'What are you doing? What have you done?'

I splashed water on my face and returned to the room.

"Oh, another good thing," I said, as I got behind my set-up, "Roy Doogan, our soundman, he's coming down to check it all out. He's a top bloke. Been with us years."

"Surprised we even need a sound man," Bluebell said.

"He's excellent with Torin's vocal," I told her, turning on my computer.

Not unlike the lads that had poked their heads around the door last week, Torin, a dot of egg yolk on his chin, looked into the room as if he'd found it by accident. Blinking confusedly at all the gear and microphones he croaked, "OK, do your worst!"

I pressed the spacebar.

Roy arrived a little after we started. He took his place on

the couch. Only once did he meet my eye, and in that moment, he transmitted a well of sympathy for the situation I'd found myself in.

"Like you said on the phone, it isn't great." We were walking from the studio together. Although it confirmed my fears, Roy's Black Country burr was a welcome old friend.

"It's so fucking average."

"What happened?" he asked. "One minute we're finishing a European tour and now, it's blimmin' Armageddon."

"I've not seen Alana since Rotterdam. Had a drink with Mick. I've lost my closest friends."

"That drive to the ferry was horrible."

Torin had been unhinged on the drive back, repeatedly leaving Conrad these garbled messages on his phone, huffing and puffing, whining about the slowness of the drive, the weather, the quality of the van's upholstery. It was like he had a forcefield of shit around him. The silences were sickening, and when they were broken you wished it was quiet again. I remember Roy asking him about some innocent detail of the sound, his monitors or something and Torin completely losing it, saying that he didn't give a fuck about the sound in some field.

"I programmed all their parts, Roy. I feel like such a traitor."

"Don't be too hard on yourself mate," he said. "I wouldn't be here if you weren't involved. I honestly thought I'd never do the sound for you guys again. Credit to you for getting it all up and running."

"Credit?"

"You know what I mean. Whatever you think about it, it's a show, a professional one."

"Sorry. I'm really stressed with all this. I dunno. We had something, and now we haven't. There isn't even a 'we.'"

"The two girls are good, but..."

I sighed. "I know man. It's shit. We're a covers band of our own band."

"The bass player?"

"Bluebell."

"She was a bit teary."

"Yeah, she'd only had one rehearsal with him and that was the beginning of last week. I tried to warn her that he could be a bit?"

"Inconsistent?"

"Ha-ha, yeah, ever so slightly. I've told her about the old nudge. I don't think she fully understood what I meant until today. She's not experienced, never 'played' anywhere near as big as this and now she's got all this pressure, with him and his fucking inconsistency."

We walked on for a bit.

"So relieved you're here to help us out, Roy. I *have* to get us through this gig. Once it's done, we'll have the template for the rest of the dates. Should be easy after that."

"I'll do everything I can, mate."

A kind smile grew from his beard, and we shook hands.

Twenty minutes later, as my train emerged from the tunnel, I forgot myself and played the eight notes. The second I concluded, Torin and Conrad's laughter flooded into the vacuum in cruel mimicry of applause. I touched my specs. It was true, I *had* fallen in love with a working girl, but the girl I'd fallen in love with worked in a shop.

***

"I got washing-up liquid and butter. You were right."

"Good."

"You OK, Daniel?"

"Yes mum."

"Did you find Torin. Did he come to rehearsals?"

"Yeah, he was staying with a friend."

Some friend. As my cannelloni pinged, I marvelled that some public school hard-nut now controlled my destiny, and he didn't even know who I was until yesterday. Spooning the steaming gunk onto a plate, I replayed his English phone call and remembered how his shirt got more and more taught and his face, more and more crimson as he snarled into his phone.

'These things happen in property, you say...? Then you'd better get your arse in gear and find us another buyer...You were so full of it in your grubby little office, now...I'm not...I'm simply telling you to do your job...OK, OK. If that's the way you feel, I'll take it across the road then. Shhh. Listen, don't let me see you and your little clipboard around here my friend…Yes, that's the perfect inference. Perhaps relocate to another branch? You don't want to see me again.'

"Did you hear me, Daniel. I got you Jaffa Cakes. For a change."

"Sorry mum, miles away. Ta." Jaffa Cakes were a treat when I got back from school in the horrendous first few weeks of bullying. There was something about eating them, their texture and taste, that seemed to calm my anxiety. Mum's too, it seemed. Between us, we must have hammered a couple of packets a day, back then.

I wolfed down the cannelloni.

"You were hungry."

"Long rehearsal."

"Torin needs you as well, Daniel. He's nothing without you."

"We used to say that about Alana and Mick."

"Oh."

"Don't worry, it's going to be alright."

My phone buzzed in my pocket. "One sec mum…Bluebell?"

Her words came through my phone in an agitated torrent as I stepped into the garden. "But it's like he doesn't know his own songs. I've seen you guys three times. He's always been brilliant, I…"

Although it was moments before sunset, a residual stripe of daylight clung to the top of the brick wall at the back of the garden illuminating the leaves of a trailing vine. I peered into its depths. "Sometimes," I said, when she'd finally run out of breath, "well quite a bit, things are not what they seem in err, 'showbiz'. When you're on the inside, and you are now, it's so flaky and hokey and things are falling apart, but the people watching don't see it all creaking and groaning under the strain of the egos and the greed, ineptitude or whatever, they see lights, camera, action!

They're sort of convinced, cos', you know, the location it's all happening in, and they love the music so much, and they've paid. Everything's gonna be fine, Bluebell. You just gotta hold your nerve, do what you do and smile."

She didn't reply.

"Bluebell?"

"Thank you. You're so strong, Daniel. Hearing that, I feel sort of OK now."

"Look, I can't deny it's not going to be challenging tomorrow, but the people will love it."

"OK."

"Yeah, we'll have a blast. See you at soundcheck."

The brick wall and the leaves had turned monochrome and featureless. The sun had set. When it rose, it would be the big day.

"Who was that, Daniel?"

"The new girl in the band."

"Oh, that's nice. Does she…" Her voice trailed off because our doorbell chimed. A most rare thing in the evening, or at any time at our house. And it was funny walking up the passage because I knew who it was before I smelled the cologne.

"Hi Conrad."

If he dominated the living room windows in Highgate, standing at my front door, he blocked out the night. "Daniel," he said.

"Who's that?"

"Someone from work, mum."

"You got ten minutes?" he asked.

I backed away to let him in. He shook his head. "We'll sit in my car."

His Porsche was parked at the end of the path. We got in. It reeked of his energy. "You smoke?"

"No."

"No, I can see you're clean-living boy. What happened to your eye?"

"Had an accident with a tub of battery acid when I was a kid."

"Bad luck. You know, you don't want to pick at those scabs, it'll only make it worse."

I shrugged. He ran his tongue along his bottom lip. "How old are you?"

"Twenty-five."

He nodded sagely. "You're quite a man, Daniel. Running that band, working with that worthless piece of shit, Torin. Keeping it all together."

I breathed in. My dinner nudged my epiglottis. There wasn't a lot of air in his cosy German cabin. "Well, people are expecting a good show. Professional."

"How was he today?"

"It's not been ideal, none of it is. He fired two of the band. They were top musicians and now it's not what it was."

"Everything he touches turns to shit."

Distracted by seeing my house from the interior of a car parked outside it, I said nothing.

"I need to know if the tour will go ahead," he said.

"Why?"

"Things are riding on it. Important things."

"Everything was ready to go, but…the tour support, the money that pays for stuff upfront…we don't have it. The musicians are owed, there's the crew, transport, hotels. People don't work for nothing. So…"

"Yeah, I get it."

"The booking agent might pull it at any time. He needs to see we have everything ready, like I said, professionally."

"So, you need how much?"

"I'm not a tour manager, Conrad, I…"

"Yeah, I know, you're only the piano player. How much?"

"Five grand?"

"Why am I not convinced?"

"I don't know."

"Ha-ha, you are a cool one. Twenty-five, living with your mum in that little semi, and you're fronting me out."

"I don't mean to…" And it was weird, because inside me I *was* laughing, laughing at the surreal nature of it all, where I'd found myself, a knob-twiddling noodler, 'fronting out' this dangerously iffy bloke. But I went on with it like an actor with a cheesy gangster script: "…disrespect you Conrad," I added.

I almost guffawed when I said that. If Mick Corbossa was sitting in the back, we'd be pissing our pants. Oh Mick. How I missed him.

"There's a 'but' coming," he said flatly.

"It's not down to me or the band. It's down to Torin. He's the singer, the frontman, the leader. Everyone – dunno, two thousand people in there tomorrow night? – will be looking at him, not me, not the backing band."

He stayed silent.

"We're replaceable. Staff, I suppose," I said, thinking of how once I'd considered myself *not* a cog in a wheel, but one of four limbs of an animal band, with blood and nerve and expression…and worth. But sitting there, I knew that that beautiful animal was stone dead, shoved to the side of the road to decompose by a storm drain. "There's only one Torin," I added quietly.

He rested his thick hand on the gear stick and tapped it with a gold-ringed finger.

"He's been doing it for years, singing for the band?"

"He has."

"Well, it can't be that bloody hard. It's what you all do, right?"

I nodded.

"Professionals," he said.

"Yes. We are."

The cabin seemed to shrink around us as he composed himself. "I'm going to speak in confidence. Frankly. Understand?"

I nodded.

He said that he and Torin had been at Eton at the same time, although he was four years older. They'd bumped into each other at a party Conrad was hosting in Knightsbridge about three and a half years ago. "These parties were not for wives and girlfriends, if you know what I mean, and I'm sure you do." With a self-deprecating shrug of his huge shoulders, he added, "I had a gift for them." He paused and shook his head. "Still can't quite get my head around Torin singing in a band…I mean, he liked to belt it out in choir practice, but he was never into music at school."

He told me his business had begun to expand. He was providing *'party girls'* for private clients, taking them to Europe for corporate dos and 'celebratory – male-only – events. He had no moral qualms, "The girls earned, the gentlemen were satisfied, and I took my cut. A virtuous circle, Daniel," he said, tapping the gear stick with his ring again. About six months ago, after an *'accident'* on one of his yacht parties, he was forced to leave that particular arena. "Don't ask, suffice it to say, an obstruction was dealt with, and we were lighter coming in than we were sailing out."

I looked up and nodded again.

He told me he moved into real estate, buying neglected properties with a group of investors. He had a crack team of builders that would do them up and have them back on the market in weeks. It didn't have the 'kudos' of his previous enterprise, he said. "But your average high street estate agent isn't going blow up your car with you sitting in it for not getting the buyer's survey in on time."

Exhaling heavily, he recounted a fateful, cokey night at the club. As he'd not been providing the entertainment Torin enjoyed, they'd not seen each other for a while. Torin's eyes had lit up when he mentioned he'd been earning a crust flipping proprieties. "I made sure he showed me his statements," Conrad said, glancing at me as if I'd think less of him for not asking for them. He'd seen two hundred thousand pounds in Torin's account. When he'd asked Torin where he got the money from, he was told it was a music payment the band received regularly from the States.

"You know about that?" Conrad asked me.

"No. Torin doesn't involve us in the money side of things."

"I bet he doesn't."

I was staring at the parade of shops before the roundabout at the top of the road. I could see the blue dot of the 'Blockbuster' sign at the end. I'd need to get a couple of videos for after the show. Something to eat too.

"Funny," he said, "at school, all Torin wanted to be was a property magnate like his dear old dad. Then he became a rock star! Most chaps, you'd think, it'd be the other way around. I remember, ages before I met him again, I was in Paris, throwing a party, and he was singing on the TV. All the girls were dancing to it. You could have knocked me down with the proverbial. Him giving that dangerous glare into the camera. Ha! Torin DeVere, the laziest, languid, most 'do nothing' bloke in his year, was giving it large on MTV. My abiding memory of him at school was as an arch bummer of cigarettes and pot. He stank too, greasy hair, leeching off everyone for a pint. Playing a mouth organ that I would have happily chucked in the river, and him after it."

The car was quiet for a moment. When he spoke again, he made sure I was looking at him.

"But he stitched me up, Daniel. The day after showing me that statement, he put the two hundred K into a timeshare in Ibiza that went tits up almost immediately."

That was what he was pleading about on the phone in Rotterdam, "Santa Eulalia, Ibiza. I'll get the money back, trust me, Conrad." At the time I thought he might be referring to one of his dad's properties, perhaps planning a break there after we came off the road.

"Why the fuck he did that, knowing that he'd promised that money to me, was not only appalling business judgement, it was hurtful too. He didn't care or think about the repercussions of his actions, that I'd worked it so we could both earn…Yeah, I can see you know *exactly* what I mean. He lied to me, said he still had the dough so, like a *cunt*, I put in an offer on the house in Highgate. The renovation was approximately four hundred thousand; two hundred K each. Mine went into the ground floor, kitchen and garden. Torin was supposed to take care of the upstairs: bedrooms, bathrooms, roof, *et cetera*. It was a loose arrangement, had to be. I dropped by the place at the beginning of the month. The lads had nearly completed my end, but upstairs was a still a wreck. I got hold of the builders. They hadn't heard from him. I tried to find him, but he'd vanished. Then two weeks ago he called me in tears, said he'd had money trouble and would I forgive him. He had ten K he could…Your band account?"

I nodded.

"What a fucker he is," he said, shaking his head. "Anyway, he said the rest would follow. I met him a couple of nights ago and, because he's such a 'rock star', I took him at his word. He told me about the huge money-making tour he had lined up. The music money I'd seen in his account had been held up, some legal issue over there?"

I shook my head.

"But the remaining one-ninety hasn't materialised. Both our buyers have pulled out, the estate agent's fucked off, and I'm left, two hundred K out of pocket, with half a house I can't sell. As you can imagine, the investors are after my blood. Well?"

This arcane sort of thing baffled me. The amounts seemed preposterous. 'Deals' had never been anything I was interested in. I focused on the blue dot at the end of the road. It was either 'The Matrix', which I really fancied, but was never in, or 'Blade', which I'd seen and would, post gig, probably sit through again.

"Daniel?"

"I don't know anything about it, Conrad. I just make music."

"Which is good, because I need 'our Torin' to do the business at these gigs, you understand me?"

"I think so."

He reached into his jacket for his pen.

"I'll make it plain. I need the money you make on this jolly to pay off my debt to the investors. I know it's going to be tough for you, but it's better to have five percent of something than a hundred percent of fuck all. I'm afraid that where Torin DeVere is concerned, *I'm* the major creditor and I need you to get him through it." He paused and tapped the gearstick. "I promise, I'll see you and your mum right when the dust has settled. OK?"

I looked at him at last.

"I'll do my best, but I'm not the singer. I'm not who everyone has come to see."

"I get that," he said, pressing the central locking system and releasing me.

"You not having your Jaffa Cakes, Daniel?"

"I'll have them in a bit mum," I said, avoiding the kitchen and climbing the stairs three at a time. I placed Conrad's cheque on the bedside table.

Back and forth, hands in pockets, I paced the six steps from the window to the door. So, the complete meltdown in the dressing room in Rotterdam had coincided with his Ibiza timeshare going 'tits up'. Where he got his two hundred thousand for the original stake in the property was a mystery to me. I was pretty certain it wasn't anything to do with the band. We'd stopped getting those sorts of payments years ago. I guessed it was family money, an inheritance, share dividend? It was all out of my experience. But however complex and fucked up the subplots were to what had happened to the band, my part was as clear now as it had ever been: I had to get Torin through this gig and the tour after it.

18

Mum slid my eggs on toast in front of me and asked if I was excited. She did not, in any way, refer to the scarring.

"Yes," I said.

"Such a shame Mick and Alana aren't in the group anymore, isn't it?"

"Well yeah."

"I know that you're upset."

I held her gaze for a second. "Life goes on, mum."

I pondered taking on some routine tasks before setting off for soundcheck later that afternoon. Returning that old CD to its shelf was one. Taking that plastic crate of nostalgia, hammering it shut and burying it, was another. I had a fleeting vision of myself on a mist-shrouded hilltop in the dead of night, bent-over gravestones, spindly church spire in the moonlight, me huffing and puffing over a spade.

"Eggs not too soft?"

"Nah, just right mum."

My thoughts turned to Blockbuster. I'd heard that 'Cider House Rules' was out, but 'The Matrix' called. I'll hire both…see how I feel and get mum to order a Chinese before it shuts. I'll call her right after I come off, then get on the tube and be home as it turns up. The scheduling excited me more than the show. I imagined the droning microwave heating my sweet and sour as I came down from the shower, the applause still ringing in my ears. Ping! Pressing open the door to a big cheer. Shuffling out of the kitchen with my tray. The dark front room, the titles coming up on the screen. The perfect end to a working day.

My new outlook was in complete contrast to the one that I'd enjoyed for the last five years. *'I can't wait to play my music to all of those people with my friends,'* was now, *'Get it done and get the fuck home'.*

I brought my breakfast things to the sink and looked up at the sky. Thunderous grey covered my quarter of London.

The grass, flaxen and wilted was shin high on my postage stamp of lawn. I'd need to get out there with the shears before mowing and trimming. Thing is, mum and me treasured that modest patch of green.

If you'd grown up on the fourth floor and was gifted a little private sunlight, you would too. But I'd be on the road on Monday with Daisy, Bluebell and Torin. It'd be weeks before I could get the mower out. I made a mental note, before anything, I'd get the grass cut.

I turned off the dripping tap. My phone buzzed on the table. Picking it up, I saw that I'd had three missed calls from the same number that had tried me a few days ago. I dialled the number. It was answered immediately, and I smiled for the first time in a week when I heard the voice on the other end.

***

Debbie nodded me towards the lone occupier of our corner table, a tanned and toned Mick Corbossa.

"You wanker," I said, sitting opposite him. "I've been calling you for yonks."

"Been in France."

I reared. "Where?"

His curls bounced on his lineless forehead as he pushed a pint across the familiar scarred surface. "France, you know the place with the snails and the Eiffel Tower?"

"You look disgustingly well too."

"I'll drink to that then, Danny boy. Cheers!"

When he set down his pint, I felt his warm brown orbs examining my face. "Never seen it so bad, Daniel."

"Best it's been for days, believe it or not. Fucking stress man. It was like I was back at school. I'm through it now," I said, confident I would be.

We paused for a moment.

"Yeah," he said, "Shepherd's Bush Empire tonight. You finally got yourself a real drummer." A surge of emotion rocketed upwards causing me to hide my face behind my pint glass. "I've been staying with Alana," he continued.

My heart thudded in my chest. "She hate me, man?"

"What are you on about?"

"Rotterdam."

"Fuck that. Ancient history. Danny, she's twelve weeks pregnant."

"Nah."

"Daniel?" I was crying now. Head in hands. I couldn't stop myself, and it was so ironic because the last time we'd sat in this pub for a drink it was Mick who was in bits. He slid beside me and put an arm around my shoulders.

"Alana loves you man. We all do."

"She's pregnant?"

"Ha-ha, yeah and loving it."

And there was me, all morning, resolutely compartmentalising all my demons, pros, cons and in two sips it had all come undone. I'd convinced myself that if I had to contort my body into a Torin-sized box and suffer Conrad's menaces (and pay his 'protection' money), I would do it, unflinchingly. I'd get this shitty thing done. *'Better to have five percent of something than a hundred percent of fuck all.'* But now I feared the pinging microwave, mum upstairs in bed, me alone with some shit film on telly. I didn't make it to Blockbuster this morning to get those two videos out.

"Going out of my mind Mick."

He'd returned to his place. "You'll be fine. How's Torin doing?"

I said nothing.

"His voice OK?"

Without mentioning the spectre of Conrad hanging over everything, I explained the whole miming sham with the girls and that Torin had promised me he'd been practising. I could tell Mick was running through the dozens of fag-paper-thin excuses our singer had presented to us over the years for something he'd said he'd done but hadn't.

"Really?" he added, with a look of amused incredulity. "You actually believe that?"

"Fuck's sake Mick, I have to," I said desperately.

Although he hadn't spoken, his follow-up question was quietly deafening. *'How the fuck do you think he is going to get through that set without Alana?'*

He sat back and lifted his glass. His shoulders and biceps were sculpted and dark beneath his shirt. The idea that he wouldn't be on the left of me on stage tonight, head back, eyes shuttered, lost in rhythm, seemed incomprehensible.

"You should see Alana man. She's shacked up with that bass player from Pink Marlin, David. Remember them, indie shoegazey? Good though. Anyway, proper loved up. Little bass player on the way. She's in Gascony. Big blue sky. All sunflowers. Goes on for miles."

I sniffed and it came to me that the losers were actually the winners in this. Him and Alana with new lives and challenges, me with this dismal old one.

"I'm glad for her."

"Daniel, she wants you to come and stay. She kinda sent me to get you."

"Really?"

"She's got something to tell you. Important. Thinks you're a hero, the way you tried to keep it all together."

"Yeah, resounding success I made of that."

Like someone else I once knew, he gently put his fingers on the back of my hand. "No one thinks bad of you."

I felt like I was losing everyone who had brought me joy or was worthwhile. I retracted my hand sharply.

"Daniel?"

I finally managed to draw breath. "Look, I'm on the road with him for the next couple of months. Can't get out of it. I'll email her. Gotta sort my gear out. You know the routine."

I stood quickly. The thing is, I could see myself sobbing in his arms any second, and that was *not* what I had in mind when I shut my front door a couple of hours ago.

Outside, the grey sheet hadn't lifted. It was one of those days when the sun will never quite get the upper hand. I switched on my phone. It rang immediately. "Torin?"

***

"This takes me back."

"What does?"

I was referencing our very first gig. Mick and me blinking with disbelief as we watched him, in his dress, stepping, arse-first, out of a cab with his lyrics on bits of paper and that unruly piece of metal trapped under his arm.

"Remember the first show? King's Cross? You brought a music stand and the lyrics all written out. Alana…".

He snarled through his cigarette smoke. "Could you shut up about that dhal-stewing lesbian and focus on this?"

"She's pregnant."

That statement paused him in his business, but only momentarily.

"Even goldfish have babies," he said. He looked at me as he flicked his fag away. "Jesus Daniel, don't sulk!"

And it was good that he'd turned on me, all grim and dark, because the hours ahead demanded my unemotional, unwavering focus. I'd been lulled into melancholy by my encounter with Mick just now. The person beside me, reading and marking bits of A4 was someone you simply could not show your soft side to. Exhibit the faintest sign of indecision or hesitancy, and his mouth will open and swallow you whole.

The sun had finally chucked in its yellow towel. We occupied a bench on Shepherd's Bush Green. I checked my phone. We'd be sound checking soon. He was mumbling away, reciting stuff from the pages laid out on the bench. Over one of his shoulders I could see the railway arches, the dank noisy rooms our sound was born in. It was poignant that over the other shoulder, 'TORIN-SOLD OUT' was writ large on the front of the hallowed theatre a few hundred yards away.

"Fuck's sake. This bit here, is it after a solo?"

I glanced at the sheet in his hand with the lyrics printed on it, and it came to me that perhaps the reason he couldn't remember the arrangements of his own songs, was that he had never loved music, at least not the way Mick, Alana and me, or even Daisy, Bluebell and Barney, did. I mean, I couldn't imagine a song stopping him in his tracks, reducing him to tears. Impassioned lyrics, instrumentals, huge swathes of classical music, even eight-bar fucking ukulele solos have the power to turn me to mush, but I'd never seen him touched by music like that. Torin enjoyed a singsong around the club piano, lots of smiles and cheers, Christmas drinks or 'happy birthday' vibes. We were at different ends of the musical telescope, me and him. However dark the scowls were beneath the spotlight, he was ultimately a singalong host, conducting, pissed up, indifferent, a fun guy. Music had only ever caused me to think and feel deeply. It had *never* been for fun.

"Stop zoning out, Daniel. You're like a fucking infant," he said, holding a sheet in front of my face. I scanned it for a couple of seconds and looked in the direction of the rehearsal room again. "It comes after my hook." I hummed the couple of the bars I played before the chorus. "One, two, three, four and then you're in. *'She told me so many times...'*"

Singing the chorus out loud reminded me of that fateful rehearsal, Alana telling him to wait for her touch before joining in. "What?" he'd said, beautifully addled beneath his purple hippy hat with the owl feather. He was blinking at us, aware that we were vexed, but oblivious as to why. Alana's voice cut through the collective astonishment. "Look," she said, moving beside him. "If you can't find your way in..."

"Way in where, exactly?"

She paused for a moment. You could almost hear her brain whirring and ticking over the speaker buzz.

"Torin, I'll start *all* the choruses. But just before I sing, I'll give you a little tap, or nudge. You have to trust me and join in, OK?"

He nodded.

On about the twelfth pass it actually happened: in the split second before Torin was supposed to sing the chorus, Alana nudged his shoulder with hers. *'She told me so many times...'* and Torin came in a fraction later, on the 'e' at the end of 'she'. This vocal flam, this musical wrongness served a dual purpose: it cued in Torin for the remainder of the chorus *and* created their unique vocal blend. And that was it. Alana's few seconds of inspiration, more than my keys, either of their voices, the drums or bass, had created the sound that made our fortune.

"Fuck!" he barked from his bench, jolting me awake.

Hunched over, fag smoke issuing from his nose, he ran a fat marker through an earlier correction.

A gust got up and I had to chase some sheets around the bench. Sifting them into a neat stack, I handed them back. "You can't go on with all this, man."

"Watch me. I'll get Barney to tape them all down."

"You fired him."

"Well some other tech, roadie, whatever."

I'd managed to call Barney, after receiving a number of missed calls from him.

"He's sacked me, Daniel."

I didn't tell him that Torin had fired better men than him, because it wasn't about that. Much like those better men, Barney had given Torin everything and been recompensed with abuse.

"I've had Barney on the phone, Torin. He's gutted. He's put so much into this, 'new way'. He was the architect, wasn't he?"

As well as Barney, there was Martin Reed, the booking agent, calling me about the viability of the tour after Barney had told him he'd been dispensed with. Reed wanted to know if there'd be 'tour support', the money to pay for everything. His agency's reputation was on the line, and he was fuming that his staff's dutiful work – getting the shows together – could all be for naught. He asked me who was in charge if Barney wasn't. In the pantheon of lies and obfuscation I dealt in, telling him not to worry as we were in the process of hiring a top tour manager, was not that high on the list.

Beside me, Torin was half mumbling, half singing, fully cursing.

"Fuck, fuck! Was that right, Daniel?"

"Yes. You got it right that time."

"Good," he said.

While he ground another cigarette under his heel, I was put in mind of a conversation with Mick. We were discussing why we never got a proper manager in for the band, and I'd said, "He can't stand to be around people that are able to do their job properly, cos he can't do his!"

While he whinged and squinted, I realised that was why he resented Alana so much.

"Mick's in good shape," I said.

He scrabbled in his pockets for a fag. *'Flick, flick'* went the lighter in the wind. "Who?"

"Mick Corbossa."

"Oh him, the plumber. Can't keep time. Replaceable."

As the wind whipped around and the traffic lurched, I hunched up my shoulders. "Just wanted to tell you."

"And?" he said, blowing a plume at the gloomy sky.

"He's been your drummer for five years. I was worried about him after he left. Well, just now, he looked like an Olympic swimmer."

"Please man, I've got to concentrate. *She told me so many times...*' Where's my bit again?"

"Just said, after my hook, yeah? Alana starts the line, you come in on the 'e' of 'she'. Don't you remember Torin? The moment it happened, over there, she nudged you with her shoulder?"

"Am I supposed to remember every shitty second of every shitty rehearsal in this fucking shitty band!" He shouted, exhaling like a dragon. "I couldn't stand that cunt touching me all night."

I shook my head and marvelled at the bottomless well of bile and resentment he retained. The bloke was born 'three nil up at half time', gifted beauty, a top-class education and he had the all the grace of a pendulum of gob on the end of your finger.

I turned away and replayed the moments before Alana came up with her brilliant solution. She had stood beside him, much like I was doing now, making him repeat the chorus over and over, but it just wouldn't stay up there. Her shoulders sagged when she looked across at me. We were all stunned that what she'd been instilling in him for the last thirty minutes had evaporated in a couple of swallows of red.

Torin, his handsome shark-wide smile had asked, "What?" He hadn't a clue.

"It's completely wrong, Torin," Mick had said gently.

He'd responded with posh-boy hurt. "How do you mean, 'wrong'?"

"Before the chorus, Daniel plays that riff."

I played that riff.

"That cues you up, man," continued Mick. "You sing, *'She told me so many times...'*"

"What riff, again?" he'd said, without a hint of guile.

The three of us blinked in wonderment.

"Don't you listen to songs, Torin? Like albums, sing along to the lyrics?"

"I don't pay much attention to what they say, do you?"

It was dawning on us that we were creating something special in there. Our sessions were addictive. Only when we were in the same place with our instruments could we experience this incredible high. And Torin, with all his shortcomings, had become an indelible part of it.

I trapped a lyric sheet that was about to be carried off by the wind. "Don't you remember how beautiful it sounded, Torin, when Alana and you combined? Second rehearsal, it changed everything. We flew from then on."

He looked up from his notes. "You have a real problem, living in the past, Daniel. You should get therapy. Perhaps your accident, or your mother being backward? I don't know, but we're playing this fuck-off show in a few hours, and you seem obsessed with some trifling episode in a rehearsal room a lifetime ago."

"But the way her voice brings yours in on those choruses. The brilliance of it?"

"Yeah, whatever…"

The insane thing was that the entire planet credited Torin for designing that brilliance. They said *his* vocal timing revealed '*a musical instinct so rare, that he was probably a genius*'. Nobody knew that it was born out of last-ditch necessity, that it was the only way we could perform without being laughed off the stage.

"Fucking hell. Daniel!"

"What?"

"You said…is *that* where it starts? That's the last line, isn't it?"

Like most people, when exasperated, I could become impatient and unforgiving, quite caustic, but I did it upstairs, in my head. No one had ever listened to me hurl down my displeasure, because, just in time, I caught it behind my clenched teeth. But something wasn't right, and it wasn't wrong either.

I swallowed and drew a disbelieving breath. "After I play the hook. I just told you, man! Fuck me! You've been telling me for weeks you've been practising!"

Torin was looking at me. The perfect wide smile had no warmth in it. I did not love that look at all. "Ooh, get you, Danny Earl," he said camply. "The mouse that roared."

A further darkness fell on him as he leaned towards me, his

breath all faggy. "Do you know what Conrad is capable of? You really don't. I've seen him do things to people. At sea? He enjoyed doing it. 'Man overboard' and all that. Ah, I see that *our* predicament is dawning on you."

He held my gaze for a second or two then peeled off his stupid notes from the bench. "Just play your fucking piano and get me through this."

19

Two hours later, watching Torin going through exactly the same part in that song's arrangement on that piece of paper, Roy poked his head round the dressing room door. "Shall we?"

I stood with a sigh, and down we all trooped to take part in the most bogus soundcheck I had ever done. There were no drums to individually check or bass levels to adjust, just poses and playback. I hit a couple of stabs on my Juno and got the band's attention. "OK everyone?" I called, from my little outcrop of synths, stage right.

The girls and Torin nodded.

For my own amusement, I whispered, "One, two, three, four," then pressed the all-powerful spacebar. As the click track ticked in their headsets, the girls got into character. Daisy, as earnestly rehearsed in Room Three's big mirror, tapped her sticks together in a mockery of a count-in, and we were off, the sound bouncing and booming around the empty auditorium. Two thirds in, the song ran away from him. Waving his pieces of A4, he shouted into the microphone, "Stop, stop, turn it off!" He was facing me. I read his lips: "Nightmare".

While he flapped around, the music belting out of the onstage monitors, I listened to my own locked-in dialogue: "Do you not get it, Torin? The minute you decided to rid yourself of people to save money, give yourself a new sound, or some other bullshit, you signed your own death warrant. The machine rules now, man, and it is *merciless*! It will not wait for you – it doesn't care if you are a cow, a lamppost or a mountain – it will plough on, inexorably, faultlessly for eternity, you foolish puny human. And if you can't keep up, you're proper fucked."

"What, *what?!*" Torin was shouting at me over the cacophony. Behind him, Daisy wore a faint smile. I squinted and tapped my ear.

He was roaring at me. "Stop the fucking music!"

I pressed the bar and silence reigned. "Did I say something?"

"You were possessed! Rambling away about lampposts and mountains."

I laughed. "Got carried away. The music's so good, don't you think?"

"Fuck your music, this is serious."

While the crew averted their eyes, he scuttled about the front of the stage picking up his bits of paper. Bluebell gawped at me. "We can't go on like this, Daniel."

Returning the cursor to the beginning of 'song one' in the set, I began composing sentences that would delicately announce that Torin had fallen ill: food poisoning, strep throat, overdose. *'I regret to inform you that Torin DeVere is unwell.'* I needed something near fatal to pull off this show with minimum opprobrium. Bomb threat! Not on my phone, of course, there were phone boxes outside…Let the support band have their twenty-five minutes first though. Power cut! A technical problem: *'iccle simfasizer run out of batteries?'*

"What are you laughing about now, man? You're fucking unhinged!"

"Sorry Torin."

He was standing in front of me with his stupid homework and at that moment, his words of last week came to me with a bang: *'You just press your little computer button, and it'll all work out, speccy boy…'*

***

To the accompaniment of the opening band's muffled soundcheck below I climbed the graceful old staircase to the balcony.

"What am I going to do, Daniel?" Torin had stopped on the landing below. He was panting, stooped, stretching out the small of his back. "It's all swirling around on stage, the noise and…it's happening so fast. The minute I think I know it, it's gone, the song's miles ahead."

I paused my ascent and turned to him, "It's gonna be OK," I said, not feeling particularly relieved or joyful that I was going to make it so.

Because of a sentence he'd thoughtlessly tossed into the rarefied air of the club last week, I'd save the day for all of us. It had hit me smack between the eyes as he floundered in the vortex of his crib sheets downstairs: *'You just press your little computer button, and it'll all work out, speccy boy.'* Perhaps they were right, he was a genius.

"You taking the piss?"

"What?"

"You just called me a genius."

Roy was already there when we got to the balcony. I took the place one away from him, Torin fell between us, swigging from a half-empty bottle of red. "Well, we're all here," he said, "What's the big idea?"

My plan relied heavily on Roy and, to a degree, Bluebell, who I knew to be diligent and reliable in a way my singer was not. It was imperative that Torin should be seen, well 'heard', to be live. The crowd hung on his ad libs, song intros and impromptu remarks during solos (invariably vocal mistakes Alana would cauterise with a look or a nudge). His posh-boy utterances were an indelible part of our gig experience. It was vital that, on those big choruses we were famous for, the audience hear his 'real' voice coming through the PA. Our public might let pass a missed cue two or three times, but the game would be up if they heard Torin singing the wrong line or melody, song after song. It would be shambolic. A hell on stage.

"Torin, Roy, here's the plan…" It had always been Roy and me who would scrutinise the gig recordings to see where we could get the best out of our live sound. Torin had never understood our attention to detail, and his disdain for what Roy did for him was evident.

"Roy, I've got Torin's vocals on playback, the album takes," I said. "It's what the girls have been rehearsing to for the last couple of weeks. So, if there's a problem…with the…"

Torin butted in, agitatedly. "If I fuck it up."

Roy remained impassive, but I read his mind: *'Not if, but when.'*

"If that happens," I continued, "I want you to bring the level of the live vocal down and raise the lead vocal on my computer."

Torin blinked in instant comprehension. "I just join in with myself. That's genius."

Roy rubbed his beardy chin. "So, as soon as I see you in err… 'trouble'," he said to Torin. Then he turned to me. "I'll back the stage mic off and bring up the vocal on the playback."

I nodded. "Should be pretty seamless." I looked at Torin. "Make sure you cover your mouth with your hand or something, turn around, I dunno, when you know you've lost the song. I'll have a word with Bluebell, she can do an 'Alana' on you in the verses. Do you understand, Torin?"

"Fuck me, yes! You keep asking. I'm not a complete imbecile."

I caught Roy's eye in the gloom and for a fraction of a second, less probably, saw the Black Country mirth glimmering in it.

***

In a shirt of diaphanous black muslin embossed with red butterflies and gold sequins, Torin reclined on the dressing room sofa reciting lyrics from the pieces of paper he'd chased around the stage earlier. Occasionally, his marker flew, underlining and excising, but since our chat on the balcony, an air of calm had come over him concerning our performance. Like the charade we were to undertake in less than an hour, him doing his homework was pretence, a pose to make him look professional, because in his heart, he knew that he wasn't.

"Daniel, this is going to be like miming, but instead of four minutes in a TV studio, it'll be an hour in front of a couple of thousand."

"Sort of," I said.

"Why had no one thought of this before? We've wasted so much time and money."

I imagined the furrowed brows beyond the lights at the front of the stage, people turning to each other, '*Sounds exactly like the album. Amazing...*'

The girls were in their own room along the corridor, and it was just me and Torin in this one. I selected a solitary apple from the fruit bowl, part of a creative display of crisps, sarnies and confectionary on the dressing room's extended pasting table. Deep below, the PA boomed as the support band gave it their all on stage. I felt none of the good pre-gig nerves I usually did. Why would I? The jeopardy had gone out of it. In this rigid playback state, with half the band miming, none of the beautiful stuff that can happen between musicians would take place tonight.

My apple core hit the bin, eliciting a sideways glare from the studious one. He'd finished his glass and was looking agitatedly at the door. I took a tangerine and began peeling it. Again, I felt *his* presence before he appeared. More bull-like than ever, a bristling Conrad filled the dressing room. With his physique testing the seams of a blue and white striped shirt, he examined our faces as if we wore masks.

I popped a segment into my mouth.

Torin was up, hopping from one foot to the other. "About fucking time, Conrad," he said. Without looking at him, Conrad passed him his little package and Torin quickly turned for the toilet.

Raising a couple of bottles from the table, Conrad squinted at the labels with comic disgust. "Vin ordinaire, Torin?" He rumbled.

"There's a couple of bottles of decent-ish Vin de Pays at the back," Torin called from behind the toilet door, his credit card tapping the porcelain. "Behind the vodka."

Pop! Conrad's neck bulged like a bodybuilder's bicep as he extracted the cork from one. His mouth shaped a thin smile at me. "Let's hope you guys sound as good," he said, pouring a generous glass for himself. After a testing sip, he took in our modest room. "The glamour never stops, does it?" he proclaimed with a sneer. "You'd think a rock star's comforts would be so much slicker, more lux, I guess. This is an utter shithole, isn't it?"

"Story of my life, Conrad." Torin had returned, blinking rheumily, his nose twitching like a bunny's.

I looked out of the narrow window into the alley at the side of the theatre. Below, with their posters rolled up, some fans were shuffling about in 'Torin' T-shirts. The thing is, I loved it here. Joy was generated within these walls. It had been for decades. He was so wrong.

"You think so?" Conrad was looking at me curiously.

"Think what?" I asked.

"You think I'm wrong?"

I shrugged. He took a step towards me. "How's he doing?"

I returned to the alley outside. "OK, I think."

"Who's *he*," Torin said, sharply from his lyrics, "The cat's fucking mother!"

Behind me, a glass exploded. Conrad had wiped it from Torin's hand with his bear paw. "Fucking hell!" I yelled, leaping across the room and pulling on Conrad's forearm. He had lifted Torin bodily from the sofa, ripping his shirt from the collar down. Satiny buttons exploded around us. Sequins dusted the air.

"Listen, you entitled prick!" His voice boomed over the opening act downstairs. "The time has come to set our schoolboy friendship aside. You had better nail this fucking gig, DeVere, *and* the ones to come. I'm three hundred thousand pounds out and *you* are going to get every penny back for me, comprenez-fucking-vous?" Torin's eyes bulged as he nodded breathlessly. "*You*," Conrad continued, spit flying, "are going to sing and dance for me and my money, you prize – bullshit – artist!"

"Let him go! How's he gonna do it if you throttle him."

He threw Torin onto the sofa and pushed me against the wall. Bile and fury wafted from his razored pores. As his tiny pupils dissected every centimetre of my skin, one heavy digit excavated the muscle fibres of my chest. His whisper was a roar, "And as for you, my scar-faced, whore-loving, ivory-tinkler..."

But as he drew breath for a further volley, an unusual sense of calm came over me. It didn't make me strong or brave, but it did make me reckless. I looked straight at him. '*Have a good fucking look, then,*' I said in my head. He stepped backed suddenly. "Sorry, Daniel that was out of order." He was gently patting down my jacket collar. "I know how hard you've worked." Shaking his head, he returned to the table, sighed and topped up his glass. "It's him, coke-head, fuck-up. He's been playing me for months."

White as a sheet, with his stage shirt ripped from collar to sleeve, Torin stared at Conrad like a trapped animal. Then as one, our heads turned towards the open door to see Martin Reed framed in it. Like his name, Reed was tall and spare, but a force in the business. He stepped in and spoke without preamble. "Torin, no Barney, big London show, no TM? I've spoken to Daniel, not a thing from you. And I only heard second hand that your label has dropped you! What the actual fuck Torin?"

"Barney's mum's not well, Martin," I said. "He..."

Reed ignored me. "It's been a shit show, Torin. What happened to communication?"

It was then that Reed noticed the scattered sequins, pieces of A4, and realised Torin's tattered garment wasn't an exclusive Westwood creation.

"Daniel?" he said, looking bemusedly at me.

"It's all good, Martin."

"Doesn't fucking look it," he replied, as Torin scrabbled around picking up his lyrics. He must be tired of doing that, I thought.

Conrad stepped in and offered his hand. "Conrad Price."

Reed regarded him coolly as he shook Conrad's hand. "I know it appears a little chaotic, but that's bound to happen during a period of transition. My company," Conrad said, fishing out a wallet from his unfeasibly tight chinos and handing Reed an embossed card from it, "is now managing Torin in all spheres. Lawyers are finalising contracts. There's been snags and that is what has caused this…'breakdown in communication'. I honestly thought Barney was taking care of things with you, and he thought I was. Glass of wine? It isn't too shabby."

"I'll have a beer."

Conrad flipped a cap off one from the vast ice bucket and handed it to Reed. "We would have informed you personally, but, as you know, with the gig and the tour to sort out, my office has been a little overrun."

Reed had not yet brought the bottle to his lips. "I need to know if the tour support is there," he said. "I'll be sued all over the place if this goes pear-shaped. It's a fucking shambles. Amateur hour."

"It's all taken care of," said Conrad. "There's money in the tour account to cover everything."

When Reed looked at me, I could tell the man the truth for the first time in forty-eight hours. "Yes, the money's definitely in there," I said.

"Torin?"

Buttoning up a shirt of pink silk, dotted with aquamarine and black polka dots while side-footing shards of glass into the skirting, Torin managed to retrieve his smile. Credit to him, I thought, although knackered, potless, and having had his life threatened just moments ago, he still ticked those Rock Star boxes.

"Conrad is the person I've been looking for…well, forever," he said checking himself in the mottled old wall mirror, "I'm really excited by the err…?"

'New way,' I said in my head.

"What way?" said Reed.

"The new one," I confirmed.

Reed's hatchet face was finally cracking. He took a swig from his bottle.

"It's good to hear," he said regarding Torin. "You've never had what I'd call, a serious manager." He paused for thought. "Always lacked a strategy. Direction. You've never fulfilled your potential."

"Perfectly put, Martin. Conrad is someone I trust," Torin said, looking admiringly at Conrad in the mirror, "He's a man with a vision for me."

"So, Martin," said Conrad. "We'll get this show done and pack these kids off on the road. Perhaps lunch next week? The Groucho. Talk budgets. The States?"

"If I'm completely honest, I came here expecting to pull the entire thing after tonight. Cut my losses. Getting rid of two amazing musicians, completely turning the thing inside out, no tour manager, well...but OK, OK, let's do that."

Conrad looked the agent in the eye. "Torin has got his head down recently, and *not* over a CD case, if you know what I mean?"

From his great height, Reed nodded. "That's been a problem, hasn't it Torin?"

Torin pistol pointed in the mirror. "Pow! I think I'm through that phase now, Martin," he said, blowing on his fingertips. He was irresistible when he turned it on.

"OK. I'm sold," Reed said, smiling at last. "What we need now is a stellar show. And I know you'll deliver that."

Torin turned from the mirror and put his arm around Conrad's shoulder. With a clenched fist, he proclaimed; "Let's fuckin' rock!"

Everyone was smiling. Reed opened the dressing room door. "Break a leg."

As he left, Conrad pushed Torin away and approached me. It was my shoulders he took in his thick hands now. "Allow me to apologise for my earlier loss of cool. *'Have a good fucking look, then,'* Ha! I admire your chutzpah, Daniel. Not only have I grown to respect you, I actually rate you as a man. This could be the start of something really productive between us. I've always got talent passing through my hands, pretty girls that can hold a tune? A person with your expertise, all that computer music you make, could capitalise on that talent. Look after your mum in *real* style. What do you say?"

The stage manager saved me from telling him that I'd rather chew off my own arm and *never* touch a keyboard again than do anything with him.

"Five minutes gents."

Conrad finished his glass and checked his phone. "I'll see you both in here afterwards."

"Conrad?" Torin was like a little boy peering up at his dad.

"Fuck's sake, Torin," he said, fishing into the pocket that did not contain his wallet and passing him a wrap.

When Torin returned from the toilet, we were alone.

'It's time to put on make-up...' I sang, Kermit style.

"What?" he snarled and sniffed.

It was what Mick would normally sing at this point in the evening.

I shrugged. "Just an old joke. It isn't funny anymore."

***

When Daisy and Bluebell met us at the side of the stage, Torin was posing, pouting and jogging on the spot. "What a couple of stunners," he said, causing them to smile through their nerves. He glugged from his bottle and leaned into my ear. "I'm actually looking forward to this, for once."

The PA boomed: "Ladies and gentlemen, opening their British tour here at the Empire… Torin!"

On we went to roaring approval.

We were two numbers in, and it was going OK. He'd blanked on a chorus and had been late for a verse, but neither episode was fatal. During the verse, Bluebell had stood in front of him and shouted the lines he'd forgotten until the penny dropped. The chorus oversight was a little more concerning. He'd turned and faced the drums, eyes screwed up listening to his own voice in the drummer's side-fill, mouthing, trying to locate where he should land. I held my breath as the thin vertical line drew inexorably towards the song's chorus on my screen. A bright yellow follow-spot hit him. His smile broadened. Swishing the mic cable left and right, he spun around and joined in with a chorus that'd almost sailed by.

At the end of the song, he sauntered over to me. "I've got this Daniel. Piece of piss."

My finger hovered over the spacebar. He bade me wait, then turned to address *his* people. "New dawns, brothers and sisters. As we grow, we realise there were never any rules to begin with. We strive for change, demand new ways and methods. We don't listen to mortals, regulators. Out with the old! We are gods. Let's get the job done!"

As he raised one fist high, I pressed play on 'Zeus Smiled Down'.

Out front, Roy was doing an amazing job, anticipating Torin's vocal glitches. The audience couldn't see the join between live mic and the one pre-recorded on my laptop.

Songs six and seven had had their vocal faux pas, but again, nothing that would cause a musician to soil themselves. I felt detached up there, close to boredom if I'm honest. My mind began to wander like it did at school after the accident. I could lose a whole lesson staring out of the window at the seagulls on the playing field crossbars.

In the middle of 'Freezing Torrent' there's a four-bar section where the drums play on their own. I glanced up to see the audience leaping and clapping to Mick's 'sampled' groove with its swing and caressed ghost-rolls. A sickening flashback saw me hunched over my computer in the shed, stealing my best friends work so Torin's pre-recorded pantomime could exist.

I snapped back. Torin was at the far edge of the stage, hip-swinging, slowly rotating the mic on the cable. The fans beneath him were melting, reaching up for a touch of his gold flares, and I remembered him moving similarly a few hours earlier on the Green when I told him about the girls having not been paid.

"...and *they* are going the way of Barney," he'd said, poring over his pages. "Bluebell is far too trappy, poking her nose in, demanding. Is she continually on the blob? miserable cow."

"She's got a kid. She was just asking for confirmation about..."

"Fucking premenstrual women are the plague of my life. *Wahlababa, oh me mensies! Oh me mumphlies!*" he squawked, swinging his hips, stage style. Then, to the amusement of the drinkers and rough sleepers on the benches either side of us, he began running around ours, clutching his stomach, fanning his crotch, performing his stock impression of a woman having her period.

He flopped onto the bench. "And Daisy, well thick is a compliment, but then she is a drummer."

"Torin, Barney hasn't been…"

"Just don't fucking Barney me, man. He should be paying *me* for the pain and suffering he's caused with his incompetence. Stalking me around *my* club. I forbid the mention of his fat little name."

"The bloke only wants what's due to him."

"Then he'll have to get in line with the rest of them. Anyway, the flower ladies are history after tonight. I know some Slavics who will do it for half *and* there'll be extras, ha-ha! What? Aw, you've gone all 'Daniel-looking'. Don't come the innocent with me, I know you're partial to an old *brass*, ha ha ha!

…Who'd have thought *she* was the coffee-chucker? Let me tell you about her…"

I was grateful for the wailing ambulance that drowned out the rest of his discourse. The siren faded. Bus brakes hissed, engines revved, and cars surged into the ambulance's wake. Torin was smiling at me through the fading, pulsing blue.

"…But I'll admit, she was a favourite of mine, Sorrow. I mean, they were all slags, of course, but she liked to read and could converse. She had a sense of…style. There was an element of ambition too. Greedy though. Never satisfied. We gave her everything she could want, but there's no pleasing some women, is there? I'm mildly envious you've tamed her."

"She's not wild Torin."

"Ha-ha. Don't think I've ever seen you so sensitive. A word to the wise: she's scum m'boy, she sells herself for money. But I can't deny you've actually holed old Torin below the water line, fucking her. And for gratis too!"

A wave of applause brought me round.

"Thank you, my friends. Are you rockin' with Torin?…I said, *are you rockin' with Torin!*…" A roar of gratitude had him nodding with slow approval. "That's more like it. We're gonna play a song now that we…"

I pressed the spacebar and zoned out. Usually, I'd be listening to my bandmates, getting the feel and intensity of the song, going with them, watching Torin like a hawk, anticipating one of his 'moments'. But there was no need for focus of that kind here, I'd designed a foolproof system that needed only a fool's concentration.

"What was he like?" I'd asked her.

"You don't want to know?"

"I do."

"One of the worst. No, the worst."

"Jesus."

"He liked us at the same time, Francine and me. Made us perform, threw notes on the floor singing that fucking 'storm' song for all the men. Cocaine everywhere. Pills, beers, wine, the mess, the chaos, bloody toilet roll, bits of tobacco and notes and cards, broken glasses, doors locked, curtains drawn…everything spilled or spilling…Poor Francine, she'd do anything, and he knew she would. God, thinking about it now, I don't know how I…"

She put her hands to her face.

"I don't blame you, Kerry."

"What did I do to myself? Oh my god, how could I?"

"It's OK."

One sad eye looked through her fingers at me. "They treated us like shit, Daniel, fed us full of drugs and booze, slapped us, burned us with cigarettes, put things up us, bottles…tied us up, pissed on us… and they all clapped because he was singing a song. Is that right? Just because you can sing a song you can behave like that?"

Through fading applause, I looked up and saw Bluebell anxiously blinking at me over her shoulder. I winked encouragingly and depressed the fingers of my right hand.

In his dimly lit cubicle in the distance, I could see Roy, his eyes tracking Torin as he stalked the stage, swishing his mic cable behind him like a lizard's tail.

Conrad was right. I was the cleverest of sods, wasn't I? Twenty-five years old and I rescued my career from oblivion, arranged a business plan for a pimp, and probably saved the life of the bloke who fucked it all up in the first place. Pat on the head, Daniel Earl, *pizza face*, recluse, bottler and studio schemer.

The vertical line journeyed relentlessly across the parallel bands on my computer screen, each one a different colour, 'playing' separate instruments: bass, strings, drums, backing vocals, lead, percussion. That this practically invisible, creeping mark was dispensing this wall of music was miraculous.

Because I seemed to be zoning out on nearly every song now, I pressed the button for my Moog Prodigy to go live. I began adding a couple of pushed darts on 'The Ship That Never Sailed'. They were edgy and sounded pretty dramatic coming through that big system. It was the sort of thing I would have discussed with Alana at soundcheck, see if she thought it felt right to jam it in during the gig. Well, Alana wasn't here to say yes or no, so I continued: '*Flick, flick*'. I counted: 'ONE, two, three, four, flick-flick, TWO, two, three, four, flick-flick, THREE, two, three, four, flick-flick, FOUR, two three, four...

"Oi Earl, you fucking gargoyle cunt."

Leaning on the alley bars after school, Craig was trying to light his fag but it was windy, and although he flicked his lighter spitefully, it just wouldn't spark. I'd been back at school a week after convalescing at home. Accepting he wouldn't allow me to cut through (and I'd have to walk the long way home), I turned, but his mate Andy blocked the way.

"You got tax for me?" Craig said, levering himself off the bar and spinning me so that the small of my back was against it.

I said no. He knew I hadn't. We were poor.

I felt his eyes on my face, loathing my appearance. I was picking very badly and in a world of pain, inside and out. He put his hands on my shoulders bending me backwards over the bar. His face was inches from mine, his breath was not Merlot, but faggy bacon. There was a packet of Jaffa Cakes in my rucksack, and they were getting squashed. I could feel my weight compressing them. My mother liked to arrange them on a plate for me. I'd smile for her (even though I hated smiling) like a kid on Christmas morning. It cheered her up that she pleased me, so it was no big deal. Poor mum, seventeen and knocked-up by a bloke she never saw again. Parents disowning her. Having a breakdown. Ending up in a mother and baby home. But through all of that, she had steadfastly loved and cared for me, the best she could. '*Flick, flick*', ONE, two, three, four, flick-flick, TWO, two, three, four, flick-flick, THREE, two, three, four...' So, I always smiled for my mum and her fan-like Jaffa Cake display. No other fucker was going to.

"I don't hate you cos of your shitty burned eye, you soppy coloured cunt. It's cos you're a half-breed Paki and your mum's a slag."

'Flick, flick...Bang!'

I was suddenly standing over him and flailing away. Big Andy had stepped back in awe of my rage. Neither of them knew that when I looked in the bathroom mirror, the thought of jumping off the balcony onto the walkway below, rigging up some knotted sheets across the loft hatch, swallowing all mum's antidepressants at once, was nothing I feared. The loneliness and ugliness of it all made living worthless, so I didn't care if they killed me. They'd be doing me a favour.

Sometimes at a gig, a big one, there's what can only be described as a 'truce' between the audience and performers. It's understood that we are all taking part in something wonderfully symbiotic, but for a moment we decide to be private. It was in one of these lulls that I saw Bluebell standing in front of me, panting, make-up running.

"Jaffa Cakes? Is that code...a song?"

Through the wash of stage lights, I felt countless eyes on me.

"You alright?" She asked, trying to get my attention.

"Yeah, I mean no. It ain't a song. Just thinking about my mum and school. You know what *he* said to me once?" I was addressing her as if we were standing by the Coke machine in a break at rehearsals. "He said, *'Nothing personal, Daniel. But the trouble with the music industry is that there are musicians involved in it'.*"

Bluebell's lips were compressed anxiously. Her eyes flitting behind her. The truce was over. I could hear groaning and mutterings of impatience. A half-hearted slow handclap began. Apart from a chorus of *'You're shit'*, it's the worst thing you can hear when you're playing live.

"Don't worry," I said, pressing the spacebar for the next song. "Here we go."

As I mimed the opening notes of 'Silent Storm' the audience went into raptures. Listening to those revered chords, and the irresistible groove born in the rehearsal room a few hundred yards from where we were, I was doused in a melancholy blueness. I wanted to get a microphone and tell everyone there that I'd created this music on the Casio my mum had given me after I came home from hospital. It had been such a brilliant thing for her to buy me. She hadn't a clue about music. But out of love and care, she'd delivered to me the thing that had made my life.

'Silent storm...' everyone sang.

Looking across the sea of heads, I pictured myself, on any Wednesday night five years ago, waiting in the pub doorway with that 'entry-level' keyboard after rehearsing with Miss Ferguson's band. Through falling snow, I could see my mum silhouetted behind the wheel of her car, and I wondered if she had just done a loop of the tarmac when I'd entered the pub and had sat waiting there for the entire two-hour rehearsal. Because the electrics were dodgy, she kept the engine turned off, so no heating either. And I'd *never* invite her in. Outside of our front door she always looked nervous and fragile, and I felt embarrassed by her. It was only a ten-minute walk from our block to the pub, but she would *always* drive me there and back.

I was embarrassed *then*, but here, now, I was proud that I had a mum who ferried me and my little set-up to that dismal car park twice a week to rehearse and play. How many hours had she stared at that 'private, no parking' sign by the bins?

"Oh mum," I muttered, looking out at the undulating waves of human joy before me.

The singer flashed across my eye-line, head back, grinning as wide as the world. He was winning. He'd always won. His kind just do. They glory in their victory, careless of people like me, Mick and Alana… Barney, Bluebell, Daisy, Francine and Kerry. They let the bodies pile high behind them as they stride towards greatness, assured that they'll never be held to account simply because of an accident of birth.

In the shady wings, Conrad was as still as stone, a look of loathing fixed on his well-razored face. I'd been clocking him ever since we'd come on. Not once did he tap his foot or nod his head. He was staring past me at Torin, who had one foot on the wedge at the front of the stage, conducting our fans in that time-honoured way.

I heard Kerry's voice through her tears: '...*that fucking 'storm'*, *song.'* The whole theatre joined in as the key shifted, a semitone up. *'One of the worst. No, the worst.'*

Raising my head, I listened in awe to our huge chorus thundering from the PA, echoing off the ceiling and snaking between the aisles. I'd never hear it this way again. I moved the cursor to the yellow band on my computer screen, studied the thin line running through it, highlighted it and pressed 'mute'.

20

Impervious to the shouts and calls at my back, I strode through the alley from the stage door. I wanted to get on the tube and get home for that Chinese I'd had mum order for me. I'd instructed her to get loads. I'd eat like a king tonight.

It had got chilly, but slaloming between the traffic, an amazing energy warmed me. I jogged onto the Green, feeling as if I could run all the way home.

Beneath a streetlight on the intersection of paths fifty yards ahead, what seemed to be a murky apparition, set against a tree trunk, was in fact a rotund woman in a mac. Her belt-ends hung by her sides like two sad doggy ears, while a stuffed rucksack dragged one shoulder down, pulling at the sinews of her neck. With her laundry bags of belongings, I thought she was another rough sleeper, beaten by life. A lot of them gathered over here. As I strode towards the station behind her, I speculated on her luckless backstory. She'd slipped through the cracks and reaching up for a helping hand, had been dismayed that there wasn't one there. Bound to have got into debt, set fire to her final bridge, ripped off the wrong people, made one bad friend too many, and now, all she had left was resting on the wet black tarmac around her feet. Could happen to any of us, right?

She'd placed herself in such a way, that I had to step onto the grass to circumnavigate. I was surprised that she wore a pale blue baseball cap. I was a few yards away before I spoke.

"Hello, you OK?"

She shivered. A yellow-hued mist rose from her mouth. "Pam's closed down the shop. She's opening one in Paris now."

"She's not taking you?"

Glancing at the bags at her feet, I watched her try to locate the old 'front of house' dazzler, but she managed only a sad shrug of acceptance. "She wants to go in another direction, sort of."

I smiled. "A new way. Yeah, heard that one myself."

I couldn't bear the way the rucksack was pulling on her shoulder, causing her to take the weight on one tired hip. Close up, the tendons were blue on her neck. Her eyeballs swam with fatigue. "Can we sit over there?" she said, nodding towards a bench a little way away.

"Fuck no," I said.

She coughed and raised her eyes towards the theatre behind me. "Sorry I couldn't make it."

"No big deal," I said, taking the rucksack from her shoulder and slinging it on mine. I picked up two laundry bags.

"Did it…?"

"Yeah, went well. Come on."

She picked up the final bag and followed me.

On the way home, she'd stared waxily into the tube window, and I worried she'd gone somewhere in her head she'd never return from. The short walk to my house was undertaken in silent endurance, but when I put the key in the lock and pushed the door open, I saw a smile finally splinter the ice around her eyes and mouth.

"I know," I said, with a smile of my own. "Chinese."

"Daniel?" my mother called as I shuffled sideways into the passage with the bags. "I got those noodles as well. I thought…" Stepping out of the front room into the corridor, her sentence froze on her lips.

"Mum, this is my friend Kerry."

"Oh. Hello, Kerry."

"Hello?"

"Mandy."

"Mandy."

Mum's eyes were on the bags.

Kerry piped up, "I've got a cab coming."

"I'll put them in the shed," I said.

I carried the bags through the house to the kitchen.

"Mum," I called, passing the steam rising from copious aluminium trays on the surface. "Can you put another plate out, ta."

Kerry was sitting at the table when I shut the garden door. I'd never seen another female sit there apart from my mum. She'd taken her mac off. There were a number of fleeces and sweaters on the other chair.

"You've shrunk," I said.

I was opening a drawer and pulling out a pair of chopsticks when my mother called my name. Bad eye and all, I actually winked at

Kerry. I did! "Get stuck in. Back in a mo."

In the front room, mum ran her beads between her fingers.

"I've been going out with Kerry for about a month. Just walking, getting something to eat. She's staying here tonight."

"Are you sure, Daniel? She's a bit…"

"More sure than anything, mum."

We paused for a moment on the stage of our living room.

"You've done the lawn," I said.

"You always do it. Thought I would."

"Done a good job, mum."

I opened the door. Exit stage left.

"You didn't say if it was a good gig?"

"Went well. I'm starving," I nodded at the sofa. "I'll be sleeping down here tonight."

"Your mum's lovely."

"Yeah, she is. Never had anyone round here before. A girl, I mean. Eat up."

I was amused at her reserve, taking a modest portion from each of the trays. If we were in Soho, she'd have been buzzing around those dishes, sauce flying everywhere.

"If you can hold on to my stuff, I can come back."

"Nah, you can stay in my room. I'll sleep on the couch. It's big enough."

Ping.

"That's the jasmine rice."

She was about to protest. I held up both palms. I'd had enough drama for one evening.

"Kerry, shall we move on."

***

Her head lay on my shoulder while a TV film droned on unintelligibly. I'd switched all the lights off. I'd had enough of those as well. We'd not spoken much, swapped some lines, mainly about dinner and how big the telly was. She didn't have one. Not watched any for months. I'd become used to her taking the lead and was unsettled (in a nice way) by her novel reticence, pausing between sentences, giving our exchanges space and time.

The adverts came and went. I turned off the sound completely.

"Why did they call you Sorrow?"

"Because I look like this." Fleetingly, she produced that waxy, vacant expression. "It was the name they gave me at the orphanage. It worked in my favour when I was little, cute, but as an adult…Ah yes," she nodded, "I told Francine, and somehow Conrad, or another of the men found out. More sport for them."

"Not surprised you prefer Kerry."

"Well, it's where I'm from. I don't want to be known for sadness."

We watched the scenes change on the screen – nighttime in a car, eyes connecting in a rear-view mirror, a door opened, a hallway light flicked on. He opens a bottle of wine by unwashed plates in a kitchen.

"You're always hungry."

"Ha, so unladylike. There was never much food when I was little. The nuns stuck to a spartan existence. I couldn't believe it when I came to London and met Conrad, the waste. I actually put on a few pounds towards the end."

"The end?"

"I'll come to that."

We watched the screen for a bit.

"We're like those actors, him and her watching telly," she said.

"We're better than them, we're not acting."

"Oh Daniel."

Her taste was chow mein and salty tears. When she drew back, I sensed a change, something unlocking behind her eyes. "OK," she said, with a sigh. "It's time."

"You can't go."

"I'm not. It's time to talk."

There then began the great cracking of Kerry. The granite hard images and reinventions splitting, tragic fissures opening, boulders of her past falling into the foam below.

"She never let me eat in the shop and I couldn't dash out for a sandwich because I was the only one there. She'd go mad if the shop was shut in the day, and you never knew when she'd come by. But I couldn't be in two places at one time, so I was always hungry. At seven, when I locked that door, I could eat a woolly mammoth. Not long before I met you, she caught me with some toast I'd made for breakfast. She had a toaster in the kitchen, downstairs. She lost it, said I'd got butter on a cashmere sweater and docked my money. She got rid of the toaster too."

Wanting to make her smile, I said lightly, frivolously, "Kerry, you will never be hungry again."

I can't tell you for how long she cried after I said that, but when we woke up on the sofa, the film had finished, and it was my turn. Energised, I just started proper babbling, four in the morning, post-gig, tour bus bollocks.

"How did you get out of it? I mean Conrad. I can't stand being near the geezer, he's like, fucking infecting me with his friendship. Wants me to go into some kind of partnership with him, producing? I'd rather pack it in…I just want to play, know what I mean? I've never told you, but I'd be happy on a desert island with my synths and a power supply, and you."

More of the edifice fell away with her tears.

"You think I'm crying because of Conrad and being prostituted, don't you?"

"Well, of course. It's an evil…"

"Oh Daniel, It's not that. I'm crying because I'm happy here with you."

My memory tripped back. I was looking out of the patisserie window when I felt her loaded fork against my lips. When I turned to face her, her eyes expanded with encouragement, and I *had* to open my mouth. She'd smiled with a sly, comedic satisfaction, reloaded the fork and joined me. It was a unique moment of intimacy, the sharing of the same fork, the enjoyment of the same taste. She had wanted to make me feel the way she did. It was twenty minutes later that we saw her friend huddled in the doorway. "I thought about Francine, on stage tonight. I mean last night."

"Francine," she groaned. "Have you seen her?"

"Not since after we had cake together. I look for her nearly every night, ask in the hostels, street people she knows."

"I'm sorry."

She felt for my hand. Her grip was desperate. "Sisters in hell," she said, exhaling hard.

"Conrad mentioned her," I said.

"She was his favourite. I was Torin's."

"Look, I don't care about..."

She silenced me with a quick shake of her head. "I became homeless when I was twenty-eight, not that I had what most people call a home before then. Because he'd said I could contact him any time, I called Conrad. I don't know when or where I'd met him, but he'd been courteous enough when I did. The weather was bad, and I had nowhere Daniel. He spun me a line about how he looked after his 'friends'. Ha ha." She laughed darkly. "I was in one of his mate's brothels within a month. It was a posh one, but they are all hellish and grim, however tasteful the light fittings. I met a man from Ireland. He seemed kind and bought me cakes and then started fucking all the girls in the brothel. When I said I'd had enough, he beat me up and started on one of the other girls. It was a disaster. I got kicked out. So, there's me again, walking around, chancing anything for food and a bed. Living out of rucksacks and holdalls. A girl put me in touch with Francine."

She smiled at the TV screen as if her friend had suddenly appeared in it.

"She was one of those people you meet…Kindness shone out of her. Nothing was ever too much trouble. I'd lost loads of weight, got run down. She nursed me. Such care and always a joke and a giggle. We shared one bed in her tiny flat in Bloomsbury and started dancing in a club at the end of Brewer Street. It was a laugh for a while, men just looking and not touching. One night there was a knock on the changing room door. It was Conrad. I'd not seen him for a year."

She saw me looking at her.

"I know, Daniel. I should have run a mile, but you can't help but be drawn to kindness when you've had so little, even though you know it's all a big lie and people are going to use you."

"But he'd put you in his mate's brothel?"

She shook her head, as if trying to unjumble her thoughts. "I suppose, you think, well, *this* could be a new start. Here is day one."

I let her stare at the TV for a minute. "But it wasn't a new start?"

"No. He took us to dinner across the road, Francine and me, this fabulous seafood restaurant, wine and champagne. We were skint, of course he knew that. Anyway, the money he offered us to 'dance' at his parties was so much more than we were earning. It seemed serendipitous. We'd talked endlessly about saving for a deposit for our own place. Here was our chance of getting a proper flat together. He said he'd help us; he knew loads of landlords. We promised ourselves that it would be a quick hit, a means to an end, but there was no end, no flat or deposit. We were back sleeping with men for money. There was a lot of coke and E around, and Francine got addicted. Conrad liked to get her completely wrecked, have his friends – and your singer – abuse her...It's just sadistic tormenting a fellow human being. Am I being too...?"

"No Kerry. Carry on."

"Francine was very fine featured, delicate. She wasn't sleeping or eating, she was constantly wired and her looks started to go. She got really thin, moody, irrational, dull. He turned on her because she *'brought the party down'* even though he'd been supplying her with the shit that made her that way. He broke her, Daniel. Turned her to mush."

A garish advert came on the screen: groups of grinning young people in pastel colours dancing along a busy street.

"What happened when he saw you the other day, at the restaurant?"

"It had to happen. I was actually relieved. I'd let him down badly on a job abroad, but he was fine. Pragmatic." She smiled dismally.

"That all?"

"He said, as long as I didn't work for any of his competitors, he didn't give a shit if I lived or died."

"Staggering."

"My 'profession.'"

"No, no, just the way your life ended up." After a pause she continued. "Eventually Francine was thrown out of the group, the 'A Class' as Conrad called us. I didn't hear from her. I hoped she'd escaped, found someone who could care for her, who she could care for, because she was so good at that, looking after people...she should have been a nurse...And then I saw her, like she is now. I was leaving for Paris, a party for Conrad. Investors, a lot of Russian money. He said there'd be a bonus for us…She was begging on the street outside King's Cross Station. It was pouring down. Cold. She looked sixty years old. My heart broke in two."

"Jesus," I whispered.

Her fingers were trembling in my hand. "It all happened on the same day – seeing Francine begging me to help her, give her money, find her somewhere to sleep – and having to go to Paris for one of those awful parties…" Her nails began digging into my palm, "…with those gross men and their stinking, pissy cocks, and I had to smile and pretend I was having the time of my life."

I blew my cheeks out. "Fucking hell."

"And I left her there in the rain. I gave her my number on a piece of paper, told her to call me. She didn't even have a phone."

She was crying hard now. I stroked her face…eventually we fell asleep.

***

Mum looked at me as the power shower did its work. We'd never heard it sitting together. There was always one of us in it.

"How long is she staying, Daniel?"

"We're working it out mum." She nodded, her eyes still on me. "We're very close," I told her.

"I don't want you to get hurt."

"Why would I be?"

"She's not a normal girl."

"Ha. I'm not a normal bloke."

Kerry took in the blinking, winking effects racks, faders and speakers in the shed at the back of my garden.

"So many buttons and switches. Looks fiendishly complicated." Her finger hovered over a red button. "What'll happen if I press this?"

"No! Not that one!" I replied, dramatically, our eyes meeting in a smile.

"Is it expensive?"

"A bit. I've spoiled myself in here."

I flicked a speck of lint from the top of a speaker. I'd always thought I'd upgrade my studio equipment, now I was thinking about the best price I could get for flogging it.

She was scrutinising the myriad channels on the mixing desk. "You never really know what goes on behind all the music."

"You don't actually need all this, Kerry," I said, then I tapped the side of my head. "It's all up here."

A slice of midday sun illuminated our half of the studio. Stepping across the room, she pressed her palm to my chest.

"No, it's all in there."

Her eyes narrowed, the green in them searching for something in the recesses of mine. I moved my mouth to hers and we kissed. But this time things got a little bit manic. Energy flowed through us as we touched, not like a comfortable couple strolling, arm in arm, through the streets of London, but like food and heat.

Standing there shy and sort of new, it was as if the edifice had fallen away entirely when I removed her sweater.

***

"You cracked something in me Daniel," she said, kissing me gently as we lay on the sofa. The room was in darkness now. I turned on the lamp.

"So, how *did* you get out of the life?"

"Paris."

"Paris?"

"I love it."

"You always spoke about you and your mum in France in such detail. It seemed so plausible."

"Everything you heard me say about my imaginary mother was stolen, taken from conversations I'd had with girls. Things I'd overheard, bits of books, scenes in films. None of it happened to me."

I leaned across and pressed 'play' on the computer. As synthetic strings eased through the speakers, I thought of all the times we had looked at shoes in shop windows, or at flats for rent in the estate agent next door, perused menus outside posh restaurants (her telling me where she'd eaten the items on it and who with), and I couldn't decide whether I should be happy or sad that her opinions and tastes had been formed by the fantasies she'd had to construct because her reality was so bleak. Sitting there, staring at that space between the speakers, I realised that it didn't matter – we were here now, and that was all that mattered.

"This is amazing, Daniel. Who is it?"

"Only me noodling about."

She shook her head and smiled. "I've met so many men who've swanned around pretending they're rock stars, 'artists', all deep and moody, posing and mouthing off and yet you, so modest and quiet, are the real deal."

"Like I said, I just love playing. It's all I've ever wanted to do." A harp and sampled choral part caused the piece to build. A cello emerged, to support the progression from beneath. I laughed at its grandiose journey. "A bit over the top, but it's kind of private, self-indulgent."

"But I love it, Daniel."

She returned her head to my chest, and we listened for a while. "There's a café, Café de Flore," she said quietly. "I heard a girl talking about it way before I met Francine and Conrad. She said she used to go there with her mother. She was from a 'good' family, ha. Ended up working next door to me." She sat up. "The day I'd left Francine at King's Cross, I got it into my head that I'd go there, visit this legendary café, before I…I don't know, joined Francine in her doorway?"

My piece had reached its climax and dissolved into a simple piano part.

"…So, I went there," she said.

When I looked at her, laughter-lines had spread from her eyes.

"It is the most Parisian café you can imagine. The tables are tiny, impractical really. They pour hot chocolate from a silver jug. It is *nectar*, Daniel, and the little tartines…" She spoke as if she were dancing, sweeping and turning in an open space. "It was fashion week, late spring, and Paris was all decked out. It was like being on a film set or in a musical. Huge displays of flowers in hanging baskets dripping water on the pavements, trendy Parisians swanning around, the courtyards all grand, and chic little stores that you never see anyone in, ha-ha."

I had noticed that her laugh had altered over the last twenty-four hours, it was deeper in tone, richer and more immediate. It no longer looked left and right to see if it was OK.

"Pastels, green and red, and the crisp white linen on the outside tables. And the waiters, like ponies, prancing." Suddenly she was standing in front me, performing an impression of a slim bloke balancing a tray, wiping a table and tilting his head, superiorly.

"I get it. I can see it."

Without make-up, or the cap pulled down, or the belt pinching, her energy was undiluted. "I've never heard you laugh like that, Daniel. What a wonderful sound."

"Yeah well, it's funny."

She retook her seat beside me and we enjoyed a comfortable pause. "You know *my* two passions are cake and fashion, right?"

"Right."

She kissed my smiling cheek. "I was walking through Saint-Germain-des-Prés, and you know those gigantic wooden doors they have? Well, I was passing one with these big metal studs in it. It had a huge knocker. I'd always wanted to know what went on behind them. I pushed it open and…there was a courtyard, pale stone walls with paper arrows taped to them, like photocopied, pointing the way, so I followed them. I could hear conversation, classical music and laughter from the building at the back of it…This boring?"

"You're joking."

"I walked up these worn steps into a hall. Huge space. You'd never have guessed there could be a room as big as that when you came in off the street. It was all faded grandeur, you know, peeling paint and giant chandeliers all twinkling. There must have been a hundred people in there. A waitress offered me a glass of champagne. She had such a lovely smile. Looked a bit like me, probably the same age and I started to feel weird, because what I'd come to the city for was so ugly and I'd left Francine curled up outside the tube station in the rain."

My track stopped as she caught her breath and gripped my hand. After a moment, she continued.

"So, it turns out I'd walked into a wholesale fashion show with designers looking to sell to retailers, place their clothes, hats, bags whatever in the shops and boutiques for that autumn. I realised that everyone around me had passes, accreditation, but no one had said anything to me."

"It's 'cos you look like you belong in that world."

She turned and stared at me intently. "Sorry, it's just that I've never told anyone about this. There was stall after stall, rows of them, a different designer at each. I stopped at this amazing display of handbags. Works of art, like bonbons, sweets in wrappers? Handcrafted wickerwork, pistachio and brown, pink pastels. God, it took my breath away. I realised that a woman, very posh in Prada, was speaking to me. 'Ne parle pas français,'" I said.

"Pam."

"Ha, always one step ahead, aren't you? Yes, Pam it was. She asked me the price and availability of the bags. She thought *I* was the designer. The person who should have been at the stall must have nipped off to the loo or something. I didn't speak for a few secs, then I told her, in English, I was browsing too. We laughed. She seemed so genuine and warm. She took some champagne from a waitress, and we started walking around. I'd not eaten breakfast and it went straight to my head. I was rabbiting on and on, like I do. But it was exhilarating talking to this woman about fashion and style, in this setting, where no one knew what I did. She thought I was in fashion, professionally, like a buyer or something. She was asking my opinion about everything there, what I thought was 'on trend' and what women were looking for these days. And because I'm such a fashion nerd, you know, read *every* magazine there is, I had all the answers. That's when she told me about her shop and how she was looking for someone to run it."

"Yeah, I get it now."

"She thought I was somebody else. Somebody who could do more than…I was walking back to the hotel about to put her business card in the bin when…There was no great fanfare, Daniel, no godly hand reaching through the clouds, I just turned and went to the station and changed my ticket. When my phone started ringing, I threw it out of the window. I bought that baseball cap when I got out at King's Cross."

"Conrad?"

"You know he's got a reputation for violence? There are stories. I've seen men wilt when he shouts at them. The way he treated Francine was inhuman. But I couldn't go back. I slept on a friend's sofa that night and called Pam first thing in the morning. Met her at the shop. I told her some flimsy story, that I was between jobs and accommodation. She said she'd help me out."

"The basement."

"Yeah. Like the nuns and boyfriends, Conrad and pimps, they all see me coming, Daniel. But what choice did I have? I had to disappear."

"It's OK, I understand."

"From the minute I stepped in there, I loved the shop, and she knew it. It's like your desert island with your keyboards. Your passions override logic and…" She shook her head trying to clear it.

"So, you told her everything?"

"It's this thing about not having a mother. The minute someone shows me kindness, even a little bit, I vomit up the truth, everything comes out. If they still want to know me after that, then…"

Our eyes met. There was no music playing, but I could hear a plane's engines roaring.

21

"Looks like you've embraced it," I said, thinking that's what you say to people who make these sorts of geographical moves. "Impressed by your language skills in the shop as well."

"I liked French at school," he said, flicking back a wedge of brown hair that had fallen over one blue eye. We'd stopped at a crossing of roads, parked and walked up a rutted track. The view from the top of the incline was breathtaking. All around us, a sea of yellow heads went on for miles. I exhaled. "Amazing."

"Helianthus is the Latin for them," he said, rubbing a nicked and scratched forearm with his palm. "You'll actually see them turn their faces to follow the sun, if you've got the time."

I hoped I had.

"So, you don't have to err, 'tend' them or anything?"

"No, but we look after the farm and fields, keep everything tidy. I've got plenty of odd-job work, building, carpentry. Loads of expats around here that need their holiday homes doing up."

"You don't miss London?"

"I do, but then I think I'd miss this more. You're not homesick already, are you? You only got here this morning."

"Not in the slightest." I sighed, "I absolutely get it."

I gazed at the hills beyond the yellow pastures. Were they hills? They could have been clouds. This morning, after picking us up at the airport in his rusty-red Renault, a cloud as wide as the sky had chased us all the way back to the farm. It deposited its load just as we shut the door.

We returned to the car. We'd made a goodish dent in the local supermarché stock. The boot, and most of the back seat, were brimming with produce: wine, champagne, cognac, a huge bird, veg, ham, cheeses, chocolates and cakes.

He refused point-blank my contribution at the checkout. "No, you're our guests," he'd said. I looked at him across the car's roof. He was tanned, but not craggy. If he lived for the rest of his life beneath the brilliant sun of Southern France, he'd remain boyish.

"Are you sure I can't chip in?" I repeated.

"Nope," he said, shaking his head.

Opening his door, I noticed his smile was secretive, downward glancing. It wasn't the first time I'd seen that smile since I'd arrived. "She hasn't told you. Not even a clue?" he said, starting up the engine.

"No. She said she'd tell me today. At dinner."

"We better get going then: I'm cooking."

We bounced over the potholes onto the tarmac. "She said she wanted to hear my story first," I said.

"She usually gets her way."

That wasn't necessarily true in my experience. I nodded at the back of the car. "That's a lot of spuds."

"Corbossa said he's hungry."

We laughed and through the window, the sunflowers tilted their heads and laughed too.

***

We'd enjoyed a monumental slap-up and I was drunk. Very. There was loads of chatter. A fair bit of Bowie and Dylan, some Miles Davis then nothing for a while.

"So quiet," I said for the umpteenth time. I was allowed a couple of seconds to double-check the noise levels until someone shifted in their chair. "I love the way that chair creaks."

My pronouncement elicited some tipsy tittering. I revelled in it: my friends were laughing at me. In the centre of the table, the huge fowl had been picked to the bone. Heavily depleted trays of veg, potatoes with sprigs and twigs of this and that, congealed in oil, surrounded it. The cheeseboard was decimated, surrounded by crumbs and crackers, empty bottles and glasses.

"What now?" someone asked because I was laughing again.

"Just thinking, probably macaroni cheese tonight…lasagne, maybe? If I'm feeling continental."

Corbossa was sitting next to me. He put his arm around my shoulder.

"Talking about my trusty microwave," I informed him.

"Man, you've been through the fucking grinder," he said, laughing.

I looked at a pastoral watercolour bookended by ornate candelabras. The dancing flames revealed the hundreds of brush strokes that made hills green and fields yellow. The painting could have been a photograph taken yesterday. You could tell that not a lot changed around here. Between a couple of hanging rugs on the bare stone wall to my left, an open window revealed the black infinite. Not a streetlight or lit window, not even a passing headlight, could be seen. Pleasantly content, my head fell back. Wooden beams crisscrossed my blinking eyes. It all looked vaguely medieval.

"I think that: knights and damsels," said David, flicking back that wedge of hair over his eye. "Or even monks, all cowls and chanting."

That's when you know you're proper drunk, when people can read your thoughts.

He stood up.

"Kerry, shall we?" She was up quickly. I watched her spin her hair into a tight bun. She did that when performing chores. The removal of the plate in front of me was accompanied by a kiss on my lips.

Kerry wasn't much of a drinker. In fact, only me and Corbossa had properly indulged. David was a bit pissed, but neither of them were in my league this night.

As often happens when very drunk, you blink, and things have moved on. A minute ago, I could have sworn Kerry and David were chatting beneath the rude kitchen strip light, The Stones blaring, water running, cutlery chinking, plates stacked on the draining board – the next minute, there was no music and the table had been cleared and wiped down.

The candles on the wall had been snuffed out. Only the ancient 'Miss Havisham' effort in the middle of the table had been left to flicker. The wax dripped slowly from it. I let some harden on my little finger. It was dark, quiet and I felt completely safe.

Mick broke the stillness. "Like being on the road."

We all smiled because it was. Unusually though, for the three of us, we weren't travelling: we'd arrived, sort of.

With her hand on her tummy, Alana winced and rested her feet on a chair. It was such an 'on-the-road' moment when she leaned forward and rubbed my knee. "Are you OK, Daniel?"

Her hair had grown out. For five years, I'd seen it, in various bottled shades, no longer than half an inch. To see her now, with a head full of brown curls, was to see, not the band's teak-tough elf, but someone queenly and open.

"Couldn't be happier," I replied.

"What happened?"

There was a pause. My ears were ringing. God, it was so insanely quiet out here.

"Did you let go, man?" Corbossa asked from his chair.

"What do you mean?"

"You know."

I did, and even though I still felt incredibly pissed, when I began speaking, I realised that I wasn't as far gone as I thought. "I pressed mute."

Alana took her hand from her tummy and put it to her mouth.

"You never!" said Mick.

"Fucking train crash," whispered Alana.

"Was..." I muttered, nodding.

David joined us on our stationary bus. "On purpose?"

"Yes."

"I'm sorry?" That was Kerry, running to catch up. Her and David were sitting in the armchairs behind us. "Daniel?"

I turned and sighed. She'd undone her hair and let it cascade over her shoulders. What must be going through her head? Forty-eight hours ago, she was homeless, shivering on Shepherd's Bush Green with all she owned at her feet, now she was sitting in a warm farmhouse in Gascony without a clue as to what anyone was talking about.

"I fucking knew it, when I met you in the pub, I *knew* that there was something else going on. It was like you were standing on the edge of a cliff. Did you plan...?"

"No Mick. I had it in my head to do the shows with Torin. Keep the thing going, make a living. 'This *had* to get done', I kept telling myself. But then I did what I did."

"Fucking hell," said Mick Corbossa. "How long did it take, for him to?"

"Instantaneous?"

"What song?" said Alana.

I batted my eyes. "Just had to be..." I said, leaving the title hanging in the eves and beams.

They both sat back in their chairs. I could tell they were trying to imagine the moment.

"You're fucking joking," said Mick. "That bridge. He's not ever, *ever* got it. How many thousands of times?"

I nodded. "Yep." Mick howled into the ceiling; Alana just kept shaking her head.

"What?" said Kerry looking from face to face.

While David explained to her the basics of programmed music and how you are able to raise and lower the volume, affect sound, delete or indeed, mute the many instruments playing on a song *while* it is playing, we kept sneaking peeks at each other, me and my old bandmates, and every time we did, we laughed.

"You turned off Torin's singing?" she asked, her wonderful green eyes smiling curiously from the grey stone behind her. "But, you said it was OK when I asked you."

I reached behind me and took her hand.

"Yeah, it was."

***

As the last of the equipment was being loaded into the trucks in the alley at the side of the theatre, I stepped out of the stage door. There was a bit of a crowd waiting. A few enquiries were aimed at my back, one or two impolite, but most just wanting to know what the hell had just happened. But I said not a word, nor looked left or right. I dodged the traffic and stepped onto the Green.

Moments before, as they'd sat shell-shocked in their dressing room, I'd again written out cheques for Daisy and Bluebell. I knew how much this gig and the tour had meant to them, but the tangible relief on their faces indicated that they were as glad as I was that it was all over. None of us had participated in anything like the events that had occurred on the stage below, and I'll bet we never would again.

"I don't understand, Daniel," Daisy had said, still gripping her drumsticks, "I know every second of that song, not just the words, but every note and beat."

"Even people who hate it know how it goes," Bluebell echoed quietly.

"It was my favourite over a whole summer holiday. Everyone was singing it."

Shaking her raven hair, she peered at me out of fashionably smudged eyeliner. "The entire audience sang that bit, *'and now I know where we're going...'* but he didn't."

"You have to believe me, Daniel." Bluebell took my hand. "I *was* telling him, shouting in his ear. The entire room was, *'Oh silent storm, your rain cleansing me...'* He was staring at me as if I was speaking a foreign language. And then, and then...he..."

"I nearly got off the drums and fucking hit him!" said Daisy.

Transfixed from my keyboards, I'd watched as Bluebell, her face a mask of anguish, bellow the lyrics at him as he faced his crowd. He was singing the verse over the chorus of our signature hit, shaking so much he appeared to levitate. He *knew* he was imploding and that made his torment worse. Then, as the chorus was about to repeat, a white blinding wash coated the stage and s*mack*, his hand recoiled, and Bluebell was staggering sideways.

Our great anthem was belting out, and the bass player was holding, not her instrument, but her face. Daisy had stopped drumming and had stood up. The whole room was listening to music and nobody on stage was playing anything. I could see Conrad, blinking and blinking in the wings, the vein in his neck throbbing like an angry python as Torin frantically tore off pieces of paper that he'd taped to the front of the stage. As he mumbled random lines into the mic, it struck me that Roy hadn't muted the microphone and I imagined his Wolverhampton smirk broadening at the justice the music gods were meting out.

Alana (manfully trying to keep the show on the road) asked me what the next song was. I told her...'The Ship That Never Sailed'. By then I had stepped back from my gear to watch the catastrophic denouement play out in front of me, unimpeded.

"That's the most challenging one in the set," Mick said to David. "It goes from fours into six-eight and the melody goes with it, then there's half a bar break, one two, and it goes back to fours. Alana practically sings it all on her own, live. He's never had a scooby."

"And?" said Alana, peering at me between her fingers.

"Well, to their credit, Daisy and Bluebell got stuck back into miming. Bluebell doing your vocal, but by then half the crowd were booing him. I mean smacking the bass player in the mouth, right at the high point of the concert, it was fucking nuclear."

"She OK?"

"Yeah, not a scratch. She said she didn't even feel it. But if they thought it was just part of the show, the fucking nightmare of 'Ship' absolutely killed it."

"'*This is why you love me...*'" Mick sang drunkenly, shaking his head. "He's never got it."

"It was as if some dyslexic, dunno, extrovert, pissed out of his head, had dressed up like Torin and wondered on stage by mistake," I told them. "By the key change, there was all kinds of shit flying in… sarnies, T-shirts, spraying beer."

"No," said Mick. "What happened then?"

I laughed.

"What man?"

"He started abusing them. He called them all cunts and walked off."

"He never!"

"We played, well, mimed on and they sort of clapped a bit and everyone started drifting away. People were laughing a lot more that I thought they would. Must have been only about twenty people left in there at the end, kicking plastic pots about and that."

It was indeed very quiet in that farmhouse now.

"Roy said he'd take care of my gear, I paid everyone, and just left."

As the night absorbed my tale, I looked through the window and saw myself stepping onto the Green and seeing Kerry, rotund with all that padding under her mac, in the glow of the streetlamp.

"Daniel? *Daniel!*"

Alana and Kerry were standing over me. Corbossa was laughing.

"He's hardly slept at all," said Kerry.

"Let's get him to bed."

I shook my head, befuddled. "No. Alana, you said you'd tell me something…something to tell me…*Oui?*"

***

I was sitting in the garden in the ambient midday heat – didn't mean I felt particularly chipper, though. Even drawing breath was taxing. It was as if I'd climbed ten flights and there were twenty more to go. Sheep (could have been goats) were bleating a few fields away, birds chattering above. It wasn't so quiet now.

I was struggling to concentrate on what was being said. With an effort, I looked up.

"Sorry. Just, can't think properly. I was floating, then I pressed mute…it's like I've landed. Not sure where, though."

Alana smiled at me from across a substantial wooden table. Mick was one side of her, David the other. It felt like boardroom business.

"Well, we're all glad you've come back down."

"Ta," I said hoarsely.

She winced slightly as she adjusted her hands on her tummy. "OK. I'll tell you again. I saw that something odd was happening to the band account, yeah?"

"Yes."

"After Rotterdam, I was never going to speak to him again, never mind get on a stage with him. I wanted to get my tour money and just get out, but they wouldn't let me have it. Not even let me see the statement. That obnoxious accountant."

"Pinky bleedin' Forbes."

"Him. He's as dodgy as fuck, but we knew that. He wasn't answering any of my calls. So, I went to the bank, showed them my passport, signature, and they finally let me see it. There were some very odd movements, money in and out. James, David's brother, is an accountant."

I regarded the funky, floppy-haired guy sitting there. "I'm the black sheep," he said with a wink. "Sister's a lawyer. As soon as my little bro looked at it, he said the account should be closed."

"So, me and Mick went down there and closed it," Alana said.

I rubbed my hand across my face. I was starting to get the picture.

"I couldn't get into it either. Neither could Barney, Torin's gofer. I thought it was Torin."

"Daniel, there was nothing in it to get."

"Really embarrassed in Denmark Street," I told them. "They locked us out of the room. All the gear in it. No one had paid them for weeks. Thought Barney had taken care of it, it was his job. Ends up he hadn't been paid either, couldn't access the account. I had to foot the rehearsal bill from with my own money *and* sort him out, the girls as well. I'll be in bother when I go home…" I sipped from a glass of water and peered into the whorls of old wood. "…if I've still got one. Gonna have to talk to the bank about the mortgage, get some kind of deferment?"

I sensed, rather than saw, glances and smiles being swapped around me, but felt too lethargic to investigate. I didn't want thoughts of what I'd do when I returned to London – selling everything, retraining, evening classes, or whatever – to infect these few days down here with my girl and best friends.

I'd got up half an hour ago, had a couple of headache pills, and was on my second cup of strong coffee and third pint of water. The priority was to get some energy back and absolutely rinse out this experience, because when I did go back, there'd be mum to deal with and God knows what else.

When I lay my head on my folded arms, I saw the beginning of a narrow track through the middle of the sunflower fields that hemmed in the property. I began to silently count the steps it would take to reach it.

"Daniel, you're counting."

"Sorry. I'm listening."

I glanced at the path again. New priority: once my old band had done with me, I'd explore it with Kerry.

David noticed the direction I was looking in. "Down there, half a mile, you come to a lake."

"Oi! Dopey. Wait till you fucking hear this." From the cloudless sky, Corbossa was peering down at me.

"James looked at the statements," continued Alana. "It was gobsmacking. About three months ago, we'd had four hundred thousand pounds come in and then go out in twenty-four hours."

My sluggish, apathetic brain sparked momentarily. "That's just mad. There's never been more than a few grand in there for gigs and rehearsals, emergencies."

"Have you heard of a film, an American film, called 'My Perfect Seventeenth'?"

"Yes!" yelped Kerry. She was sitting on the bench beside me. "I've got the soundtrack. Sorry," she said quietly. "It's a bit tacky."

I could see she felt embarrassed piping up amongst the 'cool' musos, so I took her hand and pressed myself against her. She'd been quiet all morning. Exhausted by events, probably. Clinging on, as she'd done all her life.

"You asked me about it, Daniel, when I threw the coffee over you."

"You did what?" Corbossa said.

"Tell you later, mate."

Alana left for the kitchen. David began rolling a fag.

"Gonna be warm today," he said, looking across the fields.

I lay my head on Kerry's shoulder and looked at the path between the sunflowers.

Alana returned to the table with a couple of CDs and a portable player. She put a disc in and selected a track. I could see it was one of those mix CDs they sell for a couple of quid down Camden and Portobello: 'Sebtronic', it was titled.

An unremarkable dance beat played for a few bars and then my eight notes. But the rhythm was all wrong, the piano lurid and clumpy, the barked 'heys' a nuisance.

"That's 'Foss,'" I said. "I wrote that."

David looked at me quizzically. "*Foss*?"

"Means waterfall in Icelandic."

Even as I explained how I'd used foreign names for titles for the two-minute sketches I'd written (and remembered how crushed I'd felt sending all this music to Torin and not hearing anything back), I sensed something in Alana's noon DJ set that had portents beyond a remixed old demo.

"I'd send these ideas, ten, twelve sketches to Torin, they were for the third album. The one that never got made," I told David, then I met Alana's eye. *'Ideas are the currency.'*

She nodded ruefully as we listened. It wasn't the most sophisticated mix you'd ever heard. Some club producers had just plonked my hook, eight notes on the SH-101, on top of a generic techno beat with a lot of claps and sampled 'Heys'. They'd shifted the octaves around, dropped bits out. Cut and paste job, really. I hadn't a clue where or how they'd got hold of my music and I didn't care.

Alana stopped the track, took out the CD, inserted another and pressed 'play'.

"'My Perfect Seventeenth,'" Kerry said.

"This was playing when we met," I said, smiling at the shmaltzy West Coast pop production.

"And you wrote this too."

I felt the hairs on the back of my arms begin to tingle, imagined the rocking of a tube carriage. A voice said, 'I heard it'. The voice was mine.

"It's the same," Kerry said, her eyes widening, looking at Alana and then back at me.

Alana stopped the CD, removed it and placed it front of me. The garish 'My Perfect Seventeenth' logo was plastered across it, characters from the film beaming behind, but I was drawn to the tiny credit.

"Sebtronic?" I said.

Looking gravely at me, the way she might have done before the red light in the studio, or as a stage curtain inched slowly open, Alana said, "It's Torin and a couple of his mates from down the club. A little side project to help him with his dealer's bill. All our demos, bass lines, Mick's beats, have been used by him and Pinky to get 'solo' publishing advances. That's why we never heard anything back from him."

"The fucker sold off our album piecemeal for drugs."

"Alright, Mick," said Alana, patting his hand and focussing on me again. "But this one…'Foss', right?"

"Right," I said quietly.

"Someone in the publishing company must have been doing

their job and anyway, bingo! I don't think Torin ever dreamed it'd get taken up and used in a huge Hollywood movie. But..." she said, glancing at Kerry then peering at me, "you already knew that, right?"

My brain thrummed in protest. I'd assumed Alana had invited me here for a break, tell me about her, her baby and David, get me away from Torin and his madness. But now I felt the tow of my old singer, the music business and all its dark chicanery dragging me back to London. More than anything, I wanted to disappear into the sunflowers with Kerry, tell her that this was the happiest I'd ever been in my life and that I loved her and would be with her forever.

"Well, I'd heard Kerry playing it that morning..."

Did I know that I'd written it? I must have done. After all, I'd been playing those eight notes in my head for weeks. That sequence formed one of the first melodies I'd created – part of the 'Water' album I'd played to the school that morning in assembly. It was years later I gave it the title, 'Foss'.

I felt the air around me warming and my eyes beginning to close. In my micro-sleep I was in my garden studio slotting Mick's beats onto the computer program. I tasted cardamom in my microwaved korma and felt my fingers swishing the curser. Then I paused as from the grey-black soundproof foam between my speakers, the authorship of those eight notes came to me. But I refused to accept the evidence of my ears. The shredded guitar samples, oilrig drum fills and inhumanly tweaked girly chorus repelled me. I felt like spitting out my food. Convinced I could never write something like that, I steeled myself and continued replacing Mick's drums. In that moment, my focus was entirely on survival – getting this shitty 'new way' over. To hear 'Torin' in all its glory was painful and shaming. It had become the sound of betrayal and cowardice.

But sitting here, in the South of France, it came to me that 'the past' had not only meant the band but all the music I'd created before it.

"Daniel!"

I looked up. "What? Err...yeah?"

"You own this."

Behind Alana's three short words was a mountain of complexity and toil: lawyers, accountants, meetings, a hundred and one emails. I'd had enough. I'd already mapped out an exit strategy. On my return to London, I'd put the entire contents of my studio up for sale and retrain. The next century would be run entirely on computers. The phones they were making were works of technical genius, and the laptops thinner and lighter than a couple of magazines.Soon, the entire planet would be viewed on something slipped into your back pocket, no thicker than an After Eight mint. Surely it wasn't beyond me to transfer my music programming skills to the 'real' world? There'd be a future for me in that. I could convert my studio into an office and save money on tube fares. The love of my girl and seeing mum right was all I cared about.

I drew breath. "Look Alana, I've sort of had enough of it all. I played cos I loved it, and if anyone gets joy from what I did, I'm happy for them."

"Listen man." Mick was trying to get my attention, but I just wanted to say my piece and walk away.

"Hang on Mick, these weeks without you two have been horrible and I've fallen out of love with it. I just want to be with Kerry now, start again. Was thinking of going into programming, admin. I'm optimistic I can make something of myself."

"Alana," Kerry said, "Daniel's had to take on so much. He's very tired."

She was holding my hand tightly, and I realised that her apparent reserve was her way of looking out for me, guarding me. She'd never seen me in the company of anyone else and I had never seen her away from the West End. I had so much to tell her about the way I was and wanted to be, and I knew she would sit and listen patiently. Kerry would love and accept the shonky and unfinished me unconditionally, because I loved and accepted her in the same way.

I returned her reassuring squeeze. It was as if we were two kids turned out into a hostile, friendless world, but that was a ludicrous notion. The people sitting opposite me cared about me just as much as she did.

"What's so fucking hilarious Corbossa?" I asked; he was laughing, and I couldn't help laughing too. He'd always cracked me up. "This is serious. You're such a knob, mate."

"Alright, alright…"

Alana was trying to contain a smile but couldn't. *That* was unusual. David had got up and walked away. I'm pretty sure he was smiling as well. Kerry's grip tightened. I sensed the fear in her, and my tired heart began thudding.

"Daniel, this is for you." Alana passed a single oblong piece of paper across the table, face down.

I picked it up and turned it over. Kerry caught her breath. I blinked at it. "This right?" I asked.

"Daniel, you've written the theme song for a huge Hollywood movie. Fifty thousand is just the start. David's brother is retrieving all the money that 'you know who' has defrauded from us over the last three years. This is from the people behind the film. They are mortified. They don't want it to get out that they've been using your music illegally."

I blinked and shook my head.

"He stole your music and forged all our signatures. The police are involved and everything."

***

Kerry and I entered the sun-dappled path. "It's a lot of money," she said, swinging my hand in hers.

"Remember your lipstick?" I said. "You lost it when we met at the cafe that first time." She nodded. "Well, I kind of nicked it. Put my foot over it."

"I saw you do it," she said.

I laughed, and on we walked through shade and light, patches of blue above. "Think about it, Kerry, we're gonna walk and not hear a car, see a building, road or another person. Mad, isn't it?"

"What *is* mad…is that the song that was playing when we met, you wrote! Didn't you know?"

"I heard it, yes, but I just couldn't, wouldn't?…with the shock of the coffee and then you running up the escalator after me, I thought I'd imagined it, or wished it? I was overwhelmed, I suppose. The band was disintegrating. It was like a family splitting up and I felt guilty staying with…but there was mum and the house… and then there was this huge shift to the 'new way', rehearsing the girls and feeling so shit about Mick and Alana… And then baffled by you, Pam and the shop, us splitting up, picking again, thinking I was gonna lose the house… I was just trying to survive, couldn't see the wood for the trees. Kerry, my head was a mess."

She undid her fingers and ran on.

"You'll find clarity now," she called over her shoulder.

How different she was to the woman I'd walked with through the Soho streets. In the sunshine, without the city foundation, her skin was less taut, and the lines appeared more deeply etched: she looked the age she was. Yet, watching her skipping ahead, performing graceful, uninhibited sweeps of leg and arm, she seemed more youthful than she'd ever been in London. Breathlessly, she turned to face me.

"Ha-ha, you've gone all red," I said.

"I don't care," she panted.

We linked arms and on we went.

"What did you say to Torin afterwards? He must have been devastated."

Through the flashing sunflower stems, I had a brief vision of him onstage, the terror on his face as he floundered like a drowning man in his own song.

"The last thing I said to him was, 'You ready?'"

She stopped walking and waited for me to explain.

"Highly technical," I said with a smile, tugging her along. "It's what you say before you start a song."

"Oh. What about Conrad?"

"I don't remember…"

As I'd come off stage, he'd actually shaken my hand and apologised for Torin's ineptitude and behaviour. The last time I saw my singer was in the dressing room corridor. His pose was that of a vulture, head sunk low between his shoulders as he slumped against the wall. Conrad was standing over him, puce, screaming.

"That's water!" she said, running into the sunlight at the track's end.

Beyond a short pasture, and encircled by boulders, was the lake David had told us was there. Overhanging branches, poplar and ash, edged into the scene, randomly darkening the impossibly clear blue